HIGH IS THE EAGLE

This Large Print Book carries the
Seal of Approval of N.A.V.H.

THE KANE LEGACY, BOOK 3

HIGH IS THE EAGLE

AL AND JOANNA LACY

THORNDIKE PRESS
A part of Gale, Cengage Learning

GALE
CENGAGE Learning™

Detroit • New York • San Francisco • New Haven, Conn • Waterville, Maine • London

FIC
LAC

LIBRARY OF CONGRESS CATALOGING-IN-PUBLICATION DATA

Lacy, Al.
  High is the eagle / by Al & Joanna Lacy.
    p. cm. — (Thorndike Press large print christian historical fiction) (The Kane legacy ; bk. 3)
  ISBN-13: 978-1-4104-1143-3 (alk. paper)
  ISBN-10: 1-4104-1143-5 (alk. paper)
  1. Mexican War, 1846–1848—Fiction. 2. Texas—Fiction. 3. Large type books. I. Lacy, JoAnna. II. Title.
PS3562.A256H54 2009
813'.54—dc22
                                  2008040831

Published in 2009 by arrangement with Multnomah Books, a division of Random House, Inc.

A72005177744

*This book is sincerely dedicated to our
dear friend,
Steve Cobb,
president and publisher
of the WaterBrook Multnomah
Publishing Group.*

— 1 Corinthians 16:23

INTRODUCTION

The series of fierce nineteenth-century battles between the armies of the United States and Mexico, which historians aptly call the Mexican-American War, are sometimes dated April 1846 to February 1848. However, the majority of historians who have written on the subject agree that the war between the United States and Mexico that began in April of 1846 and extended until February of 1848 actually stemmed from the Mexican army's surrounding the fighting Texans and their Tennessee friends at the Alamo in San Antonio, Texas, on February 23, 1836, and launching the fierce attack on March 6.

This attack, which was led by Mexico's president and chief military leader, Antonio López de Santa Anna, was in retaliation against the Texans for declaring themselves independent of the Mexican government.

In 1835, the people of Texas had formed

their own government and issued a declaration of independence from Mexico at a large meeting in Washington-on-the-Brazos in southeastern Texas. David G. Burnet was chosen as president of the new Republic of Texas, and General Sam Houston was appointed to be its military leader.

Thus, the majority of historians who have written of these events actually date the Mexican-American War from February 23, 1836, to February 2, 1848.

A bit of history: The land known as Mexico was conquered in the 1540s by Spain. By the 1730s, Spain had sent several expeditions into the land called Texas and claimed it for their own since Mexico had claimed it before it was conquered by Spain. The city of San Antonio, Texas, which since 1758 had housed a military post and a Franciscan mission known as the Alamo, had become the administrative center.

Anglo-American colonization gained impetus in Texas when the United States government purchased the Louisiana Territory from France in 1803 and claimed title to all the land from the Sabine River as far west as the Rio Grande. All of Texas was then claimed by the Anglo-Americans.

Mexico had remained in Spain's control

until 1821, when the Mexican people rose up in determination to be free. They declared their independence from Spain and adopted a federal constitution modeled after that of the United States of America.

There was trouble between the Mexicans and the Spaniards because of this, but no blood was shed. The Spaniards quickly withdrew peaceably when a Mexican revolt in 1833 placed Antonio López de Santa Anna in power. By military might, Santa Anna became the undisputed leader of Mexico.

Thus on February 23, 1836, in retaliation against the Texans for declaring themselves free from Mexico in 1835, Santa Anna and his troops surrounded the Texans who were fortified at the Alamo defending their freedom. On March 6, Santa Anna's army attacked the Alamo and killed every man behind its walls. The Mexican-American War, then, actually extended from February 23, 1836, until a peace treaty was signed between the two countries on February 2, 1848.

During the twelve-year period of 1836–1848, it was never the American government's desire to be at war with the Mexican government, but it seemed that the United States was caught in a web of destiny that forced them to fight Mexico, no matter how hard they tried to avoid it.

PROLOGUE

In mid-1835, when the people of Texas declared themselves independent of Mexico and established their own republic, the government of Mexico was angry. As time passed the anger did not subside. On December 4, 1835, Mexican General Martín Perfecto de Cos brazenly led his fourteen hundred troops into San Antonio, Texas, and occupied the old Franciscan mission known as the Alamo.

The townspeople were frightened and sent riders to the nearest Texas army outpost to inform the leading officers that General Cos and his troops had taken over the land and buildings of the Alamo. The riders made it clear that the people of San Antonio were in grave danger.

On the morning of December 5, a well-armed band of some 300 Texan soldiers surrounded Cos and his troops in the Alamo.

Five days of battle ensued, and by Decem-

11

ber 10, 115 of Cos's men had been killed and 185 had deserted him and run away. Cos and his 1,100 remaining troops threw down their weapons and surrendered to the 290 Texans who were still alive and strong.

When word of the rout reached General Antonio López de Santa Anna in Mexico City, he gathered his military leaders for a joint conference. News of the conference reached Texas with reports that Santa Anna had declared that he would personally lead his Mexican troops on a punitive sweep across Texas. He would begin by punishing the people of San Antonio for backing the Texas troops in their attack on General Cos and his men.

At the time, Texas army headquarters under General Sam Houston were located at Washington-on-the-Brazos in southeast Texas. Houston received the news of Santa Anna's threat and knew immediately that he would have to enlarge his army considerably to defeat Santa Anna's troops when they came to punish the people of San Antonio. Knowing they were going to San Antonio, Houston feared they would use the Alamo as a fort as General Cos had.

General Houston knew it would take Santa Anna better than two months to lead his army from Mexico City to San Antonio.

He sent word by Texas newspapers and by word of mouth that he needed at least five thousand volunteers to join the army by March 1 so they could meet Santa Anna and his troops head-on when they arrived at San Antonio.

Time passed, and in mid-February 1836, Houston sent Lieutenant Colonel William Travis to go into Texas towns and challenge Texas men to go with him and destroy the Alamo before Santa Anna and his troops got there. However, as related in book 1 in The Kane Legacy, *A Line in the Sand,* Colonel Travis and the few men he could gather with him were forced to use the Alamo as a fort when Santa Anna and his huge number of troops surrounded them for twelve days and attacked them on the thirteenth day.

In the first book of The Kane Legacy, readers were introduced to the Kane family of Boston, Massachusetts, in early April 1834. Forty-nine-year-old Abram Kane and his four sons — Alex, twenty-eight; Abel, twenty-six; Adam, twenty-three; and Alan, twenty — were dock workers in Boston Harbor. The Kane brothers also had a sister, Angela, who was twenty-one. Abram's wife, Kitty, the mother of his five children, was quite ill with tuberculosis.

Born the son of Abner and Elizabeth O'Kane in Ireland on February 21, 1785, Abram was brought to Pawtucket, Rhode Island, in 1792. Neighbors in Pawtucket invited the O'Kanes to a Bible-believing church a short time later, and eight-year-old Abram found Jesus Christ as Saviour, as did his parents.

Within a year, Abram's paternal grandparents, Alexander and Maureen O'Kane moved from Ireland to Pawtucket and soon received Christ also. Abram was brought up in that solid church, and in his Christian home was taught the value of family living and hard work.

In 1793, since they were now living in the United States, the O'Kanes decided to change their last name to Kane.

In 1804, when Abram was nineteen, he married eighteen-year-old Kitty Foyle, who was also Irish and a fine, dedicated Christian who belonged to the same church in Pawtucket as the Kanes. The young couple moved to Boston shortly thereafter and joined a good Bible-believing church there. Abram found employment as a dock worker in Boston Harbor. As Abram and Kitty's children came along, they gave them names that started with an *A*, which had been a tradition in the O'Kane family in Ireland for over a hundred years.

As their sons grew up, they joined their father as dock workers. In time, however, Adam and Alan decided they wanted to get into a business of their own. Alan had become well acquainted with a wealthy Texas cattle rancher who often brought cattle hides to the East Coast to sell. The rancher's name was William Childress. A Christian himself, he offered Alan and Adam jobs as ranch hands on his large ranch in Texas. The two brothers felt sure that if they took the jobs, one day they could have their own cattle ranch in Texas and do well.

Kitty Kane died in late April 1834. As time passed, Alan went to Texas first and was soon followed by Adam. On the trip that Alan took with William Childress, he and the rancher stayed with some close Christian friends who owned a large cotton plantation just outside New Orleans, Louisiana. Alan met their lovely daughter Julia and fell in love with her. Unaware of Alan's feelings for her, Julia Miller showed him kindness and spoke of the two of them being very good friends. She even allowed him to call her Julie, which her close friends did. When Alan reached the big ranch in Texas and went to work, his thoughts were on Julia continuously.

Before Adam was able to make the trip to Texas, rancher William Childress died. Alan learned then that because he had saved Childress's life a short time earlier at the risk of losing his own, Childress — who was a widower and had no children — had willed the ranch to him. Alan also came into a great deal of money, which Childress had in bank accounts.

A short time later, Adam made the trip to Texas. William Childress had told him earlier that the Millers would let him stay in their home in New Orleans while he waited for the boat that would carry him to Texas. When Adam and Julia were together those few days during his stay, they fell in love. But neither told the other how they felt. Adam went on to Texas, not knowing that his younger brother was also in love with Julia.

When Adam arrived at the ranch in Texas, he was surprised to learn of Childress's death, that the ranch and Childress's money had been willed to Alan, and that Alan had already legally made Adam half owner of the ranch and was giving him half the money.

During the time since Alan had left Boston, much had been in the newspapers about serious trouble between the people of Texas and the government of Mexico, which was led by dictator Antonio López de Santa Anna. It seemed that war was inevitable.

Since the ranch now belonged to Alan and Adam Kane, they sent for their father; their sister, Angela; their brothers, Alex and Abel, and their wives. They offered jobs to Alex and Abel and houses for them and their wives. The offer was gladly accepted.

As time passed, Alan decided that he must go to New Orleans, tell Julia that he now was wealthy and that he loved her, and ask her to marry him. However, Adam — who did not know how Alan felt about Julia — took time off to go to New Orleans first. There, Julia admitted that she was in love with him, and they were married.

When Adam came home to the ranch with Julia and announced that he and Julia were now married, the news hit Alan with a powerful jolt. He kept his love for Julia a secret, not wanting in any way to hurt Adam or his new bride.

Time passed and in early 1836, it was certain that Santa Anna and his Mexican army were coming to Texas to take it over. Alan and Adam learned of the need for volunteers to go with Colonel William Travis of the Texas army to San Antonio. Leaving their family at the ranch, they went, and at the old Franciscan mission just outside of San Antonio, known as the Alamo, they ended up facing the fact that Santa Anna and thousands of his troops were on their way from Mexico. In late February, the Mexican troops had the Alamo surrounded, but they were waiting for more troops to arrive before they attacked.

Alan was sent by Colonel Travis to bear a message of their need of help to General Sam Houston, leader of the Texas army, who was situated on the Brazos River in east Texas. Even though Alan must ride through the camped Mexican troops at night, risking his life to do so, he willingly went.

At dawn on March 6, 1836, the 182 men in the Alamo were attacked by thousands of Mexican soldiers, led by Santa Anna. By nine o'clock that morning, every man in the Alamo had been killed. One woman had been at the Alamo, Susanna Dickinson, the wife of Captain Almeron Dickinson. She and her fifteen-month-old daughter were spared by Santa Anna and allowed to ride away on her husband's horse.

Susanna and her baby were some five miles outside of San Antonio, on their way to Gonzales, Texas, when she came upon a camp set up by citizens of San Antonio when they had fled their homes several days earlier, in fear of the approaching Mexican troops. Moments later, Alan Kane came riding up on his way back to the Alamo. He was shocked to hear of the attack and that his brother Adam was dead, along with all the other men in the Alamo.

Susanna knew of the danger Alan had faced in order to ride through the Mexican troops at night, and in front of the crowd said she thought Alan's name ought to be changed to Alamo because of the risk he took in going for help. The people agreed. Alan told Susanna and the people that it would give him a special closeness with his brother Adam, who had been killed.

When Alan arrived home at the ranch, he gave his family the bad news about Adam being killed, along with all the other men at the Alamo. He then explained why he had not been there and told them of Susanna Dickinson's suggestion that he now be called Alamo Kane. The family also agreed.

Alan "Alamo" Kane still had deep love in his heart for Julia, of which she had no idea. While spending some time alone that night with the grieving, brokenhearted Julia, Alan was informed that she was expecting a baby, which would be born in late September or early October. Alan said he wished that somehow Adam could have known about the baby. Julia said that maybe in heaven the Lord had already told Adam that his little son or daughter was on the way.

Alan agreed. Then after Julia had reminded him that they were still good friends and that she still loved him, Alan went to his room in the ranch house and knelt in prayer. *Lord, You know I am still in love with Julie. The love she feels for me is a friendship love. Maybe — maybe someday, Lord, when she is over the jolt of losing Adam and becoming a widow expecting a baby . . . You could change that love in her heart toward me so it is like the love I have felt since I first met her. Maybe — maybe someday she could become Mrs. Alan — er — Mrs. Alamo Kane.*

In book 2 of the Kane Legacy, *Web of Destiny,* the Lord answered Alamo Kane's prayer. One day in April 1838 — just over two years since his brother and Julia's husband, Adam, had been killed at the Alamo — Julia admitted to Alamo that she had fallen in love with him.

Ecstatic, Alamo asked her to marry him.

On Saturday, June 16, 1838, they were married at their church in Washington-on-the-Brazos by Pastor Patrick O'Fallon, who had married Angela, making him their brother-in-law.

On the following Monday, Alamo legally adopted Julia's son, Adam, whom she had named after his father the day he was born, September 30, 1836.

As time passed and the Diamond K Ranch flourished, Julia presented Alamo with their first child, Abram — who was named after his paternal grandfather, Abram Kane — on October 7, 1840. Another son, Andrew, was born on January 16, 1842. On little Abram's fourth birthday, October 7, 1844, Julia presented Alamo with a beautiful baby daughter, whom they named Amber.

The historic relationship between the Republic of Texas and Mexico broke off completely when Texas became the twenty-eighth state of the United States on December 29, 1845. This angered the Mexican government, and by the spring of 1846, serious trouble was brewing between the United States and Mexico. Knowing that military combat was inevitable, President James K. Polk knew he must build up the military forces, so he called for men of his country to join the U.S. Army.

Alamo, Alex, and Abel had fought with the Texas army as volunteers in the Battle of San Jacinto on April 21, 1836, where the

Mexican forces were defeated. Because of their love for their country, the Kane brothers responded to President Polk's request. They joined the United States army immediately, leaving the Diamond K Ranch in the care of foreman Cort Whitney.

The Kane brothers fought in the Battle of Palo Alto on May 8, 1846, and the Battle of Resaca de la Guerrero on May 9, 1846, under the leadership of General Zachary Taylor.

Official word came to General Taylor on May 15, where he and his troops were stationed at Fort Polk near the border between Texas and Mexico, that President Polk and the United States Congress had officially declared war on Mexico on May 14.

When news of the declaration of war reached the Diamond K Ranch, the Kane family and the ranch hands were stunned. They learned of Private Alamo Kane's brave deed in the Palo Alto battle when he saved the life of a fellow soldier at the risk of his own and that as a result of his deed, General Zachary Taylor had promoted him to first lieutenant.

Julia Kane's tear-filled eyes sparkled as she said, "My darling husband just never ceases to amaze me. He is such a wonderful man! I'll be glad when this war is over and he can come home to his wife and children!"

1

As dawn was breaking at the White House in Washington, D.C., on Monday morning, May 18, 1846, President James K. Polk was slumped in an overstuffed chair, clad in a robe and slippers. He was rubbing his face with his palms when he heard his wife, Sarah, sit up in bed and say, "Darling, what are you doing?"

Polk turned to look at her in the shadows. He gently cleared his throat. "I-I couldn't sleep."

Forty-three-year-old Sarah climbed out of bed, picked up her robe from the back of the wooden chair where it was draped, put it on, and walked to where her husband sat by one of the bedroom windows. The dim light of dawn revealed the fifty-year-old president's totally white hair and his receding hairline.

"It's this Mexico situation, isn't it?" she said softly.

James Polk looked up at her with dull eyes. There was a tight knot in his chest, a gnawing of dread, which accompanied his sinking heart. "Yes, dear. When darkness fell last night, it had been three days since I'd sent that telegram to Mexican president Mariano Paredes. It takes only a matter of minutes for a telegram to reach Mexico City. The very fact that he has not replied to my message yet tells me that he is ignoring it. There is going to be a bloody war, Sarah. Paredes is not going to surrender."

Sarah bent down and caressed her husband's cheek. "You tried, darling. There is nothing else you can do."

The president sighed. "I know. I was hoping that with the way our troops whipped the Mexican troops at San Jacinto, Palo Alto, and Resaca de la Guerrero, the new Mexican president would realize the price Mexico will pay if they do not heed my declaration of war and surrender before it is too late."

Still bent down, Sarah looked him square in the eye. "But James, dear, if we *do* go to war with Mexico, much American blood will be shed too."

Polk nodded. "I know, but since Paredes leaves us no choice but to go to war against them, I guarantee you, there will be much more Mexican blood shed than American blood."

Sarah's features pinched. She licked her lips nervously. "I'm sure that is true, dear. I just wish there didn't have to be any war between us and Mexico."

The president nodded again. "Me too. But as I've said, we're caught in a web of destiny. We have no choice but to fight Mexico. This is why Congress and I have taken the offensive position. Since they give us no choice, we will fight them. And even though many of our men will be killed in battle, *they* will lose many more!"

Sarah stood up and thumbed away a tear from her cheek. "Oh, darling, why does there have to be war?"

"Because of greed, honey. It was so under Santa Anna, and it is so under Paredes. They want our land." Polk took a deep breath. "Well, they're not going to get it! We're going to attack Mexico, and they'll have to bury their troops in their own sod!"

Sarah thumbed away more tears. "Y-you are right, James. We are caught in a web of destiny. We have no choice but to fight them."

The president rose to his feet, embraced his wife, and kissed her cheek. "It will be daylight pretty soon. I'll go ahead and shave so we can eat breakfast together. I need to get to my office shortly. I have work to do."

By the time President Polk entered his office and looked out through the large, south-facing windows, along the bold outline of the horizon appeared a strong rose color, herald of the sun. Polk dug into the paperwork that faced him on his desk, and time passed slowly.

At noontime, the president had lunch with his wife in the dining room of their large living area in the White House, and when they had taken their fill, he returned to his office.

At midafternoon, the president was still working at his desk when he heard a knock on his office door. He recognized the rhythm of the knock and called out, "Please come in, Mr. Vice President!"

The door opened, and Vice President George M. Dallas entered holding two sheets of paper. Polk noticed the sour look on Dallas's features as he moved toward the desk and said evenly, "Mariano Paredes's return telegram was just sent to us from Colonel Rex Ballard in Laredo, sir."

Polk's thick eyebrows arched. "Oh? So Paredes *did* finally reply?"

"Yes sir. The second sheet of paper here is

Colonel Ballard's message to *you.* He says he had one of his soldiers who knows Spanish well, Lieutenant Roger Allison, translate Paredes's message into English."

Polk rose to his feet. "I know about Lieutenant Allison. I'm glad he was there to translate."

Dallas smiled, nodded, and handed both sheets to the president. He waited silently while the president read Colonel Ballard's telegram first, then concentrated on the translated message from Mexico's new president.

The vice president watched blood rush to Polk's angular face as he read Paredes's words. Polk then lowered the hand that held the message, his eyes cold against his reddened features, and said in a dead-level tone, "As you know, George, this is what I expected. It makes me angry, but it is still exactly what I expected."

Dallas nodded. "Yes sir."

Lips pulled into a thin line, Polk said, "George, I want you to contact Speaker of the House Ralph Miller right away and tell him that I want to meet with Congress at eight o'clock tomorrow morning."

"Yes sir," replied Dallas as he hurried out of the office.

Alone now with the translated telegram in

29

his hand, President Polk sighed. "Well, Sarah dear, as I said, I guarantee you there will be much more Mexican blood shed than American blood."

The next morning, Tuesday, May 19, at precisely eight o'clock, in the congressional auditorium of the United States Capitol Building, with Vice President George M. Dallas sitting on the platform a few feet behind him, President James K. Polk stepped to the rostrum after being officially introduced by Speaker of the House, Ralph Miller. The congressmen could tell by the solemn look on the president's face that he was emotionally perturbed.

"Gentlemen," the president said in a tight voice, "I have called you together this morning to give you news about the message I sent to President Mariano Paredes of Mexico on May 14. I remind you that Mexico has had a telegraph system for three years now between some main border locations and the government offices in Mexico City."

The president paused for a few seconds, then said, "You will recall that you voted one hundred percent on May 13 to declare war on Mexico."

Heads all over the auditorium nodded.

Polk went on. "The very next day, May 14, I wrote out the declaration of war in English, then had Julio Espada, a Mexican American who is one of the caretakers of the White House grounds, translate it into Spanish."

The congressmen were exchanging glances and nodding to each other.

The president went on. "Once the declaration of war had been translated, I sent a personal telegraph message to Colonel Rex Ballard, who is the commander of the United States troops at the army post in Laredo, Texas. I told the colonel that I was sending a second telegraph message in Spanish, addressed to Mexico's president, Mariano Paredes. The colonel was to take my telegraphed message across the Rio Grande and into Nuevo Laredo, Mexico, which is one of the main border locations I referred to a moment ago. I told him to take a band of soldiers with him, and with guns pointed at the Mexican telegraph operator, they were to see that he sent the message to President Paredes in Mexico City."

The president's mention of guns pointed at the Mexican telegraph operator had the congressmen exchanging glances again.

Polk continued. "I also told Colonel Ballard that along with the band of soldiers he would take into Nuevo Laredo, he was to include Lieutenant Roger Allison and have him make sure the Mexican telegraph operator sent the message exactly as it was written." The president then took a folded slip of paper from his inside coat pocket. "I want to read to you in English the declaration of war I sent to Mexico's president."

As President Polk carefully and clearly read the declaration of war to Congress, they learned the facts he had wired Paredes: Because Mexico had invaded United States land and shed American blood at the Alamo near San Antonio in a thirteen-day siege from February 23 to March 6, 1836, and had also shed American blood at San Jacinto on April 21, 1836, at Palo Alto on May 8, 1846, and at Resaca de la Guerrero on May 9, 1846, the United States was responding decisively. Therefore, on May 13, 1846, the president and the United States Congress agreed to declare war on Mexico and were now, on May 14, 1846, declaring it to President Paredes and the Mexican government.

While President Polk went on reading to Congress his declaration of war, the congressmen learned that he had told Paredes if Mexico would surrender to the United States immediately, the country would forthwith be occupied by American troops, who would oversee the Mexican government and disarm all of their military forces. Otherwise Mexico would be invaded by American troops and captured at the expense of Mexican blood.

Once again, the men of Congress exchanged glances and agreed that President Polk had been appropriately firm with President Paredes and the Mexican government.

Polk then read Paredes's telegraphed reply, in which he angrily declared that Mexico would not surrender but would fight the Americans *and win the war.*

The congressmen looked at each other, all verbally agreeing that this was what they had expected.

When the sound of voices throughout the auditorium finally faded, President Polk said loudly, "Gentlemen, as commander in chief of our armed forces, I have already wired word to major newspapers all over the country, asking them to put a message in bold print on the front pages of their next issue concerning the pending war with Mexico. In the message I have quoted President Mariano Paredes's violent reply to my declaration of war, and I am asking for fifty thousand new men to join the

United States Army from every possible state and territory for the duration of the war, whom I will use in addition to our present army to conquer Mexico."

At that moment, Vice President Dallas stepped up from behind the president, laid a hand on his shoulder, looked him in the eye, and said loud enough for all to hear, "Mr. President, you are doing the right thing! Mexico must be conquered!"

All over the auditorium, congressmen were rising to their feet, applauding the vice president's words and shouting to the president their approval for what he was doing.

While the applause and shouting continued, the congressmen saw President Polk's secretary, Arthur Fleming, coming through a rear door of the auditorium. People watched Fleming as he hurried up some side steps and rushed toward the president.

Polk then caught sight of Fleming from the corner of his eye and noticed that he had a telegram in his hand. Vice President Dallas and the men of Congress looked on with interest as the secretary placed the telegram in the president's hand. All of them watched closely as the president silently read the message. His face turned beet red. He cleared his throat and thanked his secretary for bringing the telegram to him, then stepped back to the rostrum.

Clearing his obviously tight throat once more, Polk said loudly, "Mr. Vice President, gentlemen of Congress, this telegram just delivered by my secretary, Arthur Fleming, came to the White House less than an hour ago from General Lester Matheson, commander of Fort Santa Cruz in south-central Texas. General Matheson says here that since receiving the telegram I sent to him on May 14 informing him of Congress and myself declaring war on Mexico, he has been sending patrols from his fort to scout out any Mexican troops. Just yesterday one of his patrols returned from west Texas and reported that they saw at least three thousand Mexican troops heading toward New Mexico."

By the sudden twisted faces among the men of Congress, it was obvious to the president that their minds were racing forward with crisscross impulses.

As if reading their thoughts, Polk continued. "I know what you're thinking, gentlemen. The same thing has been on my mind ever since we declared war on Mexico. Since Mexico claims New Mexico as one of its territories, I have wondered if they might send troops there right away in order to keep it under their power. I know now that I figured correctly — and you did too. I can see it on your faces."

The majority of the congressmen were nodding, and several spoke out, telling the president they had feared this would happen.

Polk removed a handkerchief from the hip pocket of his suit and mopped his moist brow. "I must send troops to New Mexico as quickly as possible!"

Vice President Dallas was only a step behind the president. He moved forward hastily and laid his hand on the president's shoulder again. "I agree, Mr. President! Send troops to New Mexico as soon as you can!"

The congressmen leaped to their feet, shouting their agreement, many of them waving their arms for emphasis.

Polk raised both hands over his head. When the congressmen had quieted and sat down, he said, "My friends, I will send troops from somewhere in this country other than Texas, since Texas may become a main target in the eyes of President Paredes."

One congressman shouted, "That's the thing to do, Mr. President! Texas will no doubt be *the* main target in the mind of

Paredes! We must not weaken our military numbers in Texas!"

There was an instant roar of voices, with the men of Congress shouting out their agreement that the president should send troops to New Mexico from army camps and forts in other states and territories of the United States.

Polk mopped his moist brow once more. "I will get on this right away, and I will keep all of you posted on my actions. Now, since I must get busy, I hereby declare this meeting adjourned!"

All of the United States Congress and Vice President Dallas were on their feet, cheering the president and shouting out that America would have the victory.

In southeast Texas, on the bright spring Sunday morning of May 24, the sun was shining above the few white clouds that drifted on the light breeze as the Kane family and the Christians who were employed at the Diamond K Ranch headed for their church in Washington-on-the-Brazos. Some of them were in wagons, others on horseback. The group was cheerful as they bounced along the well-worn trail eastward, in the sunshine beneath the azure blue sky.

The Kane family occupied one wagon,

with Abram at the reins. His three grand-sons, nine-year-old Adam, five-year-old Abram, and four-year-old Andrew, sat on the driver's seat with him. On one of the seats that had been built for the wagon's bed, Julia Kane sat holding her one-and-a-half-year-old baby girl, Amber. Facing Julia and Amber, Alex Kane's wife, Libby, and Abel Kane's wife, Vivian, sat on an identical seat. The Kane women chatted among themselves as they rolled along with other Diamond K wagons on each side of them. The twelve wagons were three abreast, from the front of the line to the rear. The Kane wagon and those on each side of it were second in line. The ten men on horseback were riding alongside the lines of wagons on both sides.

For those on horseback and in the wagons, the topic of conversation soon turned to the pending war with Mexico. A pall fell over the Diamond K group as they talked to-gether about the president and Congress's declaration of war on Mexico. The conversa-tion included the names of the three Kane brothers and other men from their church who were already in the army and were soon facing combat in a full-scale war with the Mexican troops.

Abram Kane waited until the conversation among the others began to wane, then hipped around on the driver's seat and said so all could hear, "What do you think about President Polk's nationwide request that fifty thousand men join the army to fight alongside the present troops that are stationed in a number of forts and army posts in the country?"

"I like it, Mr. Kane," spoke up the Diamond K foreman, Cort Whitney, who was in his saddle just ahead of the Kane wagon. "The more men we can get in the American army, the quicker Mexico will be conquered and the sooner those who volunteered to fight for the duration of the war can go back home."

"Right!" called out one of the ranch hands driving his wagon. "I like the way the president is handling the situation!"

There was a sudden eruption of voices — male and female — voicing their agreement with the foreman.

Abram smiled, nodded, and shouted, "Good for you! I know we all want this war to be over in a hurry! Yes, there will be a lot of battles, and some of our men will be killed and others wounded, but the quicker we get our number of troops boosted, the sooner the war will be over!"

While the Diamond K people were speaking out their agreement with Abram's words, in the rear of the Kane wagon, Julia, Libby, and Vivian fell silent as they contemplated their father-in-law's words: *"Some of our men will be killed and others wounded . . ."*

The morning sunshine glistened off of Julia's long dark brown hair as she clutched her baby daughter close to her heart and set her deep blue eyes on Libby and Vivian.

Libby drew a shaky breath. "Ou-our husbands are already in the army and living far from home. They've already faced combat with the Mexicans."

Tears welled up in lovely Julia's eyes, and as they began streaming down her cheeks, she said quietly, "I sure hope this big war is short-lived and all of our husbands and loved ones will be home with us very soon."

Julia pulled a snowy white handkerchief from her drawstring bag and dabbed at her eyes. She fixed her eyes on her sisters-in-law. "My children and I want Papa Alamo home with us."

Libby wiped her own tears from her cheeks. "I want Alex home too."

Vivian was also weeping as she said with a quiver in her voice, "I want Abel home so very, very much."

"We must continue to pray that this war will be a short one and that while they are fighting with the Mexicans, the Lord will protect them and bring them home unharmed." Julia dabbed at more tears.

"Yes," said Vivian, "and we will do that."

Libby sniffed and wiped away more tears. "Yes! We most certainly will! And we will pray for a swift and final end to the war with Mexico!"

"Amen!" said Vivian.

"Amen and amen!" Julia agreed.

In the wagon on their right were two ranch hands and their wives. They had been able to hear what the Kane women were saying above the thump of hooves and gentle clatter of wagon wheels on the soft trail.

The man who held the reins looked at them. "We and our wives want you dear ladies to know that we will pray daily that the Lord will keep our boss, Alamo, safe, and his brothers as well."

The Kane women thanked them.

On the front seat of the Kane wagon, young Adam looked up at his grandfather. "Grandpa, Papa and our uncles are really going to be in danger when that war starts, aren't they?"

Abram saw the stricken look on young Adam's face, then noticed that little Abram's and Andy's faces looked just as stricken. The boys had picked up on the fact that their father and uncles were in grave danger.

The aging Abram Kane looked down at them and gently cleared his throat. "Now, boys, your papa is a very brave man, and your uncles are brave men too. They've been in battles with the Mexican troops already, as you know. They know full well how to protect themselves in combat, but even more important than this, many people on our ranch and in our church are praying for them. Our family is praying for them too. I've heard you boys praying for them many times. We must continue to pray our Lord's shield of protection around them and trust Him to safeguard them as well as the other men from the ranch and our church who will soon be fighting the Mexican troops."

Abram could see instantly that his grandsons were encouraged by his words.

As he had many times before, young Adam brought up how he wished he was old enough to join the army and fight alongside his papa and uncles. Adam drew a short breath. "Grandpa, I would gladly go fight the Mexicans beside Papa Alamo, Uncle Alex, and Uncle Abel!"

Abram smiled down at him. "Well, I'll tell you this, Adam. You're probably a better shot with a rifle than a lot of those men who are about to join the United States Army!"

Two of the young ranch hands who were on horses close to the Kane wagon — Bob Krayson and Cody Proctor — heard what Abram said.

"You are indeed a crack shot with your rifle, Adam," said Bob.

"That's for sure!" Cody agreed. "You really are a crack shot . . . especially for a nine-year-old!"

Adam smiled and looked down at his hands. "Thanks for your kind words."

Bob looked at gray-headed Abram. "Tell you what, Mr. Kane. I've been thinking that maybe I should honor President Polk's request and join the army."

Abram's bushy eyebrows lifted. "Oh really?"

Cody set his gaze on the old man. "Well, sir, the truth is that Bob and I have both felt this way for a while, and we've been praying about it. We'd like to help make the war a short one."

Just ahead of them was foreman Cort Whitney, who had picked up on the conversation. He pulled rein until Bob and Cody were beside him. Then, keeping his horse in step with theirs, he said, "If you fellas feel that's what the Lord would have you to do for your country, I promise you'll still have jobs when you come back."

Noting that they were now entering Washington-on-the-Brazos, Cody and Bob both thanked him and said they would let him know if and when they decided it was the Lord's will to join the army and fight against Mexico.

Soon the Diamond K people were drawing up to the church. A few minutes later, as they walked toward the front door of the church building, one of the ranch hands said, "I wonder what Pastor O'Fallon is going to preach about this morning."

Another ranch hand said, "Well, I'll tell you this. Whatever his subject is, it'll be good . . . as are *all* of his sermons."

2

As the Diamond K people entered the vestibule of the church building, they were greeted by other members, some of them speaking encouraging words about their daily prayers for the safety of the Kane brothers as the time of full-scale war drew near.

Julia, Libby, Vivian, and Grandpa Abram thanked them warmly.

Nine-year-old Adam patted his mother's arm. "Mama, I'll take Abram and Andy to their Sunday school classrooms."

Holding nineteen-month-old Amber in her arms, Julia smiled down at her oldest son. "Thank you, Adam. We'll see you boys in the church service."

Adam led his brothers down the hall to their left. Julia's cook and housekeeper, Daisy Haycock, had ridden to church as usual with one of the older ranch hands, Horace Ludlum, and his wife, Beatrice.

Daisy turned to Julia and said, "Miss Julia, I didn't tell your boys, but we're having their favorite meal for Sunday dinner."

Julia's face lit up. "You mean, as Andy puts it, 'fried chicken and all the neat fixin's'?"

Daisy fluffed her silver hair and smiled. "Yes ma'am. That's it!"

"Well, I won't tell them until we're pulling up to the house."

Daisy giggled. "Okay! As usual, the Ludlums and I will head for home after church a little faster than the rest of you so's I can get dinner on the stove."

Julia patted Daisy's wrinkled cheek. "Thank you, Daisy dear. You're the best cook in all the world."

Daisy's face flushed. "I'm glad you feel that way."

"It's not just me, honey. Not only do my boys feel that way, but Papa Abram does too."

Suddenly Abram, who had been talking to some friends near the door, moved up behind Daisy in time to hear the conversation between her and Julia. "I sure do, Daisy!" he said. "I sure do!"

A bit startled, Daisy drew a quick breath, whirled, and gasped. "Oh, Papa Abram! I-I'm so glad you do!"

Abram's lined face was beaming. "So what are we having for Sunday dinner?"

Daisy smiled. "Your three grandsons' favorite meal."

"Oh! Fried chicken and all the neat fixin's?"

"That's it," she said.

"But don't tell the boys, Papa Abram," Julia said. "I'm going to tell them just as we're pulling up to the house. Otherwise they might not pay attention during church because they'll be thinking about lunch!"

Abram put a finger to his lips and whispered, "I'll keep it a secret, sweetie. I promise!"

Julia laughed. "Good! Well, Papa Abram, I'm going to take Amber to the nursery now. See you in Sunday school class."

As Julia headed down the hall to the right, speaking to people as she met up with them, Abram joined Libby and Vivian, and together they walked into the sanctuary, where the adult Sunday school class met.

A few minutes before eleven o'clock, the Kane family met at their usual pew, which was in the center section, four rows from the front.

The three boys shared with their mother, aunts, and grandfather what they had

47

learned in their Sunday school classes, and as Andrew continued to talk about his lesson, the piano and organ on the platform began playing. Seconds later the choir members came from a side door onto the stage, followed by the pastor and the music director. When the choir members had taken their places in the choir loft, they remained standing.

A hush came over the crowd as the music director led the choir in a rousing gospel song, which uplifted the Lord Jesus as the Captain of the Christian's salvation. By the time the choir's number concluded, the congregation was showing their joy in its message.

The music director then had the congregation stand and led them in two songs from their song books. At the close of the second song, the pastor stepped to the pulpit and called for more music from the piano and organ while the people shook hands with those all around them, especially welcoming the visitors.

When everyone was seated again, the pastor returned to the pulpit, made the normal announcements, read the names of first-time visitors from the cards they had turned in to the ushers earlier, welcomed them warmly, then asked the ushers to come to the front. When they reached the designated spot at the front of the sanctuary, the ushers picked up the offering plates from a small table directly below the pulpit, where a vase of fresh-cut flowers was sitting. The pastor asked one of the ushers to pray for the offering, and when he had done so, the pianist played a beautiful solo.

When the offering had been taken, Pastor Patrick O'Fallon stood at the pulpit. "I want us to have special prayer for the men of our church who are in the United States Army and are soon going to be in furious combat with the Mexican army. Very soon the war that President Polk and Congress have been forced to declare against that country will begin."

Pastor O'Fallon then listed the names and ranks of the men from the church who were in the army, having their families stand as he listed each one. He purposely left the Kane brothers until last. When he named them and the Kanes were all on their feet, he turned and pointed to his wife in the choir. "For you folks who are visitors, this is my wife, Angela. She is also a Kane. The men I just listed are her brothers." A smile spread over his face. "Because of who I married, I am related to Lieutenant Alamo Kane, Private Alex Kane, and Private Abel

Kane and proudly so."

There were "amens" from the crowd, and a few people applauded.

Heads were then bowed as the pastor led in prayer for the men of the church who would soon be in mortal combat with the army of Mexico. When he finished, many people were wiping tears from their faces.

The pastor then introduced a young lady in the choir — Sarah Denison — who was going to sing a duet with Angela before he preached his sermon. He smiled. "I have asked Mrs. Denison and my dear wife to sing that great hymn written by John Newton, who is now in heaven, 'Amazing Grace.' "

The piano and organ played together as the two young ladies sang the powerful song, which had touched so many hearts since Newton wrote about the amazing grace of God that had saved his hell-bound soul. When the ladies finished the heart-touching song and made their way back to their places in the choir, a chorus of "amens" could be heard throughout the crowd, and many were wiping tears from their faces.

Pastor O'Fallon then went to the pulpit and spoke for a few minutes about the war between the United States and Mexico. He told how he had read articles in some church newsletters from across the country that declared it was sin for a Christian man to become a soldier, go to war, and kill other human beings.

"Ladies and gentlemen," Pastor O'Fallon opened his Bible, "those church newsletters are wrong. It is *not* sin for men to protect and defend their country in battle when their enemies would steal their land and kill their families, friends, and fellow country-men if not stopped."

There were many "amens" from the congregation as people nodded their heads.

Pastor O'Fallon then said, "Open your Bibles to Psalm 144."

The sound of fluttering pages filled the auditorium as people turned to the designated passage.

"We are going to read verse 1 in this psalm," the pastor said, "but before I read it to you, please note that in the last verse of Psalm 143, David mentions his enemies. He then writes, 'Blessed be the LORD my strength, which teacheth my hands to war, and my fingers to fight.' Please note the word *war* and the word *fight.* God knew the enemies of Israel were out to make war with them and with David, their king. They would not hesitate to kill as many Israelites as possible, including King David. Thus David says that the Lord is his strength and teaches his hands to make war and his fingers to fight. What we read here would be true of any Christian man when he joins the army of his country and makes war against those who have made themselves enemies. It is to protect his land, his family, and his country. When he uses deadly weapons to do so, it is not wrong, nor is it sin."

There were more "amens."

Pastor O'Fallon then had the people turn to Romans 13. When the sound of fluttering pages stopped, he read verses 1 through 3 and then pointed out that the "higher powers" that are spoken of here are government rulers who represent the law.

He then pointed out that these rulers, who are men of the law, "are not a terror to good works, but to the evil." He read again the words in verse 3: " 'Wilt thou then not be afraid of the power? do that which is good, and thou shalt have praise of the same.' Now, look at verse 4. Of the lawman it says, 'For he is the minister of God to thee for good. But if thou do that which is evil, be afraid; for he beareth not the sword in vain: for he is the minister of God, a revenger to execute wrath upon him that doeth evil.' "

Pastor O'Fallon went on to explain that the "sword" is a weapon of death. A man who wields the sword must be part of the government that has made him a swordsman. He may wield the sword only by the authority of civil government. No man can be a private swordsman. But when he wields a sword by the authority of the law, he is a "minister" of God to punish crime. He must use the sword righteously, as responsible to God, for the suppression of evil.

The pastor then proceeded to compare a soldier in the army of his country with the lawman who serves the civil law, also bearing a weapon of death such as a sword or a gun. In the same manner, the soldier is a "minister" of God to punish the crimes of enemies who would attack his country.

Referring to the church newsletters he had mentioned earlier, Pastor O'Fallon said that these papers use the sixth of the Ten Commandments, "Thou shalt not kill," to prove they are right. He directed the congregation to Matthew 19:17–18, where the Lord Jesus interprets "Thou shalt not kill" as "Thou shalt do no murder." He then gave them the definition of *murder* from Webster's Dictionary of 1840: "To kill a human being with premeditated malice; to slay feloniously." He pointed out that *feloniously* means to commit a crime. The pastor reminded them of the Scriptures they had read moments before about God Himself having taught David's hands to war, and his fingers to fight . . . and how a lawman who bears a deadly weapon is a minister of God. According to Scripture, it is not a crime to kill as a soldier in battles of war, defending one's own country; nor is it a crime for a law officer to kill criminals in defending the citizens of his town, city, or country.

The pastor ran his gaze over the crowd, noting the few soldiers in attendance who had been assigned to the army post in Washington-on-the-Brazos. "I want to commend you men who are in the uniform of the United States Army for your willingness to put your lives on the line when you go into battle against enemy troops who are determined to kill American people and take away our land."

People in the choir and in the congregation nodded and applauded the soldiers, eying them with admiration.

Pastor O'Fallon reminded the congregation of the song the choir had sung at the opening of the service about Jesus being the Captain of the Christian's salvation, then took them to Matthew chapters 27 and 28, where the crucifixion story is told, followed by Jesus' glorious resurrection. He then took them to 1 Corinthians 15:1–4, showing them that the gospel is the death, burial, and resurrection of Christ. He quoted Romans 1:16, which defines the gospel of Christ as "the power of God unto salvation," then showed how the Captain of our salvation fought a battle with the devil when He went to the cross, shed His precious blood, and died . . . then rose from the dead three days later in victory over Satan.

He explained that salvation takes place only when a guilty, lost sinner believes the gospel, comes to the living Saviour in repentance of sin, calls on Him, and receives Him into his heart, trusting Jesus — and Him alone — to save by His grace. He reminded the crowd of his wife and Mrs. Denison singing, "Amazing Grace," then gave the invitation for lost sinners to come forward, receive Jesus as Saviour, and be saved by His amazing grace.

Regular attendees and visitors, including some of the soldiers from the army post in Washington-on-the-Brazos, walked the aisle to receive Jesus as their Saviour. While they were being led to the Lord by counselors at the altar, several Christian men came forward to let it be known that they were going to follow President Polk's request and join the army to help defend their country from Mexico.

After the service, Bob Krayson and Cody Proctor, who had gone forward in the invitation to declare that they were joining the army, approached Diamond K foreman, Cort Whitney, and told him that they would come back to Washington-on-the-Brazos tomorrow morning and join at the U.S. Army post there in town.

Cort smiled and shook their hands. "I'm proud of you fellas! And I guarantee you that when the war's over and you return, your jobs will be waiting for you."

Bob chuckled dryly. "Just pray that we'll live to return, Mr. Whitney."

"Yes, please," said Cody.

Cort nodded solemnly. "I sure will."

As the Diamond K people climbed into their wagons and mounted their horses, many of them commended Bob and Cody for deciding to join the army.

Some of the same people looked toward the Kane wagon, where Julia's three sons were climbing up on the driver's seat while Abram helped Libby into the rear of the wagon. They spoke of Alamo, Alex, and Abel, saying that after hearing the pastor's sermon, they were prouder than ever of them.

Julia was standing near the rear of the wagon next to Vivian holding little Amber in her arms and noted the Ludlum wagon on the road about two miles west of the church property. Daisy was with them. She indeed was going to get home and have dinner cooking by the time the Kane family arrived at the ranch.

Grandpa Abram helped Julia and Amber into the wagon, and while they settled on the seat, he helped Vivian aboard. Vivian made her way to the seat Libby occupied and sat down next to her. As Abram climbed up onto the driver's seat, Adam looked back at his mother. "I sure wish I was old enough to join the army and fight the Mexicans alongside Papa Alamo and Uncle Alex and Uncle Abel."

"Well, Adam," Vivian said, "I hope by the time you're old enough to join the army, there isn't any more war for us to face."

"Yes," agreed Libby. "Me too."

Julia ran her gaze to both women and nodded. "War is such a horrible, tragic thing. It all stems from greed. Wars have been fought since the early days after God put human beings on this earth. They have all been over jealousy and the greed in men's hearts. I'll never understand why people in this world can't be satisfied with what they have. Instead they want what someone else has as well."

"That's true," Vivian said. "It's too bad people won't listen to the Bible. Like Hebrews 13:5, where God says we are supposed to be content with such things as we have and He will never leave us nor forsake us."

Julia sighed heavily, pressing her baby girl close to her. She looked out over the prairie, and a silent prayer went from her heart to her heavenly Father.

Abram put the horses in motion, then looked back over his shoulder at Vivian. "Honey, what you just said is so true. It's too bad people won't listen to God's Word and be content with what they have. But there is so much greed in this world. This is why God's Word says in Romans 12:18: 'If it be possible, as much as lieth in you, live peaceably with all men.' Note the phrase 'if it be possible.' Sometimes it is not possible to live peaceably with all men. They are so often greedy, and because of that greed, they make war on people who want to live peaceably with them.

"As Pastor pointed out in his sermon this morning, sometimes we are forced to fight in order to protect ourselves and what we have. War is indeed a horrible, tragic thing, like Julia said, but it would be worse if we just lay down and let evil, mercenary people take over our country, our land, and all that we've worked for."

"You're right, Papa Abram," Julia said. "Sure, I wish there wasn't any greed in this world and what it causes, and I wish there wasn't any war. But that's only wishful thinking. I'm thankful that our God is able to keep us in His care, even in the midst of war and fighting."

As the wagon rolled on toward the Diamond K Ranch, Abram, his daughters-in-law, and his grandsons fell silent, lost in their own thoughts. After a while, the wagon pulled onto the ranch, and a few minutes later, Abram guided it to a halt in front of the big ranch house.

Sensing the sadness that had overtaken her family with the talk of war, Julia said with a wide smile, "Well, who's hungry?"

The adults chuckled, and Julia's three boys turned around in the driver's seat and looked at their mother.

Adam grinned. "I am, Mama!"

"Me too!" said young Abram.

"Yeah, and me too!" spoke up Andy.

Julia held the gazes of her sons. "Guess what we're having for Sunday dinner? Daisy told me at church . . ."

Andy's face lit up. "Mama, is it fried chicken and all the neat fixin's?"

Little Amber was giggling, as if she knew the answer to the question.

Julia laughed. "You got it, Andy! Fried chicken and all the neat fixin's!"

"Oh boy!" shouted Andy, who was sitting at the right end of the driver's seat, with his brothers between him and his grandfather. "Hey, Adam, Abram, let's go to the kitchen right now and give Aunt Daisy a hug for cookin' our favorite meal!" He jumped down to the ground and looked back at his brothers, who were scrambling downward behind him.

"Let's do it!" young Abram said excitedly.

"Yeah!" said big brother Adam. "Let's go tell Aunt Daisy how glad we are she's cooked us fried chicken with all the neat fixin's!"

Moments later, when the adults entered the kitchen, they found the three boys still hugging Daisy. She was smiling as she looked at Julia, Libby, Vivian, and Grandpa Abram. "I really like these hugs I'm getting! Think I'll cook fried chicken and all the neat fixin's more often!"

The boys laughed and agreed that she should do that.

Everyone in the family went to the washbowl on the kitchen cupboard and washed and dried their hands.

In just a short time, dinner was on the dining room table. When everyone had sat down at the table and little Amber was in her high chair next to her mother, they held hands around the table, bowed their heads, and closed their eyes.

Though little Amber bowed her head like the others, her eyes were open as Grandpa Abram led them in prayer. He thanked the Lord for His gracious provisions and choked up a bit as he prayed earnestly for his three sons who were in the army and about to face combat.

When the "amen" had been said, platters and bowls of delicious food started around the table with much chattering and laughter filling the room.

Seeing the happiness of her loved ones in spite of the pending war with Mexico, lovely Julia Kane thought to herself, *This is as it should be. We must not overpower the boys with gloom and doom. They are so young and should be allowed to enjoy their childhood. I will do my best to make it a happy one for them. I know that's what Alamo wants. That's what he is fighting for.*

Julia looked around the table at her children, her sisters-in-law, and her father-in-law. Her heart swelled within her chest. *Thank You, Lord,* she said in her heart. *Thank You that we can all be here together. Please protect us and Alamo, Alex, and Abel.*

A peaceful smile graced Julia's lips as God filled her heart with peace.

3

On Monday morning, May 25, at the capitol building in Mexico City, *el presidente* Mariano Paredes stood on the platform of the colorful carpeted assembly room and observed as fifty-two government leaders made their way into the room, chatting with each other and settling onto the thinly cushioned chairs.

When everyone was seated, Mexico's new president stepped up to the podium, ran his eyes over the group, and smiled at them. *"Buenos días."*

Fifty-two voices chorused, "Buenos días."

Paredes was forty-eight years of age, stood barely over five and a half feet tall, and was quite slender. He had a thick head of black hair, long sideburns, a mustache, heavy eyebrows, and a long, slender face. His eyes were a deep, dark brown.

Speaking in Spanish, Paredes warmly welcomed the government leaders to the meeting, then called the meeting to order. He spoke of Mexican general Manuel Armijo and the three thousand Mexican troops he had sent with Armijo to New Mexico to keep the contemptible Americans from taking the territory away from Mexican rule. Paredes went on to say that he had no doubt that General Armijo and his troops would be successful in defeating the American troops if they invaded New Mexico. The government leaders loudly spoke out their agreement, which made Paredes smile broadly.

Still smiling, Paredes told the group that America's president, James K. Polk, would be embarrassed and ashamed when his troops were defeated in New Mexico. The Mexican government leaders cheered Paredes, waving their arms.

Paredes then talked to them about how Mexico was once under the rule of Spain, but in 1821 became independent of Spain. At that time, the Mexicans took over property in California from the Spaniards and claimed California for Mexico.

Paredes's mouth then sagged at the corners, and his expression displayed bitterness as he went on to say that at that time, in 1821, the United States had people in California, and just recently, in early 1846, the Americans claimed California as *their* territory. The Mexican president's eyes filled with fire as he went on to say that at that same time the contemptible Americans declared California an independent republic. And now the American flag was flying over every major city in California.

A grinding feeling of injustice seemed to sweep over the crowd of Mexican government leaders, and it exploded into waves of wrath. The whole group jumped to their feet, their eyes inflamed and their dark faces flushed.

One of the high-ranking men, who was in the front row, set his wild eyes on the slender man at the podium. Paredes noted his clenched fists hanging at his sides, his twisted, swarthy features, and the cruel angle of his jaw as he shouted to him, saying that Paredes must send troops to California to take it back from the Americans.

The rest of the government leaders shouted their agreement, demanding that the president do just that.

Paredes raised his hands palms forward to silence them. When the loud voices went quiet, he assured them that he would send troops to California to take it back from the Americans, and they cheered him.

On that same day at Fort Polk, near the Rio Grande, which the American government had declared was the border between Texas and Mexico, army medics continued to care for the 136 American soldiers who had been wounded in the Palo Alto and Resaca de la Guerrero battles on May 8 and 9.

At the same time, their leader, General Zachary Taylor, was waiting for orders from President Polk as to when and where the president would command the troops at Fort Polk to begin their attacks on Mexico's military forts, towns, and cities now that the United States had declared war on Mexico.

Each day since returning to the fort after the Palo Alto and Resaca de la Guerrero battles, General Taylor had sent out patrols on horseback to keep watch for Mexican troops that might be coming to attack the fort. So far none had been seen, but five patrols were sent out daily as a precautionary measure.

On this day, Lieutenant Alamo Kane was leading one of the five patrols General Taylor had sent out early that morning. There were eight men in Lieutenant Kane's patrol, including himself and his two brothers, Privates Alex and Abel Kane.

It was nearing noon when Alamo, on the return patrol route, led the men to a halt at the edge of the Gulf of Mexico, just a short distance northeast of the fort. The sky was clear, and the gulf's water was a sapphire blue. The soldiers sat on their horses and took in the beauty of the gulf as the surf washed up on the shore, breaking into sheets of white foam while giving off a low, soft swishing sound.

Alamo, who at thirty-two years of age, was eight years younger than his brother Alex and six years younger than Abel. The three resembled each other very much, especially since they each stood six feet four inches tall, had sand colored hair, light blue eyes, and weighed a muscular 220 pounds.

While the surf continued to wash up on the beach, Alamo ran his gaze up and down the shore, then turned to the seven men. "Well, fellas, I'm plenty glad we didn't see any Mexican troops this morning."

The others nodded.

"I hope none of the other patrols saw any Mexicans in army uniform either."

"Yeah, me too," said one of the sergeants.

The other six men joined in verbally also.

Alamo ran his gaze up and down the shore

once again. "Men, it's time to head back to the fort. The cooks will have lunch ready pretty soon."

At that instant, movement in the sky caught Alamo's attention. He focused on a bald eagle flying high above them and pointed to it. "Look at that bald eagle up there! Isn't he magnificent?"

Every man in the patrol directed his attention to where the lieutenant was pointing and focused on the eagle, which was gliding on the wind, his wings spread to the fullest. They all commented on the beauty of the eagle. Then Abel said, "I've heard that the bald eagle flies higher than any other bird."

"Yeah, I've heard that too," said one of the soldiers.

"Me too," put in another one.

Alamo agreed. "Mm-hmm. I've also heard that they nest at the very top of the tallest trees they can find, leaving the lower limbs for other kinds of birds."

Alex nodded. "I read something in the Bible once about how when eagles perch in a tree, they do so on the highest branch."

Alamo's eyebrows arched. "Yeah?"

Alex nodded. "Mm-hmm."

"Where'd you read that?"

Alex shook his head. "Right now I can't

remember."

Alamo nodded. "Well, we'll have to look it up sometime." He looked around at the other men. "Like I said, fellas, it's time to head back to the fort."

A half hour later, as Alamo and the other seven men in the patrol unit drew near the fort, they saw the other four patrols coming from the west and the south.

As Alamo's patrol drew up to those patrols, he asked their leaders if they had seen any Mexican troops. All four answered in the negative.

"Good!" Alamo said. "Let's go report the news to General Taylor!"

Moments later the guards in the watchtower at the fort's main gate and the soldiers inside were happy to learn that the patrols had seen no Mexican troops. Alamo and the other patrol leaders dismounted, let their men take their horses to the corral, and headed for General Taylor's office.

Just as they were drawing up to the office, the door opened and the general stepped out to meet them.

"General, sir," Alamo said, "we have good news. None of us spotted any Mexican troops while on patrol."

Taylor smiled. "Good! I'm glad. Of course,

we'll have to keep watching for them. The patrols will cover the same ground tomorrow. It's better to be safe than sorry."

"That's for sure, sir," said Alamo.

The other four patrol leaders spoke their agreement.

General Taylor said, "Well, men, it's almost time for lunch." He ran his gaze to the tables, where he knew the cooks would set out the food. At that instant, he saw the cooks coming out of the kitchen building, pushing carts of food toward the tables. "Looks like the cooks are about to put the food out now."

Alamo and the other patrol leaders headed that direction. As he drew close, Alamo saw his brothers getting in line to pick up their food. He hurried up to Alex and Abel. "It'll take the cooks a few more minutes to bring the rest of the food out, so I'm going to go check on Lance Brooks and see how he's doing."

"We'll save you a place, little brother," Alex said, chuckling.

Alamo matched his chuckle. "Thanks! Be back shortly."

Alex and Abel smiled at each other as their younger brother hurried away toward the area within the fort's walls where the 136 wounded men were tended.

As Alamo neared, he saw that, as usual, some of the wounded men were sitting up, while the majority were lying on blankets on the ground. Soon he approached Corporal Lance Brooks, who was one of those lying on the ground. As he drew up, he noticed that Lance had a fresh bandage on his wounded leg.

Smiling at the man who had saved his life during the Palo Alto battle and led him to Christ the very same day, the fair-haired Brooks said, "Glad to see you back, Alamo. Did any of the patrols spot Mexican troops?"

Alamo matched Lance's smile. "No, they didn't."

"Good! I'm glad to hear that!"

Alamo squatted down beside Lance and was about to comment on the fresh bandage on his wounded leg, when Lance asked, "Why do you suppose no Mexican troops are roaming around the Texas-Mexico border yet since the United States declared war on them? They know the fort is here, and certainly after the Palo Alto and Resaca de la Guerrero battles they know we've got lots of troops. I'd think they'd want to wipe us out before we become a serious threat to them."

"I've thought about that," Alamo said. "I

71

have a feeling that the Mexican military leaders may have their troops busy building fortresses around certain cities and towns in order to keep the American troops from conquering and capturing them."

Lance looked up, met Alamo's eyes, and nodded. "Makes sense. That's probably exactly what they're doing."

Alamo then glanced down at Lance's wounded left thigh. "I noticed when I got here that you've got a new bandage on your wound. What did the medics say? Is it healing all right?"

"They said it's healing slower than they had expected."

"Oh?"

"Mm-hmm. But it *is* healing."

Alamo stood to his feet. "Well, I'm glad at least that it's healing. Praise the Lord for that."

"Yes sir!"

"Well, my friend, it's about lunchtime. Your lunch should be coming soon. I'll go now and eat with my brothers and the rest of the troops."

Lance's brow furrowed. "One thing I should tell you."

"What's that?"

"The medics have informed me that I'll never be able to walk on this wounded leg in a normal way. They say I'll limp for the rest of my life."

Alamo slowly moved his head back and forth. "I'm sorry to hear that, Lance."

Lance nodded. "They told me I won't be able to stay in the army, but they did say they're sure I will receive an honorable discharge."

Alamo smiled. "You most certainly will."

At that moment, both men observed the medics coming from the kitchen building with heaping plates of food and steaming cups of coffee on carts.

Alamo told Lance he would see him later, and a few minutes after that he joined his brothers amid the other soldiers for lunch near the food tables. Alex and Abel were glad to learn that Lance's wounded leg was on the mend, even though it was slow coming about. When Alamo informed them of what the medics had told Lance about his not being able to stay in the army, but that he would receive an honorable discharge, Alex and Abel agreed that he deserved it.

When lunch was almost over, the soldiers who were sitting on the ground and eating near the food tables noticed a lone rider coming through the front gate of the fort, which one of the watchtower guards was holding open. Another watchtower guard was hurrying ahead of the rider, heading for General Zachary Taylor's office.

Alamo focused on the face of the rider and smiled. "Recognize him?" he said to his brothers.

"Sure," Abel said. "That's Corporal Harry Newton from the army post at Washington-on-the-Brazos."

"Sure enough," said Alex.

"I've got a feeling that Corporal Newton might be bringing a telegram to General Taylor from President Polk," Alamo said.

One of the soldiers in a group close by who had heard the conversation between the Kane brothers leaned their direction. "If that's so, Lieutenant Kane, we are now about to find out what the first battle assignment of the Fort Polk troops will be in the war with Mexico."

By the time Corporal Newton spotted the Kane brothers and guided his horse toward them, all the men were rising to their feet. Their attention was divided between the lone rider in the United States Army uniform and the watchtower guard who was knocking on General Taylor's office door. The bulk of them headed toward Taylor's office.

As Newton drew rein where the Kane brothers were standing, he said, "Howdy, friends! I'm glad to see that you're alive and looking fine after those two battles you fought in a couple of weeks ago."

The Kane brothers smiled and greeted him in return.

At that moment, all eyes were turned to General Taylor as he emerged from his office with the watchtower guard at his side. The general moved hastily to a spot a few yards from where the bulk of the troops were collected and halted. The guard halted with him. The troops began moving toward the general and formed a half circle in front of him.

The rest of the men who had been eating near the food tables, including the Kane brothers, hurried to where the others were gathering.

Newton trotted his horse up to where the general stood, and Taylor motioned for him to stop. "Please dismount, Corporal Newton."

The corporal slid from the saddle, stepped up to the general, and saluted. "I guess your guard here told you who I am, General."

Taylor saluted in return. "Indeed he did. You're a messenger from the army post in Washington-on-the-Brazos. And your name is Corporal Harry Newton."

All of the troops standing in the half circle

before the general could clearly hear what was being said and looked on with keen interest.

The corporal grinned. "Yes sir." He drew a white envelope from his shirt pocket. "General Taylor, I have a telegram for you that came to our office this morning from President Polk in Washington, D.C. I rode here as quickly as I could."

General Taylor smiled and extended his open hand. "You must have pushed your horse pretty hard to do that. In fact, he's still panting."

Corporal Newton nodded as he placed the telegram into the general's hand. "Yes sir, he is. But he'll catch his breath pretty soon. I wanted to get the president's message to you as soon as possible."

Taylor patted the horse's neck. "Thank you." He removed the telegram from the envelope.

The crowd of over two thousand soldiers waited with anticipation as General Taylor silently read the lengthy message. When he was finished, he looked up at the crowd of soldiers. "Since war was declared, you've all been as eager as I have to hear the president's orders concerning where we'll make our first assault on Mexico. In this telegram, President Polk has commanded us to stand by here at Fort Polk until further notice."

The troops frowned and exchanged glances, then looked back at their leader.

"I know this is a bit of a letdown, men," Taylor said, "but I assure you we'll be in the thick of this war in the not-too-distant future. Let me tell you what else President Polk says. The American men are responding well to his newspaper requests that some fifty thousand join the U.S. Army at military posts and forts quickly so the army can move on Mexico as soon as possible."

The soldiers exchanged glances again, but this time they were smiling.

Taylor let a smile curve his lips as well. "Something else, men. You'll like this. I sure do. The president is sending some thirty-seven hundred soldiers to Fort Polk to add to the twenty-three hundred of you here under my command right now. A little quick arithmetic will tell you that will bring our total up to six thousand!"

The men cheered, some of them clapping their hands while others removed their hats and waved them.

When the cheering died down, General Taylor said, "Something else, men. President Polk says here that he will be sending troops into New Mexico first. The Mexican government claims New Mexico territory as its own, and shortly after Mexico's president, Mariano Paredes, received the official declaration of war from our president and Congress, he began sending Mexican troops into New Mexico with the purpose of keeping the United States government from claiming it."

The soldiers began talking to each other in low voices. General Taylor could make out that the men believed that the Fort Polk troops would probably be sent into New Mexico to fight the Mexican troops there.

Taylor shook his head and said loud enough so all could hear above the murmur. "No, men! President Polk says right here in the telegram that he will be sending troops from Missouri into New Mexico. So we won't be going there. Just before he ended the message, the president said the thirty-seven hundred troops he is sending to Fort Polk will arrive here in about three weeks. He then added that official word concerning the assignment of the Fort Polk troops in the war will come soon after the new men arrive."

The soldiers looked at each other and silently nodded their heads.

General Taylor sighed. "Actually, men, I'm glad for this delay before we're sent into battle. I want some of you men to use the wagons to take our one hundred thirty-six wounded men to their homes before the rest of us, along with the new troops, have to go into major battle."

Men among the soldiers in the large half circle nodded their heads.

The general went on. "Most of our wounded are from northeast Texas, and a good number of them are from the San Antonio–Gonzales area. Several are from towns and rural areas near the Gulf of Mexico. A few are from southeast Texas, but some distance north of the Gulf. I will be asking for volunteers to take our wounded men to their homes. From those who volunteer, I'll assign certain ones to drive the wagons. Some will use those Mexican army horses and wagons we confiscated after the Resaca de la Guerrero battle, the ones the Mexicans left behind when they fled."

The Kane brothers looked at each other, and Alamo thought of the wounded Lance Brooks. Lance was from Prairie View, Texas, which was some twenty-five miles northwest of Washington-on-the-Brazos and thirty-five miles due north of their home at the Diamond K Ranch.

Alex and Abel Kane could tell that Alamo's wheels were turning, and in a whisper Alex asked, "Hey, Alamo . . . what are you thinking?"

Alamo whispered his answer to them, and the older brothers instantly agreed that they would like to take Lance home to his parents. Alamo leaned in toward his brothers. "Since I had the joy of leading Lance to the Lord, I sure would like an opportunity to witness to his parents and try to lead them to Jesus."

Abel's eyes were bright with anticipation as he whispered, "Let's volunteer right now. Let's tell General Taylor that we want to take Lance home!"

4

As Abel Kane was whispering to his brothers that they should volunteer on the spot, Alamo Kane glanced toward the general and saw that at the moment he was in conversation with a lieutenant named Darrell Devries.

Alex Kane followed Alamo's line of sight then turned to Abel. "We'll have to wait till the general gets through talking to Lieutenant Devries."

Alex shrugged. "Well, we could head that way and be next to talk to the general."

"Good idea," Alamo said. "Let's go."

As the three Kane brothers casually moved toward the spot where the general was standing, Alex said, "Hey, guys, since we're gonna take Lance to his parents, seems we should spend a little time with our family at the Diamond K as long as we're gonna be that close to home."

"I had that in mind, too," Alamo said,

"since it'll be three weeks before General Taylor gets an assignment from the president for our troops to make an aggressive move on the Mexicans."

"Great!" Alex said. "Let's ask the general if we can visit the ranch on this trip."

Alamo glanced toward the general and saw that Lieutenant Devries was walking away. "Let's move, fellas!" he said to his brothers.

With Alex and Abel flanking him, Alamo hastened toward the general and raised a hand over his head. "General Taylor, may my brothers and I talk to you?"

Taylor smiled, running the fingertips of his right hand through his heavy mustache. "Of course, Lieutenant Kane."

As they drew up, Alamo said, "General, we'd like to be the ones to take the wounded Corporal Lance Brooks home."

Taylor nodded. "Well, I —"

"His home is only thirty-five miles due north of our ranch, sir," Alamo interjected. "Would you give us permission to take him?"

The general ran his gaze over the three Irish faces and smiled again. "Why, of course." He lifted his hat and placed it back on his head at a slightly different angle. "Gentlemen, since Corporal Brooks's home is so close to your ranch, I'm sure you'd like to go home and have a little time with your family."

Alex and Abel grinned at Alamo, and he grinned back. They were pleased at the general's attitude. Alamo set appreciative eyes on his commander. "We'd *love* to do that, sir!"

Taylor nodded. "Since it'll be three weeks before the new troops arrive and President Polk sends orders as to when and where we should head in aggressive attack on Mexico, you should spend a week at your ranch before coming back to the fort."

Alamo's head bobbed. "A *week,* General? We'd love that, but I don't know if we should stay that long. You see, from Fort Polk to the Diamond K Ranch is some 265 miles. I figure that traveling in a wagon with the wounded corporal aboard will require driving slower than normal. It'll probably take us about six days to get there, then another day to take Corporal Brooks to his home in Prairie View."

Taylor smiled. "That's fine, Lieutenant. I still want you and your brothers to spend a week with your family. I suggest you go to the ranch from here, spend your week there; then take Corporal Brooks to Prairie View and head back toward Fort Polk. Since you won't have the wounded corporal in the wagon on the return trip, you can probably make it back to the fort in four days. This'll still have you back in three weeks."

The Kane brothers smiled at each other. Then Alamo said, "General, sir, we appreciate your kindness in even wanting us to have some time with our family. And we'll be back well within three weeks."

"We sure will, General Taylor," Alex said. "And indeed, we appreciate your kindness."

"That's for sure, General Taylor!" Abel exclaimed. "Thank you so much!"

The general smiled and nodded. "I'm just glad it worked out this way, gentlemen. Now before you go to Corporal Brooks, I want you to wait right here while I put together the rest of the volunteers who'll be taking wounded men home. Then we'll all go over to where the wounded men are, and after I tell them the contents of President Polk's telegram, I'll inform them that they are going home."

"Sure, General," Alamo said. "We'll just move back with the other men until you're ready to go."

As the Kane brothers slipped back among the troops, General Taylor spoke to the crowd that was still gathered around him and called for volunteers to drive wagons and take wounded men to their homes. He explained that it would take around thirty wagons to get the 136 wounded men to their homes in various parts of Texas. Many of the wagons would carry 4 or 5 wounded each, and Taylor would assign men to team up in pairs so they could trade off driving. For those whose wounds were quite serious, he would assign medics to ride along. The general then informed them that Lieutenant Kane and his two brothers had already volunteered to take the wounded Corporal Brooks to his home in Prairie View.

There were immediately more than enough volunteers. Most of them had already chosen their driving partners. Soon the general had appointed enough men to work in pairs driving thirty-four wagons. He told the volunteers he had not chosen that they would be on hold in case he needed more.

At that moment, Corporal Newton approached General Taylor. "Sir, I must be heading back to Washington-on-the-Brazos. Would you like me to send a telegram to President Polk for you?"

The general nodded. "I sure would, Corporal."

Newton took a small pad of paper from

his shirt pocket along with a pencil. "All right, sir. What should I say to him?"

"Tell the president that my men and I will be waiting for the new troops to arrive and for orders as to when and where he wants us to make an aggressive move on the Mexicans."

The corporal hurriedly wrote the general's words on the pad and read them back to make sure he had it right. When the general had thanked him for his help, Newton smiled. "It's my pleasure, sir."

With that, Newton turned and bade the Kane brothers farewell, mounted his horse, and rode away. Soon he had passed from view.

General Taylor then dismissed the large crowd of troops, called for the volunteers, and led them across the fort grounds to the special area where the wounded men were gathered. Some were sitting on the ground, and others were lying on blankets. A few medics were there, moving about and caring for the injured men.

As the general moved toward a spot where all the wounded men could see and hear him, some of them began asking him what was going on. They could see the crowd of soldiers gathered in the large open area inside the fort but couldn't hear what was being said. The general smiled and told them they were all about to learn what was going on.

When General Taylor reached his intended spot, he smiled. "Men, I've got good news for you!" He then proceeded to tell them of the telegraph message from President Polk and explained that the president was sending enough soldiers to Fort Polk to bring the number of troops to six thousand. He explained that the reinforcements would arrive in about three weeks.

The general then told the wounded men of the arrangements he had made for them to be taken to their homes right away, some in American army wagons and others in the wagons confiscated from the Mexicans after the Resaca de la Guerrero battle.

This news made the wounded men happy, and they loudly spoke their appreciation to General Taylor for doing this on their behalf.

The Kane brothers immediately walked over to where Lance Brooks lay on the ground with a blanket beneath him. Alamo bent over him. "Lance, my friend, my brothers and I worked out an arrangement with General Taylor. We'll be taking you home."

Lance's face lit up with joy. "Oh good! There's nobody I'd rather have take me home than you guys! This will be great! I

want to thank all three of you for being willing to take me home. I —"

At that moment, Lance saw General Taylor passing by. "General Taylor, sir!"

The general turned around and walked
over to the wounded corporal. He smiled.
"Yes, Corporal? What can I do for you?"

Smiling in return, Lance replied, "Nothing, sir. You've already done it! I want to
thank you for allowing the Kane brothers to
take me home!"

General Taylor's smile broadened. "Let
me tell you, Corporal Brooks, I was mighty
glad when these men came to me and offered to take you home."

Lance's eyes swung to the Kane brothers.

"Corporal Brooks," the general said, "I'm
sure Lieutenant Alamo Kane has a special
place in your heart since he saved your life
on the Palo Alto battlefield."

Lance looked back at the general, smiled,
and turned his bright eyes toward Alamo.
"Yes sir, General Taylor, the lieutenant
indeed has a special place in my heart."
Lance looked at Alex and Abel. "And his
brothers have also earned a special place in
my heart by just being my friends."

The general was still smiling as he once
again set his eyes on the wounded man.
"I'm very glad the Kane brothers are will-

ing to take you home, Corporal, and I'm also very glad that in so doing they'll be able to spend a little time with their family at the Diamond K Ranch as well."

Lance's eyelids fluttered. "Really?"

"Really, Lance," Alex said. "Of course, the main thing is to get you home with your parents, but we're sure looking forward to being able to stay at the ranch a few days and be with our family."

"Something else before I move on, Corporal Brooks," the general said. "I want you to know that I'll be working on getting you an honorable discharge from the army. Since you were wounded so seriously that you have to be discharged, I want it to be an *honorable* discharge. And that's what it's going to be!"

Lance's face lit up. "Thank you, sir!"

"The papers will come by mail to your parents' home in Prairie View," said Taylor.

"Thank you again, General."

"You deserve it, son." The general walked away.

Lance smiled at the Kane brothers. "I'm sure glad you can spend some time at your ranch while making the trip to take me home."

Alamo leaned closer to Lance. "Would you mind if we go to the ranch first and stay for a few days before we take you on to Prairie View?"

Lance rolled his head back and forth against the blanket beneath him. "Of course not, Lieutenant."

Alamo grinned. "Thanks. We appreciate it. You see, Alex, Abel, and I want you to meet the Kane family and at least some of the ranch hands so I can tell them the story of how you came to know the Lord Jesus as your Saviour after at first being hardhearted toward the gospel and what the Bible says about hell."

"Oh, I'd love to meet the rest of the Kane family and let you tell the story in my presence."

Alamo patted Lance's arm. "Believe me, it'll be a tremendous blessing to be able to tell the story."

Lance swallowed hard and took a breath. "Lieutenant, when you take me home, would you try to lead my parents to the Lord while you're there? Since I've only been saved a short time, I don't think I'll be able to deal with my parents about their need of salvation as adeptly as *you* would."

Alamo chuckled softly. "Lance, ol' pal, I was already planning on doing just that when we're there!"

Tears welled up in Lance's eyes. "Why

doesn't this surprise me?"

Abel laughed and elbowed Alex. "We figured Alamo was already determined to give the gospel to your parents, Lance."

While they were talking, Alamo saw the main medic who had been taking care of Lance pass by. "Dr. Myers! Dr. Myers!" he called out.

Dr. John Myers came to a halt. "Yes, Lieutenant Kane?"

"Could I talk to you for a moment, please?"

The medic smiled and made his way toward Alamo. "Of course. What do you want to talk about?"

"Well, for the past couple of weeks, you've been the main medic taking care of Corporal Brooks here."

"Yes?"

"Well, sir, General Taylor has assigned my brothers and me to take him home in a wagon to Prairie View. It's 265 miles from here to our ranch, which is where we're going first, then another 35 miles to Corporal Brooks's home in Prairie View. As you can see, that will total 300 miles. Can he make the trip without a medic riding along?"

Myers nodded. "I believe so, but he'll have to lie down in the wagon bed during the entire trip. He should have enough pillows and blankets underneath him to cushion against the bumps. As long as the wagon doesn't bounce him hard, he'll be all right and won't need a medic."

Alamo nodded. "We plan to go slower than normal so the corporal won't be jarred and bounced around."

"Good," Dr. Myers said. "That'll be a necessity for his sake."

"Of course, driving slower means it'll take six days to get to the ranch. Will this be too much for Lance?"

Dr. Myers shook his head. "No. He's past that kind of danger. How soon do you plan to leave?"

"Well, since you've given your approval, we'll head out as planned after breakfast tomorrow morning."

"All right," the doctor said. "I'll put a fresh bandage on his leg just before breakfast. I'll let Corporal Brooks keep the crutches he's been using the past several days, and I'll send along some medical supplies for his care on the trip."

Alamo nodded. "All right, sir. That sounds good."

Dr. Myers set steady eyes on Alamo. "I strongly suggest, Lieutenant Kane, that Corporal Brooks be examined by a doctor when you get to your ranch to make sure he's all right."

"We'll do it, Doctor."

"Good." Myers looked down at Lance. "Corporal, all the best to you."

Lance smiled up at him. "Thank you, Doctor. You've taken excellent care of me."

"It has been my pleasure. I'll see you in the morning."

Lance grinned. "Yes. In the morning."

"Exactly, Corporal," the medic said as he turned and walked away.

Lance reached up, took hold of Alamo's right hand, and squeezed it tightly. "Lieutenant, thank you for being so good to me."

Alamo squeezed back. "Lance, you can call me Alamo."

The wounded man's eyes were suddenly watery. "Really?"

"Really."

Lance sniffed and blinked at his tears. "Then I'll put it this way. Alamo, thank you for being so good to me."

Alamo smiled. "Lance, we brothers in Christ are supposed to be good to each other."

"That's right," said Alex.

"It sure is!" Abel agreed.

On the afternoon of that same Monday, May 25, 1846, at Fort Clemson, Missouri, which was located on Loutre Island at the junction of the Missouri and Loutre rivers, the fort's commander, Colonel Stephen Kearny, was sitting at the desk in his office when he heard a sudden sound of excitement among his troops outside. He hurried to the office door, opened it, and saw a crowd of men coming through the fort's main gate.

Kearny smiled to himself when he laid eyes on Missouri's governor, J. D. Rockwell, who was on horseback leading the men, who were afoot, into the fort. The colonel was aware that President Polk had assigned the Missouri governor to sign up as many volunteers as possible at the state capitol building. He dashed across the porch, stepped down onto the soft earth, and moved swiftly toward the governor, who had spotted him by that time. The governor hurried his horse toward Colonel Kearny, pulled rein when they were drawing close to each other, dismounted, and extended his hand as Kearny drew up.

As they shook hands, Kearny said, "Looks like you've got a good bunch of volunteers here, Governor!"

"Well, Colonel, I wish there were more, but I'm glad I was able to bring you 856 volunteers who joined the army at the capitol building since President Polk put out his request for 50,000 thousand men of this country to join the army."

"Eight-hundred-and-fifty-six! That's great! I want to welcome them."

At that moment, Colonel Kearny noted some men on horseback following the last of the volunteers through the gate. He turned to the governor. "Who are those men on the horses?"

"Those are my 12 armed escorts, Colonel. They came with me from Jefferson City and will escort me back there."

"Oh, I see. Well, with Mexicans able to move about in this country as they please, that's a good idea."

As he spoke, the colonel headed toward the new crowd of men, who were being greeted by the men at the fort. Rockwell followed on the colonel's heels until the colonel stopped, raised both hands, and said loudly, "I want to welcome all of you men who have come here with Governor Rockwell! I am Colonel Stephen Kearny, commander of Fort Clemson."

The new men smiled and greeted the colonel.

Kearny continued. "Governor Rockwell tells me there are 856 of you. This will bring the number of men here in the fort to just over 1,700. As you know, you were inducted into the United States Army at this time to join the other men in this fort under my command and take New Mexico Territory from the Mexican troops who have been sent there by President Mariano Paredes, under the command of General Manuel Armijo. President Polk has ordered that you new men undergo combat training until the last week of June; then I am to lead all of my troops into New Mexico. This gives us a month to train you new men to fight the Mexican troops."

"We're ready, Colonel!" shouted a husky man in his midthirties.

All of the new men waved their arms and shouted the same, echoing the husky man's words.

The colonel smiled. "Our first assignment as we invade New Mexico is to capture Santa Fe, the capital city of New Mexico, for the United States and to assure the governor and his territorial leaders that we will protect them while we're battling and conquering General Armijo's 3,000 troops."

Kearny knew the volunteers had been told that the Mexican troops in New Mexico numbered 3,000. The men showed no shock at this number, but some showed concern that the Mexican troops would outnumber them by nearly 1,300.

"Let me say this to you, men," Kearny said. "In the battles of Palo Alto and Resaca de la Guerrero earlier this month, the American forces were vastly outnumbered but were still the victors. The Mexican soldiers are not nearly as well trained as our American soldiers, nor do they have the quality of weapons we do, especially cannons. Because of this, we can win over General Armijo's 3,000 troops, drive them out of New Mexico, and claim New Mexico Territory for the United States."

The men already in uniform shouted their agreement, and soon the new men were doing the same.

Smiling, Colonel Kearny immediately commanded his officers to take the new recruits to the open fields at the southern tip of the island for the rest of the afternoon and begin their combat training. He quickly explained that he would have the new men measured for uniforms that evening, and because of telegraph connections, the uniforms would be delivered from St. Louis within a week or so. He also told the new men that the guns they would be trained with would be assigned to them before they headed for New Mexico so they could use the same guns in battle that they had used in training.

By this time, the officers in charge of training the new recruits were standing before them, and Kearny told the trainees to follow the officers.

Governor Rockwell and Colonel Kearny watched as the officers and the other soldiers who had been assigned to train the Missouri volunteers lined them up six abreast, led them through the main gate, and turned southward.

5

Governor J. D. Rockwell and Colonel Stephen Kearny kept their eyes on the new army volunteers and their military trainers until they passed from view, headed for the southern tip of Loutre Island.

The sun was shining brightly on the island and the waters of the two rivers that bordered it as the colonel turned to the governor. "Governor Rockwell, since we have telegraph equipment here in the fort's office, I'll wire President Polk immediately and let him know that the new Missouri recruits have arrived and are now being trained. I'll tell him that all the troops and I will leave for New Mexico in time to take Santa Fe from the Mexican army and go to full-scale war with them by the third week of July. This is what he requested when he first contacted me with his orders to train the volunteers who were coming to Fort Clemson from all over Missouri through your office at Jefferson City."

The governor nodded and met the colonel's gaze. "I very much appreciate your sending the telegram, Colonel. And let me say that I have absolutely no doubt that you and your troops will be victorious over the Mexican troops in New Mexico and will solidly claim New Mexico Territory for the United States."

Kearny smiled. "Thank you, Governor Rockwell. I very much appreciate your confidence in me and these men."

Rockwell sighed and put on his hat. "Well, sir, I need to head back to Jefferson City."

Moments later, Colonel Kearny stood at the main entrance of Fort Clemson with a couple of army gate guards beside him and watched the governor ride away on his horse, accompanied by his twelve armed escorts.

At Fort Polk the next morning, Tuesday, May 26, before breakfast, Dr. John Myers put a fresh bandage on Corporal Lance Brooks's wounded left leg as promised.

After breakfast, Alamo Kane stayed with Lance while Alex and Abel Kane went to the corral and hitched a pair of horses to an army wagon. They placed plenty of pillows and blankets in the bed of the wagon for

Lance's use, as well as bedrolls for all four of them. When they returned to the area where other wounded men were being placed in wagons for their journeys home, they pulled rein and hopped out.

Alamo saw his brothers coming and said to Lance, "Here they come. Let me help you up."

Lance was on his feet and leaning on his crutches as Alex and Abel drew near. He smiled. "Is my chariot ready, gentlemen?"

Alex chuckled. "Sure is, your majesty!"

Alamo and Abel laughed, as did Lance.

Dr. Myers had been looking on from a short distance and hurried over to them. "How does that bandage feel by now, Corporal Brooks?" he asked.

"It's fine, Doctor," Lance replied.

"Good! I'll just make sure these tough, rugged Irishmen make you comfortable."

The men chuckled softly while the Kane brothers and the medic flanked the wounded corporal as he made his way toward the wagon on his crutches. When they got to the wagon, Abel hurried to the tailgate and let it down. While Alex was climbing into the wagon bed from the side, Alamo picked Lance up in his arms, gently placed him in a sitting position at the bed's edge, then hopped in. Abel also hopped in

101

and took Lance's crutches from him as Alamo helped him to his feet and assisted him toward the front of the wagon, where Alex was placing the pillows and blankets as directed by Dr. Myers so Lance could lie down and be as comfortable as possible. Alamo helped Lance to a sitting position on the blankets and pillows; then Lance thanked the medic for all he had done to help him.

Myers wished him the very best, told the Kane brothers he'd see them in a few weeks, and walked away.

"Well, boys," Alamo said, "it's time to get going."

At that instant, General Taylor came walking in their direction. "Not until I tell Corporal Brooks good-bye."

Other soldiers moved up to bid the corporal good-bye, including Lieutenant Ulysses Grant.

General Taylor set admiring eyes on the young corporal. "Once again, I want to commend you for the valor you showed on the Palo Alto battlefield."

Lance smiled. "Thank you, sir."

The general reached over the side of the wagon bed and extended his hand. Lance gripped it as Taylor said, "Good-bye, Corporal."

Lance nodded. "Good-bye, General."

Taylor told the Kane brothers he would look forward to seeing them when they returned to the fort.

The other men walked toward the wagon, and Lieutenant Grant said, "I want to commend you Kanes for volunteering to take Corporal Brooks home and for your example as good soldiers of the United States Army. I watched you in those battles we fought side by side and admired your courage and determination to help win those battles."

"Thank you for your kind words, Lieutenant Grant," Alamo said.

Alex nodded. "Yes, thank you, sir."

"I'll echo that 'thank you,' " Abel said. "And I'll say this, Lieutenant Grant. We saw *your* courage and determination too. You are a great leader! Maybe someday you'll be president of the United States!"

Grant laughed. "Sure, sure, Private Kane. *Me* become president?"

Alamo's blue eyes sparkled. "Why not, Lieutenant Grant? I think you're great! You'd make a great president!"

Grant shook his head, grinning. "Well, I think *you're* great, Lieutenant Kane. I want to commend you for the way you risked your own life that day at Palo Alto to carry the wounded Corporal Brooks through a field of blazing, smoking grass and save his life!"

Alamo's face flushed. "Well, thank you, sir." He ran his gaze over the small group of soldiers, then let it settle on Grant. "My brothers and I will see all of you when we return to Fort Polk."

The other men told Lance good-bye as Alex and Abel made their way to the front of the wagon and sat down on the driver's seat. Alamo helped Lance lie down comfortably, then positioned himself beside him, sitting on a pillow.

Alex took the reins in hand and put the horses into motion. The Kane brothers waved at Grant and the others, who were watching them drive toward the main gate of the fort. Seconds later, the wagon passed through the gate, turned north, and quickly disappeared.

Lieutenant Grant said to the others, "Those Kane brothers are great fellas."

The others agreed wholeheartedly.

As the wagon carrying Corporal Brooks and the Kane brothers rolled northward, Alex Kane held the horses to a steady, slow pace so as to make the bumps on the rough trail easier for Brooks to endure.

From the driver's seat, Alex and Abel heard Lance talking to Alamo softly, thanking him as he had many times before for caring about his eternal destiny and leading him to the Lord.

When Alamo had reminded him that it was his joy and pleasure to lead Lance to Jesus, Abel looked over his shoulder and said, "Since you're talking again about Alamo leading you to the Lord, Lance, I want to say what a delight it was to see you come to Him that evening after the battle at Palo Alto."

Keeping his eyes on the trail ahead, Alex turned his head a bit and spoke from the side of his mouth. "I want to add my own comment, Lance, about what a blessing it was to see you open your heart to the Saviour. I was so glad the Lord used Alamo as His vessel to bring you to salvation, as He used him to save your life amid the flames and smoke of that burning field."

By this time, there were tears in Lance's eyes. He reached toward Alamo and grabbed his arm, then looked up at the two men on the driver's seat. "Fellas, I know I've said this many times since that day, but I must say it again. If Alamo hadn't saved my life as that blazing fire closed in on me, I would've burned to death and gone to hell.

I'd be burning in the flames of hell right now, and I'd have burned in the lake of fire forever — by far worse than burning in that grass fire would've been."

As Lance spoke, he tightened his grip on Alamo's arm.

Alamo wiped at his own tears. "Lance, I'm just so thankful the Lord enabled me to get to you in time to carry you away from that deadly fire. And I'm so thankful He enabled me to bring you to Him for salvation so you would never burn in the horrible lake of fire."

There was much rejoicing and praising the Lord as the wagon rolled on.

At sunset, they stopped beside a bubbling creek for the night and ate supper a short time later by the cook fire under a starlit sky with a silver moon shining down on them. As the four men ate, they talked about the Mexican war and shared their opinions on where many battles might be fought in Mexico.

When the dishes had been washed and dried and more wood added to the fire, the Kane brothers and Lance sat around the fire's glow as Alamo read aloud from his Bible while Alex and Abel followed in theirs.

Lance read along in Abel's Bible. When they were finished reading together, Alamo looked at the bandaged man. "Lance, when we get to the ranch and go into Washington-on-the-Brazos, I'm going to buy you a Bible."

Lance smiled. "That's nice of you, Alamo, but I'd be glad to buy myself a Bible."

Alamo shook his head. "No, no. It will be my pleasure to give you a Bible."

Tears filled Lance's eyes. "You're just too much, Lieutenant Alamo Kane."

Alamo shrugged and tilted his head. "My brothers might argue with you on that one."

Lance looked at Alex and Abel questioningly.

Both shook their heads.

"No way, Alamo," Abel said.

"Right," Alex said. "No way."

Alamo smiled. "Thanks, dear brothers. Well, before we slide into our bedrolls, let's pray together."

Alamo led them in prayer, and when he asked the Lord to allow him to lead Lance's parents to Jesus when they were at the Brookses' home, the Kane brothers could hear Lance sniffling.

When Alamo closed off his prayer, Lance thumbed tears from his eyes. "I've sure been praying for my parents' salvation, Alamo. I-I just really believe they're going to open their hearts to the Saviour."

"Amen!" said Alex. "My brothers and I believe they will too!"

"Amen!" Abel and Alamo chorused.

Still wiping tears, Lance said, "I'm just so excited about seeing my parents. And I'm sure you three are excited about seeing your family."

Alex nodded. "I know that we haven't been gone all that long this time, but I sure do miss Libby and the rest of the family, the ranch, and Libby's good cooking!"

"Yeah," Abel said. "I miss Vivian, the rest of the family, the ranch folks, and Vivian's good cooking too! Ol' Cookie does the best he can with the army grub, but nothing tastes anywhere near as good as home cooking on our own land!"

"I could use a good dose of home cooking myself," Alamo said with a wide grin on his face. "But most of all I want to be with my sweet Julie and my children. Seems like I've been away from them more than I've been home with them, and that's what marriage and family is all about — being together."

"For sure," Alex said, stoking the fire. "Let's just keep praying that this war with Mexico will end quickly and we'll be able to go home and concentrate on our family, the ranch, and cattle raising."

Abel popped his hands together. "Amen

to that!"

"Yes sir! Amen to that!" Alamo agreed heartily, clapping his hands together as well. "Well, gents" — he picked up his Bible and rose to his feet — "it's time to get some sleep."

Alex rose to his feet. "Oh, Alamo! There's something I've been meaning to bring up."

Alamo frowned. "What are you talking about?"

"Remember when we were on patrol yesterday morning and you spotted that bald eagle flying over us?"

Alamo's face relaxed. "Oh sure."

"While everyone was watching the eagle, Abel said he had heard that the bald eagle flies higher than any other bird."

Alamo nodded. "And when I said I had heard that bald eagles nest at the very top of the tallest trees they can find, you said you had read something in the Bible about how when eagles perch in a tree, they do so on the highest branch. And you couldn't remember where in the Bible you had read it."

Alex nodded, opening his Bible. "Well, it came to me just now. Let me read it to you."

"Where is it?" asked Alamo.

Abel was holding his Bible, ready to open it.

Lance looked at Alex with interest.

"It's in Ezekiel chapter 17." Alex stopped at that page in his Bible. "Verses 1–3. Ezekiel says that God calls it a riddle and a parable, but look at what He says: 'And the word of the LORD came unto me, saying, Son of man, put forth a riddle, and speak a parable unto the house of Israel; and say, Thus saith the Lord GOD; A great eagle with great wings, longwinged, full of feathers, which had divers colours, came unto Lebanon, and took the highest branch of the cedar.' "

"Hey, that's good!" Alamo said. "That eagle took the highest branch of the cedar! God sure created one magnificent bird when He created the eagle."

"That He did," said Abel.

Lance nodded his head. "I find that very interesting, fellas."

Alamo looked down at him and smiled. "Lance, my friend, when you get to reading that new Bible I'm going to buy you, you'll find that book very interesting on every page!"

Alex and Abel both agreed. Then Alamo said, "Well, we'd better get some sleep. We need to get an early start in the morning."

Alex and Abel put out the fire while Alamo helped Lance into his bedroll. Moments later, after the Kane brothers had slipped into their bedrolls, a stiff wind began to blow.

Abel looked up at the night sky. "Heavy clouds are blowing in, fellas."

The others looked up to see the clouds, noting that only a few stars were visible and the clouds had totally covered the moon.

"I'd say we've got a storm blowing in." Alamo scooted farther into his bedroll.

The others spoke their agreement.

Alex yawned loudly. "Guess we'd better get some sleep while we can."

No rain had fallen by the break of dawn the next morning, but the four men awakened to see dark, heavy clouds covering the sky. Alamo suggested that they eat breakfast quickly and move out. While Alex hastily cooked breakfast, Alamo and Abel fed and watered the horses.

Soon they were on the trail with Alex at the reins, Abel next to him on the driver's seat, and Alamo sitting on a pillow next to Lance in the wagon bed.

The wind blew hard, and the heavy grass on the plains seemed to roll like ocean waves.

They had been in motion about an hour when suddenly sky-blistering lightning cracked overhead, one jagged bolt after another. They soon smelled the ozone of the lightning bolts and detected the crisp scent of oncoming rain. Soon rain was pouring down in sheets.

Alamo moved up behind the driver's seat and above the roar of the wind and rain said to his brothers, "Fellas, we need to look for a place where we might find shelter!"

Both Alex and Abel were wiping rain from their eyes as they turned to look at Alamo. "I was just thinking the same thing," Alex shouted. "We'll see what's up ahead."

Alamo went back to sit beside Lance as the rain poured down. In less than half an hour, Alamo and Lance heard the men on the driver's seat talking to each other excitedly. Before Alamo could get up to go to them, Abel turned and said, "Alamo, there's an old barn just ahead. Looks like it was once a farm, but all that's left is the barn. The roof is still on it."

"Good!" Alamo called above the roar of the storm. "Let's head for it!"

Alamo hurried up behind his brothers, and as the wagon drew near the barn, he commented that the farm indeed appeared to be abandoned. The old farmhouse and some sheds had collapsed.

When Alex hauled the wagon to a stop in

front of the old barn, Alamo and Alex quickly hopped to the ground and opened the barn doors. Alamo called out for Alex to drive inside, and seconds later the doors were swung shut behind them.

The roof of the old barn was leaking profusely, and they found it impossible to park the wagon where no water was dripping. After a few minutes, Alex parked so at least the horses wouldn't be dripped on and the side of the wagon bed where Lance lay would remain relatively dry. Then the Kane brothers found a small spot beneath the hayloft without a leak.

Alamo made Lance as comfortable as possible, seating him on a pillow from the wagon so he could lean against a feed trough.

As the storm raged outside, the four men tried to relax. Cracks in the old wooden walls allowed the chilly wind to blow through the barn, and after a while, Lance's whole body began to shake. Soon his teeth were chattering; then he started coughing. Fearful that in his already weakened condition Lance might succumb to a cold — or worse, pneumonia — the Kane brothers hurried to the wagon to try to find a couple of dry blankets. They found two blankets where Lance had been lying in the wagon bed that were only slightly damp in a few spots and hurried to cover him up where he sat at the feed trough.

When the shivering Lance had been wrapped in the blankets, he wearily snuggled down into the warmth, and after some twenty minutes, his shaking ceased and he closed his eyes in sleep.

Alamo said to his brothers in a low voice, "Thank God, Lance has quit shivering and is sleeping now. I was really afraid he might take on a serious chill, and then somehow we'd need to treat that as well as his leg wound."

Alex smiled. "The Lord is good, isn't He?"

"Amen and amen," Abel said.

"And *double* that," put in Alamo.

Both Alex and Abel grinned at their brother, then settled down to rest.

After some six hours of taking refuge inside the old barn, the storm ceased, and soon the sun was shining. Lance was awake when they placed him back in the bed of the wagon, and Alex put the team into motion.

As they moved along the trail northward, Lance told the Kane brothers he was feeling better and thanked them for how they had taken care of him.

At that moment, from where he was sitting beside Lance in the wagon bed, Alamo pointed into the sky. "Hey, fellas, look at that!"

Alex and Abel twisted on the driver's seat and noted where their brother was pointing.

"Wow!" Alex exclaimed. "What a beautiful sight!"

"I'll say!" Abel scratched his head.

Lance struggled to sit up so he could see what they were talking about. His mouth fell open when he saw it. On the horizon was a colorful double rainbow.

The four men looked on in amazement.

Abel took a deep breath and said in a voice filled with awe and wonder, "The Lord has been busy with His paintbrush today, I'll tell you!"

"That's for sure," Lance said. "I can't even imagine how beautiful heaven must be."

"Well, you'll know one day, Lance," Alamo said. "Just like the rest of us here."

"Yes," said Lance. "Praise the Lord!"

After another hour of travel, Alamo eased up behind the driver's seat and discussed with his brothers that they had lost almost a half-day's driving time because of the storm. Alex and Abel optimistically agreed that they still might be able to reach the Diamond K Ranch by late next Monday afternoon.

As the days passed, there were no more storms. The Kane brothers and Lance Brooks camped along the trail at night. As the wagon was rolling northward along the dusty road late Monday afternoon, June 1, Alex twisted on the driver's seat with the reins in hand and looked down at the wounded corporal with a dozing Alamo slumped beside him. "Lance, we're getting close to the Diamond K! We'll be able to see the ranch house when we top the next hill!"

Alex's words penetrated Alamo's light sleep, and shaking his head, he rose to his knees. Setting his gaze past the horses, he saw the familiar ridge, and said, "Yes! Julie and my children are just over the hilltop!"

6

Lance Brooks looked up at Alamo Kane, saw the smile illuminating his face, and reached toward him. "How about helping me sit up? I want to see the ranch the instant it comes into view!"

Alamo took hold of Lance's hand and gently brought him to a sitting position, and seconds later, as Lance was looking past the horse team, they topped the hill.

"There it is, Lance!" Alamo pointed to the ranch. "If you look off to the left, you can see the barns and corrals, and to the right are the ranch houses. Just a bit west of the cluster of houses, you'll see the big ranch house where my family lives."

Lance squinted against the bright, shining sun, and the big ranch house gleamed white against the cobalt blue sky. "Wow! Alamo, that's a beautiful house! And you're not kidding. It *is* a big one!"

At that instant, they all saw a buggy coming from the east. Abel smiled. "Hey, guys! It's our sweet sister and her husband — our pastor!"

"A sight for sore eyes!" Alamo exclaimed.

"Yeah!" Alex agreed, pulling on the reins and halting the wagon. "It sure is!"

Lance focused on the buggy. The Kane brothers had told him that their sister, Angela, was married to the pastor of their church in Washington-on-the-Brazos, Patrick O'Fallon. As the Kane brothers waved at the O'Fallons, Patrick and Angela smiled and waved back, and Patrick put the horse to a trot.

Seconds later, as the O'Fallons drew up, all three of the Kane brothers hopped out of the wagon. Lance noted that Angela was blond and very pretty. Her facial features bore a slight resemblance to her brothers, but in a strictly feminine way.

Patrick, who was dark-haired, was dressed in a black business suit, white shirt, and black necktie, and wore no hat. He hopped out of the buggy and helped Angela down as the three brothers drew up and dismounted. Each of them hugged his sister and kissed her cheek while joyful tears flowed; then they hugged their brother-in-law.

Patrick wiped his own tears. "Everyone in

Washington-on-the-Brazos and all over this ranch heard about General Taylor's troops fighting the Mexican forces in fierce battles at Palo Alto and Resaca de la Guerrero. Oh, praise the Lord, we're so relieved to see that all three of you are alive and unharmed!"

Alamo nodded. "Indeed we must give praise to the Lord. He has been so good to protect us in battle."

The significant roll of Alamo's words seemed to linger on the quiet air.

Patrick and Angela held each other's gaze for a few seconds. Then Patrick spoke to his three brothers-in-law. "Angela and I are on our way to the Diamond K to have supper with the rest of the family at the ranch house."

Alamo chuckled. "Well, the rest of the Kane family may be a bit surprised to be having more guests at supper."

Angela giggled joyfully. "I'll tell you this, dear brother, Papa, Libby, Vivian, Julia, and the four children will be very happy to see their surprise guests!"

Alamo chuckled again. "Alex, Abel, and I are going to be very happy to see all of them too!" He then flicked a glance toward the army wagon and noted that the wounded corporal was looking at the small group. "Patrick, Angela, there is someone over here in the wagon we want you to meet."

The couple had been facing the horse team, which blocked their view of the wagon bed. They glanced that direction as Alamo motioned and headed toward the rear of the wagon. Alex and Abel followed behind Patrick and Angela.

Alamo drew up to the side of the wagon, and the others stopped a few feet away, with Patrick and Angela setting their eyes on the young man who was sitting in the wagon bed and smiling at them.

"So this is your pastor/brother-in-law and your sister," Lance said.

Alamo grinned and nodded. "Yes. Patrick, Angela, I want you to meet Corporal Lance Brooks. He was wounded in the Palo Alto battle, and we're going to be taking him home to Prairie View after we've spent a few days at the ranch."

Both the pastor and his wife smiled at Lance and told him they were glad to meet him.

Alex then spoke up and told the O'Fallons how Alamo had witnessed to Lance on the night before the Palo Alto battle, trying to win him to Christ, and how belligerent and unbelieving Lance had been.

Lance nodded and said solemnly, "What Alex just told you is true. I was indeed belligerent and full of unbelief."

"There's more to this story." Abel went on to tell them how Alamo risked his own life in order to save Lance, who had been shot in the leg during the Palo Alto battle on May 8, amid a blazing grass fire, carrying him to safety.

Grinning now, Abel said, "And that night, after the battle was over, Alamo dealt with Lance about his lost soul again, and Lance opened his heart to Jesus!"

As Patrick and Angela were rejoicing over Lance's salvation, Patrick looked at Alamo. "Wow! You must have been flying high when you had the joy of leading Lance to the Lord!"

At that instant, squawks were heard from above, and they all looked up to see a large flock of bald eagles flying overhead.

"Oh my!" Angela said. "I've never seen that many eagles flying together before! Usually there are only about eight, nine, or ten in a group."

"Yeah." Alex shielded his eyes with his right hand. "That's really a big bunch, isn't it?"

"Sure is," agreed Abel.

Alamo had spotted one eagle flying much higher than the rest of the large flock, directly above them. He pointed up at the high-flying eagle. "Look, everybody! See that one flying alone up there, way above the rest?"

Everyone looked up where Alamo was pointing.

"Patrick," Alamo said, "when I got to lead Lance to Jesus, I was flying high like that one eagle wa-a-ay up there above the others!"

The pastor's eyes were fixed on the high-flying eagle. "Yes! I see him!"

By this time, the rest of the group was also focused on the highest-flying eagle.

Alamo kept his eyes on the magnificent bird. "As you know, Patrick, I've had the joy of leading many precious souls to the Lord, but, yes, being able to lead the belligerent, unbelieving Corporal Lance Brooks to Jesus has me flying extra high. Just like that high eagle wa-a-y up there!"

Lance wiped tears from his cheeks while the O'Fallons, Alex, and Abel were rejoicing and praising the Lord.

Patrick turned to Alamo. "I recently did a study on eagles, mainly because they are mentioned so many times in the Bible. What you said a moment ago about that high eagle wa-a-ay up there has given me an idea for a sermon. I'm going to put it together and preach it next Sunday morning. I'll call the sermon 'High Is the Eagle.' "

Patrick then ran his gaze over the faces of all three Kane brothers. "Will you still be around next Sunday?"

Alamo clapped a hand on Patrick's back. "We sure will! I can't wait to hear that sermon!"

"It's amazing what the Lord has put in His Word about eagles!" Patrick looked heavenward again. "Alamo, I hope indeed that you like the sermon."

"I have no doubt that I will," Alamo said.

The group then watched as the flock of eagles, including the high-flying one, flew toward some low clouds, entered them, and passed from view.

Alamo then explained to his sister and brother-in-law that General Taylor had allowed him and his brothers to bring Lance home because of his wounded leg. He went on to explain that since Lance's home was only thirty-five miles away in Prairie View, the general said they could come home first, stay at the ranch a week, then take Lance home and go on back to Fort Polk from there.

"This is great," said Patrick.

Alamo grinned. "And, Pastor Patrick, we'll bring Lance to church with us next Sunday."

Lance looked at the pastor and said with

a smile, "I'll be there, even if they have to carry me!"

Patrick smiled back. "Good!"

He then turned to Alex and Abel and said while Lance, Angela, and Alamo looked on, "If you don't mind, when I preach the sermon I'm planning, I'll tell the story of Alamo's witnessing to Lance, sowing the seed of the Word in his heart, how he saved his life on the burning battlefield, then had the joy of leading him to the Lord. I'll tell about what happened right here when those bald eagles flew over with the one eagle much higher than the others, how Alamo pointed out that since he led Lance to Jesus, it has had him flying high like that eagle. I'll tie in plenty of Scripture and show how a Christian who is a soul winner flies high in his or her heart like an eagle!"

Those words made Angela, her brothers, and Lance smile, and they happily praised the Lord, agreeing that they were looking forward to hearing the sermon.

"Well, let's get to the ranch!" Alamo said.

"Yes," said Patrick. "Let's do that!"

Patrick helped Angela into their buggy. Moments later, the buggy and wagon were headed down the hill toward the Diamond K Ranch.

Alamo's heart pounded with excitement

as he sat beside Lance in the wagon bed. In a few minutes, he would take his precious wife into his arms and then hug his precious children.

His mind flashed back to how he fell in love with Julia Miller the first time he met her but kept that love a secret. Then he thought of how Julia and his brother Adam met, fell in love, and married. Then Adam was killed at the Alamo, with Julia carrying his child in her womb.

Alamo's thoughts wandered to the day, some time after Adam's death, when he finally confessed to Julia — whom he was allowed to call Julie — that he had fallen in love with her the first time they met. She told him that she now had a deep love for him as well. Soon after, they married and little Adam Kane became his stepson.

Once again, Alamo's heart pounded with excitement. He and Julie had been blessed with three children in addition to her son Adam — five-and-a-half-year-old Abram, four-year-old Andy, and one-and-a-half-year-old Amber. In a few minutes, he would be with them. He would also be with his father, and he would get to see Alex's and Abel's wives, as well as his foreman, Cort Whitney, and all of his ranch hands and their families. His heart continued to pound inside his chest with anticipation.

When the wagon turned off the road onto Diamond K land, Alamo saw several ranch hands working at the barns and corrals, while others were in the fields on horseback, riding among the cattle. Others were moving about the small frame houses where they and their families lived.

Those ranch hands who were close by set their eyes on the wagon and the buggy, and when they recognized the Kane brothers, they waved and smiled. Then they also waved to the O'Fallons.

As the wagon and buggy angled westward on the ranch property, making their way past the small frame houses, they could see Julia sitting in a wicker chair on the front porch of the big ranch house, holding little Amber on her lap. Next to her in identical wicker chairs were Libby and Vivian.

The three women were chatting about the warm weather they were having and how summer was drawing near. Julia's two youngest boys were sitting on the porch steps talking about their father and uncles being in the war.

Suddenly Julia's eyes picked up on the approaching wagon and buggy, which she recognized as belonging to the O'Fallons. Then she fastened her gaze on the driver of the army wagon and thought, *It looks like Alex driving that wagon! But I must be dreaming! Probably just wishful thinking.* She rose from the chair slowly with little Amber in her arms and moved to the porch railing. *No! I'm not dreaming! It's Abel sitting beside him!*

Julia let her eyes roam farther, and there, peering over the side of the wagon bed, was the man for whom she was searching. *Oh, thank You, Lord!*

Libby and Vivian stopped talking and looked past Julia. "What are you looking at, Julia?" Vivian asked.

"It's our husbands!" exclaimed Julia. "Alex is driving that army wagon, Abel is beside him, and Alamo is in the wagon bed! Patrick and Angela are behind them in their buggy!"

Abram and Andy heard what their mother said and bounded off the porch steps. Libby and Vivian were getting out of their chairs as Julia hurried down the porch steps holding Amber tight, her boys several paces ahead of her.

As the wagon and buggy drew near, with some of the ranch hands looking on, the two boys cried out, "Papa! Papa!" and ran toward the wagon.

When the two vehicles came to a stop,

Alamo jumped out of the wagon bed, and Abram and Andy launched themselves at him. He bent over, gathered one boy in each arm and hugged them close as they clung to him. "Papa! Papa!" they continued crying out, as he told them he loved them.

At that moment, Alamo lifted his eyes and saw his beloved Julie coming toward him, holding their little girl. Releasing his sons, he reached for the woman he loved, and they were instantly in each other's arms, the squirming baby girl pressed between them.

Alamo placed a soft kiss on Julia's lips then looked into her tear-filled eyes. "I love you, sweetheart."

"Oh, darling," she said breathlessly, "I love *you!*"

Alamo then stepped back a pace and reached for his baby daughter. Little Amber gurgled and smiled up at her father. Young as she was, she recognized him, saying, "Papa! Papa! Papa!" He kissed each of her rosy cheeks, then caressed her downy head. "Papa loves his little sweetie."

Then, holding Amber in one arm, Alamo stepped up to Julia again and kissed her soft lips once more. "Oh, honey," he looked deeply into her soft blue eyes, "I've missed you, our sweet children, and our home more than you can even begin to imagine."

"We've missed you too, darling. More than you will ever know."

Alamo looked down and saw both boys standing close to him. He glanced around to see Alex and Abel embracing their wives.

Julia smiled and looked up at him. "We are so glad to see our husbands alive and unscathed. How is it that you were able to come home?"

"I'll explain later, honey. We get to stay for a week."

Julia's eyelashes fluttered. "Wonderful!"

At that moment, Patrick and Angela walked over, and the women and the boys welcomed them.

Angela turned to Julia. "I hope there will enough food at suppertime for the unexpected guests."

Julia laughed, noting the young soldier sitting up in the bed of the wagon. "Tell you what, Angela, I'll go tell Daisy there are four more mouths to feed."

Libby, who was standing in Alex's arms, pulled free and said, "Julia, I'll go tell Daisy about the surprise guests." She looked at Alex. "I'll be right back, darling." Alex watched Libby hurry toward the front door of the house.

At that moment, Alamo looked around. "Julie, where are Adam and my father?"

"Well, right now," she replied, "they are hunting birds and rabbits together on the west side of the ranch. They should be showing up pretty soon."

Alamo nodded. "Good."

Julia smiled. "They'll both be mighty happy to see the three of you alive and well."

"We'll be mighty happy to see them too."

Just then, Libby came out the front door of the big ranch house with Daisy Haycock on her heels. The silver-haired cook walked up beside Libby as they descended the steps and rushed to Alamo to hug him as he handed Amber back to her mother. "Praise the Lord! I'm glad to see you home, boss! And your brothers too!"

She then hurried to both Alex and Abel and hugged them, welcoming them home. She also went to her pastor and his wife and hugged them, saying she was glad they could come for supper.

Abel Kane looked around at the family members and Daisy. "Come over here to the wagon. We want you to meet someone." Abel motioned to the wagon.

Some of the ranch hands watched from a reasonable distance as the family group gathered at the army wagon. Abel introduced the young soldier sitting in the wagon bed.

Lance was a bit pale and somewhat weak from the journey, especially having been wet and cold and having coughed a great deal. He smiled at the group and coughed slightly. "Hello, everyone. I've heard so much about you from Alamo, Alex, and Abel. It is so nice to get to meet you." As he spoke, he rolled as if to move onto his knees, intending to get out of the wagon.

Alamo hurried to the rear of the wagon, picked up the crutches, and helped Lance down. He then situated him on his crutches.

When Alamo had introduced Lance to everyone, he told the group about the few days General Taylor had given them to come home and see their family. He explained that they would be taking Lance to his home in Prairie View to rejoin his parents when they left the ranch next Monday.

A wide smile spread over Daisy's face as she declared joyfully, "Welcome home, all three of you, and welcome to *you*, Corporal Brooks. Now if you'll excuse me, I'll get back to the kitchen. I've got a feast to prepare! I must make sure I cook enough food to include our surprise guests!" Daisy clapped her hands together and hurried away.

At the same time, some of the ranch hands — including foreman Cort Whitney —

131

began gathering around the big ranch house and looking on, desiring to hear what was being said.

Alex ran his gaze over the entire group. "Let me tell all of you about Corporal Lance Brooks here." He then told them the story of how Alamo had witnessed to Lance before the Palo Alto battle and how stubborn Lance was against the gospel and the Bible's passages about the burning, everlasting hell where all sinners go who die without Jesus as their Saviour. He then shared how Alamo risked his own life to save the wounded corporal, who lay helpless on the burning battlefield, about to be consumed by flames. That very evening, when the battle was over, Alamo had the joy of leading Lance to the Lord.

Standing beside Alamo, Lance adjusted himself on the crutches and looked at the group of people. "Let me tell you, folks, as I was lying there wounded on that blazing field, the wind blowing the flames toward me, I knew I couldn't get up and run. I thought about what Alamo had told me from the Bible about the fire of hell, and at that moment I believed it. I was filled with terror as I thought of the flames of hell that awaited me beyond the flames of the grass fire."

By this time, tears were glistening in Lance's eyes. He put his arm around Alamo and looked through his tears into Alamo's eyes. "Thank you once again, my friend, for caring enough about me to save my life at the risk of your own and then lead me to Jesus."

Several sets of eyes were shedding tears at this point. The ranch hands who had gathered close were all Christians and members of the church in Washington-on-the-Brazos. Standing close to their pastor and his wife, they rejoiced in Lance's salvation.

Cort stepped up to Alamo and patted his shoulder. "Boss, I want to commend you for risking your life to save Corporal Brooks, and even more so, for witnessing to him and finally leading him to the Lord."

Julia walked up beside her husband and looked around at the group. "Everyone, I want to ask you something. Have any of you noticed something different about Alamo?"

A quizzical look captured the faces of the group as they set their eyes on the owner of the Diamond K Ranch.

Julia chuckled as she took hold of Alamo's arm. "Since my husband was promoted from private to first lieutenant by General Zachary Taylor because of his courage in saving Corporal Brooks from the blazing fire on the Palo Alto battlefield, he just looks different!"

Julia then patted Alamo's cheek. "Congratulations, *Lieutenant Alamo Kane!*"

The others chimed in, applauding him at the same time.

Alamo's face flushed a deep red. Julia rose up on her tiptoes and kissed his cheek. He smiled as the flush on his face became an even deeper red.

7

Most of the group was smiling at Alamo Kane's red-flushed face as he smiled back. "Something I'd like to ask all of you to pray about," Alamo said. "When we take Lance home from here, we're going to try to lead his parents to the Lord. Would you be praying that the Lord will work in their hearts and make us successful in this?"

Heads nodded, and everyone in the group acknowledged that they would be praying for Lance's parents to be saved.

"Thank you." Alamo turned his gaze to Lance. "I know Lance appreciates your prayers for his parents."

Lance nodded. "Yes! Yes!"

"Lance, I-I wonder if you'd mind if we change the day we take you home to next Tuesday instead of Monday. I'd like for Alex, Abel, and myself to have Monday as our last day here instead of Sunday. Just make Monday a big day to be with our family."

Lance smiled. "Of course I wouldn't mind, Alamo. We'll go to Prairie View on Tuesday."

"Sounds good to me!" Abel said.

"Me too!" agreed Alex.

"Me too!" Libby said.

Everyone laughed.

Alamo could tell that they were going to be outside for a while. He looked at the four women. "How about you ladies go up there on the porch and sit down? I think we'll be here for a while yet."

Still carrying little Amber, Julia led Angela, Libby, and Vivian up on the front porch of the big ranch house, and they each sat on a wicker chair.

Alamo then encouraged his two sons and the men of the Kane family, including Pastor Patrick, to go up on the porch. When they had done so, Alamo helped Lance mount the steps on his crutches and led him to a wicker chair and helped him sit down.

The ranch hands who were on foot drew up closer to the porch.

Alamo, his brothers, and Patrick remained standing near the porch steps, as did young Abram and Andy.

From the ground, Cort Whitney said to

the Kane brothers, "So tell us what you think is ahead in the Mexico situation."

"Well" — Alamo scratched his head — "all of you know that President Polk and Congress declared war on Mexico almost three weeks ago. So we men in the U.S. Army will be facing big battles ahead."

From his chair, Lance Brooks said, "Alamo, I wish I could fight at your side, but that'll never happen again."

"No, it won't, Lance," replied Alamo. He then set his eyes on the ranch hands. "Let me tell you all about Lance. The army medics at Fort Polk told General Taylor that Lance will no doubt limp on that injured left leg for the rest of his life, and he can no longer be a soldier."

Cort and the other ranch hands set their eyes on Lance sadly.

Alamo went on to tell the ranch hands that General Taylor had told Lance he would be receiving official papers in the mail giving him an honorable discharge from the army.

"Well, congratulations, Lance," spoke up one of the ranch hands.

The rest of the Diamond K people, both on and off the porch, spoke their congratulations.

Cort said, "Lance, we all commend you

for doing an honorable job as a soldier of the United States Army. You were wounded while faithfully serving your country on the Palo Alto battlefield, and you deserve the honorable discharge."

Patrick stepped to where Lance was sitting and laid a hand on his shoulder. "Lance, if it weren't for brave men like you who are willing to fight for this country, none of us would be safe. I'm very proud of you."

Everyone in the group who was gathered at the edge of the porch or on the porch spoke their agreement with the pastor's words. Even young Abram and Andy Kane.

Alamo wiped a tear from his eye as he looked at Lance. "And now that you're a child of God, you are in the Lord's army, Lance. I'm sure you will serve Him faithfully."

Lance looked up at him and smiled. "I will do my best, Lieutenant Kane."

Cort looked around at the rest of the ranch hands. "Well, fellas, it's time for us to get back to finishing up the work for today." He chuckled. "We sure don't want to get fired."

The ranch hands laughed.

Alamo grinned at them. "Yeah. You'd better get that work done!"

"Yes sir, Lieutenant Kane, boss." Whitney saluted.

The ranch hands followed their foreman as he walked away, and the Kane brothers also sat down in wicker chairs. Abram and Andy sat on the porch steps.

Alamo sat in a chair next to Lance, and when he turned and looked at him, he noticed Lance wiping perspiration from his forehead. Frowning, he asked, "Are you not feeling well?"

"I'm just feeling a bit weak," Lance said. "You know I've been feeling feverish since I got soaked and chilled when it rained on us while we were coming here."

"Mm-hmm. You feeling hot now?"

"Yes. Not real bad, but it's on me. You also know that I've been coughing some since I got soaked in that storm. But the coughing has almost stopped. Don't worry about me. I'll be all right."

Everyone on the porch was looking on and listening to what was being said between Alamo and Lance.

"Well, may I remind you, my friend," Alamo said, "that your main medic, Dr. John Myers, said you should see a doctor and get your wounded leg checked while we're here at the ranch, and I assured him it would be done."

Lance nodded. "Yes."

"Well, I'll take you to see the Kane family physician, Dr. Dennis Dewitt, in Washington-on-the-Brazos tomorrow. Dr. Dewitt can check your leg, and he can examine you to see what's causing the fever and cough too."

The young corporal smiled. "Thank you. I-I don't mean to be a problem."

Alamo cuffed his chin playfully. "You're not a problem. But you *are* a blessing."

At that moment, movement off to the right some fifty yards away on the path that ran by the big ranch house caught Julia's attention. She pointed in that direction. "Look! Here come Papa and Adam!"

Every eye on the porch focused on young Adam Kane and his grandfather as they walked toward the big ranch house pushing a cart. Each was carrying a rifle.

When they came nearer, Lance squinted at the cart. "Looks to me like they've done pretty well in their bird and rabbit hunting!"

Libby chuckled. "Since Adam became a crack shot with his rifle, they always do good when they go hunting together. There are a lot of dead rabbits and birds in that cart!"

As Abram and his nine-year-old grandson

140

drew close, Alamo rose from his chair and walked to the edge of the porch just above the steps.

Suddenly, young Adam saw him and left the cart for his grandfather to push, happily dashing toward Alamo. "Papa! Papa!"

Alamo met his stepson at the bottom of the steps, and there was a sweet reunion between them.

A moment later, when the aging Abram Kane drew up pushing the cart, Alamo playfully mimicked Adam and shouted, "Papa! Papa!" as he hurried to him. There was a celebration between this father and son.

Alex and Abel rushed to their father and nephew, and there was more sweet reunion. Patrick and Angela then went to Abram and young Adam and hugged them.

The Kane brothers looked into the cart, and Abel said, "Well, lookee here! Papa and Adam did well in their hunting today!"

Alamo and Alex agreed.

Grandpa Abram smiled and tousled Adam's hair. "Well, let me brag on this grandson of mine. It was him who bagged all of those rabbits and birds with his .22-caliber rifle!"

Adam's stepfather, mother, and aunts and uncles — including Uncle Patrick and Aunt Angela — all congratulated him on his expertise with the rifle.

Alex and Abel introduced Grandpa Abram and Adam to Corporal Brooks and reminded them of the story of Alamo witnessing to him at the fort and being cut off by the belligerent, unbelieving corporal. They then reminded them about Alamo saving Lance's life on the burning field of grass during the Palo Alto battle and leading him to the Lord the evening after the battle.

"Oh, yes!" Abram swung his gaze to Alamo. "Son, that sure was a brave thing to do, to go after this young man on that burning field. But the Lord protected you, praise His name! And then you led Lance to Jesus!"

Alamo smiled.

"Papa Alamo, you really *did* show your bravery!" Adam said. "And I'm sure glad Corporal Brooks got saved!"

Alamo smiled again.

Lance ran his eyes between Abram and young Adam. "What a difference the Lord has made in my life already! What a wonderful change! And there is no way I could fully express how much I appreciate Alamo saving my life and bringing me to Jesus!"

"Lance," Grandpa Abram said, "I'm so glad for you."

"Me too," Adam said.

"Well, Adam and I need to take the cart to the nearest barn over there," Abram said, "and prepare the dead rabbits and birds so Libby, Vivian, and Daisy can have them for cooking. We'll see you later."

As Abram and his oldest grandson pushed the cart toward the designated barn, Alamo sat down next to Julia and took little Amber from her, cuddling her in his arms.

Vivian said, "It's really something that, as young as he is, Adam is such a good shot with that rifle."

"That's for sure," Libby said.

Alamo gently cleared his throat in a humorous way. "Adam is so good with that rifle of his because *I* taught him how to use it."

There was a lighthearted chuckle among the others. Then Julia turned to her husband. "Honey, where do you think the battles will be fought in this Mexican-American War that is about to begin?"

At that moment, Lance Brooks coughed, took a breath, then coughed again.

Alamo glanced at him and saw the perspiration shining on his brow. He turned to Julia. "I'll tell you about it in a few minutes, sweetheart. But right now I need to take Lance inside and let him lie down."

She nodded and smiled lovingly at her

husband. "Of course. Let's put him in the bedroom here on the main floor so he won't have to climb the stairs. I'll go ahead of you and make sure everything is in order."

"Here, Alamo." Libby opened her arms. "Let me have Amber."

While Alamo was placing the toddler in her aunt's arms, Julia made her way to the front door of the ranch house and slipped inside. She hurried down the hall and entered the bedroom. As she opened a window, she felt a soft breeze touch her face as it fluttered the curtains. She then went to the bed, uncovered the pillows, fluffed them up good, and laid one on top of the other. She avoided turning down the covers, figuring that as warm as it was, Lance would want to lie down on the bedspread without covering up.

Julia hurried down the hall to the kitchen. There she took a pitcher and cup from the cupboard, pumped the handle of the well pump at the end of the cupboard, filled the pitcher with cool water, and rushed back to the bedroom.

She found Alamo helping Lance to lie down on the bed. "Here's some water for you, Lance." She filled the cup with water, then set both pitcher and cup on the small table beside the bed.

"Thank you, ma'am," Lance said as Alamo adjusted the pillows under his head.

"There's plenty of water in the washbowl over here on the dresser," Julia said, "along with soap, washcloths, and towels."

Lance rolled his head on the pillows and looked at her. "You're so good to me, ma'am."

She smiled. "You're my brother in Christ, Lance. It's my pleasure to be good to you."

Alamo looked down at Lance. "Thirsty?"

"I could use a sip or two."

Alamo picked up the cup of water, helped Lance take the portion he wanted, then set it back on the small table. "You rest now, my friend, and I'll wake you in time for supper."

Lance smiled up at him. "Thank you. That sounds mighty good to me."

The corporal laid his head back on the pillows and closed his eyes. By the time Alamo and his beloved wife were walking out the door of the bedroom, Lance Brooks was sleeping.

Everyone smiled when the couple arrived back to the front porch and told them that Lance was already sleeping.

Julia noticed that Amber was asleep in Libby's arms. "Do you want me to take her?"

Libby shook her head. "No, I'll hold her. You just sit down and get comfortable."

Julia smiled and sat down next to her husband.

Alamo set his attention on his two brothers. "Did you tell them about the telegram from the president that General Taylor received just before we left?"

"No," Alex said. "We figured you'd want to answer Julia's question in front of all of us."

Alamo grinned and looked around at the others. "So, to answer Julie's question of where I think the battles will be fought in the coming war, let me begin by telling you that just before we left Fort Polk to come here, General Taylor received a telegram from President Polk. The general shared the message with the troops. The president said in the telegram that he will be sending troops into New Mexico first because the Mexican government is claiming New Mexico Territory as its own. The president said that since Mexico's president, Mariano Paredes, received the official declaration of war, he has been sending Mexican troops into New Mexico with the purpose of keeping the United States from claiming it."

Heads were nodding.

Alamo went on. "In the telegram, Presi-

146

dent Polk said he will be sending troops into New Mexico from Missouri. So we Fort Polk troops know we won't be fighting in New Mexico."

Heads nodded again.

"In the telegram," Alamo said, "the president also told General Taylor that he will be sending thirty-seven hundred troops to Fort Polk, which will bring our total up to six thousand. Those troops will be arriving the third week of June. The president said that further word concerning the assignment of the Fort Polk troops will come soon after the thirty-seven hundred new men arrive."

Pastor Patrick adjusted himself on his wicker chair. "So you and the other Fort Polk men won't have any idea where you'll be fighting the Mexicans until you hear from the president again?"

Alamo nodded. "That's correct. In relation to Julie's question, there's no way to tell for sure at this time just where the American units will attack Mexican forts or other military posts in that country. I can say that I'm sure there will be fighting in California because the Mexican government still claims that it belongs to them. For sure, the United States Army will have to drive the Mexican military out of California."

Alex looked at Alamo. "I'm sure of one

city that we Americans will have to take and occupy to win the war, and that is Mexico City."

"I was about to bring that up," Alamo said. "For sure, Mexico City will be the main target in the minds of President Polk and the U.S. Army leaders. When the Mexican forts and other military posts are subdued, the American army will have things pretty well under control, but there will not be total victory until the Mexican government, which is centered in Mexico City, is vanquished and crushed."

Julia looked at her husband. "So at this point, no one knows where all the battles might be fought in Mexico."

"This is correct, sweetheart. There is no way to know just where the Mexican military forces might set up defensive positions to battle the Americans, whom they will know are in their country to conquer it. President Polk and his military advisors in Washington, D.C., probably have certain strategic places where they plan to send army units, but even *they* can't know where Mariano Paredes might set up defensive positions."

Tears welled up in Julia's eyes as she clasped her husband's hand. "Alamo, I deeply appreciate that you, Alex, and Abel feel that you need to go fight in this war, but — oh, it's so hard to know you are facing Mexican guns."

A sob escaped her lips, and pent-up tears trickled down her cheeks.

Alamo squeezed her hand gently. "I know, honey. I know. It's hard on all of us, but the president has asked for our help, and I for one couldn't live with myself if I didn't respond to this need."

Alex and Abel were sitting beside their wives holding their hands. Both Libby and Vivian's lips were quivering.

"We have to look at it this way, sweetheart." Alamo hoped to help Julia fully understand. "If we don't fight for our own land, the Mexicans will take it away from us. And we sure don't want that to happen, do we? They'd like to have Texas even more than they want New Mexico and California."

Julia wiped tears from her cheeks and put on a brave smile. "Please forgive me, sweetheart. I know you and your brothers must go because you want to do your part to protect our land and our home. I-I was just having a weak moment. I'll be all right."

"Good girl, honey." Alamo stroked her cheek. "I'm glad you understand the situation." Leaning over, he kissed her tear-streaked face. "One day soon this war situation will be behind us, and we can live in freedom and enjoy God's blessings."

"Amen!" his brothers responded.

"Oh, I'll be so glad when all this fighting with Mexico is over," Julia said.

"I will too," Alamo said. "I want to come home to the ranch and go on with life as a cattle rancher."

Alex and Abel gripped the hands of their wives, who were now shedding tears, and Alex said, "Amen, Alamo! I agree with you!"

"Me too." Abel nodded. "Like you, Alex and I just want to be ranchers again and have a peaceful future with our wives, our family, and the other ranch hands."

Supper in the dining room of the big ranch house at the Diamond K was a lively occasion that evening.

Adam, Abram, and Andy sat as close to their father as possible at the large table, and Julia had little Amber between herself and Amber's father in her high chair — a stool with a back on it. Leather straps offered the toddler safety from falling. Angela sat by her aging father with her husband on her other side, and Lance sat on the other side of Patrick.

Shortly after beginning the meal, Alamo

looked up at the cook, who stood close by, and said heartily, "Daisy, you sure have outdone yourself with this meal! It's terrific!"

"Boy, that's the truth!" Alex exclaimed. "Some army food is all right; it does fill a man's stomach. But compared to *your* cooking, it's hardly palatable."

Daisy laughed and waved a hand in Alex's direction. "Oh, go on with you, Alex. Your flattery will get you nowhere!"

Everybody laughed.

A huge smile split Daisy's face as she looked around the table at her "family."

As dinner progressed, there was much joy amid the family and Daisy because Alex, Abel, and Alamo had come through the Palo Alto and Resaca de la Guerrero battles safely. There was also joy over Corporal Lance Brooks's story of Alamo saving his life in battle then leading him to the Lord.

The family assured the uniformed Kane brothers that they would be praying for them as they went back to Fort Polk and faced whatever battles lay ahead of them . . . even as they had already been praying for them concerning previous battles.

Patrick said, "Let me also assure you, Alamo, Alex, and Abel, that the people in the church have been praying for you as well as the other men from the church in the army."

The three men expressed their appreciation to their pastor for his leadership in this.

At that moment, the pastor noted tears in Corporal Brooks's eyes as he said, "Pastor O'Fallon, I sure am looking forward to coming to your church. I want to meet the rest of your people, and I certainly want to hear that sermon on eagles!"

The pastor smiled. "I'll be glad to have you, Lance. By the way, do you have a Bible?"

As Lance was shaking his head, Alamo spoke up. "I've already told Lance that I would buy him a Bible while we're here. You know, in the book section at the general store. I plan to buy him one tomorrow when we take him to town to see Dr. Dewitt."

Pastor Patrick grinned. "Alamo, may I have the privilege of giving Lance one of the new Bibles the church has on hand that we ordered from that big Christian publisher in Philadelphia? You know, the ones we give to new converts?"

Alamo nodded. "Okay, I'll go along with that." He grinned at Lance.

Excitedly, Lance said, "I'll probably read the ink right off the pages of that new Bible!"

Young Adam laughed. "It wouldn't surprise me if you really did that, Corporal Brooks!"

Then the adults at the table laughed, filling the room with warmth as happy hearts were melded together in love. A God-given peace filled the heart of each one, and for a moment, there was a sweet silence as in their hearts, they praised the Lord for His marvelous, wonderful blessings.

8

After staying to talk for a while in the parlor when supper was over, Patrick and Angela climbed in their buggy at dusk and headed for home.

When darkness had fallen and the moon and stars were adorning the night sky, Alex yawned. "Well, Alamo . . . Julia . . . it's getting close to my bedtime."

Abel yawned as well. "Yeah. Mine too."

A few minutes later, Alex and Libby and Abel and Vivian headed for their own houses a short distance away on the ranch.

Julia had already put little Amber to bed and was now sitting beside her husband. She turned to Alamo. "I think it would be good if someone slept on a cot in Lance's room just in case he should need help during the night."

Alamo nodded. "That's a good idea, sweetheart. Who did you have in mind?"

She grinned and looked toward young

Adam. "How about the boy in this family who handles a gun quite well and says he wants to be a soldier when he grows up?"

Adam's face brightened. He jumped off the sofa, where he was sitting with his brothers. "Yeah! I'll be glad to look after Corporal Brooks!"

Seated nearby, Lance grinned. "I'd be honored to have you as my bodyguard, Adam!"

Alamo stood up. "Well, Lance, I'll escort you down the hall to your room. Adam knows where the cots are kept in a closet upstairs. He'll bring one to your room and be your bodyguard, as you put it." Then looking at Adam he said, "If for any reason Corporal Brooks awakens and needs help that you can't give him, you come and get me, okay?"

Adam nodded. "Sure, Papa Alamo."

"While you're getting Lance and Adam settled, darling," said Julia, "I'll escort Grandpa Abram and Adam's little brothers to their rooms upstairs."

Nearly half an hour later, Alamo and Julia met back in the parlor. As they sat together holding hands, Alamo cocked his head as if listening to some distant sound.

"What are you listening to?"

He smiled down at his bride. "The silence.

A few minutes ago, I thought I heard the collective sighs of everyone else in the house as they snuggled their heads into their pillows. The silence tells me they are now asleep."

Julia nodded. "I think you're right."

Alamo glanced toward the parlor's largest window, noting the twinkling stars. "Hey, how about we go out on the front porch and get a little fresh air before we head for our room?"

Julia stood to her feet. "Okay. Let's go."

Alamo jumped up, took hold of her hand, and together they went into the hallway, then out the front door.

As they stepped onto the porch, Alamo led Julia to the railing and stopped. He gazed out at the bright starlit, moon-filled night and breathed in the fragrant spring air. "It's a beautiful night."

"Sure is." Julia sidled up even closer to her husband.

"And there's a reason it's so beautiful."

Julia waited for him to speak the reason and smiled when she heard it.

"It's beautiful because *you're* here, sweetheart. If you weren't so wonderfully beautiful, the night would be drab."

"Oh, darling," she said, "you certainly know how to make me feel good!"

Alamo folded her in his arms, kissed her soundly, then looked into her lovely blue eyes, which reflected starlight. "Every day of my life, I thank the Lord for giving me such a beautiful wife, both inside and out."

The moonlight made it possible for Alamo to see that his wife was blushing. He folded her in his arms and kissed her again. "Let's sit down for a little while," he whispered.

They sat down on a wicker bench, and Alamo put an arm around his darling Julie. She leaned into him and rested her head gently on his chest. They both relished the moment.

Alamo lowered his face toward her head, breathed in the sweet-smelling scent of her hair, and tried to commit the aroma to memory so that when he was far away again, he could recall the sweet smell of her hair and relive this wonderful moment.

Julia could hear the steady beating of her husband's heart, and it brought immeasurable comfort to her. She lifted her head, looked up into his dear face, and trailed the tips of her fingers over it, memorizing every nuance. "I love you so much, my sweetheart."

"And I love you more than I could ever tell you, Julie." Alamo placed a soft kiss on her lips.

She laid her head back on his chest, and they remained close for several minutes. Then Alamo said, "We'd better head to our room."

Julia nodded and together they rose from the bench and entered the house. Arms entwined, they moved to the stairway, climbed to the top, and headed down the hall toward their room . . . their own private haven.

The next morning, Tuesday, June 2, the birds on the Diamond K Ranch were chirping gaily when the sun peeked its golden head over the eastern horizon, bathing the land in a pink and yellow glow. The adults in the big ranch house began awakening to the tantalizing aromas of sizzling bacon, hot biscuits, and rich brewing coffee that made their way to the bedrooms.

In the kitchen, Daisy Haycock hummed a happy tune as she prepared a hearty breakfast for the people she called her family, plus the houseguest, Corporal Lance Brooks. Busy at the stove, Daisy had ceased humming for a moment and at the same time heard the *clump, clump* of crutches on the kitchen floor behind her. She turned around just as the corporal said, "It sure does smell good in here, Miss Daisy."

The silver-haired cook could tell that Lance's face had recently been scrubbed and shaven, and his hair, which was still a bit damp, had been combed neatly. She smiled. "You come right on in here, young man, and sit down at the table. Just pick a chair, and the rest of them will still have enough to go around."

"Yes ma'am. I'll gladly do that," Lance said, obeying the feisty little woman, a wide grin on his face.

"The others will be straggling in a bit later," Daisy said softly, "so you go ahead thank the Lord for the food, and I'll get you started on your breakfast."

Lance bowed his head, closed his eyes, and moved his lips silently as he thanked the Lord for the food he was about to receive. "Amen," he said aloud.

Daisy poured Lance a cup of steaming coffee, then placed a blue and white plate in front of him that was heaped high with bacon, scrambled eggs, fried potatoes, and brown biscuits.

"Now, son," she said, "I want you to eat every morsel of this food. You're way too thin. I can tell by your frame that you had more meat on your bones before you got shot in that battle. You don't want to scare your parents when they see you, so while you're around here the next few days, ol' Daisy is gonna fatten you up a bit!"

Lance sent an impish grin her way. "Thank you, Miss Daisy. I'll try to do right by this glorious breakfast feast."

"Good boy!"

At that moment, Kane family members began filing into the kitchen, following the delicious aroma that filled the air. Daisy quickly explained that Lance had already prayed before he began eating his breakfast.

Adam, Abram, and Andy were ahead of their parents and ran to give Daisy a hug.

"Sure smells yummy, Miss Daisy!" Adam said happily.

Daisy chuckled and hugged all three boys, telling them to sit down and she would fill their plates. The boys cheerfully greeted Corporal Brooks as they obeyed Daisy's orders.

Julia and Alamo were right behind the boys, with little Amber in her papa's arms. Grandpa Abram had trailed in behind them. Amber was placed on the special little seat. Everyone sat down, and Abram led in prayer, thanking the Lord for the food.

As the family joined Lance in eating, Alamo smacked his lips. "Wow, Daisy! I haven't had food this good since I was home last!" He took another bite, chewed it quickly, and swallowed. "In fact, I think your cooking is better than ever!"

Daisy put her hands on her hips and made a mock frown. "Oh, go on with you, Alamo. You're just full of Irish blarney!" Her eyes were sparkling happily. Her boss and his brothers were home, and she was content.

Shortly after breakfast, the Kane brothers helped Lance into the rear of the army wagon, and as usual, Alamo sat next to him while Alex and Abel hopped up into the driver's seat with the reins in Alex's hands.

Standing in front of the porch, Julia, Libby, and Vivian, along with young Adam, Abram, and Andy, and Grandpa Abram, waved as the wagon rolled away. In her mother's arms, even little Amber waved, saying, "Bye-bye, Papa!"

Less than an hour after leaving the ranch, the Kane brothers and Lance Brooks entered Washington-on-the-Brazos. They traveled down Main Street a few blocks; then Alex guided the wagon up in front of Dr. Dennis Dewitt's office and pulled rein.

Alamo helped Lance out of the wagon and handed him his crutches. They entered the office with Alamo at Lance's side as he walked with the crutches. They were warmly welcomed by Dr. Dewitt's receptionist,

Mary Woolford, a woman in her midfifties.

Alamo introduced Mary to Corporal Brooks, explaining how, when, and where he was wounded. He told her that Lance had experienced fever, chills, and coughing since being exposed to the cold rain on the trip from Fort Polk and that Lance's medic at the fort told him to see a doctor and have his wound examined when they got to the ranch. He added that he and his brothers would be taking Lance to his home in Prairie View a week from today.

Mary told Alamo that the doctor was with a patient at the moment but should be finished in a little while. She suggested they take a seat in the waiting area just a few feet from her desk.

The Kane brothers and Lance sat down in the waiting area, which otherwise was unoccupied.

Alamo looked at Lance. "Are you feeling all right?"

Lance gave him a thin smile. "I'd say so. No fever right now. Very little pain in my leg."

"Good," Alamo responded.

The Kane brothers talked about the big mystery as to where they might be sent to do battle with the Mexican army when the reinforcements arrived at Fort Polk.

Some fifteen minutes had passed when they saw an elderly man come through the rear door of the office that led to the examining room. He shuffled a bit as he walked up to the receptionist's desk. "Ma'am, Dr. Dewitt wants you to set up another appointment for me in ten days."

Mary smiled. "Please sit down, Mr. Sheffield. I must take another patient to the doctor immediately. I'll be right back."

Mr. Sheffield nodded and sat down on a chair near Alex and Abel, who remained seated as Alamo and Lance followed the receptionist toward the rear door. As they followed Mary into the examining room, they saw Dr. Dewitt making notes on a sheet of paper while seated at a small table. He glanced toward Mary and the two men, smiling when he recognized Alamo. "Hello, Alamo. Glad to see you're home. How about Alex and Abel?"

Alamo reached out his hand. "It's nice to be home, Doctor, and it's nice to see you. Alex and Abel are in the waiting area. They're both fine."

As the doctor stood to his feet and shook Alamo's hand, Mary gestured toward Lance Brooks. "Dr. Dewitt, this young soldier was brought here by the Kane brothers. He was wounded in the battle of Palo Alto and needs your attention. Lieutenant Kane and his brothers will be taking him to his home in Prairie View a week from today."

Dewitt nodded, noting Lance's crutches. "All right, Mary. I'll see to him right now."

Mary smiled, stepped through the doorway, and closed it behind her.

Dr. Dewitt said to Alamo, "I was aware that you and your brothers were in the battles of Palo Alto and Resaca de la Guerrero. Sure am glad to know that the three of you are all right. What is this young corporal's name?" He held out his hand.

"Lance Brooks," Alamo said. "He was shot in his left leg in the Palo Alto battle. The medic who took care of him told him to have a doctor check the wound after we arrived at the Diamond K Ranch."

"Well, Corporal," the doctor said, "let's get you on this examining table right over here so I can check on that wound."

As Lance was in the process of lying down on the examining table, Alamo told the doctor about Lance's getting wet and chilled during the bad rainstorm on the way from Fort Polk and about his coughing and recurring fever.

Alamo stayed at Lance's side as Dr. Dewitt laid a hand on Lance's slightly moist brow for a few seconds then carefully

164

removed the bandage from his leg and examined the wound with tender hands. Lance winced at the doctor's touch as he continued to probe. "Sorry, son. I didn't intend to hurt you, but I have to be sure you're healing properly."

"I understand, Doctor." Lance coughed a bit and tried to smile. "I'm just glad you're here to check on it." He then asked hesitantly, "How is it?"

Dr. Dewitt laid a hand on Lance's thin shoulder. "It's healing nicely, but it's still a long way from being completely well. You must go slow with it. Always use your crutches, and don't put any weight on that wounded leg. I imagine you're chomping at the bit to get back to normal, but remain cautious and take extra care. The wound will heal eventually if you do as I say."

Lance coughed again and then nodded and grinned at the kind, caring physician. "Yes sir. I promise to do just as you say."

When Dr. Dewitt put a new bandage on the wound, he said, "Let me caution you about bathing, son. Just do a 'spit bath' so the bandage doesn't get wet at this point."

"Yes sir."

The doctor used a stethoscope to listen to Lance's heart and lungs and checked him over thoroughly. He then mixed some powders and put them in a glass bottle. He handed the bottle to Alamo. "Mix two teaspoons of these powders in a cup of water four times a day, and have Lance drink it. It will loosen his cough, take down the slight fever he has, and stop his chills."

Alamo nodded. "I'll take care of him."

The doctor looked down into Lance's eyes. "I'm finished with the examination, now, Lance. You should see a doctor in Prairie View soon after you get home so he can give you a checkup and take care of you until you're well."

Lance nodded. "I'll do that, Doctor."

"He'll let you know when you can take a regular bath again."

"I'm sure he will."

Moments later, once Lance was off the table and on his crutches, Alamo walked beside him as they headed for the exam room door. "I'll go with you to the waiting area," Doctor Dewitt said. "I want to see Alex and Abel."

Alamo grinned. "They'll be happy to see you, Doctor."

The doctor and Alex and Abel shared a warm reunion in the office.

Alamo walked over to Mary's desk and looked down at her. "I want to pay Lance's bill. How much is it?"

Before Mary could speak, Dr. Dewitt said, "No charge, Lieutenant Kane. Corporal Brooks was fighting for his country when he was shot. The least I can do is make the examination and treatment free."

Alamo smiled. "That's generous of you."

Lance nodded. "It sure is, Doctor. Thank you."

"My pleasure," the doctor said. "Thank *you* for fighting for our country."

The Kane brothers escorted Lance outside to the wagon, and Alamo helped him into the wagon bed and made him comfortable.

Alex put the team in motion and headed the wagon back toward the ranch.

As the days passed, Alamo took care of Lance as he told the doctor he would, and the three Kane brothers enjoyed the time with their loved ones and the ranch hands and their families.

Young Adam Kane showed his stepfather and uncles how he could handle his .22-caliber rifle better than ever by shooting at a target that Grandpa Abram had made for him. They were amazed at how good he had become with the gun.

On Sunday, June 7, when the Kane family arrived at their church in Washington-on-the-Brazos, the people of the church welcomed the Kane brothers home and warmly greeted Corporal Brooks.

Sitting with the Kane family in the adult Sunday school class, which was held in the church auditorium and taught by a dedicated layman, Lance thoroughly enjoyed the lesson.

In the morning service, at announcement and offering time, Pastor O'Fallon stepped up to the pulpit. "Folks, we have a very special guest with us this morning." Pointing to the wounded soldier in the pew with the Kanes, the pastor said, "His name is Corporal Lance Brooks."

Alamo helped Lance to his feet, and Lance steadied himself on his crutches.

The pastor briefly told of the corporal's having been wounded in the Palo Alto battle, welcomed him warmly, and also welcomed the Kane brothers home. There were many "amens" in the crowd.

The pastor made the rest of the announcements; then the offering was taken. This was followed by a choir special, which told of "mounting up with wings as eagles."

Pastor O'Fallon then went to the pulpit and opened his Bible. "I've titled my sermon this week 'High Is the Eagle.' " He looked out at the congregation.

He began his sermon with a deeply moving passage of Scripture about eagles — Ezekiel 17:1–3 — pointing out that the eagle took the highest branch of the cedar tree.

At this point, Alex looked at Alamo and Abel, and they smiled at each other. "Guess we were ahead of him on this one!" Alex whispered. His brothers grinned and nodded.

"I want to give you the definition of the word *eagle* in a new Bible dictionary I was recently able to obtain," the pastor said. "I wrote it down in my sermon notes so I would be sure to get it right. It says, 'Eagle: a very large bird, noted for its strength, keenness of sight, speed, flying range, and ability to attain a great height.' Please keep this definition in mind as I proceed."

The pastor followed this by telling the story of how Alamo had witnessed to Corporal Brooks just before the battle at Palo Alto and how defiant Brooks was against the gospel and what the Bible says about an everlasting burning hell, where lost sinners go when they die.

He went on to tell how the corporal was shot in the left leg during battle and how he lay helplessly on the ground with the grass on the field blazing around him and the wind driving the flames toward him. The pastor dramatically retold the events — Alamo risking his own life to run to Brooks, pick him up, and carry him to safety, winding through thin open areas in the blazing, wind-swept grass.

The congregation was caught up in the story, many folks sitting on the edge of their pews, and they rejoiced aloud when they heard the preacher tell how Alamo had the joy of leading Corporal Brooks to the Lord that evening after the battle was over.

Pastor O'Fallon proceeded to share how on Monday of that past week, he and his wife came upon the Kane brothers as they were driving an army wagon toward the Diamond K Ranch. He and Angela were introduced to the wounded Corporal Brooks, and Alex and Abel told them the story of how Alamo had witnessed to Brooks, trying to win him to the Lord and how belligerent and unbelieving Brooks had been.

Pastor O'Fallon then told the crowd about the flock of bald eagles that came flying over them at that moment and about the one Alamo pointed out, which was flying much higher than all the other eagles in the flock. He went on to tell how Alamo pointed up to the high eagle and likened winning souls to flying high like an eagle. At this point, many "amens" were coming from the crowd, and the majority applauded Alamo's words as quoted by the preacher.

9

Pastor Patrick O'Fallon smiled at the congregation's reaction to Alamo Kane's words.

"Let me remind you," the pastor said, "that in my Bible dictionary, the definition of *eagle* says first that the eagle is a very large bird, noted for its *strength.* Turn in your Bibles now to Exodus 19:3–4."

When the sound of fluttering Bible pages across the auditorium faded, the pastor said, "In this passage, God told Moses, 'Thus shalt thou say to the house of Jacob, and tell the children of Israel; Ye have seen what I did unto the Egyptians, and how I bare you on eagles' wings, and brought you unto myself.' God is comparing His great rescuing strength to that of an eagle's. The eagle is indeed known for its strength."

People in the congregation were nodding, some exchanging agreeing glances.

"Now, turn to Psalm 103:4–5. Here David is referring to the Lord of heaven. 'Who redeemeth thy life from destruction; who crowneth thee with lovingkindness and tender mercies; who satisfieth thy mouth with good things; so that thy youth is renewed like the eagle's.' When youth is renewed, it means you are stronger. Once again, in His Word God pictures the eagle as strong. Now turn to Isaiah 40:31."

As before, when the sound of fluttering pages faded, the pastor spoke. "The choir gave us part of this verse in their special a little while ago. God says here, 'But they that wait upon the LORD shall renew their strength; they shall mount up with wings as eagles; they shall run, and not be weary; and they shall walk, and not faint.' Once again, we see the *strength* of eagles spoken of in the Word of God. And as you can see, it is their strength that enables the eagles to fly so high."

As people all over the crowd nodded, the pastor then commented on the wisdom eagles have and went on to give information about eagles he had read of in various books. "You see, folks, it is because of their great strength and wisdom that eagles have been a symbol of war and imperial power since Babylonian times. As I noted in the definition of *eagle* in my Bible dictionary, the eagle is known for its ability to attain a great height. Bird experts say eagles fly higher than any other bird and nest in the tops of the tallest trees. We got a picture of that from Ezekiel chapter 17, didn't we?"

Pastor O'Fallon had the full attention of the crowd as he proceeded. "I have learned in my study on eagles that the species called *Haliaeetus leucocephalus* is the bald eagle, which is the wisest, largest, and strongest of all eagles. The bald eagle can have a wingspan of up to eight feet and can weigh up to sixteen pounds. The only other eagle that comes close in size is the golden eagle. However, the bald eagle has the ability to attain the greatest height of all eagles. Bald eagles inhabit areas along rivers, big lakes, and tidewater. Various species of eagles live throughout the world, except South America. But wherever they are, all species of eagles can fly much higher than any other kind of bird. Thus soul winners, in a spiritual way, are the ones, like Alamo, who experience the truth of 'High Is the Eagle'!"

The church members looked toward the Kane pew, set their eyes on Alamo, and said, "Amen!"

Alamo's face tinted. Julia Kane smiled.

The pastor then wove the gospel into his sermon, making sure that those who might be there without Jesus as Saviour and headed for hell would know that the only way of salvation was by repenting of their sin and receiving the Lord Jesus Christ, who had shed His precious blood on the cross of Calvary, died, was buried, and rose from the dead three days later.

He then tied this with the wisdom of the eagle, pointing out that soul winners are said in the Bible to be wise: "The fruit of the righteous is a tree of life; and *he that winneth souls is wise*" (Proverbs 11:30) and "*A true witness delivereth souls:* but a deceitful witness speaketh lies" (Proverbs 14:25).

Pastor O'Fallon went on to powerfully compare the true gospel of Jesus Christ with false gospels, which teach salvation by good works and religious deeds rather than by grace through faith in the Lord Jesus Christ and Him *alone.*

He then closed the sermon and gave the invitation for lost people to come and be saved and for saved people who were not soul winners to come and dedicate themselves to becoming soul winners.

As the choir and congregation sang the invitational hymn, the powerful presence of the Holy Spirit was apparent in the service as several people walked the aisle to receive Jesus into their hearts as their Saviour. Many Christians also came forward to dedicate themselves to be soul winners. They wanted to experience the truth of "High Is the Eagle," as the pastor had described it.

In the pew where the Kane family and Corporal Lance Brooks were standing, Lance had tears running down his cheeks as he leaned on his crutches and put an arm around Alamo, who stood next to him.

In a low voice, Lance said, "Alamo, I want to thank you once again for caring enough about me, not only to save me from the blazing flames on the battlefield but to lead me to Jesus."

Alamo hugged him. "You have been such a joy, Lance. I have a strong feeling in my heart that the Lord is going to use you in a mighty way for His glory."

Lance wiped tears. "Alamo, I want to be a soul winner just like you. I want to be a strong Christian just like you . . . as Pastor O'Fallon put it: 'High Is the Eagle!' I would go forward and publicly dedicate myself, but with these crutches and this bad leg, I couldn't kneel at the altar like the others are doing."

Alamo cuffed Lance's chin playfully. "Tell you what. You dedicate yourself to be a soul winner right here and now. Bow your head and tell the Lord that this is what you're doing. You can make it public later."

Lance bowed his head, closed his eyes, and prayed in a whisper, telling the Lord he was dedicating himself to be a soul winner.

Moments later, the congregation was seated once again, and new converts were baptized in the baptistry just before the close of the service. Lance turned to Alamo and thanked him for showing him in the Bible that he should follow the Lord's first command after being saved and get baptized.

Alamo nodded.

Lance continued. "When my leg heals to the point that I no longer need a bandage, I'm coming back here to get baptized. I want to be a member of this church. The only church in Prairie View is the one where the minister teaches that hell has no fire. Alamo, he also teaches that people go to heaven if they live good lives. He says that only really bad people go to hell. That's a false gospel."

"It sure is," Alamo said. "Coming regularly to church here won't be a problem. You live five miles closer to it than we do. And as you can see, we make it just fine."

After the service, when people were filing past the pastor and his wife, shaking hands and greeting, Lance shook the pastor's hand

and said, "I will be back to attend church here, Pastor. And when my leg is healed, I want to be baptized. I will be so happy when I can become a member of this church. Coming the distance between Prairie View and Washington-on-the-Brazos will not be a problem at all!"

Pastor O'Fallon smiled. "Lance, I'll be glad to have you come to church here, and as soon as the bandage comes off, I'll proudly baptize you, making you a member."

Angela O'Fallon smiled and took Lance's hand. "Lance, I'm very happy that you want to be a member here."

"Oh, Lance!" the pastor said. "I promised to give you a Bible! Wait right here. I'm going to run to my office and get it!"

The Kane family stood close by. Only a few minutes passed, and the pastor was back with the beautiful Bible, which had a black leather cover. When he handed it to Lance, he grinned. "If you read the print off the pages, I'll give you another one."

The Kane family chuckled.

With tears in his eyes, Lance said, "Thank you, Pastor. I'll sure give it a try!"

"It'll be hard for you to carry your Bible and use the crutches, Lance," Alamo said. "I'll carry it for you."

When the Kane family and Lance Brooks passed through the vestibule door onto the front porch of the building, Alamo looked at Lance's Bible. "I don't think the general store here in town carries Bibles with covers as beautiful as this one. I'm really glad Pastor gave it to you."

Lance met Alamo's gaze and smiled. "I am too. But even if the one you were going to buy me didn't have the exquisite leather cover this one has, I'd love it because it came from you, and I would still do my best to read the print off the pages."

Alamo felt a lump rise in his throat. "Thanks, pal."

The Kane family and Lance made their way to the wagon, speaking to other Diamond K people as they walked. Soon the Kanes and Lance were loaded in the large ranch wagon, and during the ride back to the Diamond K, Lance went on and on about the pastor's sermon. "He really knows how to preach the Word and make it easy to understand."

"He sure does," said Grandpa Abram, who sat on the first seat behind the driver's seat. "And, boy, did he tell us some marvelous things about eagles!"

The others in the wagon agreed, including young Adam Kane.

As the wagon rolled westward, the Kanes and Lance discussed the many wonderful things they had learned about eagles in the sermon.

Abram turned on his seat and looked at Alamo, who was behind him holding little Amber and sitting beside Julia. "You really know about 'High Is the Eagle,' don't you, Son?"

Alamo's features tinted as he smiled. "Thanks to my wonderful Saviour, who went to the cross, shed His precious blood, and rose from the dead, Papa. If He had not gone to Calvary for this hell-deserving sinner, not only would I go to hell without hope, but I wouldn't know the joy and thrill of winning souls or of flying high in my heart like an eagle."

Abram patted Alamo's knee. "Right, Son. Praise His wonderful name!"

Everyone in the wagon responded with joy, even little Amber, who set her dark blue eyes on her father's face. "Papa! Papa!"

When everyone arrived at the Diamond K, they found the ranch hands and their families and Daisy, who were also members of the church, standing around in a group. Cort was joyfully talking about the pastor's great sermon on eagles and how he tied the things the Scriptures say about eagles to

Christians' lives in such a marvelous way.

Daisy spoke up. "And wasn't it wonderful to see those precious souls come to Jesus at the invitation today?"

There were happy "amens" all around.

That evening the Kane family, Lance, and the other Diamond K Ranch people who were members of the church attended the evening service. Lance was thrilled with the sermon he heard in that service and, watching him, Alamo and the others in the Kane family could see that he was eager to attend the church regularly and grow in the Lord.

When the service was over and the people were walking out the vestibule door, Lance let the Kanes go ahead of him while he paused before the O'Fallons, gripped their hands warmly at the same time, and said, "Pastor, that was another great sermon. It really exalted the Lord Jesus in a magnificent way. I'll never forget it."

Pastor O'Fallon squeezed Lance's hand. "I'm glad you liked it."

Still holding both of their hands, Lance looked from the pastor to Angela. "I want to ask both of you to pray for my parents, that when Alamo presents the gospel to them, they will open their hearts to Jesus."

Angela squeezed Lance's hand firmly. "We

181

sure will."

"What are your parents' names?" the pastor asked.

"Papa's name is Harland, and Mama's name is Lucille."

Pastor Patrick nodded. "All right, Lance. We will most certainly be praying for Harland and Lucille Brooks, that the Lord will give Alamo Holy Spirit power as he witnesses to them and that He will draw them unto Himself."

Angela squeezed Lance's hand firmly once more. "I'll say it again. We sure will!"

Tears misted Lance's eyes as he thanked them and hobbled away on his crutches, heading for the open vestibule door, where he could see the Kanes waiting for him on the porch.

Soon they were in the ranch wagon, with Alex at the reins as usual. Instead of Abel sitting on the driver's seat beside him, Adam, Abram, and Andy had climbed up. Abel was seated next to Vivian in the back of the wagon.

Sitting on one of the other seats in the back of the wagon next to Grandpa Abram, Lance talked about the evening sermon, then brought up the morning sermon again. "I sure want to be a soul winner like Alamo. In my heart, I want to fly wa-a-a-y up high like an eagle!"

Planning to leave the ranch for Prairie View on Tuesday, June 9, the Kane brothers made Monday a special day with the family as planned.

While Cort and some of the men took Lance on a tour of the ranch in a comfortable cart, Alex and Abel devoted the day to being with their wives.

Alamo spent the morning with Julia and the children. Then in the afternoon he spent a great deal of time with Julia alone, walking along the banks of the creek that wove its way across the ranch while Grandpa Abram kept little Amber and her brothers with him at the big ranch house.

When Alamo and Julia returned to the house just past midafternoon, they found Abram on the front porch with the four children. Amber was in Grandpa's arms.

Adam dashed up to his parents, holding his .22-caliber rifle, and said to his stepfather, "Papa Alamo, with Grandpa's help, I set up some small targets out by the side of the house. I want to show you how well I can shoot."

Alamo smiled. "All right, Son. I want to see it."

"You'd better make it fast, Adam," Julia

said. "It'll soon be Amber's nap time. And she sure can't sleep with your gun going off."

Adam giggled. "I understand, Mama. It'll only take ten or fifteen minutes."

Julia smiled and nodded. "All right. Let's go around to where you set up the targets so we can see you hit them expertly."

With his grandfather and mother keeping his brothers and sister at a safe spot, young Adam Kane used the exceptionally small cardboard targets to show his stepfather how well he could handle his rifle since his last demonstration some months earlier. Alamo was amazed at how small the targets were and even more amazed when Adam hit every one of them without fail.

Less than fifteen minutes had passed for the demonstration, and Julia excused herself, saying she needed to take Amber inside and put her down for her nap. As Julia carried Amber toward the back of the house and rounded the corner, Grandpa Abram smiled as he heard Alamo commend Adam for such excellent marksmanship.

The boy looked up at his stepfather. "Papa Alamo, I know you've heard me say this many times before, but I *still* wish I was old enough to join the army and go fight the Mexicans with you and my uncles."

Alamo hugged him. "Son, I would not want to have my boy in combat. I would be on edge every minute if you were facing enemy guns. And so would your mother."

"And so would your grandpa," spoke up the aging Abram.

Adam nodded. "I understand, Papa. But if any Mexican soldiers ever sneak into Texas and step foot on the Diamond K Ranch, I'll use my rifle on them."

Alamo tweaked his nose. "Let's hope such a thing never happens."

Alamo, his father, and the boys returned to the front porch, and only a few minutes later, Julia came back, saying that Amber was already asleep. And she sat on the wicker bench next to Alamo.

The adults and the boys enjoyed talking about when the Mexican-American War was over and how good it would be for the Kane brothers to be back on the ranch permanently.

When nearly two hours had passed since Amber had been put down for her nap, Julia patted Alamo's arm and rose from the bench. "I'm going to go check on our baby girl, honey. She's probably waking up about now."

Alamo smiled and nodded. "Sure, sweetheart."

Bending down, Julia kissed her husband and headed toward the front door.

Alamo followed her with his eyes. *She is as lovely as the first time I laid eyes on her. Uh . . . no. That's not quite right. She's even lovelier than the first time I saw her. She has such an inward beauty about her now, since bringing four children into the world. Being a mother has added that radiant glow to her that shines so beautifully from her face.*

Alamo was still lost in thought when young Adam sat on the swing beside him and cut into his cogitation. "Papa, if the Mexican war's still going when I turn eighteen, will you let me join the army?"

Abram stood up with young Abram and Andy. "You two go ahead and talk, Alamo. I'll take these boys for a little walk. Okay?"

"Sure, Papa," Alamo replied, smiling.

As Abram and the two boys walked away from the porch, Alamo set steady eyes on Adam. "To answer your question, Son, I just can't believe the war will go on long enough for you to reach eighteen. But let me say this. Right now I really need you here on the ranch with your mother and your brothers and sister. Your mother told me that you've said that since you know how to handle that rifle, you'll use it if you have to in order to protect her and your brothers

186

and sister. I appreciate your determination to protect them, Son, so I'm depending on you to do your best to watch over them."

Adam's eyes sparkled. "Really, Papa?"

Alamo put his hand on Adam's shoulder and squeezed it. "Yes, really. It makes it a little easier for me to leave knowing that I can count on you and your determination to watch over your mother and your brothers and sister."

Adam looked his stepfather square in the eye. With a very proud and serious tone he said, "I'll take real good care of Mama, Abram, Andy, and Amber, Papa. And I'll do anything I can to help take care of the ranch."

Alamo hugged him. "Good boy! I'm depending on you!"

"I won't let you down, Papa. I promise."

Alamo smiled as he looked into his stepson's deep blue eyes. "I know you won't, Son. I know you won't."

The two of them quietly sat on the swing, taking in the calm beauty of the ranch land around them. Both were deep in thought, wondering what the future might hold, when they saw Cort and a young, single ranch hand named Chad Mathis coming toward them, with Lance alongside them on his crutches.

As the trio drew near the porch, Alamo and Adam left the swing and walked down the steps. Lance's face was beaming.

When they stopped, Cort said, "Alamo, I have something to tell you."

Alamo smiled. "What's that?"

"Lance now knows from experience about flying high as an eagle in his heart."

Alamo's brow furrowed. "Oh? Tell me about it."

"You know that some of us Christians on the ranch have been witnessing to Chad since he came to work here almost two years ago."

"Yes," Alamo said. "Because I'm his boss, he was kind when he turned me away the times I preached salvation to him, but he refused to open his heart to Jesus."

Chad's lips quivered as he said, "I'm sorry, Mr. Kane. You certainly gave me enough Scripture to get me to see the truth, but I just wasn't interested. Mr. Whitney, as well as some other Christian men on the ranch, has done the same thing."

Cort put a hand on Chad's shoulder. "Tell Mr. Kane what it was that made you turn to Christ just over an hour ago."

Chad looked at Lance, then back at his boss. "It was when Lance told me about almost dying in the flames on that Palo Alto battlefield and that he was terrorized as he thought of going into the flames of hell. He told me how you picked him up and carried him off the burning field and led him to the Lord that evening. Well, that got to me, Mr. Kane. So I told Lance I didn't want to go to hell, that I wanted to be saved. He quoted some Scripture on salvation to me and helped me know how to call on the Lord to save me." His eyes sparkled. "I'm saved now, Mr. Kane! I'm not going to burn in hell! And I will be going to church next Sunday so I can get baptized."

There was much rejoicing in Chad Mathis's salvation.

Amid the rejoicing, Lance put an arm around Chad, looked toward heaven, and shouted, "Thank You, Lord, for helping me get started as a soul winner! High is the eagle!"

10

That evening, while Lance ate in the mess hall with Cort, Chad, and the other unmarried ranch hands, the entire Kane family was having supper at the big ranch house.

At the dining room table in the Alamo Kane house, everyone was trying their best to make the gathering a festive, happy occasion, but it was quite obvious that the three soldiers and their loved ones were dreading being apart once more.

Even little Amber, strapped on her high chair between her parents, seemed sedate.

The three boys were sober and quiet, often glancing across the table at their father. Julia, Libby, and Vivian chattered and forced a giggle now and then in an attempt to cover the heaviness of their hearts. Grandpa Abram found it difficult to eat what was on his plate, as delicious as it was.

As the meal progressed, Alamo ran his gaze over the faces of his loved ones and saw tears misting some eyes.

After a while, the meal they had been trying to enjoy lay congealing on their plates.

Knowing he must say something to lighten the somber mood, Alamo cleared the tightness of his own throat, and said in a steady voice, "You know, dear family, our time together this past week was really a gift from God. Alex, Abel, and I certainly weren't scheduled for an authorized leave. But our wonderful Lord, who does all things well, had a different plan for us than the army had. I'm deeply sorry that Lance was wounded in the Palo Alto battle, but the Lord was in that as well. Because of his wound and how things worked out, another soul is bound for heaven. And because of Lance's wound, we three men were given the opportunity to take him home, come here to the ranch, and spend time with all of you, whom we love so much."

"Amen, Son," said Abram.

Alamo forced a smile onto his lips. "This gloom we've been passing around the table isn't the way we should be showing our thanks to the Lord for making it possible to have this time together."

For a few seconds there was total silence. Amber had been gurgling but ceased to do so, looking up wide-eyed at her papa as if even she understood the message of his impromptu "sermon."

Julia broke the silence. She turned to look at her husband. "You're right, my love. Hard as it is to think of you, Alex, and Abel leaving tomorrow, we should be praising the Lord for His goodness, and we should be fully trusting Him concerning all our tomorrows."

After a brief moment of silence, the dining room was once again filled with genuine happy sounds.

Later that night, when Alamo had his baby daughter in his arms and was about to put her to bed, it was as if she knew he was leaving again. With a tiny whine, she put her arms around his neck and clung to him. Julia stood close by and wiped her tears.

When Alamo and Julia were alone, they prayed, thanking the Lord that they had been able to be together for the past few days. They were still filled with emotion, and both shed tears as they faced being apart once more.

Early the next morning, Tuesday, June 9, a subdued family group gathered in front of the big ranch house as the Kane brothers packed up the army wagon and prepared to leave for Prairie View. Alamo helped Lance into the rear of the wagon and made him comfortable with pillows and blankets. Lance was already feeling and looking much better than when he'd first arrived at the ranch. The medicine Dr. Dewitt had given him was, without a doubt, working.

As Alamo hopped out of the wagon, he looked at Julia and the children, then looked away, his heart heavy. *It gets harder every time I leave them. Dear Lord, You know I'm trusting You completely to watch over them, but it's still so hard to leave them. Please, God, make this war end soon. I just want to be here with my family so we can all get back to normal, everyday living. Yes, I want to make this ranch a greater success, but the most important thing is to be with my wife and raise my children. I've already been in enough battles to be tired of bloodshed and strife.*

Alamo's thoughts were interrupted when he felt someone touching his arm. He looked down to see his lovely Julia gazing into his misty eyes. "Anything wrong, love?" she asked softly. "Your mind seemed to be a million miles away."

"Not really wrong, sweetheart," he replied in a similar soft tone. "I was just asking the Lord to bring a quick end to this Mexican conflict and let us all get back to normal life."

Julia smiled up at the face she loved so much. "Amen to that, darling."

At that moment, the ranch hands, led by Cort, gathered around the Kane family. Some had their wives with them. Chad Mathis made his way up to the side of the wagon to tell Lance good-bye. When the ranch people had said their good-byes to the Kanes, they moved on, wanting to give the family some privacy before the soldier brothers had to leave.

Young Adam was holding his little sister's hand as he and his brothers stepped up to their father. Julia looked on as Alamo hugged the three boys, one at a time. Then the boys stepped back as he hugged and kissed their sister. Adam then took Amber's hand again, allowing his mother to go to the arms of his stepfather.

Alamo squeezed Julia close to him. "I love you so much, sweetheart." A sigh escaped his lips. "I'll be home just as soon as we win the victory over Mexico."

"Yes, you will, darling," she said firmly, tears welling up in her eyes. "The Lord will see to that. Don't worry about us or this ranch. We're in God's hands. Just hurry home the instant the war is over."

"I will! I promise!"

When Alex and Abel had said good-bye to

their tearful wives, the aging Abram also wept as he told his sons good-bye. Still wiping tears, Abram led the family in prayer, asking for God's protection on Alamo, Alex, and Abel in the battles to come and to bring them home safely soon.

When Abram finished his prayer, all the family members shared one more hug. Then Alex and Abel climbed into the driver's seat of the wagon as Alamo swung over the tailgate and moved close to the wounded corporal.

The family gathered around the army wagon to say good-bye to Lance. "We'll look forward to seeing you at church whenever you can get there," Grandpa Abram said.

Libby and Vivian told Lance they would be praying for his parents' salvation. Julia, Grandpa Abram, and young Adam told him the same thing. Lance thanked them sincerely.

Julia then said, "Lance, anytime you can come here to the ranch, you'll be welcomed and well fed."

Lance smiled. "I appreciate that, ma'am. Thank you. I'll come just as soon as I can."

Julia gathered her children close, and the three boys told Lance good-bye. Coached by her mother, who was now holding her, little Amber said, "Bye-bye."

At that moment, Alex put the team in motion, and the wagon rolled away in the direction of the road. More tears were shed as dust rose from the wagon wheels, and the men in the wagon waved at their loved ones, who waved back.

Not wanting Alamo's last vision of her to be a teary one, Julia adjusted Amber into one arm, wiped a hand over her face, and put on her brightest smile.

The wagon was getting closer to the road, but Alamo could see the smile on Julie's face as the boys stood close to her. The boys were waving frantically at him as Julie blew him one last kiss. He blew her one back.

As the wagon carrying the soldiers disappeared from view, Vivian and Libby went to Julia, who stood Amber on the ground next to Adam. Each gave Julia a warm embrace, then headed toward their own houses. Her father-in-law then stepped up and hugged her as well. With that, he climbed the porch steps, took a seat on a wicker chair, and looked longingly toward the spot on the road where the army wagon had last been seen.

Julia turned to look at her children and saw the woebegone faces of her sons. Adam was still holding his little sister's hand. The loving mother knew she had to cheer them up.

"Now, boys," she said, "the Lord is going to take care of your papa and your uncles. We need to do our chores here at the house and keep everything looking right for when your papa comes home for good. And I have absolute confidence that the Lord is going to bring him home safely — and hopefully real soon."

The woebegone looks faded away as they gathered around their mother. Adam said, "Papa is in God's hands, isn't he, Mama?"

Julia smiled. "Yes, he is, honey. And there's no better place to be than in His hands."

Abram and Andy smiled and nodded.

"You're right, Mama." Adam handed Amber to her. "One of my chores is to provide bird meat and rabbit meat for the family." With that, he turned and looked at his grandfather. "Grandpa, do you want to go hunting with me? We really should do our chores."

The silver-haired Abram rose to his feet, smiling. "Yes sir, Adam! I'll go get my gun from my room. I know yours is on the back porch, so I'll meet you there."

As Abram entered the house, Adam was struck with the fact that he should have cleared the hunting "chore" with his mother first. He turned her way sheepishly. "It *is* okay if Grandpa and I go hunting, isn't it, Mama?"

Knowing that her oldest son needed a diversion from the sorrow of his stepfather and uncles having gone away to battle, Julia smiled and ruffled his hair. "Yes, Son. It's okay. Bring us back some good meat."

"Oh, I *will*, Mama!" With that, he ran alongside the house and headed for the back porch.

Julia watched him until he vanished from her sight and then led her two younger sons to the front door while carrying Amber. They went down the long hall to the kitchen and found Daisy mopping the kitchen floor. Julia explained that Adam and Grandpa had gone hunting. "Can I help you do some cleaning, Daisy?"

She nodded. "If you'll take over this mopping job, I'll go ahead and clean up the pantry."

"Okay." Julia turned to the boys. "Abram, Andy, you can go out and play on the back porch."

Both boys grinned and darted out the kitchen door. Julia set Amber on her stool, strapped her in for safety, then took down a rag doll from a shelf in the kitchen and handed it to her. Amber smiled and clutched the doll to her chest.

Julia walked over to Daisy and took the mop from her hand. "After I finish mopping, maybe I can work on a nice dessert for our supper tonight."

Daisy gave her a big grin. "With Alamo gone, you need to keep yourself busy, don't you, little gal?"

Julia nodded. With a slight strain was in her voice she said, "Yes, I do. Whenever Alamo comes home from his army duties and then leaves again, I can't help but think of when I was married to Adam, and he so bravely went off to help defend the Alamo against Santa Anna and his Mexican troops. And . . . and he never came home."

Julia leaned the mop against the cupboard and blinked at the tears welling up in her eyes. "And now, Alamo —" She quickly made a fist with her right hand and pressed it to her lips to stifle the sob that was trying to come out.

Daisy gripped Julia's shoulders and looked into her tear-filled eyes. "Now, honey, I've heard you tell your children that their papa couldn't be in safer hands."

Julia swallowed hard. "I know, Daisy, dear. I know. But this fear in my heart — I just —"

Daisy took Julia's trembling hands into her own. "Honey, in Psalm 56:3, David said to almighty God, 'What time I am afraid, I will trust in thee.' This precious encouragement in God's holy book is meant for each and every saved person. Let the blessing of that verse overtake the fear that comes to you concerning Alamo, and know that whatever the Lord does is right. He has promised that He will never leave us nor forsake us. Paul wrote in 2 Corinthians 1:20 that all the promises of God in Jesus Christ are yea and amen. I know that with Alamo going into battle again soon, you are fearful, but the Lord Jesus can replace those fears with His love and promises."

A sweet peace came over Julia's heart, and a gentle smile curved her pinched lips. A glimmer touched her eyes as she squeezed the work-roughened hands that held her own. "Thank you, my dear friend. I know those words are in God's book. I-I simply failed to claim them. But now I will, and I'll repeat them often to keep my mind and heart at ease."

Daisy's eyes were welled up by then. "Isn't God good, Julia? There's always a Scripture verse for every situation in a Christian's life."

"Indeed God is good," Julia replied.

"Indeed He is!"

As the army wagon came around a bend bordering a thick forest, the town of Prairie View came into sight slightly over an hour and a half after leaving the Diamond K Ranch. Lance was sitting up in the wagon bed, and he pointed past the team of horses. "Well, Alamo," he said to his friend, "there's my town."

Alamo nodded and smiled.

From the driver's seat, Abel said, "Looks like a nice place."

Alex turned around. "When we get to town, let me know how to get to your house."

"Will do," Lance responded.

"Lance," Alamo said, "since you're a soul winner now, would you like to be the one to give your parents the gospel?"

Lance shook his head. "No sir. Chad Mathis was easy to deal with about salvation because he'd heard a lot of Scripture verses from those of you who'd witnessed to him. With my parents, it's a different story. I still want *you* to talk to them, Alamo."

The lieutenant grinned. "Be glad to."

Soon they were in Prairie View, and Lance gave Alex directions to his home. Moments later, they turned onto the dusty street Lance had named, and he pointed down the block to the right. "The fourth house from the corner, Alex."

"Gotcha," Alex said.

Lance immediately saw his parents, who were in their late forties, on the front porch. "That's them. Pop is about to leave for work."

When the wagon drew near the house, Lance called out, "Hello, Mom! Pop!"

Harland and Lucille Brooks turned at the sound of their son's greeting, and their eyes widened when they saw Lance sitting in the bed of the wagon, holding a pair of crutches.

"Lance!" His mother gasped as the wagon came to a halt at the porch. "What happened to you?"

"I was wounded in battle, Mom," Lance replied.

Alamo smiled at Lance's parents and quickly helped him to the ground. A weeping Harland and Lucille hurried to their son and embraced him.

Lucille's voice shook as she said, "Lance, honey, when were you wounded?"

"A month ago yesterday, Mom. May 8. In the Palo Alto battle. Did you read about the battle in the newspaper?"

"We sure did, Son," Harland said. "How

bad are you hurt?"

Lance quickly explained his wound, telling them that a Mexican bullet hit him in the left thigh. He quickly introduced his parents to Privates Alex and Abel Kane, who now stood beside their brother. He then introduced them to Lieutenant Alamo Kane, telling them how Alamo saved his life when he was wounded on the battlefield, unable to move, trapped amid burning grass. Lance emphasized how the lieutenant had risked his own life to pick him up and carry him to safety.

Harland and Lucille tearfully thanked Alamo for risking his own life to save their son.

Alamo smiled as he laid a hand on Lance's shoulder. "I was glad to do it."

Lance told them that Alamo owned the Diamond K Ranch west of Washington-on-the-Brazos. He explained that when the Kane brothers left Fort Polk to bring him home, they went by the ranch first so they could see their families. He told them about Alamo's wife and four children and about Alex's and Abel's wives.

Harland smiled. "I hope Lucille and I will get to meet your family sometime."

"Yes," Lucille agreed. "I'd like that."

Lance turned to his parents. "The Kane

brothers have to head back to Fort Polk in a little while. Could we all go into the parlor for now? Something very wonderful and important happened to me just after the battle at Palo Alto, and I want to tell you about it with the Kane brothers present."

"I definitely want to be in on this, Son," Harland said. "I'll hurry down the street to Ben Fisher's house and tell him to advise the boss that I'll be a little late to work this morning. I'll tell Ben why too!"

As Harland hurried away, Lance looked at the Kane brothers and explained that his father was employed at the Prairie View Hardware Store, as was Ben Fisher.

"Gentlemen" — Lucille motioned with her hand — "why don't you come in the house now? Harland will be back in just a few minutes." As she spoke, she headed for the front door.

"All right, ma'am." Alamo quickly turned to the wagon, reached into the wagon bed, and picked up his Bible.

Lance hopped on his crutches alongside his mother as she led the Kane brothers a few steps down the hall to the parlor door. When they entered the parlor, Lucille noticed the book with the black cover in the lieutenant's hand and smiled. "Lieutenant Kane, why did you bring your Bible in?"

Alamo smiled back. "Ma'am, what your son is going to tell you and your husband has to do with the Bible, so I brought it along."

Still smiling, Lucille nodded and told the Kane brothers to sit down on the sofa. She took a seat in an overstuffed chair, and Lance did the same in another overstuffed chair, leaving one for his father.

Lucille asked questions about the Diamond K Ranch, which the Kane brothers gladly answered, and after a few minutes, Harland returned. As he sat down next to his wife, he noticed the Bible on the lieutenant's lap but said nothing about it. He turned to Lance. "All right, Son, tell your mother and me about the important thing that happened to you just after the Palo Alto battle."

Lance then told his parents that Alamo had talked with him about his need to know the Lord Jesus Christ as his Saviour a short time before the Palo Alto battle and how he had blatantly insulted the lieutenant's beliefs about salvation and about hell being a real place of fire. The parents exchanged furtive glances, apparently remembering when they had heard this same opposition to hell being real fire preached right there at the church in Prairie View.

Lance then told his parents about the exploding cannonballs setting the grass on fire at Palo Alto in the field where he was firing his rifle at the Mexican soldiers, and how a Mexican bullet tore into the thigh of his left leg. He went on to tell them how terrified he was while lying wounded and helpless on the blazing battlefield, certain that he was going to be burned to death as the wind blew the flames toward him.

Before the battle, Alamo had warned him of an everlasting, fiery hell if he died without receiving Jesus Christ as his Saviour. That conversation came to his mind while he lay on that burning field. After Alamo had rescued him, he was so thankful that he had been saved from the flames on the battle-field. He was ready to repent of his sin, receive Jesus as his Saviour, and escape burning in hell forever when Alamo brought up the subject of salvation that very evening.

Lance sleeved perspiration from his brow. "Mom, Pop . . . Alamo showed me in the Bible how to be saved and led me to the Lord."

Harland and Lucille looked at their son in absolute silence, not knowing what to say.

All three Kane brothers were praying earnestly in their hearts.

Lance went on to tell his parents that this

past Sunday, the Kane family took him to their church in Washington-on-the-Brazos, and he loved it.

"You see, Mom, Pop, after I received Jesus into my heart, Alamo showed me in the Bible that my first step of obedience to God is to be baptized as a testimony of putting my faith in Jesus, who died for me on the cross, was buried, and rose from the dead three days later. So I'm planning on being baptized at that church as soon as my leg heals. I plan to be a member of the church and go there regularly. In fact, I plan to go there regularly even before I'm a member."

Harland and Lucille were still looking at their son in silence, obviously deeply touched by his story.

Lance went on. "And I intend to go to Washington-on-the-Brazos regularly to Dr. Dennis Dewitt, who treated my leg while I was there with the Kane brothers. I like him much better than that crabby doctor here in our town."

Harland and Lucille smiled and exchanged glances.

Alamo then looked at Harland and Lucille with steady, compassionate eyes. "Mr. and Mrs. Brooks, I must ask you . . . have you ever repented of your sin and received the Lord Jesus Christ into your hearts as your

Saviour?"

Harland shook his head. "I have not, Lieutenant."

Lucille shook her head in the same manner. "Neither have I."

Harland wiped a nervous hand over his mouth. "Lieutenant Kane, Lucille and I have never understood how to be forgiven of our sins or how to come to the place where we could say we *know* we're going to heaven. We have only gone to the church in town a few times, but we never accepted what the minister says about hell not being real fire."

"Good," Alamo said.

Harland went on. "The pastor teaches that the really bad people who go to hell won't suffer in everlasting flames. He says salvation comes when we are religious and do good deeds. The problem I have with this is just how religious do we have to be and how can we be sure when we've done enough good works to offset our bad works so we know we're going to heaven?"

Alamo nodded and ran his eyes between the couple. "If I show you from the Bible how you can be saved and forgiven of all your sins and know you're going to heaven without *any* doubt, are you willing to obey the Word of God and, like your son, do what it says?"

Both parents nodded, saying, "Yes."

"Good!" Alamo said. "Then you will have this most important matter settled in just a little while."

Tears were running down Lance's cheeks, and a wide smile broke across his face.

11

Excitement was obvious in Alamo's eyes as he quickly shifted some chairs around so he could sit between Harland and Lucille Brooks and show them what the Bible says about how to be saved.

Alamo opened his Bible to Luke chapter 16. "First, let's hear it from the lips of the Lord Jesus Christ Himself about hell being real fire. In this passage, He talks about a man who died and went to hell. Look at verse 23. Jesus says, 'And in hell he lift up his eyes, being in torments. . . .' He is suffering torments in hell, right?"

Both Harland and Lucille nodded.

"Now, look at verse 24. He is crying for water to cool his tongue and then says, 'I am tormented in this flame.' Flame is *fire*, is it not?"

"It sure is," Harland said.

"Then according to Jesus Christ, hell is real fire, correct?"

Both of them nodded again.

"I could show you plenty more verses that say hell is real fire, but since Jesus says it is, that's enough for me to know it's true."

Alamo then flipped the pages of his Bible to the book of Ephesians. "Mr. Brooks, you asked a moment ago that if salvation were by works, how could we be sure we've done enough good works to go to heaven. You're on the right track. Salvation is not by works at all. Look here at Ephesians 2:8–9: 'For by grace are ye saved through faith; and that not of yourselves: it is the gift of God: Not of works, lest any man should boast.' You see, salvation is by grace — unmerited favor — *not* works. It is by faith — faith in the Lord Jesus Christ, who purposely died on the cross of Calvary while shedding His precious blood, was buried, and then raised Himself from the dead."

The couple's eyes were fixed on Alamo. He then turned to Mark 1:15. "Jesus said while preaching to lost people here, 'Repent ye, and believe the gospel.' "

He explained that repentance is sorrow for a person's sin and a change of mind, which leads to a change of direction. He showed them that Jesus said human beings come into this world already walking on the broad road that leads to hell. They must

211

believe the gospel, turn around 180 degrees
to Him, open their hearts to Him, and follow Him on the narrow road that leads to
heaven. When they make that pivot, they
are repenting of their sin, turning from it,
and turning from whatever religion they are
following unto Him.

Alamo took them to Galatians 1:13–14
and showed them that the apostle Paul
made it clear that when he was lost, he was
religious. "So you see, Mr. Brooks," Alamo
said, "you said the problem you have seen is
just how religious do we have to be? God
doesn't want *anybody* to be religious. He
wants them to be saved. A person must
repent of their religion and turn to God's
virgin-born, only begotten Son, Jesus Christ,
in order to be saved. Do you both believe
that Jesus is God's virgin-born, only begotten Son?"

Harland and Lucille were drinking it in.
Lance, Alex, and Abel could see it. "Yes!"
the couple said at the same instant.

"All right," Alamo said. "Jesus said we are
to repent and *believe the gospel.* Now let's
see what the gospel is."

He then turned to 1 Corinthians 15. He
showed them that in verse 1, Paul reminds
the Christians at the church in Corinth that
when he came to that city, he preached the

gospel to them. In verse 2, Paul says of the gospel, "By which also ye are saved."

Alamo then showed them what Paul says in verses 3 and 4: ". . . how that Christ died for our sins according to the scriptures; and that he was buried, and that he rose again the third day according to the scriptures."

"So you see," Alamo said, "the gospel is Christ's death, burial, and resurrection. Nothing added. In Romans 1:16, Paul writes of the gospel of Christ that it is 'the power of God unto salvation to every one that believeth.' Remember, Jesus said in Mark 1:15, 'Repent ye, and believe the gospel.' Salvation for lost, hell-bound sinners was made possible by Christ's blood-shedding death on the cross, His burial, and His glorious resurrection. Nothing else. Not good works. Not baptism. Not doing religious deeds. None of these are in the gospel."

Lucille smiled. "It's becoming clear, Lieutenant."

"It sure is," said Harland.

"Good." Alamo flipped pages again. He then read to them from John chapter 3, where Jesus spoke to a religious man named Nicodemus: "Except a man be born again, he cannot see the kingdom of God." He explained that the kingdom of God is heaven and that the reason we need to be born again is because we were born wrong the first time — spiritually dead. We must be made spiritually alive, and we must become God's children in order to avoid hell and go to heaven. It is the Spirit of God who gives us spiritual life and makes us God's children, as John 3:6 teaches: "that which is born of the Spirit is spirit."

Alamo flipped back a page. "Now, here in John 1:12, we are told how to become born again . . . become God's child. Of Jesus Christ, it says, 'But as many as received him, to them gave he power to become the sons of God, even to them that believe on his name . . .' "

Alamo looked at Lucille, then at Harland. "What do you have to do in order to be born again?"

"Well," Harland said, "believing on Jesus' name has to include believing the gospel, because it is the gospel of Christ that is the power of God unto salvation. So repenting of our sin, turning to Jesus because we believe that because of what He did in His death, burial, and resurrection, He is the only way of salvation, we receive Him."

Lucille was nodding. Lance was smiling and shedding tears. Alex and Abel were smiling as well.

"You've followed it well," Alamo said. "Now let me show you just where you are to receive Jesus in order to be saved — to be born again."

He turned to Ephesians chapter 3 and pointed to verse 17. "Here Paul is writing to saved, born-again, heaven-bound people. Look what he says. 'That Christ may dwell in your hearts by faith.' Where does Christ dwell in saved, born-again people?"

"In their *hearts,*" said Lucille.

"That's right," Alamo said. "So if a lost person sees his or her lost condition, believes the gospel of Christ, puts his or her faith in Jesus and only Him for salvation, and receives Him as his or her own personal Saviour, that person is instantly saved — and saved forever — because the Bible says He gives saved people *eternal* life."

Harland and Lucille were both blinking at tears in their eyes.

Lance's heart pounded as he prayed silently, asking God to work on their hearts and bring them unto Himself.

"Now, one last thing," Alamo said. "You may be wondering just how you receive Jesus into your hearts."

"Yes!" Lucille said.

"Exactly!" Harland said.

Alamo turned to Romans chapter 10.

Holding his Bible so Harland could clearly see, Alamo said, "Here's how you receive Jesus. Read verse 13."

Harland brushed the tears from his eyes and focused on the verse. His voice shook a bit as he read, " 'For whosoever shall call upon the name of the Lord shall be saved.' "

"So we repent of our sin by turning to Jesus and believing the gospel of Christ — we *call* on Him, inviting Him into our hearts as our Saviour!" Lucille said.

"That's it," Alamo said. "You repent, you call and ask Jesus to come into your heart and save you, and it's done!"

"I want to do that right now!" Lucille said.

"So do I!" Harland chimed in.

Lance looked on through a wall of tears as Alamo led them in the sinner's prayer of repentance and faith as they asked Jesus to come into their hearts and save them.

When it was done, Lance was on his feet, leaning on his crutches as his parents both embraced him. All three wept with joy as they rejoiced together.

Alex and Abel looked on with tears in their eyes as Harland, Lucille, and Lance celebrated. Alex swung his gaze to Alamo, who was also watching the scene with elation. "Well, Alamo, I can just imagine where you are right now — 'High Is the Eagle'!"

Alamo wiped tears from his cheeks and nodded. "You're right, big brother! I'm wa-a-ay up there!"

Abel smiled and dabbed at his own tears with a handkerchief. "Alex and I are so proud of you, Alamo! And we're proud to be your brothers! Yes! 'High Is the Eagle'!"

"Amen and amen!" Alex said, his voice breaking from the joy in his heart.

When everyone's emotions had settled down, Alex and Abel went to Harland and Lucille and welcomed them to the family of God. Alamo then opened his Bible and showed the new babes in Christ that their first step of obedience to God now that they were saved was to be baptized.

Harland responded immediately. "We'll just do that. We want to be members of your church there in Washington-on-the-Brazos."

"Yes!" Lucille said. "We'll go next Sunday with Lance and ask to be baptized."

Lance was overjoyed. Leaning on his crutches, he told his parents how glad he would be to take them to the church and introduce them to Pastor Patrick O'Fallon. He then added that Pastor O'Fallon was brother-in-law to the Kane brothers — he was married to their sister, Angela. Harland and Lucille smiled with pleasant surprise and agreed that this was wonderful.

217

Lance looked at Alamo, and as he saw the light shining in Alamo's eyes and the joy on his face, he said, "I think I see a high-flying eagle again!"

Alamo grinned. "You're right, Lance. Seeing your parents saved has me up there! 'High Is the Eagle'!"

Alex put his arm around Alamo's shoulder. "Lance, you were so engrossed in rejoicing with your parents that you didn't hear us, but Abel and I just told Alamo the same thing."

Lance chuckled. "Okay. I guess great minds run on the same track."

As Alex and his brothers were laughing at Lance's words, Lance turned to his parents. "Well, now that the most wonderful thing possible has happened to both of you, I guess I should tell you about the results of this wounded leg and my relationship with the army. I'm having to leave the army because the medics told General Zachary Taylor that I will limp on this leg for the rest of my life."

Lucille's hand went to her mouth. "Oh dear."

Lance smiled. "It's all right, Mom. The Lord has His plan for my life. Anyway, I wanted to tell you and Pop that General Taylor said he is going to get me an honorable discharge."

His parents smiled at each other, then looked back at their son. "I'm happy to hear about the honorable discharge, Son," Harland said, "and I want to tell you that I'm proud of you for being such a good soldier."

"Me too, dear." Lucille patted her son's hand.

Alamo turned to his brothers and pointed to the grandfather clock. "Fellas, I really hate to cut into this happy time, but we'd best be heading in the direction of Fort Polk."

Alex and Abel nodded.

Harland and Lucille walked over to the Kane brothers. "We'd love to have you stay right here for a while," Harland said, "but we understand that you need to get back to the fort."

Both Harland and Lucille hugged Alamo and thanked him for leading them to the Lord. They would be praying for the Kane brothers as they returned to war.

"We should have prayer with Lance and his parents before we leave," Abel said.

Alamo nodded. "I agree, Abel. You lead us in prayer."

Lance positioned himself on the crutches so he could have one arm around his mother and the other around his father. Abel led the group in prayer, thanking the Lord for Harland's and Lucille's salvation and praying that they and their son would be significantly blessed in their new Christian life.

A few minutes later, the Kane brothers were loaded in the army wagon with all three in the driver's seat and Alex at the reins. Alamo sat between his older brothers. The Brooks family stood beside the wagon and with expressive eyes looked up at the three soldiers. Lance was standing between his parents, leaning on his crutches.

"We'll be looking forward to seeing all three of you at church when the war with Mexico is over and we're back home on the ranch," Alamo said.

"Mom, Pop, and I will look forward to it also, Alamo," Lance said. "And we'll be praying for the safety of all three of you as you head to battle."

Harland and Lucille nodded their agreement.

The Kane brothers thanked them and bade the family farewell. Alex put the horses in motion, and the three brothers waved back at the Brookses as they headed up the street.

When they were out of town, Alex turned the wagon southward. Because he could drive it faster without the wounded Lance

Brooks aboard, they made better time than on the drive from Fort Polk to the Diamond K Ranch.

The sun shone down from a clear sky, and after traveling several miles in silence, each brother lost in his own thoughts, Alamo removed his hat and with a sleeve wiped away the perspiration beading on his brow. He placed the hat back on his head and sighed deeply.

Gripping the reins, Alex turned to Alamo. "What's troubling you, little brother?"

All that could be heard was the clomping of the horses' hooves on the soft earth and the rustling of the leaves on the big trees that grew close to the road.

Alamo shrugged. "Oh, it's just this war situation. I think I know how you and Abel feel, and I feel the same way. I'm just getting real tired of having to leave our home and family and go off to fight a war. Why can't people live peaceably in their own territory? Why do they have to want what someone else has?"

"You already know the answer to that, Alamo." Abel removed his hat and, running his fingers through his thick, sandy hair, said, "Greed."

"That's it exactly." Alex mopped his brow with a large red and white handkerchief.

"Greed. If we don't fight this war, there won't be any Diamond K Ranch. The Mexicans will take it all."

A smile curved Alamo's lips. "Silly me. Sure, it's greed. I know that. Guess I'm just not thinking straight. But I sure wish those Mexicans would leave us alone."

"Me too," Alex quipped. "But until they change their minds about wanting Texas, I'm gonna keep fighting them."

Alamo's square jaw jutted forward. "Well, me too, but I'll sure be glad when we've won this war and put the Mexicans out of the greed business."

As the days passed, the Kane brothers made good time on their journey. They camped Tuesday, Wednesday, and Thursday night along the road and arrived at Fort Polk late in the afternoon on Friday, June 12. When they pulled up to the main gate, the guards looked down from the tower and welcomed them. The gate opened, and the guards shouted at soldiers inside the fort that the Kane brothers were back.

Alex had barely gotten the wagon inside the fort when their soldier friends swarmed around them, welcoming them back. Alex pulled rein.

One of the sergeants hurried to the wagon

and looked up at the three men on the driver's seat. "How's Corporal Brooks doing?"

Others joined in, wanting to know the same thing. They were pleased when Alamo told them about taking him to their family doctor in Washington-on-the-Brazos and the medicine he gave Lance, which had made him much better. Every man who heard Alamo's words showed that he was glad to hear this.

Alex shook the reins and clicked his tongue, heading the wagon toward the barns and corrals, but before he could get very far, more soldiers came rushing up, welcoming them back. In the crowd was Lieutenant Ulysses Grant. Alex pulled the wagon to a halt, and he and his brothers greeted the group.

"What's new concerning American troops going into New Mexico?" Alamo asked the men encircling the wagon.

Lieutenant Grant spoke up. "Well, President Polk sent a telegraph message to General Taylor through the army post at Washington-on-the-Brazos on May 29. The president told General Taylor that he had just sent Colonel Stephen Kearny from Fort Leavenworth, Kansas, to take his troops to New Mexico, along with troops from Missouri army posts. Kearny has a total of fifteen hundred troops, and their goal is to free the territory from Mexico's grasp."

At that moment, General Taylor, who had been made aware that the Kane brothers were back, walked up. "Hey, welcome back!" Taylor smiled. "Everything go all right?"

"Yes sir," Alamo said. "We had a good time with our family, and Corporal Brooks is now home with his parents. His wound is healing well."

"Good. I heard what Lieutenant Grant just told you. At this point, I'm still waiting to get orders from the president of where to lead my troops from Fort Polk to attack Mexico once our reinforcements arrive and the New Mexico situation is taken care of."

Alamo nodded. "All right, sir. We'll wait for those orders with the rest of your men. Right now, we'll put this wagon and the horses where they belong."

As Alamo turned back toward the wagon, his attention was drawn to two buildings being constructed inside the fort's walls. He pivoted and asked, "General, what are those new buildings?"

Taylor smiled. "That large one is the new barracks so we'll have plenty of room to house our present troops and those who are coming. The other is the new mess hall so we can all eat our meals inside."

"Great!" Alex Kane exclaimed. Abel spoke his agreement.

The general said again that he was glad the Kane brothers were back and headed for his office. The crowd broke up, and Alex drove the wagon to the area inside the fort where the horses and wagons were kept. They put the horses in a corral, seeing to it that the men in charge would feed and water them. Then the Kane brothers gathered the Christian soldiers together and told them about Lance's parents coming to the Lord. There was much rejoicing in this good news.

The next morning, the Kane brothers were assigned to one of the scout units that went out daily to see if any Mexican troops were anywhere near the fort. So far, since the president and Congress had officially declared war on Mexico, none had been seen.

As time passed, the soldiers at Fort Polk, as well as American soldiers in army posts all along the Mexican border, waited for word from President Polk as to when and where they should attack Mexico. They soon figured out that this would depend on what happened in the battle to make New Mexico Territory completely free from the control of the Mexican government.

The new barracks and mess hall were completed on Saturday, June 13, which made the men very happy.

On Monday, June 15, the thirty-seven hundred new troops promised by the president arrived and were warmly welcomed by General Taylor and his men. Taylor was glad to have the number of his troops up to six thousand.

On Friday, July 3, General Taylor received official word by telegram through the U.S. army outpost at Corpus Christi Bay that Colonel Stephen Kearny and his fifteen hundred troops had already moved into New Mexico in late June and were currently doing battle with Mexican forces in many places throughout the territory.

12

At the Diamond K Ranch, on Monday, July 6, foreman Cort Whitney and two ranch hands returned from Washington-on-the-Brazos with a copy of that day's edition of the *Washington Post* in Cort's saddlebags.

"I'll go on over to the big ranch house and read the article to Julia and Mr. Kane," said the foreman. "Then I'll head over to the other Kane houses and read it to Libby and Vivian. You fellas can join your team working on that section of new fence out on the west pasture."

"Sure enough," Wiley Fordham said. "See you later, Cort."

"Sure enough." Cort nodded as the two men rode away at a rapid trot.

Cort headed for the big ranch house, and a few minutes later, he was pleased to see Libby and Vivian sitting on the front porch with Julia. Libby was holding Amber, and young Abram and Andy were playing

"Americans and Mexicans" on the side of the house with toy wooden guns, making firing sounds with their mouths.

Julia rose from her wicker chair as the foreman dismounted. "Hello, Cort. Everything all right in town?"

Cort nodded as he reached in his saddlebag and pulled out the newspaper. "Yes ma'am. Everything's fine." As he moved toward the porch and started up the steps, he held up the newspaper. "This is today's edition of the *Post*. I'm sure you ladies will be interested in the article on the front page. I'm glad you're all here. That way I can do this in one reading."

Julia sat down. "All right. We're ready to hear it."

Cort snapped his fingers. "Whoops. Is your father-in-law here? I'm sure he'll be interested in the article too."

"He's hunting birds and rabbits with Adam," Julia said. "I'm not sure when they'll be back. I'll share the information with him later."

Cort nodded. "Okay."

He proceeded to read the article to the women, which told of Colonel Stephen Kearny and fifteen hundred troops entering New Mexico Territory in late June and that they were presently engaged in battles with

Mexican troops in many places throughout the territory. The article reported that all the other American troops President Polk had ready to attack Mexico would be sent in once the New Mexico situation was in hand, which the president expected would be soon.

When Cort had finished reading the article to the Kane women, he said, "I felt that you ladies and Mr. Kane should know about the New Mexico situation and what the president says about American troops who are ready to attack Mexico being sent soon. Alamo, Alex, and Abel will soon be in battle somewhere in Mexico."

Biting their lips, Libby and Vivian looked at each other in silence.

Julia rose to her feet. "We appreciate your reading the article to us, Cort," she said, her voice a bit tight. "I'll tell my father-in-law about it. I-it's hard to face the fact that Alamo, Alex, and Abel will soon be facing Mexican guns again."

Cort nodded. "Yes. But I knew the four of you would need to know where things stand right now."

Julia swallowed hard. "Of course. Thank you."

"You're welcome," Cort said with a thin smile as he descended the porch steps. He swung a leg over his horse and rode away.

Libby stood up and placed a drowsy Amber on the small pallet of quilts that was next to the chairs. Vivian rose to her feet. Together they put their arms around Julia, and all three women wept.

As they stood there clinging to each other and weeping, that same old fear wended its way back into Julia's heart. But instantly, she thought of the Scripture verse Daisy had quoted to her. With a shaky voice, she said, "Libby . . . Vivian . . . when I was having a hard time with this war thing not long ago, Daisy quoted Psalm 56:3 to me: 'What time I am afraid, I will trust in thee.' We need to cling hard to that verse. If we fall apart now, we aren't trusting the Lord to keep His promises to us."

"What a precious verse that is, Julia," Libby said quietly.

"And another thing. We promised our husbands we would keep things running as smoothly as possible here at home, and we can't do that if we fall to pieces when some news about the war filters back to us."

Vivian let go of her sisters-in-law and wiped the tears from her face. "Then we'd better dry these tears, trust God to fulfill His promises, and storm the gates of heaven with prayer, which is our best weapon."

"I agree." Julia sniffled as she picked Amber up from the pallet. "Let's go inside." Moments later, the three women were on their knees in Julia's parlor doing that very thing. As they prayed together, they asked the Lord to protect their husbands in every battle. They also asked for strength and comfort from the Lord for themselves, telling Him they knew He understood the load they were carrying.

In Washington, D.C., on Wednesday morning, July 8, President James K. Polk was at his desk in his office when he heard a knock on the door. As usual, he recognized the rhythm of the knock and called out, "Come in, Mr. Vice President!"

The door swung open, and Vice President George M. Dallas stepped in. As he closed the door behind him and headed toward the president's desk, Polk saw a strange look on his face. When he drew up to the desk, the president asked, "Something bothering you?"

The strange look disappeared. "Uh . . . uh, no sir. It's just that something quite different — and you might say amazing — is happening."

Polk frowned. "Well, what is it?"

"Well, Mr. President, a very important

man from Cuba has just arrived in Washington, and he is asking to see you."

Polk's frown deepened. *"Cuba?* Did you say the man is from *Cuba?"*

"Yes sir."

"Well, who is he?"

"His name is Colonel Alexander Atócha. He is the official Cuban representative of the exiled Antonio López de Santa Anna. He showed me his identification papers."

The president's frown vanished. "Hmm. Has Colonel Atócha said what he wants to see me about?"

"No sir. I guess he wants to tell just *you.* He knocked on my office door a few minutes ago, introduced himself in perfect English, and said he had come to me, the vice president, because he felt it would be the best way to get to talk to President Polk."

"Is anyone else in the White House aware that Atócha is here?"

"Not as far as I know, sir. He asked if I wanted to search him to see if he was carrying a weapon. I told him I did, but I found no weapons. I left him in my office with the door locked."

"All right." Polk straightened some papers on his desk. "Go get him and bring him here to my office."

Dallas hurried out the office door, and in less than five minutes, he returned with Colonel Atócha at his side. Dallas introduced Atócha to the president. After shaking hands with the president, Atócha presented his identification papers. Polk was amazed that the dark-complexioned Cuban, indeed, spoke perfect English with absolutely no Spanish accent.

When the president had looked over Atócha's papers and handed them back, the colonel asked, "Mr. President, may I have a conversation with you now?"

"Mr. President," Dallas said, "I'll go now and let you and Colonel Atócha talk."

Polk shook his head. "No, I want you to stay."

"That is perfectly all right with me, Mr. President," Atócha said.

The three men sat down on overstuffed chairs, facing one another. "All right, Colonel Atócha," the president said. "What do you want to talk to me about?"

"Sir, Antonio López de Santa Anna approached me a short time ago and asked if I would go to the United States capital and talk to President Polk for him. He asked me to tell you that he knows if he were allowed to return to Mexico, he could bring peace between Mexico and the United States and stop the bloodshed that is coming. He believes the Cuban government would release him if he wanted to go. And, Mr. President, he is correct. He will just need someone to provide a way for him to make the trip, and he feels sure that you will do that in order to allow him to return to Mexico and keep the war between Mexico and the United States from happening."

George Dallas sat still like a statue, his mouth half open.

James Polk rubbed his forehead for a moment deep in thought. He looked at the Cuban. "Colonel Atócha, this is quite a surprise. I mean a *big* surprise. I'm going to have to think it over."

The colonel nodded. "I can understand why, Mr. President."

Polk looked him square in the eye. "Will you wait in Washington for a few days? If I decide that Santa Anna means business, I will take it before Congress, and a decision will be made."

Atócha smiled. "Certainly. I will stay until you give me your decision, Mr. President. I completely understand why you have to think it over. I know that Santa Anna has showed himself to be an enemy of the United States on several occasions. But let me say this. I really do believe that Santa

Anna is being honest now. I feel certain he wants to bring the hostilities between his country and yours to an end."

Polk sighed. "I sure hope you're right, Colonel."

Atócha smiled again. "Me too. I am staying at the Victorian Hotel, just a few blocks east of here."

"I know exactly where it is," Polk said.

"I will remain there until I hear from you, Mr. President, and I'll talk to no one else about it."

"Fine. I appreciate that," the president said.

Colonel Atócha rose from his chair, thanked the president for talking to him, told both men he would look forward to seeing them again, and walked out the door.

On Thursday morning, July 9, President Polk was sharpening a pencil in his office when he heard a knock at the door. Recognizing the rhythm of the knock as well, he laid the pencil down. "Please come in, Arthur!"

The president's secretary, thirty-four-year-old Arthur Fleming, entered, holding the door open behind him. "Mr. President, Congressmen Whalen, Allison, Jones, and Tharp are here asking if they can see you."

Polk rose to his feet and nodded. "This is a good time, Arthur. Bring them in."

The secretary smiled as he turned and stepped back through the door. The president heard Arthur saying they could go in, and the four congressmen — Matthew Whalen, Eugene Allison, Michael Jones, and Douglas Tharp — filed in. Their faces showed that they were deeply concerned about something.

Polk gestured toward two chairs beyond the two that sat in front of his desk, telling the men to pull the chairs closer.

When they were seated, Polk eased into his own chair behind his desk. "What do you gentlemen want to see me about?"

Congressman Jones, the oldest of the four, spoke up. "Mr. President, we're deeply concerned about this pending war with Mexico, and we've been talking about it. We want to make a suggestion."

"All right," said the president. "What is it?"

"Sir," Jones replied, "we've heard rumors about what Antonio López de Santa Anna is saying to the Cuban authorities of late. If he were freed from his exile there, which the Mexican government put him in last year, he would find a way to return to Mexico. He is saying that if he returned to

Mexico, he could resume power again and bring Mexico to peace with the United States without further war. We believe he would do that, Mr. President."

The other three congressmen nodded their agreement.

Polk smiled. "You know what, gentlemen? I've been thinking the same thing. Not only have I heard the same rumors, but just yesterday, I was visited by Colonel Alexander Atócha, Santa Anna's official Cuban representative."

Surprise showed on the faces of the four men.

"Really?" Eugene Allison said.

Polk nodded. "Really. Atócha told me that Santa Anna himself asked Atócha to come to Washington, D.C., and present his case to me."

The four congressmen looked at each other. With a smile on his face, Congressman Tharp said, "Mr. President, do you think it's possible the Cuban government will let Santa Anna go free?"

"I don't think, my friend," said Polk. "I *know.*"

"Really?"

"Yes. Colonel Atócha assured me that the Cuban government would definitely release Santa Anna if he wanted to go."

The four congressmen looked at each other, smiling.

The president went on to explain in detail the things Santa Anna had asked Colonel Atócha to tell him, including the fact that he would need someone to provide a way for him to make the trip from Cuba to Mexico, which he felt that the president would do in order to keep the war between the United States and Mexico from happening. He told them that Atócha was in the Victorian Hotel right now waiting to hear from him as to what decision he has made about helping Santa Anna to return to Mexico so he could bring Mexico to peace with the United States without further war.

Polk smiled. "If I understand correctly, all four of you are willing to trust Santa Anna to fulfill his promised deed if he is allowed to return to Mexico."

The four men nodded, affirming that they were willing to trust Santa Anna.

"All right." Polk rubbed his chin. "I'll take it before the entire Congress first thing tomorrow morning. We'll meet at nine o'clock."

Whalen, Allison, Jones, and Tharp showed their excitement.

Polk added, "If the majority of Congress

feels the same way, I'll see that Santa Anna has transportation to Mexico."

The congressmen left the president's office in a happy state, encouraged by President Polk's determination to bring peace between the United States and Mexico.

The president then called Arthur Fleming into his office and told him to notify all the other congressmen immediately that there would be a very important meeting with him tomorrow morning at the capitol building.

On Friday morning, July 10, 1846, at precisely nine o'clock, President Polk stood before Congress in the congressional auditorium of the United States Capitol with the vice president seated behind him. He told them of the visit he'd had on Wednesday from Colonel Alexander Atócha of Cuba, whom he explained was the Cuban representative of the exiled Antonio López de Santa Anna. He told them of Santa Anna's desire to return to Mexico, regain political power, and bring the pending bloody war between Mexico and the United States to a halt.

When the president told Congress that Colonel Atócha was waiting at the Victorian Hotel for him to give him an answer as to whether he would help Santa Anna get back to Mexico to could carry out his noble purpose, one hundred percent of the congressmen joyfully spoke their agreement. Without question, the president saw that, eager to prevent full-scale war, Congress felt that Santa Anna had learned his lesson about being an enemy of the United States and could be trusted to do as he said.

Smiling, President Polk ran his eyes over the crowd of congressmen and said loudly, "All right, gentlemen. I will get right on it!"

Every man stood up, cheered, and applauded in reaction to the president's words.

When the ovation finally faded, they all sat down once more. "I will immediately tell Colonel Atócha the decision that has been made here," President Polk said. "Then I'll have a crew ship of the United States Navy take the colonel back to Cuba. The navy officer I'll put in command of the ship is Captain Alexander Mackenzie, who has been to Cuba often and is fluent in Spanish."

Recognizing the name of Captain Mackenzie, the congressmen applauded.

The president went on. "Captain Mackenzie will be given authority from me to have a serious talk with Santa Anna. If Mackenzie is convinced that Santa Anna can and will do what he says regarding the relationship between Mexico and the United States, the captain will be authorized to take Santa Anna back to Mexico City with a naval escort." He paused. "Everyone still in agreement?"

Every congressman jumped to his feet once more, giving the president a standing ovation for what they believed was a wise and splendid move.

The president pronounced the session finished, and he and the vice president returned to the White House. President Polk called a member of the White House staff into his office and sent him as a messenger to the nearby naval base to bring Captain Mackenzie to his office.

It was midafternoon when the messenger escorted Captain Mackenzie into the president's office, where the president and the vice president were waiting.

President Polk welcomed the captain and had him sit down beside George Dallas. The president then explained the situation to the captain, told him that Congress was behind the plan one hundred percent, and gave him his orders.

The captain, who was in his late forties, smiled and said, "Mr. President, this is excellent news! How exciting! It'll be wonderful when this war threat is over! I am pleased to accept your orders."

The president smiled back. "Your enthusiasm is an encouragement, Captain Mackenzie."

"I'm glad, sir. And let me say this. I feel sure that Santa Anna will keep his promise if he is taken back to Mexico. Certainly he has seen enough war and bloodshed in his military career."

The president nodded. "I sure am counting on that."

"Me too," spoke up Vice President Dallas.

"I'm eager to carry out your orders, Mr. President," Mackenzie said. "I'll go to work on it immediately. My ship and naval escort boats will pull out for Havana, Cuba, tomorrow morning."

"Good!" Polk's eyes sparkled.

"And, sir," the captain said, "I'll send one of the escort boats back to the naval base so a message can be brought to you quickly about how it went with Santa Anna and if we take him to Mexico and when."

On Tuesday, July 24, a naval officer came to the president's office in the early afternoon and told him that the boat sent back to the naval base by Captain Alexander Mackenzie carried a message for the president. Captain

Mackenzie wanted the president to know that all went well with Santa Anna and that Mackenzie's ship and the naval escort ships would be leaving Havana for Mexico with Santa Anna on board the first week of August.

The next morning, at a brief special session in the congressional auditorium, Vice President George Dallas and Congress were pleased to hear this report from President Polk.

Upon leaving the capitol building, the president returned to the White House and entered his office. When he sat down at his desk, he opened a drawer, looking for some papers that needed his attention. His White House staff had been facing some problems with visitors who would appear at the vestibule, wanting to meet the president, vice president, or some other government official.

Noting that the papers weren't in the drawer he thought he'd left them in, President Polk closed the drawer and opened the one just below it. When he saw the folder that contained the desired papers, he picked it up. At that moment, his eyes fell on another folder that was quite familiar. He remembered putting it there several months previously.

Laying aside the first folder and picking up the second one, he laid it before him on the desk and opened it. A bitter taste came to his mouth as he looked at a number of newspaper clippings he had put in the folder regarding Generalissimo Antonio López de Santa Anna's open hatred for the defenders of the Alamo and how he gleefully led in the slaughter of every man in the Alamo on March 6, 1836. With those clippings were others disclosing the vile hatred Santa Anna had shown to American forces when he led the Mexican troops in the battle at San Jacinto on April 21, 1836.

A sick feeling came over Polk. Suddenly, everything was fresh again. Santa Anna was a hate-filled, bloodthirsty killer of Americans.

Polk's brow furrowed, and an arrow of fear pierced deep into his heart. "Ohhh," he said in a half-whisper, "I hope I've made the right decision about transporting Santa Anna back to Mexico."

13

In the days that followed, President Polk began to ponder his decision to help Santa Anna get back to Mexico. He continually asked himself if Santa Anna had truly been honest in saying that he wanted peace between his country and the United States.

The president hid his misgivings from his wife, Sarah, not wanting her to know that he was thinking he might have made a mistake in trusting Santa Anna, who had certainly shown that he was an enemy of the Americans when he led in the slaughter of the men at the Alamo and led a vicious attack on the U.S. soldiers at San Jacinto.

On the night of Friday, July 31, Polk had a nightmare about Santa Anna: the Mexican dictator was now back in power in Mexico City and was sending troops to wipe out every United States fort and army post anywhere near the Texas-Mexico border. In the midst of the nightmare, Polk watched as

American soldiers were shot down by the dozens by a large Mexican force that was attacking an army post.

At that moment, Sarah sat up in bed and began shaking her husband, who was moaning and tossing and turning beside her. Bright moonlight filled the room through two large windows as Polk opened his eyes, feeling his wife's hands on him. "James! James! Wake up!"

Polk blinked, swallowed hard, and squinted at her twisted face. "Honey, what's wrong?"

Sarah took a deep breath. "You were having a nightmare, darling."

Her husband sat up and blinked as he looked at her again. "Yes, I was. It was really bad."

Frowning, she asked, "What were you dreaming?"

"Well, honey, I was dreaming about Santa Anna. It really was a nightmare. I dreamed he went back to Mexico on the transportation I provided as president of this country, and instead of making peace between this country and his, he was leading his troops to attack our army posts and forts near the border and wiping them out." Polk paused and took Sarah's hand. "I-I've been having solemn thoughts that maybe that is exactly what he might do."

Sarah squeezed his hand. "But, honey, you trusted Santa Anna to do as he said and lead his country to make peace with us. Why are you doubting him now?"

The president shared with his wife the feelings that had overwhelmed him when he looked at the newspaper clippings he had placed in his desk drawer that focused on Santa Anna's hatred for Americans. He told her about his fear that possibly he had made a mistake in trusting the man and providing the transportation to get him back to Mexico City.

Sarah rubbed her husband's arm. "But, sweetheart, George Dallas and Congress agreed with you completely on this. Like you, they want peace between us and Mexico. Even with as much hatred as Santa Anna has shown toward this country in the past, all of you were willing to take this chance on him having a change of heart because you want peace for our country. Please don't blame yourself. You've only done what you thought was best for the United States."

Polk wiped a hand over his sweaty brow. "I know, honey, but if Santa Anna has been lying and leads his army against us, I'm the one the people of this country will blame."

Sarah nodded. "Because you're the president."

"Yes." Polk shook his head. "Oh, if only I could hear soon from Captain Mackenzie that all is well with Santa Anna, it would help tremendously."

Sarah leaned close and embraced her husband. "We'll just trust that it will be that way."

Polk nodded. "Let's see if we can get some sleep."

They lay their heads back down on their pillows, and soon both were asleep.

Weeks passed, and still there was no word from Captain Mackenzie.

On Friday morning, August 21, President Polk and Vice President Dallas were looking at each other across the president's desk, discussing Santa Anna and his trip to Mexico City.

"I'm in agreement with you, Mr. President," Dallas said. "It's about time for Captain Mackenzie to be returning to let us know how things went when Santa Anna arrived in Mexico City."

At that moment, there was a knock on the office door. Polk looked past Dallas. "Yes, Arthur?"

The door swung open, and the president's

smiling secretary stepped inside. "Mr. President, Captain Mackenzie has returned from Mexico and wants to see you. Is now all right?"

Polk pushed his desk chair back, rose to his feet, and said with a smile, "It sure is! Bring him in!"

Arthur turned toward the hall, gestured, and the captain instantly appeared in the doorway. The president and vice president both welcomed him back, and the three sat down together. Mackenzie reported that when they had Santa Anna aboard the ship, he was allowed to pass through the American blockades of Mexican ports with no problem. They were willing to take Mackenzie's word that President Polk had authorized the navy to transport Santa Anna back to Mexico.

"That's good," said Polk.

"Then," Mackenzie continued, "when my naval escorts and I used horses from the final port to take Santa Anna to Mexico City on dry land, he was warmly welcomed by Mexican soldiers and civilian citizens along the way. He greeted them in a friendly manner."

Both men nodded and waited to hear more.

"Upon reaching Mexico City, Santa Anna

was welcomed by a few of the present government leaders. When he told them he was back permanently to take control of the country, they instantly called for a meeting of all the government leaders. President Mariano Paredes was immediately deposed of his office, and Santa Anna was made president and full commander of the Mexican military."

Polk's eyes widened. "That fast, eh?"

"Yes sir."

"That was fast, all right," Dallas said.

The captain adjusted himself in his chair. "Mr. President and Mr. Vice President, I want you to know that it looks very much to me as if Antonio López de Santa Anna is going to be working toward making a lasting peace with the United States."

Polk smiled. "I'm glad to hear it, Captain." He set his eyes on the vice president. "I want you to go to the *Washington Tribune* for me and see if reporter Jason Dunne is there. If so, and if he's free to leave his work, bring him back quickly. If not, make an appointment for him to come to my office as soon as possible so he can interview Captain Mackenzie. Dunne is the best reporter out there, and I want the *Tribune* to publish the captain's comments about his optimism concerning Santa Anna's dedication toward making a lasting peace with the United States."

George Dallas nodded and hurried out the door.

In less than an hour, Dallas returned with Jason Dunne, and the interview with Mackenzie took place as the president desired. Before leaving the president's office, Dunne told Polk that he would immediately pass this story to other major newspapers so it could be spread quickly all over the country. The people of the United States needed this good news.

At the Diamond K Ranch on Monday afternoon, August 24, Julia was in the kitchen of the big ranch house talking to Daisy. Her three boys were playing "Texans and Mexicans" with their wooden guns at the front of the house, and little Amber, who would turn two in October, was napping on her small bed in the master bedroom upstairs.

As Julia was telling Daisy that she was finding Psalm 56:3 so comforting, they heard rapid footsteps in the hall coming from the front of the house. Julia knew it was her three sons and turned toward the open kitchen door as the boys skidded to a halt and stepped into the kitchen. "Mama,"

Adam said, "Aunt Libby and Aunt Vivian came to see you. We had them sit down in the parlor."

"Thank you, boys," Julia said. "I'll go to them right now."

Daisy said, "Would you boys like some oatmeal cookies?"

"We sure would!" Andy exclaimed.

Julia smiled and moved out the door as Adam, Abram, and Andy rushed up to Daisy, who was opening the cupboard.

When Julia walked into the parlor, her two sisters-in-law were standing just inside the door, happy looks on their faces. Vivian was holding a folded newspaper in her hand. "Well, you gals look joyful," Julia said. "Is there some kind of good news in that newspaper?"

"There sure is!" Vivian unfolded the paper. "A couple of the ranch hands, Bobby Wilson and Hal Smith, gave this to us when they rode in from town a few minutes ago. We want you to see the article on the front page."

As Julia was taking the paper from Vivian, her three sons entered the parlor, chewing on oatmeal cookies. Speaking around his cookie, Adam said, "What's in the paper, Mama?"

"I don't know yet. Your aunts just brought

it to me, but I'm about to read it and find out."

While her sisters-in-law and sons looked on, Julia read the article aloud. It told about Captain Mackenzie of the United States Navy, who under orders of President Polk, escorted the exiled Santa Anna from Havana, Cuba, to Mexico City in early August. The article expressed how likely it appeared that the new president Santa Anna was going to see that peace was made between Mexico and the United States.

When Julia finished reading the article, Libby brushed at the tears on her cheeks and said gleefully, "Isn't it wonderful? Now there will be no war between our country and Mexico! Now Alex, Abel, and Alamo will be coming home to settle down as ranchers!"

The boys jumped up and down clapping their hands, and Adam shouted with joy, "Papa's coming home! Papa's coming home! And so are Uncle Alex and Uncle Abel! They'll never have to face Mexican guns again!"

Julia, Libby, and Vivian embraced each other with happy tears streaming down their faces. The boys kept jumping up and down, clapping their hands.

When the excitement eased, Julia said,

"Let's go tell Daisy!"

With tears spilling down their cheeks, the three women hurried down the hall toward the kitchen with the exultant boys still cheering. When they entered the kitchen, Abram was there eating an oatmeal cookie. He was elated by the good news, as was Daisy.

The three young women filed out the kitchen door onto the back porch with Abram and the boys behind them. Together they hurried to some of the ranch hands and their wives, showing them the newspaper article. The ranch hands took off running, wanting to tell everyone else on the ranch the good news, including Cort. Soon, all over the Diamond K Ranch, there was jubilation in the hearts of all who had received the encouraging news.

After being gone for better than an hour, Julia and her boys mounted the steps of the back porch and entered the kitchen.

Working at the cupboard counter, Daisy smiled. "Julia, I heard Amber making some noises up in her room just now. Sounds like she's awake."

The boys followed their mother upstairs to her bedroom, and when Julia picked Amber up from her small bed, she excitedly told her that Papa would be coming home soon, and he would never go away again. Even little Amber seemed to understand. She giggled and clapped her hands.

That night after supper, when the children had been bathed and the boys were asleep in their room and Amber was snuggled in her bed near where her mother lay, Julia settled her tired head on her own soft pillow. Her mind wandered over the events of the day. She thought of her sons' cute antics when they heard the good news in the *Washington Post* and how at the supper table Papa Abram and the boys had had such happy faces.

Julia adjusted her head on the pillow, sighed, and smiled into the darkness. Thinking of the day when her precious husband would return home, her heartbeat quickened. Though exhausted from the toil of a long day, her body crying for rest, Julia's mind was alive with the excitement that Alamo would soon be home to stay.

After tossing from side to side in bed for over an hour, Julia finally gave up on sleep. She tossed back the sheet that covered her and slipped from the bed. Clad only in her summer nightgown, she padded barefoot to the open windows. Looking out at the night sky, she gazed at the innumerable stars twinkling brightly.

These same stars, she mused, *are shining over the fort where my love is sleeping. Please, Lord,* she prayed in her heart, *bring him home soon. I love him so very, very much.*

Breathing in the sweet-smelling night air, Julia lowered herself into the overstuffed rocking chair that faced the windows. She enjoyed the fluttering of the curtains created by the soft breeze. Pulling her legs up under her, she wrapped her arms around herself, thinking of the nights not long from now when it would be Alamo's arms wrapped around her.

Julia's mind wandered back to the day when she learned that her first husband, Adam, had been killed in the battle of the Alamo. The grief and sorrow had been almost more than she could bear. She thought of God's promise in Psalm 30:5: *"Weeping may endure for a night, but joy cometh in the morning."* "Lord," she whispered, "You so compassionately turned my mourning over Adam's death into joy when You brought Alamo and me together. We have such a precious marriage, Lord. Alamo is so much like his brother Adam, and my son Adam is so much like him too. That boy is almost a complete replica of his father."

These kinds of sweet thoughts continued

to roam through Julia's mind as she gently set the chair to rocking and closed her weary eyes. Soon her head dropped downward and jerked her awake. She yawned. "Oh, my. I'd better get back in bed and get some real sleep. Tomorrow will be another busy day."

As Julia walked quietly past Amber's small bed, she looked down and smiled. In a whisper, she said, "Sleep on, sweetie. Your mama's going to try to follow your example."

As Julia lay down on the bed and pulled the sheet up over her, a troublesome thought filtered into her tired brain. She bit down on her lower lip. "Please, dear Lord, make Santa Anna keep his word to President Polk about making peace with our country."

Another negative thought entered her mind. *Okay now, Julia Kane,* she said to herself. *God is in control. He will handle it as He sees fit.*

A Scripture suddenly came to mind. *"Be still, and know that I am God."*

Resting in that truth, Julia fell asleep.

In New Mexico, by early September victory had come on every hand for Colonel Stephen Kearny and his troops. General Manuel Armijo and his troops were driven out of New Mexico, which then was claimed by President Polk and Congress as an official American territory. In the battles that took place, just over three hundred Mexican soldiers were killed, and some three hundred were wounded, compared to American losses of only one soldier killed and five wounded.

On Friday, September 4, when President Polk received the news of the overwhelming victory, he sent a telegraph message to President Antonio López de Santa Anna in Mexico City, telling him he was glad the New Mexico hostilities between American and Mexican forces were over. He asked if Santa Anna felt the same.

Polk eagerly waited for a reply, which would signal to him that Santa Anna had been honest when he said he wanted peace between Mexico and the United States. Polk waited for a full day, but no reply came. This worried him.

The next day, Polk received word that Mexican military forces in California territory were attempting to claim it for Mexico. The president quickly sent another telegram to Santa Anna, asking why his military forces were trying to claim California.

Again, even after two days, there was no reply. Since Polk had not received any word from Santa Anna within a reasonable time, he feared that the Mexican leader had been dishonest all along.

When by Wednesday, September 9, President Polk still had not received a reply from Santa Anna, anger overtook fear, and he wired a message to Colonel Kearny in New Mexico through a nearby U.S. Army post, ordering him to take his troops immediately to California and do battle with the Mexicans who were attempting to secure California as a Mexican territory. Kearny wired back that he and his troops would leave for California immediately.

Alone in his office, after reading the telegram, Polk laid it on his desk, knowing that American blood would be shed in California. Polk was now fully convinced that Santa Anna was not interested in a peace settlement between Mexico and the United States. If he were interested, he would've called the Mexican troops in California back to Mexico. And certainly by Santa Anna's refusal to reply to his telegraph messages, the big war was going to take place.

A heavy gloom descended on Polk, and he sat dejectedly at his desk, his head in his hands. *What a fool I've been,* he said to himself. *I should have listened to my inner voice that I should not trust Santa Anna. I just wanted peace between us and Mexico so very much . . .* He rubbed his forehead and said to the empty room, "Never again will I allow myself to be swayed in such a matter!"

Still weighted with gloom, Polk went to the office door and opened it. He told Arthur to tell Vice President Dallas he needed to talk to him immediately. Moments later, as the two men sat privately in the president's office, Polk shared his conclusions about Santa Anna being an acid-mouthed liar and a warmonger. The vice president agreed that they were on the verge of a bloody war with Mexico.

Dallas was about to return to his office when there was a knock on the door, and Arthur entered at the president's invitation. He approached the desk with a yellow envelope in his hand. "Mr. President, here is a telegram from some of the spies you sent from those few Texas army posts into Mexico to keep watch on what was happening."

Polk nodded, accepted the envelope, and opened it. Arthur left while the president read the telegram.

When Polk had finished reading the message from his spies, his eyes were filled with rage as he looked at the vice president. Irritation came up from its shallow bed and exploded into gusty, whistling words. "Santa Anna has ordered one of Mexico's outstanding military leaders, General Pedro Ampudia, to take ten thousand troops to the northern Mexican city of Monterrey and from there to head northward toward Fort Polk and attack General Taylor and his six thousand troops and wipe them out!"

The vice president's face reddened, and anger glimmered in his eyes as he blared, "You were right! That dirty Santa Anna *is* an acid-mouthed liar and a warmonger!"

14

Early on Thursday morning, September 10, two U.S. soldiers rode up to the front gate of Fort Polk and looked up at the two guards in the tower next to the gate. One of the riders was a lieutenant, and the other a sergeant.

"Good morning, gentlemen. I am Lieutenant Jasper Caldwell, and this is Sergeant Richard Anderson. We are from the army post at Corpus Christi Bay. Our new commander, Colonel Oscar Benson, received a telegram from President James K. Polk late yesterday afternoon to be delivered here to General Taylor as soon as possible. We've been riding all night."

While one of the guards was heading down the tower stairs, the other one said, "General Taylor is eating his breakfast in the mess hall with the men. Corporal Dudley will open the gate and lead you there."

■ ■ ■ ■

In the new mess hall, the Kane brothers were eating breakfast at a table with Privates Bob Krayson and Cody Proctor, the two young men from the Diamond K as well as members of the church in Washington-on-the-Brazos who had recently joined the army and had been assigned to Fort Polk. Upon their arrival at the fort, the Kane brothers and the other soldiers from their church had warmly welcomed them.

Seated at the next table was, among others, Captain Jett Bannock. The captain picked up the conversation at the adjacent table while eating his breakfast and heard the men talking about how wonderful it was to know that whenever they died they would go directly to heaven.

Alamo noticed Captain Bannock listening in and smiled at him. Bannock smiled back nervously then quickly concentrated on his breakfast.

At that moment, Corporal Chester Dudley entered the mess hall, followed by Lieutenant Caldwell and Sergeant Anderson. Dudley led them to the table where General Taylor was eating with some of his officers and said, "General Taylor, these men are from the army post at Corpus Christi Bay. They have a telegram for you from President Polk."

The lieutenant and sergeant introduced themselves to the general; then the lieutenant handed Taylor the envelope that contained President Polk's telegram.

The officers at the general's table and the soldiers sitting nearby could hear what was said and watched the general as he took the telegram out of the envelope and began reading it. Taylor's face blanched, and his mouth seemed to go dry.

Those men who were aware of what was going on noted the pallid look on the general's face as he kept reading the message and finally stood to his feet. By this time, word had spread all over the mess hall about the telegram that had just been delivered to the general.

The general walked to a central position where he could address all of the men in the mess hall. "Men! I want your attention!" Running his gaze over the crowd, he could instantly see that he had it.

Speaking loudly enough that all could hear him, General Taylor said, "I have just received a telegram from President Polk by two messengers from the relatively new United States Army post at Corpus Christi

Bay. I assume it was sent there instead of to Washington-on-the-Brazos because it is somewhat closer."

General Taylor began telling them what was in the telegram, emphasizing loudly Santa Anna's orders to General Pedro Ampudia to take his ten thousand troops through Monterrey, Mexico, northward toward Fort Polk and to attack General Taylor and his six thousand troops and wipe them out.

The troops in the mess hall showed a definite reaction of anger toward Santa Anna's orders. When everyone had settled down, the general spoke again. He told them that Santa Anna had been lying all along about wanting peace with the United States and had proved it shortly after arriving in Mexico City. He was now at war with the Americans.

The heat of anger spread even stronger through the mess hall, and after a few minutes the general lifted his hands in a gesture that showed he wanted silence.

When the angry men had quieted, the general told them that per the president's orders, they would leave the next day at dawn and head for Monterrey. From what Polk's spies had told him, the president was confident that if they left Fort Polk quite soon, they would find General Pedro Ampudia and his troops pausing for a short period at Monterrey before heading for Fort Polk. There they could make a surprise attack on the Mexican troops.

General Taylor then told his men that President Polk said in the telegram that he would be sending General William Worth and his two thousand troops to Monterrey from an outpost near the Mexican border to join their six thousand troops in battling Ampudia and his ten thousand men.

The men cheered, some of them shouting out that their eight thousand troops could defeat Ampudia's ten thousand.

The general then gave orders to some of his officers to carry this news to the men who weren't in the mess hall at the time. The officers hurried away to do so.

A few minutes later, as soldiers filed out the doors of the mess hall, Alamo stepped up to Captain Bannock and said, "Sir, I guess you heard the discussion about heaven we were having at our table and how we are so glad to know that whenever we leave this world, we'll go to there."

Bannock nodded. "Uh, yes."

Alamo smiled. "The Bible says there are only two places people can go to when they die . . . heaven or hell. Captain, do you know if you're going to heaven when you die?"

Bannock kept a friendly look on his face. "No one can know for sure that they are going to heaven. They can't know if they've done enough good works to offset their bad works."

"Salvation is not by works, Captain," Alamo said. "For instance, God says in Ephesians 2:8–9, 'For by grace are ye saved through faith; and that not of yourselves: it is the gift of God: Not of works, lest any man should boast.' Did you get that? *Not* of works?"

The captain only stared into Alamo's eyes.

Alamo continued. "Salvation — that is, going to heaven when you die rather than an everlasting burning hell — is a *gift.* You can't earn it by good works. It all depends on whether you have received the Lord Jesus Christ as your Saviour, trusting Him and Him alone to save you. If you have received Him, Christ is in you, and you are in Him. There are only two ways to die — in Christ or in your sins. And Captain, the person who has received Jesus into his heart as Saviour *knows* he is going to heaven."

Captain Bannock shook his head. "That doesn't make sense to me, Lieutenant," he said curtly and walked away.

Alamo called after him, "Die without

Christ, Captain, and it's eternity in hell!"

Bannock kept walking and did not look back.

On that same morning, Thursday, September 10, an angry President Polk was pacing the floor in his office as Vice President Dallas sat in a chair and looked on. Polk was snapping out heated and acrimonious words against Antonio López de Santa Anna for his deceitfulness about wanting peace between Mexico and the United States. Breathing hard, he stopped in front of Dallas. "George, indeed we are caught in a web of destiny. We have absolutely no choice but to go to full-scale war with Mexico!"

Dallas rose to his feet and sighed. "You are right, Mr. President. That deceitful Santa Anna has left us with no choice."

At the break of dawn on Friday morning, September 11, General Taylor and his six thousand troops were preparing to pull out and head for Monterrey, Mexico, which was just over a hundred and sixty miles south of Fort Polk. The general had estimated that they could make about eighteen miles a day, which would bring them to Monterrey on September 20.

They had over a hundred cannons on

wheels attached to the rear of wagons, which also carried ammunition for their weapons and food for the troops and their horses.

Both cavalry and infantry were eager to show Santa Anna that he had made a mistake in leading Mexico to war against the United States.

When Taylor was about to mount his horse and lead the troops to Monterrey, the Kane brothers stepped up to him. "General Taylor," Alamo said, "we want you to know that we're ready to fight those Mexicans."

"That's right, General," Alex said. "We sure are."

"Yes sir," Abel put in. "We want to make that Santa Anna wish he'd been honest when he said he didn't want war with us."

The general nodded grimly. "That's what we're going to do."

Alex wiped the back of his hand over his mouth. "General Taylor, I don't understand why President Polk trusted Santa Anna. He should have known better."

Taylor jutted his jaw. "You're right, Private. He never should have trusted a man who led in the slaughter of those few brave men who were defending the Alamo. Even afterward, Santa Anna showed his hatred for our country over and over again."

"Well, what's done is done," Alamo said. "We can't change that now. But we sure can change Santa Anna's plans to have General Pedro Ampudia and his troops wipe us out."

"Right!" Taylor took hold of the reins and lifted his left foot into the stirrup. "Let's go!"

As the general swung onto his horse, the Kane brothers hurried to get in line with the men with whom they would march to Monterrey. General Taylor led the troops out of the fort, with the wagons directly behind him. The infantrymen were next on foot, followed by the cavalry on horseback.

Dawn was now a ruddy gold as the Fort Polk troops moved southward on the lonesome Texas plains toward the Mexican border. Long patches of green grass waved in the morning breeze amid the undulating bronze slopes of bare land that were soon reflecting the great white flare of sunlight.

As Alamo marched alongside Lieutenant Grant, he pointed forward with his square jaw. "You know, Lieutenant, I sure am glad those cannons are with us. Since we already know that the Mexican army has very few cannons and that they are so old they hardly work properly, we're going to have a good advantage at Monterrey."

Grant nodded. "Sure looks like it to me,

Lieutenant Kane. It'll be a real battle, of course, facing ten thousand Mexican troops, even though we'll be joining up with General Worth and his two thousand men. But those cannons of ours could mean the difference for us and give us the victory."

At the Diamond K Ranch on Saturday, September 12, the Kane family was being visited by Lance Brooks and his parents. At the church services in Washington-on-the-Brazos the previous Sunday, Julia Kane had invited them to come for lunch the following Saturday. Because Lance had led ranch hand Chad Mathis to the Lord and they were now close friends, she had invited Chad to lunch as well.

Libby and Vivian were there, as well as Julia's four children and Abram. Little Amber was strapped on her stool, next to her mother.

As they ate the delicious lunch Daisy had prepared, the two families talked about the baptisms of Harland and Lucille the very next Sunday in June after Alamo had led them to the Lord, and that Lance had been baptized in early July when Dr. Dewitt told him he was healed up enough to do so.

Chad, who was sitting beside his friend Lance, looked at him and grinned. "Yeah,

Lance. I got to beat you getting baptized. I was baptized on June 14, the Sunday after you led me to Jesus."

Lance chuckled. "Yes! Praise the Lord! This eagle is still flying high over your getting saved!"

While the Kanes, the Brookses, and Chad were eating their lunch, Cort and ranch hand Wiley Fordham were riding onto the ranch, returning from Washington-on-the-Brazos. Cort had purchased that day's edition of the *Washington Post,* which gave detailed information on the pending battle at Monterrey, Mexico, in which Alamo, Alex, and Abel would be fighting.

When Cort and Wiley were nearing the big ranch house, Cort said, "You go ahead and get your lunch, Wiley. I'll take the paper to Julia so she'll know what's happening with the Kane men and can pass it on to the rest of the family."

Wiley nodded. "Okay, Cort." He veered his horse in the direction of the ranch's mess hall.

In the dining room of the big ranch house, those around the table were just finishing their lunch when they heard a knock at the front door. Young Adam looked up at his mother. "I'll go to the door, Mama."

Julia noted that he was not quite finished with his meal. She rose from her chair. "I'll go, honey. You finish your sandwich."

"I'll go," Grandpa Abram said.

Julia smiled. "You've still got food to eat too! I'll see who it is."

Julia left the dining room and hurried to the door just as the knock started again. When she opened the door, she noticed the folded newspaper in Cort's hand and the dismal look on his face. One look at his troubled eyes told Julia that he was not there with good news. Her heart seemed to fall to her toes as she braced herself for what he was going to tell her.

"What is it, Cort?" she asked in a low voice, a tingle of fear snaking its way down her spine.

The ranch foreman lifted up the paper. "This is today's edition of the *Post,* Julia. There's something in here you need to know about. I thought I'd show it to you first. Then you can pass it on to the rest of the family whenever you wish. May I come in?"

"Oh, I'm sorry." She took two steps back. "Of course. Please come in."

As Cort stepped in, Julia glanced at the newspaper, then back up at his face. "The

Brooks family is here, as well as Chad. So are Libby and Vivian, and of course Abram and the children. We're just finishing lunch."

"I want to let you all know what is happening with General Taylor's troops, which of course include Alamo, Alex, and Abel."

Julia's spine tingled again, and her brow furrowed. "Is it bad news?"

Cort nodded solemnly. "Yes, it is. Since the rest of your family is here, maybe I should tell everybody at once? Your guests are welcome to hear it too."

Julia nodded. "Of course. You can go on into the parlor and sit down. I'll bring the others."

As Julia hurried down the hall, a million fearful thoughts tumbled about in her mind.

Moments later, as everyone made their way to the parlor, Julia carrying little Amber, Cort rose to his feet.

"I told them about the news you said is in the *Post,* Cort," Julia said.

Gripping the folded newspaper in his right hand, Cort nodded and ran his gaze over their faces. "Please, all of you, sit down."

While the others were choosing their seats, Julia placed Amber in her little play area in the parlor and then sat down beside Grandpa Abram.

"As Julia probably told you," Cort said,

"this is today's edition of the *Washington Post*. I'll read the front page article to you."

Cort then unfolded the newspaper and showed the front page to them. The headline of bold, black letters read:

FIERCE BATTLE PENDING AT MONTERREY, MEXICO,
BETWEEN AMERICAN AND MEXICAN TROOPS

Cort noted the stunned look on the faces before him as he continued with the article, which told of General Taylor's six thousand troops and General Worth's two thousand troops traveling to Monterrey to face General Ampudia's ten thousand troops. When Cort finished the article, he could see great disappointment among the Kanes, the Brookses, and Chad.

The elderly Abram's voice quivered. "I had so hoped that Santa Anna was being honest and would work for peace between Mexico and the United States."

"Me too," Harland said. "I doubted it to a degree, of course, but I sure was hoping he meant business."

"I'd say we were all in that same state of mind, Harland," Abram continued. "And now we must live with the fact that Alamo,

Alex, and Abel will once again face enemy guns in battle and that the American troops will be outnumbered by some two thousand Mexican troops who are being led by one of Mexico's top military leaders, General Pedro Ampudia."

"One thing really bothers me." Cort shook his head. "If General Ampudia fortifies his troops inside the city of Monterrey, they'll have protection that our troops won't have out there in the open."

Harland sighed. "I'd think Ampudia would be against putting all those civilians in the city in danger."

"Well, he really doesn't have any choice in the matter, Papa," Lance said. "If that heartless Santa Anna tells him to do it, he has to obey — or else."

Harland nodded. "Yes. You're right about that, Son."

Abram looked around at the group. "Let's pray together right now and ask the Lord to protect Alamo, Alex, Abel, and the other American soldiers in this fierce battle."

"Yes," Julia said. "Prayer is our most powerful weapon."

Abram looked at the foreman. "Cort, will you lead us?"

Julia glanced at Amber and saw that she was asleep in her play area. She motioned for her three sons, who were standing, to come and sit on the floor at her feet, which they did. Heads were bowed, and Cort led the group in prayer. His voice choked up as he asked the Lord to protect Alamo, Alex, and Abel as they once again headed into battle.

There was sniffling among the group as Cort prayed, and when he closed off in Jesus' name, young Adam stood up beside his mother, who was sitting on a small couch beside his grandfather. "Mama, I wish I was old enough to join the army and use my rifle to fight alongside Papa Alamo and my uncles."

Tears misted Julia's eyes as she rose from the couch and wrapped her arms around her oldest son. "Adam, dear, I am very proud that you would be willing to fight the Mexicans, but you heard what I said to Grandpa a few minutes ago when he suggested that we all pray together and ask the Lord to protect your papa and your uncles in the fierce battle that is coming. And I've said the same thing to you many times. *Prayer is our most powerful weapon.*"

The group looked on, deeply touched by Julia's words about prayer and her sweet tenderness.

The room was silent as Julia held Adam

tightly in her arms. The emotion of the moment gripped her, and her thoughts went to young Adam's father, Adam Kane, who had been killed in the Battle of the Alamo more than ten years ago.

She then thought of Alamo, who was now her husband, and trembled at the thought of his being killed.

She saw both Libby and Vivian weeping. The same fear for their husbands in the upcoming war was in their hearts as well.

Deep in her heart, Julia said, *Oh, dear Lord, please forgive me for this fear I'm having about Alamo in the war. I just said that prayer is our most powerful weapon, and here I am experiencing fear again. Help me cling to that fact — prayer is indeed our most powerful weapon. Thank You, precious Lord. Thank You.*

15

Young Adam broke the silence of the moment as he looked up into his mother's face. "Mama, if I was old enough to join the army, I would do it. My papa and Uncle Alex and Uncle Abel believe that prayer is our most powerful weapon too, but they also have to use guns to fight the enemies or else they'd kill us and take our ranch. I wish I could take my rifle and go join Papa and my uncles right now."

Julia took hold of Adam's shoulders with both hands and eased him back at arm's length. Smiling, she looked into the eyes of her firstborn. "Honey, like I said, I'm very proud that you would be willing to fight the Mexicans, but remember what Papa asked you to do?"

Adam nodded. "He asked me to help take care of things here on the ranch while he's gone, meaning you, my little brothers and sister, and the rest of the family."

Julia nodded. "Yes, and you do such a good job of it, especially providing meat with your rifle for this family and for Aunt Libby and Aunt Vivian too. That is a very important job, and even though it's not as exciting as using your rifle to fight the enemy on the battlefield, it's still very important and very needed."

Adam smiled. "Yes, Mama. I'm glad I can do it."

"Son, I pray that our country will get settled into a lasting peace very soon and that even when you're old enough to join the army, you'll never have to do it and experience the horror of war."

The nine-year-old boy nodded, then gave his mother a lopsided grin, which reminded her so much of his father's grin. "Okay, Mama, I'll do my best to be satisfied with doing my part around here. At least it's a pretty safe occupation!"

"Good," she said. "I'm glad to hear it."

Adam looked up and fixed his eyes on hers. "Mama, can I ask you something?"

"Of course, dear. What is it?"

"I know you try to hide it from us kids, but even with all the prayer that goes up for Papa Alamo, you *do* worry about him getting killed like my own papa did, don't you?"

Julia let her deep blue eyes travel over her

precious son's adorable face — a face so reminiscent of his father's. Her hand smoothed the boy's wayward sand-colored hair as she studied his features. "You know, Son, when Papa Alamo first went off with the army to fight the Mexicans, I worried myself sick over it. It was this way for me until not long ago, when Daisy quoted me a Scripture verse that has been such a blessing to me. I had seen it before, of course, but it didn't really penetrate my heart until Daisy quoted it."

"What verse is it, Mama?"

"Psalm 56:3: 'What time I am afraid, I will trust in thee.' "

Adam's brow furrowed. "I-I don't remember that one, but I sure like it."

Julia ruffled his hair, then began smoothing it again. "Now when Satan tempts me to be afraid, I open my Bible, and that verse is still there, strong and true."

She paused and ran a shaky palm over her face. "I have to admit, Adam, that sometimes I'm still very much afraid that Papa Alamo will get killed fighting Mexicans like your real father did. Then I quote Psalm 56:3 to myself, turn my eyes from that fear, and look to my heavenly Father, knowing that His promises are *always* the same. There is not a shred of doubt in any of them. I-I often have to confess my sin of worry and fear to the Lord, and He reminds me of the everlasting promises in His Word by putting thoughts in my mind. He knows I will sometimes worry and be afraid, but when it happens and I ask Him to forgive me, He does — and then He comforts me with the psalmist's inspired words: 'What time I am afraid, I will trust in thee.' A sweet peace fills my soul, and once again, I pray and place Papa Alamo in God's tender care."

Adam sighed heavily. "Thank you, Mama. That helps me a whole lot!"

Julia wrapped her arms around Adam again and pressed a kiss on his forehead. "You are very welcome, Son. I'm glad it is a help to you."

Late in the afternoon on Sunday, September 20, General Taylor and his troops drew near Monterrey, Mexico, though the city was not yet in sight. The land was rough and rugged with many hills, and tall ridges and flat-topped mesas could often be seen. As usual, Taylor was on his horse, riding at the head of the troops.

General Taylor had sent two cavalry scouts ahead of the rest of the troops over an hour earlier, and when he saw the scouts atop a hill about a half mile ahead galloping toward him, he turned in the saddle and signaled for everyone to come to a halt.

The message was carried back through the lines so those who could not see the general would know he was signaling for everyone to halt. Most active in the few wagons that carried them were the medics, who were riding next to the drivers. They stood up on the seats and waved signals over the canvas tops of the wagons to the infantrymen behind them, and the infantrymen did the same for the cavalrymen, who were last in line. Wagons, infantry, and cavalry soon came to a stop.

Up front, the two scouts reined in and were greeted by General Taylor, who then asked if they'd seen General William Worth and his troops.

"We sure did, sir," replied the sergeant. "General Worth and his two thousand troops are gathered on the other side of a high hill with lots of rocks on top just west of the city, waiting for us to arrive. We spotted them easily coming from the high country here in the north."

Taylor nodded. "I know the hill well."

"We told General Worth where you and our troops are, sir, and he asked us to hurry on back and tell you that, indeed, General

Ampudia and his ten thousand troops are barricaded in the city."

Taylor swung a fist across his chest. "Uh-huh! Just as President Polk figured they would be. And so did I!"

The sergeant went on. "General Worth asked us to tell you where he and his men are hiding, sir, and since he knows that you are already familiar with this area, he wants us to come back and let him know where they should meet us before we get together and attack the city."

"All right," Taylor said. "There are some more high hills farther west of Monterrey, only a couple of hundred yards away. Go tell General Worth to stay where he is, and I'll guide our troops around the backside of those hills and come to where they're located. As close as we are now, it'll only take us about an hour and a half to get there."

The sergeant saluted. "Yes sir! We'll meet you there, sir!"

The general watched the scouts gallop toward the hill just ahead; then he turned and rode along the lines of troops and told them what was happening.

The sun's heat eased slightly as it lowered its red disk behind the far-distant hills to the west when Taylor and his troops arrived at the spot where Worth, his men, and Taylor's two scouts were gathered waiting for them.

The two generals shook hands. "You and I need to sit down and plan the attack on Monterrey, General Taylor, but how about we put our cooks to preparing supper for us first?"

"Sounds like a good idea to me," Taylor replied. "Of course, we'll have to keep the cook fires small so smoke doesn't rise over these hills and give away our position to General Ampudia and his troops."

Worth chuckled. "You're right about that, General. We'll have to keep the fires *very* small."

There was a small creek at the spot, and the Fort Polk troops carried water in buckets to the wagon horses and cavalry horses while supper was prepared. The horses were then fed from their food that was carried in the wagons.

When the troops sat down on the ground to eat their evening meal, the sun sank behind the hills to the west, and twilight stole over the land, slowly turning to gloom.

By the time the two generals were sitting down on the creek bank to discuss the attack they would launch the next morning, the vault of blue black overhead began lightening to the blinking of myriads of stars. Then fell the serene, silent, luminous night.

The two generals got down to business and agreed that Worth and his men would attack Monterrey at dawn from the west side while Taylor and his larger number of troops would attack the city from the east, south, and north sides at exactly the same time. They felt that this would give them an advantage over General Ampudia and his larger number of troops, who were barricaded inside the city.

When the generals had passed the attack plan on to their troops, officers assigned certain privates, corporals, and sergeants to trade off keeping watch during the night.

It so happened that Privates Alex and Abel Kane had been chosen for the first watch.

Lying on his back in his sleeping bag, Alamo looked up at the serene, luminous stars and the few puffy white clouds as he heard snoring begin all around him. He thought of his family back at the ranch and pictured the children one at a time, in order of age. When he had pictured Adam, Abram, and Andy and whispered that he loved them, his mind went to little Amber. He whispered his love to her as a father would do to his baby daughter.

Then . . . Alamo's thoughts settled on his lovely wife, Julie.

Instantly he felt a gentle throb in his chest. As he watched the clouds make different formations at the will of the breeze, he pictured the phantom of Julie's sweet face formed by the clouds. It took his breath, it was so real.

Oh, Julie, darling. I love you so very, very much. I know that you are praying, as I am, that this war will be a short one and I can come home to you. We'll just keep praying and trusting that our precious heavenly Father will make it happen. Good night, sweetheart. I love you, I love you, I love you.

Alamo turned on his side and began praying. Soon he fell asleep.

At dawn the next morning, Monday, September 21, the American troops launched their attack with General Taylor's large number of cannons booming from three directions, rifles and revolvers barking from all four directions, and gun smoke filling the air.

From their barricades, the Mexican troops fought back as the sun rose in a golden blaze, but the American cannons took a toll on them. Many went down under the barrage. The battle went on hour after hour until dark. Then both sides stopped firing.

The two American generals stood before their men by starlight that night and agreed that they were glad they hadn't yet seen any Mexican civilians while blasting away at the troops they could see all around the city. Apparently General Ampudia had the civilians inside buildings at the center of the city in order to protect them.

On Tuesday, September 22, the battle raged on. At one point late in the day, with bullets and cannonball shrapnel flying, Alamo and his brothers were lying flat on the ground on Monterrey's east side, firing along with many of their infantry companions at Mexican soldiers on the city's edge.

A few yards from the Kane brothers, Captain Jett Bannock and men under his command were also lying flat on the ground blazing away at the Mexican troops.

As darkness was falling, the gunfire on both sides began letting up. Suddenly Captain Bannock, who had risen up on one knee to fire a shot at the shadow of a Mexican soldier, took a slug in the chest and went down, dropping his revolver.

Alamo was reloading his own revolver at the moment and saw Bannock fall. He holstered the revolver and dashed to him, dropped to his knees, and called for a medic, who was crouching behind a tree stump nearby. Guns were still firing on both sides but not as rapidly. The medic dashed to the fallen captain, carrying his medical bag and a length of soft wood he would use as a torch.

Alamo looked at the medic in the gathering darkness. "He's hit in the chest! From what I can see, it looks bad!"

The gunfire had almost stopped as the medic pulled a match from a shirt pocket, lit the torch, and held it so he could examine Bannock's wound. "I'll try not to hurt you, Captain," he said softly.

Bannock swallowed hard and nodded.

The medic studied the wound, shook his head, and looked at Alamo. "The slug hit the right side of his heart, Lieutenant Kane. There is nothing I can do to save his life. He will die very soon."

The voice of another American soldier several yards away abruptly called for the medic in the darkness, saying they had a man who was seriously wounded. The medic looked at Bannock. "I'm sorry, Captain, but I must go to him. As I just told Lieutenant Kane, there is nothing I can do for you." With that, the medic took off running, carrying his medical bag and the burning torch.

The firing had stopped on both sides by that time, and Alex and Abel drew up and knelt down, flanking Alamo.

"How bad is he hit, Alamo?" Alex asked.

"Doc Spaulding just examined him," Alamo replied in a tight voice. "He's got a bullet in one side of his heart. He's not going to make it."

The dying captain said weakly, "Lieutenant, I-I have been thinking about what you said to me on the day before we left the fort. Y-you know. When you tried to talk me into receiving Jesus Christ as my Saviour." He swallowed with difficulty and took a short breath.

Alamo nodded. "Yes."

"A-as I walked away, you called to me, 'Die without Christ, Captain, and it's eternity in hell!' I-I don't want to go to hell. Please . . . help me."

Alamo took hold of the captain's hand. "Remember, I quoted Scripture to you, showing you that salvation is not by works. 'For by grace are ye saved through faith; and that not of yourselves: it is the gift of God: Not of works, lest any man should boast.' I just want to be sure you believe that."

Alamo and his brothers could barely make

out the captain's image in the darkness, but they saw him nod. "I believe that, Lieutenant. A-as you told me, salvation is a gift."

"Yes. Now, listen as I quote some more Scripture. Romans 3:23 says, 'For all have sinned, and come short of the glory of God.' That includes *you,* doesn't it?"

"Yes," Bannock choked out. "It does."

"Now, listen to Romans 6:23: 'For the wages of sin is death; but the gift of God is eternal life through Jesus Christ our Lord.' Eternal life is a gift, Captain, purchased by the Lord Jesus when He was crucified on Calvary's cross, shed His precious blood, and died for the sins of the whole world. Did He stay dead?"

"No. He came back from the dead."

"Right. His death on the cross, His burial, and His resurrection comprise His gospel. On that cross, He made it so that every sinner in this world can be saved if they will believe His gospel, repent of their sin, and receive Him into their heart as their own personal Saviour, trusting Him — and Him alone — to save them. It is not by trying to add religious deeds and good works to get to heaven. Do you believe that?"

The dying man licked his lips. "I didn't before you quoted Scripture to me, but I do now."

"Good. John 1:12 says you must receive Jesus, and Ephesians 3:17 makes it clear that you must receive Him into your heart. Are you willing to repent of your sin and ask Jesus to come into your heart and save you?"

The captain tried to speak, choked, then tried again. "Yes. I want to be saved."

Alamo then told him to close his eyes and call on the Lord for salvation. Captain Bannock closed his eyes and called on the Lord Jesus Christ, telling Him he was repenting of his sin and asking for forgiveness. He then asked the Lord Jesus to come into his heart and be his Saviour, saying he was trusting only Him for his salvation. He thanked the Lord for saving him and choked out an "amen." Then he said weakly to Alamo, "Lieutenant Kane, thank you for giving me the truth about salvation. I . . . will . . . meet you in . . . heaven." He coughed and stopped breathing.

Still on his knees, Alamo pressed fingertips to the side of the captain's neck and looked at his brothers. "There is no pulse." He then laid his head on the captain's chest, pressed his ear close, and waited a few seconds. Sitting up again, he looked toward the dark forms of his brothers. "No heartbeat. He's with Jesus now."

Alex and Abel looked down at what they could see of the lifeless form in the darkness and hugged their brother, who said, "Praise God! Another precious soul snatched from the devil!"

"Yes sir, Alamo," Abel said. "Once again, 'High is the Eagle'!"

At dawn the next day, Generals Taylor and Worth unleashed their troops' guns on Monterrey once more, doing their best to crumble the Mexicans' barricades and take out more soldiers. General Taylor had sent several of his cannons and the men to fire them with General Worth so as to do more damage to the Mexican troops on the west side of the city. After some seven hours of bombarding Monterrey as the Mexicans fired back with their rifles, General Taylor gathered some of his officers into a low spot on the south side where they would be safe from Mexican guns. Included in the group of officers was Lieutenant Alamo Kane.

The general faced the group of officers as the firing continued all around the city. "Men, I've noticed that for the past hour, the Mexicans aren't firing their guns as much as they did Monday and Tuesday. Not even as much as up to an hour ago. Have you picked up on that?"

"I noticed it, all right," Lieutenant Grant said. "And I commented on it to the men who were positioned close to me."

"He sure did, General," spoke up Alamo. "I had already noticed it too."

Other officers spoke up, saying they had also been aware of it.

"Good," Taylor said. "This has to mean one thing. They're running low on ammunition and are being careful to fire only when they think they have definite vulnerable targets in their gun sights."

All the officers spoke their agreement.

"You men are all aware that some six hundred of the thirty-seven hundred Texas troops who were sent to us by the president when we were still at Fort Polk were instructed on the tactics of city fighting by the Texas Rangers."

The officers nodded.

"What I'm going to do," Taylor said, "now that Ampudia's troops are obviously running low on ammunition, is send those six hundred men into the city, guns blazing. I believe we can cut down some more Mexican soldiers that way."

The officers nodded their agreement.

The general dismissed the officers to return to their positions as the battle went on. He then went to the officers who were among the Texas Ranger–trained men, gave them his theory as to why the Mexican troops were firing their guns less than usual, and sent them to lead the others into the city.

In less than an hour, the full number of chosen troops returned and gathered around General Taylor. He was happy to see that not one man had been killed or wounded. The officers told the general that in the brief time they were inside Monterrey, they had been able to cut down at least fifty Mexican soldiers, and for sure the Mexican troops were running low on ammunition.

The fighting went on, and by the time darkness fell, Taylor and Worth learned that one hundred and twenty Americans had been killed in the day's battles, but the generals were assured that a much larger number of Mexican soldiers had been killed.

At dawn on Friday morning, September 25, the American troops were preparing to spread out and attack the city again. Generals Taylor and Worth were in conversation, as were Lieutenants Grant and Kane. Suddenly, Alamo caught movement at the city's main gate in the corner of his eye. He squinted and pointed that direction. "Lieutenant Grant, look at that!"

They both saw a rider coming out of Monterrey alone, bearing a white flag on a stick. He was headed their direction. Others then noticed the rider, as did General Taylor, who pointed him out to General Worth.

Taylor immediately moved out ahead of the other soldiers some ten yards, and while they looked on, he waited for the rider to arrive. When the rider drew up and pulled rein, General Taylor took another couple of steps toward him.

Since Alamo was an officer, he knew it would be all right if he joined General Taylor. He quickly left the crowd of soldiers, hurried to the general, and drew up beside him. Taylor looked at him, nodded, and smiled.

The man on the horse had a colonel's insignia on his Mexican army uniform. He looked down from his saddle, still holding the white flag, and with the other hand he saluted General Taylor. Speaking in clear English, he said, "Sir, I am Colonel Francisco Moreno. I am to speak to the officer in charge of these troops."

Taylor nodded. "You are speaking to him. I am General Zachary Taylor."

Moreno nodded. "All right. I am delivering a message to you from General Pedro

Ampudia. He wants to surrender to the American troops."

Taylor smiled. "I am very glad to hear this, Colonel, but I must ask why General Ampudia is surrendering."

"Because we have no more ammunition, sir, and can no longer defend ourselves against the attacks by the United States. Three hundred and sixty-seven of our men have been killed and many more wounded."

Taylor looked around at his men and at Worth and his men, then turned back to the Mexican. "Colonel Moreno, I will seriously consider accepting the surrender of the Mexican troops, but I want to talk to General Ampudia."

"All right. I will bring him immediately. I'll have to interpret for him. He knows no English."

The colonel quickly turned his horse around and galloped toward the city's gate.

Worth walked over to where Taylor and Alamo were standing and watching the Mexican colonel gallop toward the city. Smiling, he said, "General Taylor, I am elated at what is happening!"

"We are too, sir!" came the voice of a soldier in the forefront of the crowd of troops.

The rest of the crowd began shouting with

joy. General Taylor turned and smiled at them.

Everybody waited in anticipation of the surrender. They watched Colonel Moreno draw up to the city gate, which swung open for him at the hands of Mexican soldiers. He guided his horse through the gate, which was closed behind him.

Some five minutes later, the gate opened again, and this time the colonel, still carrying the white flag of truce, had a sharply decorated, uniformed man on a horse beside him.

As the two riders trotted toward them, General Taylor called for the rest of his officers to come and join him, General Worth, and Lieutenant Kane.

When the two Mexicans drew up and pulled rein, General Taylor demanded that they dismount. They did, and Colonel Moreno then introduced General Pedro Ampudia to him.

With Colonel Moreno interpreting for him, General Taylor firmly demanded an unconditional surrender, saying it included turning over all weapons belonging to the Mexican troops to the American forces.

When the obviously disconcerted Ampudia readily agreed, General Taylor told him through Colonel Moreno that he would send a large number of his men as well as wagons with them right now to confiscate all their weapons. Ampudia agreed, and then Taylor told him that he wanted both Moreno and Ampudia to return with the American troops and all the weapons for further discussion.

Five thousand well-armed American soldiers accompanied the general and the colonel, along with fifty wagons and ten old Mexican cannons. Some two hours passed, and Ampudia and Moreno returned with the American soldiers.

With the nearly six thousand American soldiers gathered close by, General Taylor told General Ampudia that he must send some of his officers to a U.S. Army post at Corpus Christi Bay, where they would send a telegram to President Polk to tell him of Ampudia's unconditional surrender. In the telegram, Taylor would ask the president what should be done with the large number of Mexican prisoners. He told Ampudia that he and Moreno must wait right there until he received a reply from the president.

Taylor explained that it would take his officers about eight hours to ride to the army post and the same amount of time to return. If President Polk sent his reply within an hour after he received the telegram, which would be typical for him, it would be midnight before the officers returned to Monterrey.

General Ampudia nodded solemnly, agreeing that he and Colonel Moreno would stay as General Taylor demanded.

Taylor asked Ampudia how many of his men had been killed since the Monterrey battles began and was told the number was about eight hundred. Taylor quickly wrote out a message to be telegraphed to President Polk, including the number of Americans and Mexicans killed so far in the Monterrey battles, and sent three of his officers to ride to Corpus Christi Bay, send the telegram, wait for the president's reply, and bring it back as quickly as possible.

The officers galloped away. Ampudia and Moreno were kept under guard while the nearly eight thousand American soldiers destroyed all the rifles and revolvers that had been confiscated from the Mexican troops in Monterrey, plus the ten old cannons.

After this, the American soldiers who had been killed in the battles at Monterrey were solemnly buried in a large mass grave. The Kane brothers were so glad to know that the soul of Captain Bannock was in heaven.

It was almost midnight when the officers

returned from Corpus Christi Bay. With all the American soldiers gathered around, they handed President Polk's telegram to General Taylor, and he quickly read it. In the telegram, Polk congratulated the generals for a job well done and told Taylor that since he had confiscated all enemy weapons, he was to accept the surrender of General Ampudia and allow him to take his remaining troops back to Mexico City. Worth and his nearly two thousand troops were to remain in Monterrey and occupy it until further notice. Taylor and his troops were to return to Fort Polk and wait for orders as to where to go next.

Taylor read the telegraph message word for word to Moreno, who passed it on to Ampudia in Spanish, and all the American soldiers shouted for joy when they heard the message.

Ampudia and his beaten, unarmed troops left for Mexico City in the middle of the night. Taylor and his troops left for Fort Polk just before dawn, and Worth and his troops moved into Monterrey and took control just after sunrise.

16

On Monday, September 28, newspapers all across the United States carried the story of the Monterrey, Mexico, victory.

Naming Generals Zachary Taylor and William Worth, who had combined and led their separate troops in the fierce battles under his orders, the president told in the article that more than three times as many Mexican soldiers were killed than American soldiers in the Monterrey battles, giving the exact numbers of those killed on both sides.

He spoke well of both generals, saying he had congratulated them by telegram for a job well done. They had indeed conquered the enemy troops and even confiscated all of their weapons.

Polk reported that he had directed General Worth and his nearly two thousand troops to remain in Monterrey to occupy the city until further notice and that he ordered General Taylor and his larger number of troops to return to Fort Polk for further orders as the war with Mexico continued.

Further, the president reported, he had received a telegram from General Worth saying that once he and his men had occupied Monterrey, they learned that no Mexican civilians were killed or wounded in the battles. The Mexican soldiers had placed them in buildings in the central part of the city. However, many houses and businesses around the edges of the city were damaged, and some were completely destroyed by American cannonballs and gunfire. Only Mexican soldiers were killed and wounded.

Polk then explained that in his telegram, he told General Taylor that since the defeated Mexican troops under General Ampudia had been totally disarmed, rather than hold them as prisoners of war, he was to allow them to return freely to Mexico City. He further explained that he did this in order to show President Antonio Lopez de Santa Anna that the Americans have never wanted to be at war with Mexico but want peace between the two countries.

On the afternoon of Monday, September 28, Julia Kane was sitting alone on the front porch of the big ranch house. Amber was taking her nap upstairs in Julia's bedroom on her small bed. Adam, Abram, and Andy were playing tag in front of the house, laughing and having a good time.

Julia's mind was on her beloved Alamo as she wondered if he and his brothers were in the midst of the battle that had been reported as pending at Monterrey, Mexico, in the *Washington Post* almost two weeks ago.

Her attention quickly turned to two ranch hands riding their horses from the road and apparently heading toward the big ranch house. Seconds later she recognized the young cowboys — Ken Hillman and Rob Ulrich. Standing a few feet from the porch, Adam, Andy, and Abram stopped their game and looked on.

As the two riders drew up, Julia rose from her wicker chair and stepped to the top of the porch steps.

Both ranch hands greeted the three boys, then looked toward Julia as she said, "Hello, Ken. Hello, Rob. Did you want to see me?"

Rob slid from his saddle with a folded newspaper in his hand. "Yes ma'am." He headed toward the porch. "I have a copy of today's edition of the *Washington Post.*"

"It has President Polk's story about how our troops conquered the Mexican troops at Monterrey, Mrs. Kane," said Ken from his saddle.

Julia's face lit up. She clapped her hands together. "Oh, praise the Lord!" Looking down at her sons, she asked, "Did you hear that, boys?"

"We sure did, Mama!" Adam replied. "That's good news!"

Rob walked up the steps and handed Julia the newspaper. "We bought several copies so we could hand them out all over the ranch, ma'am. They're in our saddlebags. This one is especially for you."

Gripping the paper, Julia smiled. "Thank you both for thinking of me."

"Our pleasure, ma'am," Rob said and headed back to his horse.

As the two young cowboys rode on, Julia's three boys walked toward the porch, eyes fixed on their mother. Julia eased onto the same wicker chair, and unfolded the paper. Her eyes were drawn to the big headline:

U.S. VICTORY AT MONTERREY, MEXICO

"Oh, thank You, Lord!" breathed Julia. "Thank You! One more victory for our country! And Alamo, Alex, and Abel had a part in it!" She took a short breath. "Lord, I am assuming that Alamo and his brothers are all right. Oh, please bring them home soon!"

Then to her sons, who were now climbing the porch steps, she said, "Maybe with this victory, the war and bloodshed will be over. What a blessing that would be!"

"It sure would, Mama!" Adam said. "We'll wait for you to read the president's story, then you can tell us about it."

Julia then began reading President Polk's article, which was on the front page. By the time she finished, her eyes were brimming with tears. "Boys, go fetch Aunt Libby and Aunt Vivian for me. You can hear the president's story when I read it to them. Oh, and stop at the Wilson cabin and get Grandpa too. Tell him I have some real good news."

"Okay, Mama," Andy said. "Let's go, boys!"

As the boys ran from the porch together, Julia sat down again on the wicker chair and thanked the Lord once more for the good news. She let her mind wander as she daydreamed of Alamo, Alex, and Abel coming home to stay. She thought of how wonderful it would be for Alamo and her to raise their children in peace, see the ranch prosper more than ever before, and together give God all the glory for His love and for His mercy on them.

Julia heard Amber crying upstairs and

hurried to her. The sweet toddler had awakened from her nap and wanted her mother's attention. With Amber in her arms, Julia headed back downstairs. When she stepped out onto the front porch, she saw her sons coming toward the house with their aunts and their grandfather.

The boys were ahead of Libby, Vivian, and Abram as they stepped up onto the porch. Adam went to his mother. "Mama, I told Aunt Libby, Aunt Vivian, and Grandpa about the newspaper and that our army won the victory over the Mexicans at Monter-rey."

"And are we ever eager to hear the whole story!" said the silver-haired man.

"Well, all of you sit down, and I'll read it to you," Julia said with a smile.

Abram opened his arms to Amber. "Grandpa will hold you, sweetheart."

Julia extended Amber to Abram. She giggled as he took her into his arms, and said, "Gampaw! Gampaw!"

Everyone sat down, and Julia stood before them, showing them the bold headlines on the front page of the newspaper.

"Praise the Lord!" Vivian said.

"Amen!" said Libby.

"Double amen!" Grandpa Abram said.

"All right." Julia smiled. "Now I'll read

the story to you."

When she was finished, the family rejoiced at the surrender of General Ampudia and his troops.

Tears flooded Abram's eyes. "I'm very glad to know that the Americans won the Monterrey conflict, but I wish I knew that Alamo, Alex, and Abel weren't part of the hundred and twenty soldiers killed — or even if any of them were wounded."

"I feel the same way," Vivian said.

"Me too." Libby looked down at her hands. "It would be devastating news if any of them were killed or wounded, but I would still want to know."

Julia wiped tears from her cheeks. "Of course, there's no way to know at this point."

"Right," said Abram. "We'll just have to wait to find out." He took a deep breath. "Tomorrow is Adam's tenth birthday. I wish his papa and his uncles could be here for the big occasion."

"Me too!" Adam said.

Even little Amber, hearing Grandpa use the word *papa,* looked toward her mother and said, "Papa! Papa!"

On Wednesday morning, September 30, Julia Kane entered the boys' bedroom an hour after sunrise with Daisy at her side. All three boys were still sound asleep. Stepping close to the three single beds, Daisy and Julia clapped their hands and, having practiced earlier, shouted in unison, "Adam! Adam! Happy birthday!"

Abram and Andy stirred first and quickly awakened. Julia and Daisy repeated the shout; then Adam's brain cleared. He popped up and smiled. "Thank you, Mama. Thank you, Daisy."

Both women hugged Adam, and wished him happy birthday again. Then Daisy said, "Breakfast will be ready in about twenty minutes, boys. See you then."

At breakfast Julia looked around at her sons. "Do you remember at church last night that Uncle Patrick reminded the people that the reason he scheduled the midweek service on Tuesday this week was because he was going to be occupied with something very important on Wednesday night?"

All three boys nodded.

Julia set her eyes on Adam. "Do you have any idea, Son, what that 'something very important' is?"

A smile suddenly spread over Adam's face. "Mama! You mean . . . you mean . . . *my birthday party?*"

Julia chuckled. "Yes, Mr. Ten-Year-Old. Your birthday party, which will take place this evening shortly after supper!" As she spoke, she reached under the table next to her feet, lifted a beautifully wrapped package into view, and handed it across the table to Adam. "This present is from me, Son. You can open it right now."

Excitement twinkled in Adam's blue eyes. "Okay!"

Adam tore the package open and lifted out a shirt that was colored and patterned after U.S. Army officers' shirts. "Wow! Mama, did you make this shirt for me?"

Julia giggled. "I sure did!"

"Oh, I love it!" he said as he left his chair, went to his mother, and gave her a big hug.

That evening, Adam's uncle Patrick and his aunt Angela arrived a half-hour before suppertime. The family was gathered in the parlor, knowing that Daisy wanted them to enter the dining room together at precisely six o'clock. Adam was wearing his new army officer's shirt.

Only minutes before everyone was to leave the parlor and go to the dining room for the special supper Daisy had cooked, the adult family members were in a festive mood and carried on conversations with each other.

Angela was holding her niece Amber while talking to Libby, and young Abram and Andy were talking to Grandpa Abram.

Not involved in a conversation at the moment, the birthday boy drifted toward the large, lace-curtained parlor window, which offered a full view of the ranch road that led to the public road some hundred and fifty yards away. Adam casually parted the curtains and instantly spotted three riders trotting up to the house. They were exchanging greetings with some of the ranch hands as they dismounted.

Adam gasped. "Oh! It can't be, can it?"

From where Julia sat, she looked toward him and said, "Adam, what are you looking at?"

His eyes were bulging as he set them on his mother. "It's not *what*, Mama. It's *who!* Papa Alamo, Uncle Alex, and Uncle Abel are here! They're home!"

There were gasps all over the room as the rest of the family headed that way. Young Adam dashed to the parlor door and into the hallway and ran to the front door of the house. He threw the door open and lunged onto the porch, into his stepfather's arms.

As the rest of the family came through the door, with Libby and Vivian rushing into their husbands' arms, Adam said loudly,

"Oh, Papa Alamo! Now my birthday is absolutely perfect! Just perfect!"

Julia was right on Adam's heels and within seconds was in Alamo's arms. Alamo gently kissed the sweet smile on Julia's lips, and as they embraced, she said, "Yes! Adam is right! This does indeed make the day perfect!"

While the three soldiers embraced their wives, the children, and the O'Fallons, there was tremendous joy among the family to see that all three were alive and unharmed after the combat at Monterrey.

When emotions began settling down, Alamo asked if they had heard the news of the American victory at Monterrey. He learned quickly that they indeed had heard the news. Alamo then explained that as General Taylor was about to lead his troops back to Fort Polk from Monterrey, he had told the general that his oldest son was going to turn ten years old on September 30, so the general gave him and his brothers permission to ride for the ranch. They had to head back toward Fort Polk on Friday morning, but they could stay until then.

Alamo hugged Adam again, wishing him happy birthday, then eyed his new army officer's shirt while Daisy welcomed the Kane brothers home. She called everyone into the dining room, where she had already set three more places at the table.

They all sat down, and Abram asked Patrick to lead in prayer. The pastor thanked the Lord not only for the food and for His blessing on ten-year-old Adam, but also, with flowing tears, that Alamo, Alex, and Abel had been protected by His almighty hand in the Monterrey battles.

Most of the talk during the meal was about Adam turning ten that day and how good he looked in the new army officer's shirt his mother had made him.

When supper was almost over, Julia stood up, looked around the table, and said in a mock formal voice, "Ladies and gentlemen, it is my pleasure to announce that the birthday party for a certain young man who turned ten years of age today will begin in the parlor in exactly fifteen minutes."

The whole family was smiling — even little Amber, who was on her own little stool.

Julia then gestured toward her husband. "I am asking that Lieutenant Alamo Kane formally introduce the birthday boy at the party."

"It'd be my pleasure!" Lieutenant Kane saluted.

Everyone laughed, even little Amber.

Within a few minutes, everyone, including

Daisy, filed into the parlor and took their seats. A table was stacked with wrapped birthday gifts. Adam sat down beside his mother, who was holding Amber. Abram and Andy had Grandpa Abram sitting between them.

Alamo stood beside the table filled with gifts, faced the group, and smiled. "Ladies and gentlemen, it is my pleasure to present Mr. Adam Kane, who was born ten years ago today, September 30, 1836. His father, Adam, went to heaven before this birthday boy was born, but the Lord was so good to me. He allowed me to become this marvelous boy's stepfather by marrying his beautiful, charming, wonderful mother."

Julia blushed and everyone saw it.

Alamo then gestured toward Adam. "All right, birthday boy, come and stand before these wonderful people. After you say a word or two to them, I'll hand you your gifts to open one by one."

The Kane family broke into applause and loud cheers. All eyes were fastened on ten-year-old Adam as he left the chair next to his mother, stepped up to the table beside Alamo, and faced the group with a big smile on his face. The cheers and applause continued.

Dipping his chin and lifting his palms

forward in a mock display of humility, Adam shouted above the applause and cheering, "Please! Please, ladies and gentlemen!"

The applause and cheering faded out.

Adam went on. "I realize that turning ten years old is a great and magnificent accomplishment. It is certainly an achievement worthy of your admiration . . . but . . . but all this applause and cheering! I hardly feel worthy of it!"

While Alamo and Julia exchanged glances with raised eyebrows, Adam continued. "However, if you wish to display your delight by applauding and cheering some more, who am I to stop you? After all, I really don't think I'm so great, but then what is my humble opinion against thousands of others'?"

Everyone laughed and broke into another round of cheering and applause. When it finally faded out, Julia stood up and said loudly, "Adam! How did you come up with a mouthful of words like that?"

Grinning broadly, the sandy haired boy said with an impish grin, "I've been practicing for weeks, Mama. I knew that I'd have a chance to come out with it at my birthday party. I just didn't know that my papa and uncles would be here to enjoy my words too!"

After more cheering and applause, Alamo handed Adam his first birthday present. Each gift had a small piece of paper attached to it, telling the boy who it was from. Everyone enjoyed watching Adam open his presents, and he thanked the benefactor each time he opened one.

When Adam had opened the last present, Alamo, who still stood beside him, looked down into the boy's happy eyes. "I want you to wait right here, Son. I have a special birthday present for you."

Alamo left the room hastily and returned in less than five minutes. In his hands was a brand-new rifle.

Adam's eyes bulged with surprise and pleasure as his stepfather held it before him and explained that he had bought the rifle at a new gun store in Corpus Christi on the way home from Monterrey.

Alamo went on to explain that it was a .25-caliber rifle and showed Adam that it had two barrels, one above the other, and two triggers. "Now, Adam, you can bag even more birds and rabbits because you have two barrels to fire, one right after the other, instead of firing one shot and then having to reload."

Alamo then handed the boy the gun. "I also bought you several boxes of cartridges.

"You can really supply your mother and your aunts with plenty of meat now!"

There was more applause and cheering.

There was much joy on the Diamond K while the Kane brothers were home.

On Thursday night, when everyone else in the big ranch house had gone to bed, Alamo and Julia were sitting together on one of the small sofas in the parlor. They had enjoyed their short time together, but all too soon, it would be time for them to part the next morning.

As they sat there holding hands, tears began to trickle down Julia's cheeks.

Alamo squeezed her hand and set loving eyes on her. With his free hand, he thumbed away her tears. "Sweetheart, don't cry. Hopefully after our victory at Monterrey, Santa Anna will see the futility of continuing against us and decide to make real peace."

Julia sniffed. "I hope you're right, my love. Having to tell you good-bye over and over is almost more than I can bear."

Tears threatened again, and she hastily blinked them away.

"I'm sorry, love." She sighed deeply. "I-I know all these good-byes we've had to say to each other are hard for you too, as well as being gone from your family and the ranch and fighting in the war. Please forgive me. I'm just being selfish, I guess."

"There's nothing to forgive, sweetheart. War is hard on everyone involved. There have been wars and rumors of war for most of the history of mankind. But I have a feeling that this war we're in is not going to last very long. Thank the Lord that He has kept my brothers and me from harm thus far, and as long as the war does last, we must continue to trust Him for His grace, mercy, and protection."

Julia leaned closer to him and looked at him with adoring eyes. "Oh, I love you, Alamo Kane. You always know just how to make me feel reassured."

He smiled and looked into her eyes. "I'm glad, my precious one. I try." He took a shallow breath. "Well, Julie darlin', it's time to get some sleep."

The next morning, many tears were shed as Alamo, Alex, and Abel rode away from the big ranch house, where the family, including Patrick and Angela, had gathered.

The ranch hands and their families stood some distance away, also waving good-bye to the three riders.

17

As October came, the fighting in California between the United States Army and the Mexican army continued, with President Antonio López de Santa Anna sending more and more troops to battle the American forces there.

Santa Anna had made it clear to the people of Mexico that he would do everything he could to keep California in Mexico's control, and he would see to it that the American soldiers were wiped out. Mexican American spies that President Polk had sent into Mexico reported this message to him by telegraph.

On Wednesday, October 7, in Washington, D.C., Polk called a special meeting of Congress with Vice President Dallas at his side and informed them of the message he had received from his spies.

An obvious cloud of anger settled over the congressmen. Glad to see how the message affected them, the president stated that because of the Mexican leader's actions and words and what his troops were doing in California, there was no question in Polk's mind that Santa Anna was going to make aggressive moves against the United States by again moving troops into Texas from northeast Mexico.

Polk then told the angry congressmen that the United States government must prevent this by sending U.S. Army troops into northeastern Mexico to occupy the larger towns, which might provide food and supplies to the oncoming Mexican troops from Mexico City. The congressmen rose to their feet and shouted out their agreement. The president went on to tell Congress that his spies in Mexico had also reported that Santa Anna had ordered troops to set up military posts at some of the larger towns in order to fight off American troops that might be coming into Mexico to occupy them.

The congressmen continued to loudly voice their agreement — to prevent Mexican troops from once again entering Texas, U.S. troops should be sent into northeastern Mexico.

On Friday, October 9, at Fort Polk, General Taylor received a lengthy telegram from

President Polk, which was delivered by messengers from the army post at Corpus Christi Bay. In the telegram the president told Taylor the same things he had told Congress about what his Mexican American spies had reported and of the aggression of Santa Anna's troops, which he was expecting to enter Texas from northeast Mexico.

The president went on to explain that Congress agreed with him that he should send U.S. troops into northeast Mexico to occupy the larger towns that might provide food and supplies to the oncoming troops from Mexico City. The president told Taylor that Santa Anna had ordered his troops to set up military posts at some of the larger towns in order to fight off American troops that might be coming into Mexico to occupy the towns.

Gathering all of his nearly six thousand troops together, Taylor announced the entire contents of the president's telegram, explaining that they now had orders from President Polk and Congress to rush to the areas in northeast Mexico he had named in the telegram where Santa Anna had ordered Mexican troops to establish military posts. Polk would be sending additional troops to the same areas to help Taylor and his men accomplish the task.

Like all of the soldiers at Fort Polk, the Kane brothers wished they could somehow let their families know what they would be doing in Mexico, but it was impossible.

Taylor led his troops into northeastern Mexico as directed by the president, and as they and several thousand other U.S. troops occupied the larger towns, they did battle with Santa Anna's military forces.

Time moved on, and by the last week of November, almost all of northeast Mexico was occupied by U.S. troops as ordered by President Polk. What Mexican troops had not been killed had fled back to Mexico City. With more than enough troops occupying the towns, the president sent a telegram to Taylor, ordering him and his troops to return to Fort Polk and await further orders from him.

The second day they were back at the fort, General Taylor received a telegram from President Polk informing him that General Stephen Kearny and his troops had gained complete victory in California. The Mexican soldiers who were not killed in battle were now imprisoned in a secret place in the Sierra Nevada. California had been set free from Mexico's domain.

At his headquarters in Mexico City, President Antonio López de Santa Anna received word from a few Mexican soldiers who had escaped from General Kearny and his troops of the disastrous defeat and imprisonment of his soldiers in California. He met immediately with his military leaders.

In a rage over the California defeat, Santa Anna stood before them and ordered that a number of Mexican soldiers be sent into Texas dressed as civilians. Since many Mexican Americans lived in Texas, the disguised soldiers would not be detected. Santa Anna's assignment for them was to sneak onto farms and ranches and set fire to houses, barns, and sheds and to kill as many Texans as possible.

When the military leaders had gathered their chosen men for this assignment and explained Santa Anna's orders, the devious Mexican impostors were happy to carry out the plan, knowing that when they set the fires, they would have plenty of opportunities to kill the Texans exposed to their guns as they attempted to put out the fires.

In the second week of December, the Kane family at the Diamond K Ranch and their employees learned of fires being set on Texas farms and ranches by unknown felons. Apparently, the criminals hid near the fires and gunned down the farmers and ranchers when they tried to douse the fires and keep their houses, barns, or sheds from burning down. Cort Whitney put his men on guard to watch for any strangers coming onto the property.

A few days later, word spread among the farmers and ranchers of that part of Texas that some of those whose houses, barns, and sheds were set on fire had been able to fight back and had killed and wounded some of the men, who were Mexicans. Wanting mercy and medical help, the wounded ones confessed in broken English that they had been sent by President Santa Anna to set fire to ranches and farms and to kill as many Texans as possible.

When Cort talked to some of the nearby ranchers who'd caught the Mexican infiltrators, he went back to the Diamond K and gathered the Kane family and all the ranch hands and their families together in a grassy area surrounded by cottonwood and elm trees, which was used as a picnic area in the spring, summer, and early autumn. There were several benches where the ladies and some of the children could sit. Everyone dressed warmly for the chilly December air.

Julia and Libby sat on a bench together with Vivian, who was holding two-year-old

Amber. Across the table from them were the three Kane boys and silver-haired Abram. The married ranch hands stood close to the tables where their wives were sitting, and their children stood nearby.

Taking a central position before the crowd, Cort told them that the felons who were caught by some of the other Texas ranchers were Mexican soldiers dressed like civilians. They had been sent to Texas by Santa Anna to do their fire damage and kill as many Texans as possible.

The crowd was stunned to hear this.

"Some of you have questioned how these men could so easily set fire to the houses, barns, and sheds," Cort said. "I was wondering too, but I learned from some of the farmers and ranchers that the fires are so easily set because of a new invention by a man from France named Charles Sauria that has found its way to the United States and Mexico in the past year. It's called a wooden phosphorous match, and by merely striking its tip against wood or stone, it immediately produces flame. One of the ranchers told me he discovered a couple of months ago that the United States Army cooks and medics are now using them."

"That's interesting, Cort," Grandpa Abram interjected. "I wonder why Alamo,

Alex, and Abel didn't tell us about those matches when they came home."

Cort smiled. "I think I know. When they're here, their minds are totally on being with their families, and they just haven't thought about wooden phosphorous matches!"

There was light laughter all around.

"Anyway, folks," Cort said, "the phosphorous matches are making it quite simple for these disguised Mexican soldiers to set various structures on fire. So you can see that we must keep careful watch for any Mexicans who come on the ranch dressed in civilian clothes, appearing to be Mexican Americans."

"We'll keep our eyes peeled, Cort," spoke up ranch hand Chad Mathis.

The others joined in quickly, assuring the foreman that they would be on the lookout for any such men coming onto the ranch.

There was a quiet hush while Cort spoke solemnly to all the men employed by the ranch, urging them to have their guns with them at all times and to always be alert. He paused briefly, thinking about his next words. "If you find yourself facing those felons on this property, try not to shoot to kill unless it's unavoidable. If you can, shoot to hurt him enough to stop him. And ladies, I'm asking you to stay close to your homes.

Until this danger is over, don't go for walks here on the ranch unless you are accompanied by an armed man.

"Even when you're indoors, keep an eye on your surroundings by looking out your windows. If you see anything that looks suspicious, ring the dinner bell on your back porch as loud as you can for about twice as long as usual, and then go back inside. I guarantee you'll have help from Diamond K men in a hurry. These culprits mean to burn us out and even kill us. We've got to keep that from happening. All of us — men *and* women — must work together to protect this ranch in every way!"

Everyone spoke their agreement.

Cort then told the men he would work out a schedule so that every man, including himself, would have night guard duty until this threat was over. He then dismissed the crowd.

When most of the crowd had left, young Adam said to his mother, "Is it still all right for me to go hunting here on the ranch, even when Grandpa can't go with me?"

Julia's brow furrowed as she considered his question. She looked at her father-in-law. "What do you think, Papa Abram? With the possibility of these disguised Mexican soldiers showing up on the ranch, should

Adam be hunting out there in the fields alone?"

Abram thought on it for a few seconds. "I don't think he'd be in any danger, Julia. After all, there are always ranch hands moving about on this place. There's always one of them close by just about anywhere he'd be hunting. I guarantee you, with this threat facing us, they'll all be carrying guns just like Cort asked them to."

Julia nodded and looked at her oldest son. "Okay, honey, you can still go hunting, even when Grandpa can't go with you."

Adam smiled. "Thanks, Mama."

Julia looked at her sisters-in-law and sighed. "Oh boy, another worry to carry."

Vivian shook her head. "No, honey, not a worry — a challenge. God doesn't want us to worry."

"Right," added Libby. "The Lord is able to keep us and this ranch safe from harm."

Julia put her hand to her forehead and sighed. "Both of you are right." She looked toward the sky. "Please forgive me, Lord. Sometimes I seem to panic so easily. I know Psalm 56:3 is still in Your Bible, and I know I can depend on what it says!"

After a moment of silence, Julia said, "I just miss Alamo so much, and I want him and your husbands to come home for good and for all of our lives to get settled down."

Both Libby and Vivian nodded.

"I'll say 'amen' to that, sweet Julia," Abram said.

Julia stood up with Amber in her arms. "Well, I guess I'd better get little sister here and her brothers back to the house."

Adam was on his feet first, and while the others were rising from the wooden benches, he said to himself with fervent determination, *Those disguised Mexican soldiers will have to get past* me *to get to my family! If they show up on this ranch, they'll face the new rifle Papa Alamo bought me!*

A few days later, during breakfast at the big ranch house, Adam looked across the table and said, "Grandpa, would you like to go hunting with me this morning? Daisy and my two aunts need some more bird and rabbit meat."

Sipping at her coffee, Julia swung her gaze to her father-in-law, who had told her earlier that morning that he wasn't feeling well. Young Abram and Andy looked on as their grandfather swallowed the last of the biscuit he was chewing and set his eyes on his oldest grandson. "I-I'm not feeling real well this morning, Adam. I'd sure like to go with you, but I'd better not try it."

Adam's brow furrowed. "What's wrong, Grandpa?"

"I'm just feeling kind of weak, like happens to men my age, Adam," he said, smiling faintly.

"I'm sorry, Grandpa," the boy replied. Then he turned to his mother. "It's still okay if I go alone, isn't it, Mama?"

Julia nodded. "Yes, Son. Just be sure you do your hunting where you're close to some of the ranch hands, all right?"

Adam nodded. "Sure, Mama."

"Adam," Grandpa Abram said, "I'm so proud of the way you've become such an expert shot with your new .25-caliber rifle. You've already been outshooting me for some time, and with that new rifle, you bag more birds and rabbits than ever. You provide even more food for the Kane family."

Adam grinned. "Thanks for the compliment, Grandpa. I'm just so glad Papa gave me a rifle with two barrels, which makes it easier to bag more game."

When breakfast was over, Abram went out on the back porch of the big ranch house and sat down. Moments later, young Adam came out the back door carrying his new rifle. He paused to say he wished Grandpa could go with him, then stepped off the porch and headed for the area where the barns and the corrals were, planning to go past them out onto the fields, where he did most of his hunting.

As Abram watched the boy sauntering away with his rifle in one hand, he looked toward heaven. "Thank You, Lord, that Adam is such a good boy."

Late that morning, Adam had bagged rabbits, pheasants, and wild turkeys within sight of a few ranch hands who were working on fences. Heading for the house, which would take him past the corrals and barns, he dragged the full gunnysack behind him.

Just as he came around the backside of the largest barn in the corral area, Adam saw two civilian-dressed Mexican men starting a fire with a match and a handful of dry grass. He had never seen the men before. He knew they must be the Mexican soldiers Cort had told everybody about. They had opened the barn door on that side, and Adam was sure they were about to toss the burning grass inside to set the barn on fire.

His face muscles tightened, and a fighting rage welled up inside him as he let go of the gunnysack, raised the double-barreled rifle, and cocked both hammers. The Mexicans were so intent on what they were doing that they hadn't noticed him. So he immediately got their attention by shouting, "Hey! Drop that burning grass and stomp out the fire, or I'll shoot!"

As the clump of burning grass fell to the ground, one of the Mexicans whipped a revolver from the holster on his side. But before he could fire it, Adam squeezed the trigger of the top barrel. The rifle fired, and the bullet struck the Mexican in the right shoulder, dropping him.

Adam then shot the other Mexican, who already had his revolver in hand and was bringing it up to fire at him. The slug plowed into the Mexican's left shoulder. He let out a howl, dropped his gun, and fell on his back.

Adam dashed to the spot where the Mexicans lay on the ground. Both were bleeding from their wounds and crying out in agony. He quickly picked up their guns, tossed them several yards away, and began stomping out the burning grass.

At the same time, Adam saw several ranch hands, who had obviously heard the gunshots, coming on the run.

As the Diamond K men drew up, they stood over the wounded Mexicans, whose faces were twisted in pain as they lay on the ground, gripping their bleeding wounds.

Adam stomped out the last of the flames, then told the men how he had come upon the Mexicans and saw that they had opened the side door of the barn and were obviously planning to throw the burning grass inside and set the barn on fire.

The Mexicans looked at the boy with angry, pain-filled eyes.

At that moment, more ranch hands who had heard the gunshots came running up, including Cort. Directly behind them were Julia, Libby, and Vivian.

Julia dashed up, looked at the wounded Mexicans, then turned to her son. "Adam, what happened?"

"I caught these two Mexicans about to set fire to the barn, Mama. Just like they've been doing to other Texans' property! I had to shoot them! They were pulling their guns to shoot *me!*" He looked at a couple of the ranch hands and pointed to where he had thrown the Mexicans' revolvers. "I threw their guns over there."

The two ranch hands saw the guns and went to pick them up.

Taking hold of Adam's shoulders with trembling hands, Julia asked, "Are you all right?"

He nodded as he looked up into her eyes. "I'm fine, Mama. Please stop shaking. No harm was done to me or to the ranch."

With God's help, Julia gained control of her emotions, smiled at her plucky son, and caressed his cheek. "I'm so proud of you, Adam. You did just as your papa said he wanted you to do. You were very brave to take on two grown men and overcome them. Your papa will be very proud of you too. The Lord has been so good to us today!"

"Boy, what a day this has been!" Adam exclaimed.

"Indeed it has," Julia said. "It is one that will be remembered and talked about for a long, long time." Julia hugged her son, thanking the Lord for His merciful protection over Adam.

Cort took his eyes off the bleeding, moaning Mexicans to look at the boy. "Adam, I commend you for your courage and for your adeptness with that rifle. You sure put them down! I know you could have killed them if you wanted to."

Adam nodded as his mother released him, stepped back, and turned toward Cort. "Yes sir. I could have. But like you told us, we should aim to stop them, not to kill them. So I only aimed at their shoulders."

Cort heard the three Kane women talking in low voices. Julia stepped forward and said, "Libby, Vivian, and I agree that we need to bandage them up so they don't bleed to death. We can't remove the slugs Adam put in them. It'll take a doctor to do that, but we can at least slow the bleeding down to a minimum."

The foreman nodded. "Fine. As soon as you can get their bleeding in check, we'll put them in a wagon and take them to Washington-on-the-Brazos and turn them over to the military authorities there. One of the army doctors can remove the slugs."

Julia hurried to the big ranch house and returned quickly with the needed medical supplies.

The wounded Mexicans, who apparently knew no English, did not attempt to talk to the women as they bandaged them up. The job was done in about twenty minutes, and the ranch hands placed the wounded men in the bed of a ranch wagon, jumped in, and sat with them. Cort was in the driver's seat, holding the reins. He put the two horses in motion.

As the wagon rolled up the lane toward the road, the rest of the ranch hands went back to where they had been working before they heard the gunshots.

Adam's mother and his aunts turned to him. Julia put an arm around the boy.

Beaming proudly, she said, "I know you have wished you could be in the army and fight alongside your papa and your uncles, but you see, Adam, the Lord wanted you here to help protect this ranch and your family. You did a very brave thing, and we are grateful."

Adam blushed, his heart pounding in his chest. He gave his mother that famous, adorable lopsided grin. "Oh, it was nothing, Mama. I was just doing my job."

Libby chuckled and kissed the boy's cheek. "You did your job well, Adam."

Vivian kissed the other cheek. "You sure did. I'm so proud of you."

Three days later, four men in U.S. Army uniforms rode onto the Diamond K Ranch. As they neared the area where the houses stood, they came upon a couple of ranch hands on foot and pulled rein.

"Hello," said the man with colonel's insignias on his coat collar. "I'm Colonel William Branden, commander of the army post at Washington-on-the-Brazos."

"Yes sir," responded the taller of the two ranch hands. "I've heard of you. What can we do for you?"

"Where can we find young Adam Kane?" he asked. "We also need to see foreman

Cort Whitney."

The same ranch hand said, "Tell you what, sir, we'll take you to Cort, and he can take you to Adam."

Nearly a half hour later, the Kane family and a large number of ranch hands and their families had gathered in front of the big ranch house, knowing only that Colonel Branden had something very special he wanted to share with all of them.

He stood before them with his three soldiers and Cort standing nearby. The colonel looked at Adam and asked if he would come to him. Cort had introduced Adam to the colonel, but Adam hadn't been told what the colonel was going to do.

A bit nervous, young Adam left his mother's side and approached the officer. Smiling down at the ten-year-old, Colonel Branden laid a hand on his shoulder and said loud enough for all to hear, "Son, I have come here today because when those two Mexicans you wounded were brought to the army post in Washington-on-the-Brazos, Mr. Cort Whitney told me what you did to stop them from burning down one of the ranch's barns."

Adam's face crimsoned, and he swallowed hard. "Y-yes sir."

The colonel then reached into his coat

pocket and took out a shiny silver medal that reflected the sunlight. "Adam," he said so that everyone could hear, "this medal is the kind we give men in the United States Army who show supreme courage and valor in battle." As he pinned the medal on Adam's jacket, he added, "This is for the supreme courage and valor you showed when you wounded and captured the two Mexican soldiers who were about to set fire to one of the barns on this ranch. Despite the fact that they were drawing their revolvers with the intent of shooting you, you used your own rifle to cut them down. I am very proud of you, Adam."

The crowd broke into cheers and applause, many calling out words of congratulation to the ten-year-old boy.

Cort stepped up, patted Adam on the back, and dismissed the crowd. The ranch people formed a line and passed by Adam to personally commend him for what he had done.

When it was the Kane family's turn to approach the boy, his mother let his two brothers, his grandfather, and his aunts speak to him first. Then she dashed to him, folded him into her arms, and kissed his cheek. "Oh, Adam, I can hardly wait till Papa, Uncle Alex, and Uncle Abel come home and learn of your brave deed in capturing those Mexican soldiers and stopping the fire!"

The United States troops that garrisoned in northeast Mexican towns and in military posts along the Texas-Mexico border as well as in Texas forts wished they could be home for Christmas. But because President Polk felt certain there would be more battles with Santa Anna's military forces, he ordered all the U.S. troops to remain where they were stationed, telling them to be alert and ready.

During Christmas week and early in the last week of December, more Mexican soldiers disguised as Mexican American civilians were caught in the act of starting fires on Texas farms and ranches, and some were even killed. By the end of December, no such incidents had happened again.

18

On Sunday, January 3, 1847, at the church in Washington-on-the-Brazos, Lance Brooks was sitting in the pew next to his parents as Pastor O'Fallon was preaching during the morning service. His sermon was about the ministry of the apostle Paul, and the pastor told how God called Paul to preach shortly after he received Jesus as his Saviour.

Harland and Lucille Brooks had been secretly sharing with each other their belief that the Lord was dealing with their son about becoming a preacher. They based this on the looks they had seen on Lance's face the past few months whenever the pastor mentioned in a sermon how God called men to preach.

Lance's parents were thrilled that their son, who was employed at the Prairie View Hardware Store with his father, had led their boss, Harold Smith, and his wife, Rachel, to the Lord, as well as the other two male employees at the store, all who were now members of the church in Washington-on-the Brazos.

Harland and Lucille kept glancing at Lance during the sermon that Sunday morning. Pastor O'Fallon's vivid description of Paul's call to preach was quite obviously holding Lance spellbound.

In the sermon, after the pastor had presented the gospel for those who were there without Christ, he took the crowd to Titus 1:3, where Paul referred to how God manifests His Word through preaching. Paul said this preaching had been committed unto him according to the commandment of God. At that moment, Harland and Lucille saw strong conviction on Lance's features and smiled knowingly at each other. They were sure that God was speaking to his heart, calling him to preach.

This was confirmed when, during the invitation, Lance turned to his parents and said loud enough for them to hear above the sound of the piano, organ, and singing, "Papa . . . Mama . . . God is calling me to preach. I'm going to go tell the pastor."

His parents' eyes moistened as they looked at each other and then both nodded at him.

The pastor was just turning over to a counselor a man who had come forward to be saved when he saw Lance coming toward him.

The crowd saw Pastor O'Fallon grip Lance's hand and then listen as Lance spoke to him. He immediately led Lance to the altar, and they knelt down to pray together. After some three or four minutes of prayer, they rose to their feet. The pastor said something to Lance, who nodded. Then the pastor ascended the steps of the platform and stepped up to the song leader, who was behind the pulpit, still leading the crowd in the invitational hymn. No one else was walking down the aisle by then. The pastor spoke to the song leader, who closed off the invitational hymn when they reached the last line of that particular verse.

Pastor O'Fallon was then handed cards that had been filled out for the four adults who had walked the aisle to receive Christ as Saviour. There was much rejoicing as the pastor read the names on the cards to the congregation, and those four were taken to the rear of the building to be prepared for baptism.

Lance Brooks waited at the spot the pastor had designated until the new converts had been baptized by the pastor. While still standing waist-deep in the baptistry, Pastor O'Fallon pointed to Lance and announced that he had come forward because he knew God was calling him to preach and had just surrendered to do so.

Lance's parents, as well as the rest of the church members, were thrilled as "amens" came from all over the auditorium.

While the pastor was leaving the baptistry to change back into his suit, the song leader stepped to the pulpit and asked the crowd to be seated while the pianist and organist played a rousing gospel song.

A few minutes later, the pastor returned to the platform, asked the people to rise, and led them in a closing prayer. As people began filling the aisles and heading for the rear of the auditorium, Julia Kane looked around at her relatives and said, "Isn't Alamo going to be happy when he learns that Lance has been called to preach? He's the one who led Lance to the Lord!"

Abram smiled. "Yes! This news will make Alamo fly high like an eagle too!"

Julia and the rest of the family spoke their agreement, and young Adam said loudly, "Yes! When Papa comes home and hears about it, it will be 'High Is the Eagle' again!"

On the following Sunday morning, January 10, Lance Brooks sat next to Pastor O'Fallon on the platform. When the pastor

went to the pulpit at offering and announcement time, he turned and gestured for
Lance to stand up. "I want to remind all of
our members that last Sunday, this young
man walked the aisle and surrendered to
God's call to be a preacher."

There were many "amens" from the
crowd.

Smiling as he spoke again, the pastor said,
"I am going to personally tutor Lance and
train him for the ministry." There was more
pleasant vocal reaction from the people. "I
want all of you to know," Pastor O'Fallon
said, "that I just hired Lance as my assistant
pastor, and I will diligently train him to one
day pastor his own church."

More "amens" were heard.

The pastor pointed down in the audience
to Harold Smith. "I talked to Lance's boss
at the hardware store about this, and he is
all for it, even though he says he will miss
having Lance as part of his staff."

Smith smiled, nodded, and waved a hand.

After a bout of laughter from the congregation, Pastor O'Fallon said, "In addition to
the salary my new assistant will receive, the
church is going to rent him a small house
here in town so he can live close to his
work."

The people were all thrilled at this exciting news.

That following week, Julia Kane had the joy of leading a young woman in her early twenties to the Lord. Andrea Voss had been raised in a small town several miles from Washington-on-the-Brazos and had moved there a few months previously to take a job as secretary to the president of the town's only bank. Julia had met Andrea shortly after she started working at the bank, and they quickly struck up a friendship. Each time Julia was in town on a workday, she stopped by the bank to see Andrea and began witnessing to her of her need to be saved. On Thursday, January 14, they had lunch together, and after lunch was over, Julia had the joy of leading Andrea to Jesus.

The next Sunday, January 17, Andrea came to church with Julia. At the close of the Sunday morning sermon, with Julia at her side, Andrea walked the aisle and gave Pastor O'Fallon testimony of having been led to the Lord by Julia. She was coming now to be baptized.

When the pastor told the story to the congregation, everyone applauded and cheered.

In addition to Andrea, two men and a teenage boy were to be baptized that morning. Before the baptismal candidates were taken to the dressing rooms at the rear of the building to prepare, Pastor O'Fallon ran his gaze over the crowd, "Folks, those of you who were in the midweek service will remember that we voted to give our new assistant pastor, Lance Brooks, authority to baptize. This will be his first time ever to baptize someone."

People all over the auditorium smiled and nodded.

Moments later, when Lance was standing in the baptistry, ready to baptize those who were prepared, Pastor O'Fallon stood at the pulpit and said, "We have one young lady, two men, and one teenage boy to be baptized. At this church, we go by the old adage 'ladies first.' Pastor Lance will now baptize the young lady.

Two women led Andrea Voss to the edge of the baptistry. Lance took her firmly by the hand and helped her descend the steps into the waist-deep water.

Lance smiled at Andrea and said loudly so all in the auditorium could hear, "Pastor O'Fallon told us about this young lady, Andrea Voss, being led to the Lord by Julia Kane."

There were smiles and nods all through the crowd.

Lance smiled at Andrea again and whispered, "You are very special, Miss Andrea, because you are the very first person I have ever baptized."

She returned the smile and whispered, "You are very special too, Pastor Brooks, because you are the man of God who is going to baptize me."

Lance felt a fluttering in his heart, and it took a few seconds for him to proceed with the baptism. When all four had been baptized and the service was over, Lance was standing with Pastor and Angela O'Fallon in the foyer at the front door of the church building, shaking hands with people, when those who had been baptized came out. He shook hands with the teenage boy and the two men, then set his eyes on Andrea as she drew up to him.

The two of them talked for several minutes and struck up a friendship. He asked her if he could take her out to dinner sometime soon. She warmly consented.

Within the next two weeks, Lance took Andrea out to dinner five times, and they became quite well acquainted. By the time the third week came around, they found themselves very much attracted to each other.

The pastor and the people of the church

saw it, and as they talked about it among themselves, everyone agreed that Lance and Andrea made a nice couple.

Since Julia had been privileged to lead Andrea to the Lord, Andrea held a very special place in Julia's heart. Julia watched the growing romance with keen interest. She was especially happy to see Lance and Andrea spending a great deal of time together and shared with her family that she had no doubt Lance and Andrea were falling in love. Libby, Vivian, and Abram agreed.

At Fort Polk, General Taylor sent out scouts every day to keep watch for any Mexican troops that might be sent by Santa Anna to attack the fort. Taylor was glad that so far none had been seen.

Early on Tuesday morning, February 2, General Taylor gathered some forty-four of his soldiers together and, standing before them, said, "Men, because there's been a lull for several weeks in the war with Mexico and our scouts haven't seen any sign of Santa Anna sending troops our direction, I thought of something that might interest you since your homes are within a reasonable distance from the fort. All the other men here at Fort Polk, including myself, are too far from our homes, but how would you like to take a few days and go home to your families?"

Smiles spread through the group, and the men responded affirmatively in almost perfect unison that they would like to go visit their families.

The general smiled. "I knew you would! You men here can get to your families within a few days' ride, and you can return to the fort, at the most, in eleven days. So . . . I'm going to allow you to go home for a short visit. Just make sure you're all back here at the fort by sundown on Friday, February 12. Those whose homes are closer will get to have more time with your families than the others, but at least all of you will have a day or so."

Taylor gazed at their faces. "Get yourselves ready, and ride out of here as quickly as you can."

When the group had been dismissed, Alamo and his brothers stepped up to the general, and Alamo said, "We want to thank you for giving us this leave, General Taylor. Our ranch is just within the reasonable distance you mentioned."

Taylor grinned. "I know. I figured that out. Don't tell anybody, but I set the eleven-day trip for your sakes."

Alex said, "As you know then, General

Taylor, it's a four-day ride from here to the Diamond K Ranch, which will give us three days to be with our family."

The general smiled and nodded. "Yes, Saturday, Sunday, and Monday. I wish I could give you longer, but it's best that you be back here by sundown on the twelfth. So you'll need to head back here on Tuesday, the ninth."

"We'll do it, sir," said Private Abel Kane. "You can count on it."

Taylor grinned again. "Have a good time."

"We will, sir." Alamo turned to his brothers. "Let's go!"

While the Kane brothers were saddling their horses and filling the saddlebags with food and water, they gave thanks to the Lord for making the trip possible.

Moments later, they galloped through the main gate of the fort and headed north.

On Saturday afternoon, February 6, Julia Kane had little two-year-old Amber seated beside her on a sofa in the parlor of the big ranch house and was curling her hair as Libby and Vivian looked on from overstuffed chairs.

"My, my, Amber sweetheart," Vivian said, "your hair gets prettier every time your mama curls it."

"It sure does," put in Libby.

Amber smiled. "Fank you, Aunt Bibian. Fank you, Aunt Wibby."

Vivian smiled. "She's talking more every day, isn't she?"

"That she is," Julia replied, smiling down at her precious daughter.

Adam, Abram, and Andy were playing "Texans and Mexicans" in front of the house, and though the front door was closed because of the cool air, the women and the little girl in the parlor could hear the boys making firing sounds with their mouths.

Julia was making a curl on the left side of Amber's forehead when suddenly the Kane women heard the sound of horses' hooves coming to a halt, and they heard Adam cry out, "Papa! Uncle Alex! Uncle Abel!"

Julia's heart thudded in her chest. She laid the comb and curler down on the hearth, stood up quickly, and took Amber up into her arms. Libby and Vivian were already on their feet, looking out the big parlor window.

"It's *them!*" Vivian gasped.

The three women rushed through the parlor door into the hallway and dashed to the front door. Libby swung the door open and allowed Julia and Amber to pass onto the front porch first. Vivian and Libby hurried out behind them.

Alamo, Alex, and Abel were off their horses, hugging the three boys.

Julia's eyes brimmed with grateful tears as she fixed them on Alamo. He spotted her standing on the porch with Amber in her arms and smiled. He quickly hugged the one boy he had not gotten to yet, then dashed up the stairs with his brothers on his heels.

Libby and Vivian were instantly in their husbands' arms, and the three boys looked on, wiping tears, as Alamo wrapped Julia and little Amber in one big embrace. Holding them tight, he said, "Oh, Julie, I've missed you and my children so much!"

Alamo then eased his hold on his wife and daughter, kissed Julia soundly, and planted a fatherly kiss on Amber's cheek, saying, "Your hair sure does look pretty, sweetie!"

As Amber was saying, "Fank you, Papa," Julia stepped back a pace and looked into Alamo's eyes. "Darling, it's wonderful to have you, Alex, and Abel home, but why are you here? Is something wrong? Have any of you been wounded?"

Alamo smiled. "No, darling, none of us has been wounded. We're fine."

Alamo folded Julia and Amber in his arms again and noticed that Libby and Vivian were in their husbands' arms and listening to what he was about to tell Julia. "General Taylor let us and several other soldiers whose homes are within reasonable riding distance from the fort go home for a short visit because there's a lull in the war right now."

"Wonderful!" Julia said.

"Yes!" said Libby.

"Praise the Lord!" Vivian looked up at her husband.

At that instant, Abram came around the corner of the house. "Hey! My boys are home!" The silver-haired man made his way up the porch steps, and all three of his sons hugged him good. Looking at them with tears in his eyes, he asked, "How come you're home?"

Alamo explained about the lull in the war and General Taylor allowing them and other soldiers who lived within reasonable distance to go visit their families.

"This is great!" exclaimed Abram. "How long can you stay?"

Alamo cleared his throat gently. "I was about to explain to everyone that the general gave Alex, Abel, and me eleven days' leave. We rode as hard as we dared, and of course we had to rest the horses and ourselves at night. It still took us four days to get here, and it'll take us four days to get back. So we'll have to leave at daybreak Tuesday morning."

"Well," said Abram, "we'll take whatever we can get!"

"Yes!" Libby wrapped her arms around Alex again.

"For sure!" declared Vivian, hugging Abel once more.

Julia used her free arm to hug Alamo and looked up into his sky blue eyes. "Oh, darling, I'm so happy to see you again! I've missed you desperately! Welcome home, my love! Welcome home!"

Alamo took her and Amber into his strong arms and held them tight as he laid his cheek on top of Julia's head, breathing deeply the sweet scent of her shining hair. "There is truly no place like home," he whispered.

To add to the sweet reunion of the Kane family, at that moment several ranch hands and their families who had learned that the Kane brothers were back came rushing up to the big ranch house to welcome them. They were led by Cort.

Alamo then had to explain once more why they were home and when they would have to leave again. After some twenty minutes or so, Cort led the ranch people away, saying that the Kane family needed private time together.

As the Kanes watched the ranch people fading from sight, Julia said, "Alamo, Alex, Abel . . . there is something I want to tell you. Let's go inside where it's warm."

When the Kane family was all seated in the parlor, with Grandpa Abram holding little Amber on his lap, Julia told her husband and her brothers-in-law of young Adam's heroism in using his .25-caliber rifle to wound the disguised Mexican soldiers who were about to set fire to one of the barns. She explained that the wounded Mexicans were now being held as prisoners at the army post in Washington-on-the-Brazos.

Both Alex and Abel looked at Adam, who was seated on the floor beside his two brothers.

"Adam," Alex said, "I'm mighty proud of you!"

"So am I!" Abel choked on the emotion in his voice.

Alamo was sitting on a sofa beside Julia. He rose to his feet, looked down at Adam, and walked toward him.

Adam stood up, meeting his stepfather's loving gaze.

Swallowing the large lump that had risen into his throat, Alamo studied the young lad before him. "You did a very brave and honorable thing, Adam. Were you in a position where you could have killed those Mexicans?"

Adam nodded. "Yes, Papa Alamo. I could have put bullets into their hearts, but I only wanted to wound them and stop them from setting the barn on fire. So I shot them in their shoulders."

"Well, nobody would've blamed you if you took their lives because they came here purposely to destroy as much of this ranch as they could and no doubt kill anybody who tried to stop them."

"You need to know this, Alamo." Abram bounced Amber on his knee. "Both of those Mexicans were going for the guns in their holsters when they saw Adam. This boy still purposely only wounded them. You're right — nobody could have blamed him if he'd killed them. And as good as he is with that gun, he definitely could have!"

Tears flooded Alamo's eyes as he folded young Adam in his arms. "Son, if those Mexicans could have started that fire, who knows how much it would have spread? You very well may have saved this ranch and our livelihood. I commend you for the way you handled yourself in that situation. To take another person's life is a horrible thing to have to live with. You did well, Son. I'm proud of you. And I know your real father would be proud of you too."

Adam's face was beaming from the praise of his stepfather. "Thank you, Papa Alamo."

"You've done us all proud, Son," Alamo said. "You did as I asked you to do. Without regard for your own safety, you bravely did your part to protect this ranch."

The boy nodded and licked his lips. "I will always do that, Papa Alamo."

Julia's thoughts went to her oldest son's real father. *Indeed, you would be proud of your son, Adam. He is one fine boy!* She ran her gaze to Alamo and then to his brothers. "I knew all three of you would be proud of Adam. Now I have something else to tell you that will bless your hearts . . . especially *yours,* Alamo."

Alamo, Alex, and Abel set their eyes on Julia.

"Is it as good as what you just told us, honey?" Alamo asked, walking back to the couch where she sat.

"It's totally different." She smiled. "But it's going to bless your heart, I guarantee it!"

Alamo sat down next to her once again on the sofa and grinned. "I can hardly wait to hear it!"

19

The anticipation on the faces of the Kane brothers was quite obvious as Julia Kane looked at Alex and Abel, who were sitting next to their wives, then turned to her own husband on the sofa next to her.

Julia kept her twinkling eyes on Alamo. "It's about Lance Brooks, honey. Something tremendous happened to him on Sunday morning, January 3."

Alamo adjusted himself on the sofa, turning completely toward the woman he loved, and fixed his eyes on her. "What was it?"

Alex and Abel looked at their wives questioningly, and both wives smiled, then looked at Julia. Alex and Abel then did the same thing.

Knowing what was coming, Abram, Libby, Vivian, and the three boys felt their hearts pounding as Julia focused on Alamo's waiting eyes. "None of us knew it," Julia said, "not even Pastor Patrick, but the Lord had been working on Lance's heart for some time about becoming a preacher."

Alamo's eyes widened. "Really?"

"Mm-hmm. And in that morning service on January 3, Lance walked down the aisle during the invitation and told Pastor Patrick he was surrendering to preach!"

If ever delight was written visibly on the face of a man, it was written on the face of Alamo Kane. His eyes lit up. He popped his palms together and shouted, "Hallelujah! Glory to God! Hey, this puts me back in the sky! 'High Is the Eagle'!"

Julia giggled. "Well, get ready to fly higher, Mr. Eagle! In the morning service the next Sunday, January 10, Pastor Patrick announced that because of Lance's surrender to the ministry the week before, he had hired him as assistant pastor of the church, and he would begin tutoring him right away and training him for the ministry so that someday Lance could pastor his own church!"

Alamo's eyes filled with happy tears, and he put his fingertips to his mouth, his entire face glowing with joy.

"Yes sir, Alamo!" said Abram. " 'High Is the Eagle'!"

While Alamo was wiping tears from his cheeks with the handkerchief from his hip pocket, Julia said, "There's something else for you, Alex, and Abel to know too."

"Tell us!" Abel exclaimed.

"Does this also have something to do with Lance?" Alex asked.

Julia nodded. "It sure does. It involves a lovely young lady named Andrea Voss."

Alamo blinked. "Honey, do you mean — do you mean —"

"Romance?" asked Julia.

"Yes!"

"Just let me tell you the story."

"Go for it!" said Alamo.

The Kane brothers listened intently as Julia told them about Andrea Voss coming to work at the bank in Washington-on-the-Brazos a few months previously as secretary to the bank president. She explained that Andrea had been born and raised in a small Texas town several miles from Washington-on-the-Brazos.

Julia went on, telling how she and Andrea had become friends and how she eventually had the joy of leading Andrea to the Lord. She then told about Andrea being the first person Assistant Pastor Lance Brooks baptized, how they had become attracted to each other instantly, and how a romance was definitely now going on between them.

"Oh, this is great!" exclaimed Alamo.

"It sure is!" Alex said.

"Yes!" said Abel. "We'll look forward to meeting Andrea at church tomorrow!"

The next morning, at the church in Washington-on-the-Brazos, the Kane brothers were heartily welcomed by other members as they alighted from a Diamond K Ranch wagon with their family. They explained why they had been allowed by General Taylor to come home for a brief visit.

When the Kane family entered the church building, Alamo, Alex, and Abel saw their sister, Angela, talking to a pair of teenage girls. While Angela was speaking, her head turned casually, and her eyes widened as she saw her three brothers.

"Hi, Sis!" said Alex.

Angela said something briefly to the girls, who smiled and nodded. Then she headed toward her uniformed brothers. Alamo stepped ahead of Alex and Abel, opened his arms, and folded Angela in a close embrace. When Alamo released her, Alex and Abel hugged her at the same time while Alamo explained about their brief visit home.

Blinking at her tears, Angela sniffed. "Oh, praise the Lord you could come home, even if only for little more than a day!"

At that moment, Angela's husband stepped up. "Well, lookee here! Three wandering sheep of my flock are back!"

The Kane brothers hugged their pastor and brother-in-law and explained to him why they were home and that they would have to head back for Fort Polk on Tuesday morning.

Then Lance appeared with Andrea at his side and said with a broad smile, "Hey! Welcome home, Alamo, Alex, and Abel! I've got someone I want you to meet!"

Julia moved quickly from among the family members and stood in front of Lance and Andrea. "Lance, I want to be the one to introduce Andrea to my husband and brothers-in-law."

Still smiling, Lance said, "Well, Julia, since you are the one who led Andrea to the Lord, which resulted in my meeting her and being the one to baptize her, I owe it to you to let you introduce her! Go for it!"

After the Kane brothers and Andrea had been introduced, the brothers told Andrea how glad they were that she had become a Christian and that she was the first person Lance baptized. Then they turned to Lance and told him how glad they were that God had called him to preach and that he had surrendered to do so.

Alamo hugged him, then eased back. "Yes sir, Lance. As your spiritual father, when I heard from Julia that you had surrendered to God's call to preach, I was instantly flying high as an eagle!"

Lance looked deep into Alamo's eyes. "I am so glad. For sure, if you hadn't led me to Jesus, I certainly never would have been called to preach."

Even as he spoke, Lance wrapped his arms around Alamo and said in a choked voice, "Thank you for caring about where I would spend eternity. Thank you for leading me to Jesus!"

Alamo smiled. "My pleasure, Lance. You've been a real blessing to me ever since you got saved!"

The Sunday school class and the Sunday morning service were a blessing to the Kane brothers, and Sunday dinner that afternoon was a large family affair as they all sat down at the long table in the dining room of the big ranch house.

Daisy had surprised the Kane brothers by cooking a feast in their honor, remembering each of the brothers' favorite dishes and including them with the fabulous feast. During the meal, the big ranch house was once again filled with chatter and laughter.

Sweet Daisy stood in the dining room doorway, grinning from ear to ear. " 'Tis a happy home when the three brothers are back from the war and out of danger, if only for a few days," she whispered to herself.

The Sunday evening service was a blessing to the Kane brothers as well. Before they left the church for the Diamond K with the rest of the family, Alamo, Alex, and Abel hugged their sister and pastor/brother-in-law and told Patrick how good it was to hear him preach again.

When the Kane family went to their wagon and horse team in the parking lot, Lance was standing there in the moonlight to tell Alamo, Alex, and Abel good-bye. Tears spilled down Lance's and Alamo's cheeks as they hugged each other.

Lance wiped tears from his face. "Alamo, you and your brothers are in my prayers every day. I'm asking the Lord to bring all three of you home safely when this war is over."

Alamo smiled. "Just keep praying, Lance."

"You can count on that," Lance replied, wiping tears again.

Alamo grinned. "I'll be praying that things will work out for you and Andrea."

Lance matched his grin. "Just keep praying, Alamo."

"You can count on that," Alamo said, wiping his own tears.

Early on Tuesday morning, it was once again time for the three soldiers to leave their loved ones and head for Fort Polk. Their horses were saddled and ready to go, and the ranch people had already told the Kane brothers good-bye.

A few steps from where the rest of the family stood, Julia clung to Alamo and said in a tone low enough that only he could hear her, "Darling, please tell me that this war is almost over."

Alamo looked deep into her lovely eyes. "I think it's safe to say that within a few months, we'll be coming home to stay, sweetheart."

Julia sighed. "Oh yes! Please, Lord, let it be!"

She then placed a sweet kiss on her husband's lips.

When Alamo had hugged his children and told them good-bye, he kissed Julia one more time. Then the Kane brothers rode away as their loved ones dabbed at their tear-filled eyes and waved at them.

It was early afternoon on Friday, February

12, when the two corporals on duty in the tower at Fort Polk's main gate saw three riders coming from the north.

"I'd say that's the Kane brothers," said Corporal Ed Taggert.

"Well, since they're the last ones due back at the fort, I'd say it is," replied Corporal Bob Caldwell. "When they get closer, we'll be able to tell if it's them."

After keeping their eyes on the approaching riders for another five minutes, Ed Taggert said, "Yep, Bob. That's them."

Bob smiled as he focused on the riders. "It sure is!"

Moments later, the Kane brothers pulled rein. All three of them looked up to the gate tower and smiled.

"Howdy, fellas," said Alamo.

"Howdy, sir," Corporal Caldwell responded. "We're glad you're back safely. You're the last of the men to return. Did you have a good time with your family?"

All three brothers nodded, saying they did.

"Good," said Caldwell.

"I'll get the gate open for you." Taggert quickly headed down the narrow stairway toward the ground.

With his eyes on Corporal Caldwell, Alamo asked, "Have any of our scouts spotted Mexican troops coming this way yet?"

"No, sir, but about three hours ago, two soldiers from the army post at Corpus Christi Bay came with a telegram for General Taylor from President Polk. And it's not good news."

"Well, tell us," Private Abel Kane said.

Caldwell shook his head. "Since you men need to report to General Taylor and let him know you're back, it'd be best to let him inform you what was in the telegram."

"Oh. All right," said Alamo. "We'll do that."

The Kane brothers rode through the open gate and headed toward the building that held General Zachary Taylor's office. Several soldiers along the way spotted the Kane brothers and welcomed them back.

The Kane brothers drew up a few feet from the door of the general's office, and as they were dismounting, Lieutenant Ulysses Grant walked out the door with the general standing behind him.

Grant smiled at the Kane brothers as they headed toward the office door and turned to the general. "You were just saying that you hoped the Kane brothers arrived before sunset, General. Here they are. About four hours before sunset."

Taylor looked past Grant and smiled at

the Kanes. "Welcome back, men! Come on in."

Alamo, Alex, and Abel warmly greeted Grant and entered the general's office as Grant walked away.

When the Kane brothers were inside the office, General Taylor had them sit down in chairs that faced his desk and eased into his own desk chair. "Did you have a good time with your family — even though it was short?"

The Kane brothers assured him that they did. Then Alamo said, "General, Corporal Caldwell at the gate told us that you received a telegram today from President Polk that was not good news."

Taylor nodded solemnly. "That's right."

"May we hear its contents?"

"Certainly." The general nodded. "Everyone else in the fort knows, so you need to know too." Taylor paused a few seconds and bit his lower lip as he picked the telegram up from the top of his desk. He held the folded paper. "The president says he just learned that Santa Anna himself is leading some fifteen thousand troops from Mexico City to the city of Buena Vista in the state of Coahuila in Mexico, and they will arrive there in less than ten days. Santa Anna is daring the American military to try to stop

him and his troops from setting up headquarters there so they can begin taking over
the Mexican towns and cities that are currently under American control.

"In this telegram, the president has commanded me to take my fifty-eight hundred
men and stop Santa Anna and his troops
from making Buena Vista their headquarters."

"I've heard of Buena Vista, sir," Alamo
said. "Coahuila is due west and a bit south
of Fort Polk, isn't it?"

"Yes. Buena Vista is almost exactly two
hundred miles from here. Our troops are
preparing the wagons and cannons right
now. We plan to leave at dawn tomorrow
morning. We'll have to cover better than
twenty miles a day to arrive as soon as possible after Santa Anna and his troops get to
Buena Vista from Mexico City."

The Kane brothers' faces were solemn.
"This could be a real battle, sir," Alex said.

Taylor nodded. "I know. In the telegram,
President Polk told me that he has studied
a map of the Buena Vista area. He warned
me to be careful because of the steep mountainsides and rough terrain that make up a
large part of the area, even lining two sides
of the city. I was told to avoid battling the
Mexican troops in that rugged area. The

president prescribed exactly how I am to lead our troops straight into Buena Vista to attack the Mexican forces *inside* the city in order to kill a great number of them and drive the rest of them away in defeat. He has described the entire layout of the land at Buena Vista and makes it clear that I am to follow his instructions to the letter in taking the battle to the Mexican troops there."

Alamo frowned. "We're to attack by going *straight* into the city, sir? Did I get that right?"

"Yes."

"Yet there are steep mountainsides and rough terrain lining two sides of the city."

"Yes."

Alamo shrugged his shoulders. "Well, I'd say it would be better to put our cannons in the steep mountains and fire them at the troops in the barricades that they no doubt will erect in Buena Vista."

General Taylor licked his lips but said nothing.

Alamo shrugged his shoulders again and smiled slightly. "I wish we had more troops, sir, but under your leadership, I'm sure we can defeat the Mexicans with our smaller number of troops as we've done before."

Alex and Abel looked at each other, then nodded at the general.

■ ■ ■ ■

At dawn the next morning, General Taylor led his somewhat more than fifty-eight hundred troops out of Fort Polk with cannons tied behind ammunition and food wagons, and he pushed the cavalry and infantry hard for the next eight days. They arrived at the north edge of Buena Vista at dusk on Saturday, February 20.

Even though it was almost dark, the Americans could make out Mexican soldiers who were observing them from behind barricades on the north side of Buena Vista.

"What do we do, now, General Taylor?" asked Major Byron Blair, who stood close by with many other men. "Do you think they'll attack us in the dark?"

"I seriously doubt it," Taylor replied, "but we'll stay on guard during the night just in case. If there is no attack tonight, at the break of dawn I'll take some of the officers and look the area over so we know exactly what it looks like all around the city. Then we'll prepare to do as the president said and begin our assault into the city as soon as possible."

There was no attack on the American forces

by Santa Anna's troops that night. As planned, at the break of dawn on Sunday, February 21, General Taylor took some of his officers, including Lieutenants Ulysses Grant and Alamo Kane, Captains Jack Lambert and Delton Raynor, Majors Edgar Phillips and Byron Blair, Colonels Herbert Weber and Vince Leyden, and led them up on one of the steep mountains on the west side of the city.

From where they stood, they had a full view of Buena Vista and the rugged terrain on the east side of the city. Every man carefully studied the sight before him.

After a few minutes of meticulously examining the scene, General Taylor said, "Men, the best way to battle the Mexican troops, since we're outnumbered by almost ninety-two hundred, is from these steep mountainsides here on the west side of the city and those rugged hills on the east side. Both of them offer good defensive cover."

"I agree, General," said Major Phillips, "but this isn't the way President Polk told you to do it."

Taylor sighed. "I know, Major, but if we charge straight into the guns they have positioned at many places in the city, as the president said to do, we'll have hardly any defense. They'll mow us down. I have to put it like this — with all due respect to the president of our country, he has no military experience. His background is as a lawyer and a politician."

Phillips nodded. "I see what you mean. You're right. We'll have to attack with our cannons and rifles from the mountains here and those hills on the other side. That way we'll have good defenses."

"I agree, General," said Colonel Leyden.

Taylor ran his gaze to the other officers. "Are you men in agreement with my plan?"

"I don't like to go against the president's orders, General," said Lieutenant Grant, "but if we do as he said, indeed, those Mexicans will mow us down. Let's do it your way."

The other officers quickly spoke their agreement.

Pleased to hear that all officers present agreed with him, General Taylor said, "All right. We'll have to move to these positions immediately, before Santa Anna can send his troops to attack us."

Taylor then assigned Colonel Weber and Major Phillips each to take a certain number of troops and cannons to different positions in the rugged area east of the city and make their attacks. Then he assigned Major Blair to command troops and cannons in the mountains on the west side of the city, saying he would command another unit of troops and cannons on the same side at a different spot. He pointed out that Colonel Leyden would be with him and his soldiers.

The officers quickly hurried back to the rest of the men. The general explained to them his plan of using the mountainsides and the rugged terrain as points of attack on Santa Anna's soldiers, who were barricaded in Buena Vista.

Soon the troops were following the men the general had assigned to lead them, using the steep mountainsides and rugged hills to set up the defenses from where they would be firing the cannons and the cavalry and the infantry would be firing their rifles. They also made their defensive positions secure for an offensive attack on the Mexican troops within the city when it was time to do it.

Within an hour, as the sun was rising, all American soldiers were positioned as directed by Taylor, with the cannons, cavalry, and infantry in place.

In Buena Vista, at the Coahuila Hotel, Mexican president Antonio López de Santa Anna was shaving when he heard a knock at his hotel room door. With shaving foam still covering half his face, he laid down his straight-edge razor and made his way to the door.

When he opened it, he saw one of his leading officers, Colonel Ramón Lugardo, whose features were showing strain.

Speaking in Spanish, the colonel told Santa Anna that the Americans had set up their cannons, their infantry, and their cavalry on both sides of the city. He should come and see immediately.

With the foam cream dripping from his face, Santa Anna walked with Colonel Lugardo to a choice spot on the hotel's roof where he could see the American troops positioned strategically on both sides of the city, on the steep mountainsides of the west and in the areas of rugged terrain on the east.

Santa Anna's face went deep red with fury, and a fierce wildness blazed in his dark eyes as he spoke in a defiant voice, saying all the American soldiers deserve to die. He then told Colonel Lugardo to bring all the leading officers to the front of the hotel. He would finish shaving quickly, and meet them down there.

20

When President Antonio López de Santa Anna stepped out the front door of the Coahuila Hotel some twenty minutes after sending Colonel Ramón Lugardo for the designated Mexican army officers who were inside Buena Vista, he was pleased to see the colonel and the other officers there waiting for him.

Santa Anna took the officers up onto the hotel roof so they could clearly study the four positions of the enemy army units — two on the steep mountainsides to the west and two on the rugged terrain to the east. All four units were established in strong defensive positions with clear shots toward the city for their great number of cannons and rifles. Santa Anna noted that an American flag was visible with the unit on the lower side of the mountainous area. He told himself that General Zachary Taylor would probably be leading that particular unit.

While the Mexican officers were assessing the four different American army units, Santa Anna told them begrudgingly that the positions where General Taylor had placed his men offered the greatest defensive possibilities to allow tremendous offensive attack even though they only had about six thousand men.

After Santa Anna had studied the enemy troops for a long moment, he decided that the strength of the American positions was so clearly apparent that if he ordered an assault by his fifteen thousand troops, the Americans could easily kill many Mexicans. This put fear into Santa Anna's heart. He must come up with some way to conquer the Americans without losing a great number of his men.

Thinking on it another few minutes, Santa Anna made a decision. He turned and called for one of his officers who could speak English well, Captain Juan Talifero. When the captain came to him, Santa Anna told him that he wanted Talifero to accompany Santa Anna to his hotel room, where he would dictate a letter to General Taylor. The captain would write it in English and deliver it to the American general.

The rest of the Mexican officers were sent back to their posts in the city, and Santa

Anna and the captain went to his room. There Santa Anna dictated the letter, in which he lied and said he had twenty thousand soldiers in Buena Vista and he knew Taylor only had around six thousand. He pointed out to Taylor that no matter how good the American positions seemed, they were hopeless against twenty thousand Mexicans, and he offered Taylor the opportunity to surrender.

Santa Anna told Taylor that if the Americans would surrender, he would allow them to return to Texas unharmed. Otherwise they would all be killed. If Taylor was willing to surrender, he should inform Captain Talifero, and there would be no bloodshed.

At his position in the lower mountain areas west of Buena Vista, General Taylor heard one of his infantrymen, who was bellied down between two rocks and looking toward the city, call out to him. "General Taylor! There's a Mexican soldier on horseback carrying a white flag coming our way!"

The general ran to where the infantryman lay and caught sight of the Mexican horseman, who was now close enough that four American soldiers stepped out from behind huge rocks, rifles in hand, to face him. The Mexican drew rein and began speaking to the soldiers.

"He probably wants to talk to you, General," said the man on the ground.

At that instant, one of the four soldiers, Sergeant Mack Ross, nodded and pointed toward the area where General Taylor was located. He then walked beside the horse, escorting the mounted man toward the general.

"Looks like it," Taylor agreed, moving past the huge rocks his men were using for defense. He stepped out into the open and waited for Sergeant Ross and the Mexican officer to draw up. Immediately, the man on the ground and ten other men who were close by joined Taylor. Included were the Kane brothers, Lieutenant Grant, and Colonel Leyden.

Less than a minute later, when the Mexican drew rein and Sergeant Mack Ross stepped ahead of his horse, Ross said, "General Taylor, this is Captain Juan Talifero. He has a letter for you from Santa Anna. It's in English."

Taylor looked up at the captain, who said in perfect English, "You *are* General Zachary Taylor, correct?"

"Correct," Taylor said flatly.

Leaning from the saddle, Talifero handed the folded letter to General Taylor. "This is indeed from President Santa Anna. I will wait until you read the letter, General Taylor. I will need your reply to the president's message."

The twelve men gathered around Taylor waited for him to read the letter. Hundreds of other American soldiers in Taylor's division were looking on from their positions among the rocks, but they couldn't hear what was being said.

Talifero looked on, as did those men gathered close to him, while the general silently read the letter. They watched his facial features flush with anger. He then turned to his men and told them its contents.

Lieutenant Grant scowled at Talifero, then turned to General Taylor. "I know you're not going to surrender."

"Of course he's not," spoke up Alamo.

Taylor's jaw was set in an angle of indignation as he nodded at Alamo then looked up at Talifero and said crustily, "You can go back and tell Santa Anna that I will not surrender, and neither will any of my men."

The captain's features darkened. "You are a fool, General! You and your troops have no chance against our twenty thousand!"

"I don't believe you've got twenty thousand, Captain." A core of fury welled up inside Taylor. "Our scouts counted some fifteen thousand. Santa Anna is a liar."

A flash of wrath crossed Talifero's dark features. "Then you will all die!" he hissed. With that he wheeled his horse about and galloped back toward the city.

General Taylor led the men with him into the steep, rocky mountainous area where those directly under him were waiting to learn what had happened. With the letter still in hand, he told all of them its contents and what he had told Santa Anna's messenger. He then sent his own messengers to the other American positions in the mountains west of the city and in the rugged terrain on the east side to tell them of the letter's contents and his answer to Santa Anna.

When the messengers returned, they assured General Taylor that every one of his troops was in agreement not to surrender. None of them believed that Santa Anna had twenty thousand soldiers in Buena Vista, and they did not believe the lying Santa Anna when he said that he would just let the Americans ride away if they agreed to surrender. All agreed that they wanted to stay and fight the Mexicans as ordered by President Polk.

Nothing happened that day as the American

soldiers prepared themselves for battle, but the next morning, February 22, the Mexican troops attacked all four of the American positions.

American cannons roared, along with rifles and pistols from all four positions. Many Mexican soldiers were going down under the American cannons and guns, and a few Americans were dropping when struck with Mexican lead.

Late that morning, in the lower rocky area of the mountains on the west side of Buena Vista, where General Taylor and his unit were blasting away at Mexicans who were firing their rifles and attempting to climb closer, the gunfire on both sides was making a drumming roar as many bullets struck the rock walls and whined as they dangerously ricocheted.

At the spot where Alamo, his brothers, and Lieutenant Grant were hunkered low, they were firing their guns at the Mexicans who were climbing toward them and firing in return. Colonel Leyden was several feet to their left, in a standing position, using two revolvers to shoot at the oncoming Mexicans from between two tall, sharp-tipped rocks.

From every direction in the lower rocky, mountainous area, the sounds of battle grew louder and more pronounced. Great puffs of gun smoke rose into the air and were carried away slowly by the slight breeze.

While the Kane brothers and Grant fired away at the Mexicans below them, they failed to notice that eight Mexican soldiers had crawled slowly into the small area like rattlesnakes, moving up behind Colonel Leyden.

At the same instant that two of the Mexicans rose to their feet and surprised Colonel Leyden as they grabbed him, Alamo was just reloading his revolver and caught sight of them from the corner of his left eye.

"Hey!" Alamo shouted as he unleashed his gun on the two infiltrators. Both Mexicans buckled from the impact of the slugs and went down.

Alex, Abel, and Lieutenant Grant heard Alamo's shout and his gun roaring. They turned to see the other six Mexicans scrambling to their feet and bringing up their rifles, ready to fire. A volley of shots came from the two Kane brothers and Grant, striking the six Mexicans. Every one of them took slugs in their chests and dropped their guns on the ground as they fell.

Colonel Leyden stood in awe at what he had seen as the Kane brothers and Ulysses Grant examined the eight fallen Mexicans, agreeing that they were all dead.

As his rescuers moved up to him, Leyden said, "Th-thank you, my friends. You risked your own lives to save me from harm and death."

Alamo smiled thinly. "You would have done the same for any one of us, sir."

Leyden matched Alamo's smile and ran his gaze over the faces of the four men who had saved his life. "I'd like to believe I would have."

The roar of guns all around them continued. The five American soldiers quickly returned to their places and opened fire on more Mexicans who were attempting to climb up and kill them.

The fierce battle raged all around them. When darkness finally fell and the fighting halted for the night, General Taylor gathered the men of his unit together and asked a particular dozen of them to count how many of their troops had been killed. Just before they spread out to find the bodies by moonlight and make the count, Colonel Leyden stepped up to the general. "Sir, something happened where I was fighting today that you need to know about."

All the men of that unit looked on as the colonel told General Taylor how the Kane brothers and Lieutenant Grant had saved his life at the risk of their own by sheer courage and fighting ability when eight Mexican soldiers sneaked into the spot where they were positioned in the battle and two of them had grabbed him. When Leyden reported that all eight of the Mexicans had been killed, the general looked at the four heroes and commended them, saying he was very proud of them.

General Taylor then sent some of the men from his unit to ask the commanders of the other three units how many of their men had been killed in the day's battle and told the appointed dozen of his own unit to begin their body search.

At the break of dawn on Tuesday morning, February 23, General Taylor was saddened to tell the soldiers in his unit that 76 men in their unit had been killed in yesterday's battle. The reports he'd received after midnight from the other three units was 252 killed, making a total of 328 American soldiers killed. His voice catching in his throat, Taylor remarked that the only thing that helped him was to know that the toll all four of the units had taken on the Mexican troops was larger — much larger.

The men from Taylor's unit were also saddened at their losses, but were encouraged to learn that many more enemy soldiers had been killed.

At sunrise, a desperate Santa Anna sent his great number of troops in a savage attack against all four American positions, hoping to somehow overcome them. However, the troops under General Taylor and Major Blair in the mountainous area on the west side of Buena Vista, and those of Colonel Weber and Major Phillips in the rugged terrain on the east side, held their fire until the Mexicans had come well within range, as commanded by Taylor, and opened a devastating and sanguinary bombardment that quickly broke the Mexican charge and forced them to fall back, leaving hundreds of their soldiers lying dead behind them.

Things were quiet until about noon, when Santa Anna sent his soldiers against the American positions again. Allowing the Santa Anna–driven Mexicans to advance even closer than in the previous attack before opening fire, Taylor's men suddenly shot a deadly barrage of cannon fire, followed by rifles and revolvers.

Mexican soldiers were going down in a vast bloodbath, and some of those who were still untouched by shrapnel or bullets stopped dead still in the midst of this biting fire, as though deliberately seeking their own destruction. Under command of their unit leaders, the Americans rushed upon them using rifles and revolvers and even bayonets at close range. Every one of those Mexicans was killed.

The Americans prepared for another attack to come, saddened that more of their men had been killed. The Kane brothers and other Christians in their unit had a time of prayer, asking God to protect them in the next attack and to help them to defeat Santa Anna and his troops in Buena Vista soon.

At four o'clock that afternoon, Santa Anna sent a massive Mexican attack against the American positions, still hoping to wipe them out with his larger number of troops. At first the defenders in the mountainous areas and rough terrain areas were almost overwhelmed by the sheer numbers, but as their massed artillery began to tear large holes in the advancing columns, Santa Anna had his leading officers recall his troops. In less than an hour, the fighting was ended.

Several more Americans had been killed, but a huge number of Mexicans lay dead all around the American positions.

A count of their dead was made by soldiers in all four positions. When the count was completed, Taylor sadly reported that since coming to Buena Vista, 746 Americans had been killed.

Colonel Leyden went to the Kane brothers and Lieutenant Grant and told them if it hadn't been for them saving his life, the count would have been 747. He thanked them once more for saving his life at the risk of losing their own.

Early in the evening, in the center of the city as many citizens of Buena Vista looked on, Santa Anna had some of his officers get a count of his men who were still alive. He knew he had actually brought 15,000 troops to Buena Vista, and when the officers reported that 13,337 of their men were still alive, including some 300 wounded, Santa Anna, as well as his unscathed men and the citizens who were present, knew that the Americans had killed 1,663 of his men. Badly shaken, Santa Anna realized he must either risk another battle in the morning or retreat with his troops before dawn.

While the Americans were sleeping — except for the assigned sentries — a broken Santa Anna stealthily led what was left of his army out the north side of Buena Vista so the American sentries could not see them leaving in the moonlight.

At sunrise the next morning, the sentries reported to their commanders that there were no Mexican soldiers at the east, south, or west edges of the city. This was strange and different, so General Taylor took a large number of his men to Buena Vista and found peaceful civilians in groups at the edge of the city. They told the general and his men that Santa Anna and his remaining troops had fled from the north side of the city during the night. They reported that Santa Anna had said 1,663 of his soldiers had been killed in the Buena Vista conflict.

Taylor and the men with him hurried back to their positions in the mountains and the rough terrain on the other side of the city and gathered all the troops together near the south side of Buena Vista.

Taylor faced all of his men as they formed a semicircle before him and told them of their conversation with the peaceful citizens of Buena Vista, in which they learned that 1,663 Mexican soldiers had been killed in the battles. He then shared the news that Santa Anna had fled with the remainder of his troops out the north side of Buena Vista during the night. He was sure they were headed back to Mexico City.

A victorious, rousing cheer of elation rose from the troops. Then the general told them that after they buried their dead soldiers in a mass grave about a half mile from the south side of the city, they must hurry back to Fort Polk. They would cross the Rio Grande on the way, and he would send President Polk a telegram from the army post at Corpus Christi Bay and report the results of the Buena Vista battles.

Taylor looked over at the Kane brothers, then at Lieutenant Grant, then at Colonel Leyden. He spoke loudly so all the soldiers could hear. "Men, I have an announcement. Because I have the authority to do so, I am promoting the three Kane brothers and Lieutenant Ulysses Grant because of the courageous and unselfish deed they did in battle on Monday. They took out eight Mexican soldiers who had closed in on Colonel Vince Leyden and were no doubt going to kill him. They most certainly saved the colonel's life."

There was a round of cheering and applause among the crowd of soldiers.

The general went on to tell his troops that Lieutenants Alamo Kane and Ulysses Grant would be promoted to captain, and Privates Alex and Abel Kane would be promoted to first lieutenant. The men cheered them.

The general then told his men that once they had buried their dead, they would head for Fort Polk. Since they would lose some time because of the mass burial, they would travel an extra two hours a day so they could get to Fort Polk within seven days. Taylor went on to say that they had 54 wounded men, and they would be loaded in some of the wagons so the medics could care for them on the trip.

The troops were then dismissed to lay hold of as many shovels as were available and begin digging the mass grave while the rest began bringing the bodies to the burial ground.

Late in the morning on Saturday, February 27, General Taylor and his troops arrived at the army post on Corpus Christi Bay, where they were warmly welcomed. The soldiers there rejoiced when they heard of the victory over Santa Anna and his troops at Buena Vista.

General Taylor then went to the telegraph office and sent a telegram to President Polk, telling him of the large number of Mexican soldiers who were killed in the two days of fierce battle and that Santa Anna had taken the others and fled. He gave the president the number of American soldiers killed and told him they would be back at Fort Polk within three days.

Taylor added in the telegram that he had promoted the Kane brothers and Lieutenant Grant for bravery and courage beyond the call of duty in saving the life of Colonel Leyden in battle. He told the president the new ranks he had given to each of the four men.

Since it was now almost noon, the general decided that he and his men would eat lunch before they moved on.

Just over an hour later, as Taylor and his men were finishing their lunch, the post telegrapher walked up to where the general was eating with some of his officers and handed him a telegram. "Sir, this is from President Polk. In a telegram to me, he said this telegram would follow and that if you and your men had already left, I was to send a rider to catch you and deliver the telegram."

Taylor smiled as he took the folded paper in hand. "Thank you, Corporal."

The officers sitting close to the general observed his face while he silently read the telegram.

Taylor read it slowly. A hot lump rose in his throat when he read that President Polk was very upset that 746 American soldiers were killed in the two-day battle. He asked the general if he had obeyed his command to avoid battling the Mexican troops on the steep mountainsides and rough terrain around Buena Vista.

Quite irritated at the president's question, the general suddenly stood up and walked away. The officers exchanged curious glances as they watched him walk stiffly to the telegraph office and step inside.

Sitting down with the telegrapher, Taylor said, "You recall the question that the president asked me in the telegram, don't you?"

"Yes sir," the corporal replied. "He asked if you had obeyed his command to avoid fighting the Mexicans on the mountainsides and in the rough terrain around Buena Vista."

"Then you will understand the reply I want you to send him right now."

The telegrapher frowned a bit and nodded. "All right, sir."

The corporal scribbled the message down on a piece of paper as the ruffled general dictated it. Taylor told the president that he *did* lead his troops to do battle on the steep mountainsides and in the rough terrain and that that was why they were victorious. He explained that upon arriving at Buena Vista, he could see that he and his troops would have an advantage over the Mexican soldiers if they barricaded themselves in the rough terrain, and he was right. Had he not done that, they wouldn't have killed 1,663 Mexican soldiers and defeated Santa Anna and the rest of his troops and sent them running away.

The general waited until the telegrapher had sent the message to President Polk. Then he returned to his men, who had finished their lunch. Moments later, General Taylor led his troops with all their cannons and wagons away from Corpus Christi Bay and headed toward Fort Polk.

As planned, General Taylor and his troops arrived at Fort Polk early in the afternoon on Tuesday, March 2. They had only been there a couple of hours when a rider from the army post at Corpus Christi Bay arrived with a telegram for General Taylor from President Polk. The general read the telegram alone in his office.

President Polk was very upset. In the telegram, Polk told Taylor that if he had handled the battle at Buena Vista like Polk had commanded, not nearly as many American soldiers would have been killed. Polk said he was glad they were victorious, but as commander in chief of the United States Armed Forces, he was relieving Taylor from his position because of his disobedience. He commanded Taylor to head for Washington,

D.C., immediately and to report to him upon arrival.

Polk went on to say that he had sent General Winfield Scott and some sixty-eight hundred troops to land an amphibian assault on the Gulf of Mexico shores of Vera Cruz, Mexico. He was placing Colonel Vince Leyden in charge of the five thousand Fort Polk troops, and they were to head out immediately toward Vera Cruz and join General Scott in carrying forth the battle against the Mexican troops there. Taylor was to put this telegram in the hands of Colonel Leyden so he would know his new official position as appointed by the president of the United States and follow its instructions to the letter.

The president went on to explain that under his orders, General Scott would halt the ships carrying him and his troops on the beach at Collado, Mexico, some three miles southeast of Vera Cruz, on March 9. Scott would be expecting Colonel Leyden and his Fort Polk men to be there to join him in attacking Vera Cruz.

With a cold, sinking feeling gripping him, General Taylor found Colonel Leyden and placed the telegram in his hands, telling him to read it right then. Taylor watched as the colonel's head bobbed as he silently read the telegram. When he was finished, he looked at Taylor and said, "General, I'm so sorry this has happened. You don't deserve to be treated like this."

Taylor shrugged, trying to keep calm. "Well, it's been done now, my friend. I'm riding out of here immediately for Corpus Christi Bay. I'll leave the horse at the army post there so you can have it picked up later, and I'll take a boat from Corpus Christi up to Galveston. I can catch a train there that will take me to New Orleans, where I can catch a train to Washington, D.C."

Leyden frowned. "Do you want to call all the men together so you can tell them good-bye?"

Taylor's features paled. "It would be too hard. I'll just casually saddle my horse and ride away without explaining anything to anybody, even the guards at the gate. When I get to the army post, I'll send a telegram to President Polk, telling him you have taken over as he requested and that I am on my way to see him."

Colonel Leyden gathered his troops together after Taylor had ridden away and read them the telegram from the president. Within an hour, he had moved them out of Fort Polk. As they headed in the direction of Vera

Cruz, the colonel rode up to the Kane brothers and Captain Ulysses Grant and once again thanked them for saving his life at Buena Vista.

Feeling bad that General Taylor had been removed from his position of leadership over the Fort Polk troops but pleased that the stalwart and capable Colonel Leyden was alive to be assigned the position, Lieutenants Alex and Abel Kane, and Captains Alamo Kane and Ulysses Grant replied that they were very glad they had been able to subdue the eight Mexican soldiers that day and save his life.

21

On Thursday morning, March 4, Julia Kane, her children, and her sisters-in-law were in Washington-on-the-Brazos buying groceries and other household supplies at the general store. Julia was pushing a wheeled chair, provided by the store for small children, with two-year-old Amber strapped on it. Angela O'Fallon had met them there.

While the women were walking past the grocery shelves looking at different items, they saw a young man come into the store and place a stack of that day's edition of the *Washington Post* on a small table.

As the young man hurried away, Angela walked to the table and picked up a copy. When she saw the headlines, she gasped, turned toward her sisters-in-law, and held up the newspaper so they could see. Eyes wide, she said, "Look! Our soldiers were victorious over Santa Anna and fifteen thousand of his troops in two big battles at Buena Vista! One of the battles was on Monday, February 22, and the other on Tuesday, February 23!"

The other women, as well as the boys, rushed to Angela, their eyes bulging.

Angela still held the paper so they could read the headlines. "See? General Zachary Taylor and his troops did it! They were victorious over Santa Anna and fifteen thousand of his troops!"

The women and the boys knew that Alamo, Alex, and Abel served under General Taylor, so of course, they had been in the battles at Buena Vista.

"There's a large article about the Buena Vista conflict right here under the headlines," Angela said, skimming the text. "It's a report from President Polk giving the details of the battles that took place there. I'll read it to you."

Julia, Libby, Vivian, and the boys listened intently as Angela read the article to them. When they heard that 1,663 Mexican soldiers had been killed in the battles, and that Santa Anna had fled in the middle of the night after the battle, taking the remainder of his soldiers with him, they were amazed. But when they heard that 746 American soldiers were killed, everyone's face dropped.

Angela's lips began to tremble as the reality of this horrible news hit her heart. With tears of frustration welling up in her eyes, she took a quick breath and swallowed hard. "Oh . . . m-my b-brothers may have been among those 746 American soldiers killed! There's no way for us to know!"

Shedding their own tears, Libby and Vivian took hold of each other, their lips trembling and their brows furrowed.

Julia drew her boys close to her side, next to the wheeled chair that held little Amber. Tears spilled down her cheeks. "You're right, Angela," she said, her voice quivering. "There's no way for us to know."

Realizing that their father and uncles might've been killed, six-year-old Abram and five-year-old Andy began crying as well. Two-year-old Amber looked wide eyed at her weeping brothers.

Ten-year-old Adam bit his lower lip and kicked at the floor. He fought the tears that were working their way into his eyes. He took his role as the "man of the house" while his stepfather was away seriously and felt it would be wrong to let the others know of his own fears about his loved ones. He must put on a brave front, displaying his trust that God was taking care of his stepfather and uncles.

Julia could see that Adam was trying to be brave about the situation, and she admired him for it. She looked down at her two youngest sons. "Abram, Andy . . . we must trust that the Lord has taken care of your father and your uncles as we ask Him to every day."

Adam nodded his agreement.

Clinging to Libby, Vivian looked around at Angela and Julia and said in a quivering voice, "I think it's almost worse to stay home and wonder what's happening in this war than to be in the midst of the battles."

Wiping at her own tears, Julia wanted to encourage Angela, Libby, Vivian, and her two youngest boys. Taking a deep breath, she reached into her purse and took out the small Bible she carried with her. "Let's not jump to conclusions. Let me read you something here in Psalm 28 that has been such a help to me lately. I pray many times a day for Alamo's safety in this war, as well as Alex and Abel's safety. Listen."

Julia then read Psalm 28:6–7 to them: "Blessed be the LORD, because he hath heard the voice of my supplications. The LORD is my strength and my shield; my heart trusted in him, and I am helped: therefore my heart greatly rejoiceth; and with my song will I praise him."

Angela, Libby, and Vivian were sniffling and wiping tears.

"Now, listen again to these words," Julia said. " 'My heart trusted in him, and I am helped.' Let them sink in. 'My heart trusted in *him,* and I am helped.' Our hearts must trust in our wonderful God to hear our supplications on our loved ones' behalf. And how wonderful that right here in verse 6, it says that the Lord indeed *has* heard the voice of our supplications!"

Angela wiped at her tears. "You're right, Julia! Our wonderful Lord *has* heard our prayers for my brothers! We must believe that they are still alive and well!"

Libby and Vivian spoke their agreement, as did Abram and Andy.

"That's good preaching, Mama!" Adam said. "Those two verses are really what we need right now!"

Julia smiled and patted his head as Angela said, "Thank you, Julia, for pointing out those verses to us. I am very encouraged now!"

"Me too!" said Vivian.

"And me too!" Libby chimed in.

Six-year-old Abram clapped his hands together. "Mama! I know it's okay! Papa 'n' Uncle Alex 'n' Uncle Abel are alive!"

A wonderful peace came over the Kane family, and they went on with their shopping.

As scheduled, on the morning of March 9, Colonel Vince Leyden and his 5,000 troops, with their wagons and cannons, arrived at Collado, on the beach of the Gulf of Mexico. At the same time, out on the gulf, they could see ships carrying General Winfield Scott and his 6,800 troops heading toward the beach.

Moments later, General Scott and his men were walking down the gangplanks of the ships. The troops carried guns and ammunition.

Colonel Leyden and General Scott had met before and warmly shook hands as Leyden greeted the general at the bottom of the gangplank.

The two commanders discussed the approach they would take to surround the city of Vera Cruz, which was three miles up the Gulf Coast. General Scott and Colonel Leyden then stood before all 11,800 troops while the general gave them the plan. He explained that Vera Cruz was built on the edge of the Gulf of Mexico, with some beach on its east side between the city and the water. Thus they could surround the city on all four sides.

Scott went on to explain that on the beach side, there were some large rock formations they could use for cover. He then told them that on the three other sides, in addition to rock formations, there were ditches and low spots and many places with trees and bushes on the edge of the low spots that would make good cover. He had learned this from doing a study on Mexico's towns and cities.

Colonel Leyden's cannons would take positions on all four sides in order to bombard the city from every direction.

Scott then made it known to everyone that the last he knew, General Juan Morales was in command of the Mexican troops inside the city and it was estimated that he had about 4,000 men. Scott explained that their task, as commanded by President Polk, was to capture Vera Cruz and hold the Mexican troops captive so they could move inland without hindrance from the troops in that city. They would have other cities to capture as they moved inland — the ultimate goal was to attack and capture Mexico City, which would result in the Mexican government being controlled by the United States.

Scott went on to tell the troops that his plan was first to surround the city, which of course would be seen by the Mexican soldiers and civilians. Although Vera Cruz had specially built twelve-foot-high rock walls all around the city, there were many gates in each wall. General Morales's soldiers would be on the walls and at the gates. Also, the civilians would be able to see the American troops from rooftops and the windows of tall buildings.

Once the city was surrounded, Scott would attempt to negotiate a surrender, but if it was refused, the Americans would bombard Vera Cruz with Colonel Leyden's cannons and back it up with rifle fire. They would keep it up despite the return fire that would certainly come from General Morales's troops until the Mexicans were forced to surrender.

With the plan understood by all 11,800 troops, they were led up the beach by General Scott with Colonel Leyden at his side.

When they reached Vera Cruz and began to spread out to surround the city under General Scott's orders, the Mexican troops, under the command of General Morales, immediately began firing rifles from the walls. The American troops had to scatter quickly to find protective positions from which to fire back, and soon the battle was on.

As commanded by General Scott, the cannons on all four sides of the city began unleashing cannonballs, some blasting the rock walls that surrounded it and some soaring over the walls to blast houses and tall buildings.

The American infantry and cavalry were firing away with their rifles from protective places in the surrounding fields and from the rock formations on the beach side. By the time darkness fell, many of the houses and business buildings inside the city were burning. Many moans and cries could be heard coming from behind the walls.

Having stayed with General Scott during the battle, in a ditch just south of Vera Cruz, Colonel Leyden turned to him and asked, "Sir, do you want to keep firing even though it's dark?"

"I think not, unless the Mexicans keep firing," replied the husky, thick-bodied Scott. "Let's send word to our troops to cease fire and see what happens."

Soldiers who were fighting from nearby positions were sent to carry the "cease fire" order. As the general and the colonel waited for the order to be carried to the troops, Scott said, "Well, Colonel, my plan to negotiate a surrender from General Morales once we had the city surrounded didn't pan out. The Mexican troops began firing immediately. So I'll send a messenger with a white flag to the front gate at sunrise and give Morales a chance to surrender."

"All we can do is try, General," the colonel replied. "Who are you going to send?"

"I have a sergeant who has done this kind of thing for me before. His name is Wade Jorgensen. He's good at it. Wade was born and raised in Georgia, and his family had neighbors from before the time Wade was born who moved there from Cuba and spoke Spanish. He picked up on it at a young age and speaks it fluently. He's perfect for this particular white-flag job."

Leyden nodded. "Sounds like it."

Moments later, when the American guns stopped firing, the Mexican guns followed suit. Many loud voices could be heard from behind the walls, however, as soldiers and civilians labored to douse the blazing fires from so many buildings inside the city.

At the same time, all around the outside of Vera Cruz, the American soldiers began building small fires in order to cook their suppers. Many men were delivering food from the wagons.

Several yards from the spot where the general and the colonel were eating their supper, Captain Alamo Kane, his brothers, and a number of other men who had fought in that particular area during the day's battle were also devouring their food.

While they ate and talked in the firelight, a corporal entered the area, looked around, and fixed his attention on a man he knew. The corporal stepped up to him. "Sergeant Jorgensen, General Scott wants to talk to you whenever you've finished eating."

The sergeant stood up and smiled. "I can talk to him now, Corporal Edwards. Do you know what he wants?"

Edwards nodded. "Yes. Since you are experienced at 'white flagging' and you can speak Spanish, he wants you to do so in the morning and offer General Morales the opportunity to surrender."

The men close by, including the Kane brothers and Captain Grant, noted that the corners of the sergeant's lips took on a tough, sharp set.

"All right," said the sergeant. "Let's go."

When the sergeant and the corporal walked away into the darkness, Alex looked at a lieutenant who had come with General Scott and said, "Takes a lot of courage to 'white flag' it in a situation like this. What's the sergeant's first name?"

"Wade," the lieutenant replied, looking up from his meal. "All of us who know Sergeant

Wade Jorgensen deeply admire him. He's got a lot of courage."

"Good for him," spoke up Alamo.

Many of the other men within the circle nodded and spoke their agreement.

Alamo noticed that Grant's eyes were abruptly fixed on the lieutenant. Suddenly he jumped to his feet, looking at the lieutenant. "Tom Jackson! I haven't seen you since West Point!"

Jackson smiled and rushed to Grant. They shook hands and talked about when they were students at the U.S. Military Academy together. This brought a blond-headed captain to his feet, who rushed to them and introduced himself as Robert E. Lee, saying he also had attended West Point.

All the other soldiers looked on and listened to the conversation between the three West Point graduates. The men learned that Captain Lee had graduated from the academy in 1829 and that Captain Grant and Lieutenant Jackson knew each other because they were at the academy together in 1843, the year Grant graduated. Jackson had graduated in the spring of 1846.

The next morning at sunrise, General Winfield Scott, Colonel Vince Leyden, and several of the men who were positioned for battle where they'd been the day before looked on as Sergeant Wade Jorgensen talked with General Juan Morales at Vera Cruz's main gate. Among those watching were the Kane brothers, Captain Grant, and Lieutenant Jackson.

Jorgensen had borrowed a cavalry horse to ride and was still in the saddle holding the white flag as General Morales looked up at him, fury written on his face. Scott, Leyden, and the men with them could hear the anger in Morales's voice but couldn't understand what he was saying.

"I don't understand Spanish at all, General," Leyden said, "but for sure, Morales doesn't like what Sergeant Jorgensen is saying."

"That's obvious," replied Scott just as they saw the sergeant wheel the horse about and gallop back toward them.

Just as Jorgensen was drawing up to Scott and Leyden, guns on all four sides of the city's walls opened fire. Jorgensen looked back toward the city, then slid from the saddle. "General Scott, I guess you can see that General Morales has refused to surrender."

"Yes, I can see," said the general as American troops opened fire on all four sides as well, cannons booming and rifles barking.

Within three minutes, Scott and Leyden and the fighting men in their area were in their positions among trees, bushes, and in ditches, also returning fire against the Mexicans.

As Mexican bullets chewed up dirt, striking rocks, trees, and bushes, and whistled all around them, Sergeant Jorgensen fired his rifle from a ditch with Alamo, his brothers, and Jackson.

Between shots, Alamo, who was closest to him, asked Jorgensen how he knew Spanish. The sergeant was aiming at a Mexican atop the wall. He squeezed the trigger, and the Mexican buckled as the slug hit him and he fell from the wall. More rifle fire came from the Mexican soldiers along the wall as Jorgensen said, "I learned Spanish from some Cuban neighbors we had when I was growing up."

Alamo fired his revolver in return and was about to say something else to Jorgensen when the sergeant suddenly took a bullet in the chest and fell to the bottom of the ditch.

Alex, who was closest, fired a shot toward the Mexicans, then looked down at the sergeant. "He hit bad, Alamo?"

"I'm not sure," Alamo replied. "I'll check on him."

Abel Kane and Thomas Jackson both fired

their guns while turning to look at Jorgensen at the bottom of the ditch.

"Alamo's going to see about him, Lieutenant," Abel said to Jackson.

Jackson nodded and fired his gun toward the wall again.

The firing went on as Alamo dropped to his knees beside the fallen sergeant and examined his wound. Alamo was sure the slug had hit Jorgensen in his heart. He was still alive and gasping for breath, but Alamo feared he was dying.

The sergeant's eyes were still clear as he looked up at Alamo, clutching his chest wound.

Alex looked down between shots and asked again if the sergeant was hit bad.

Alamo nodded. "Yes. Pretty bad."

Both Abel and the lieutenant heard Alamo's words.

Speaking loud above the roar of the battle, Alamo bent low and said, "Sergeant, tell me something."

"Y-yes sir?"

"Do you know the Lord Jesus Christ as your Saviour?"

Jorgensen grimaced from pain and rolled his head back and forth. "No sir, but one of my aunts used to talk to me about being saved when I was in my late teens. She even showed me in the Bible several times about salvation."

Encouraged that the incorruptible seed spoken of in 1 Peter 1:23 had been sown in the sergeant's heart, Alamo quoted Scripture after Scripture, giving the wounded man the gospel and God's plan of salvation.

Between shots, Alex and Abel heard their brother quoting the verses to Sergeant Jorgensen, as did Jackson.

There was a sudden lull in the exchange of gunshots between the Mexicans and the Americans on that side of the city. At the same instant, Alamo bent his head low, putting his lips close to Jorgensen's left ear and telling him what to say to the Lord if he wanted to be saved. Alamo heard the dying man, in repentance of his sin, immediately call on the Lord Jesus, asking Him to come into his heart and save him.

The Kane brothers and Jackson also heard the dying sergeant call on the Lord to save him.

Still kneeling over Jorgensen, Alamo saw him take his last breath. His eyes closed, and his body went limp. Alamo felt for a pulse. There was none. Sergeant Wade Jorgensen was dead.

A lump rose in Alamo's throat when he saw a smile on the dead man's lips.

There was still a lull in the exchange of gunfire, which gave Alex, Abel, and Thomas Jackson a moment to rush to where Alamo was still kneeling over Wade Jorgensen's body.

Alex said, "Alamo, Abel and I heard him call on Jesus to save him!"

"Yes, we did!" said Abel. "How's he doing?"

Alamo ran his gaze between them. "He just died."

Alex blinked. "Oh, Alamo, I'm so glad you were able to bring him to salvation before he died."

"Me too!" said Abel.

Alamo nodded and looked at the dead man's face. "Do you fellas see anything amazing here?"

"Oh! Look at that smile!" exclaimed Abel.

"Yes!" gasped Alex. "Look at the smile on his lips!"

Lieutenant Jackson leaned past Alex and Abel and looked at the dead man's face as Alex said, "Well, Alamo, I can say again, 'High Is the Eagle'!"

The Kane brothers noticed tears in Jackson's eyes as he said to Alamo, "Captain Kane, I commend you for what you did. No wonder that smile is on Sergeant Jorgensen's lips! He saw the Saviour's face as he was dying, and he's with Him in heaven right now!"

Alamo smiled. "Lieutenant Jackson, it sounds to me like you know what being born again is!"

Jackson smiled and brushed tears from his cheeks. "I sure do! I received the Lord Jesus as my Saviour shortly after I graduated from West Point."

"Wonderful!" said Alamo. "I'm glad to know that you're my brother in Christ!"

Alex and Abel said "amen" to that as well.

Jackson then asked Alex about his words to Alamo: "High is the eagle."

Since there was still a lull in the firing between the Americans and Mexicans, Alex told Lieutenant Jackson the story of Alamo's leading Corporal Lance Brooks to the Lord after the Palo Alto battle and of the sermon their pastor preached soon afterward, with Lance in the congregation. In it he commended Alamo for winning Lance to Jesus. Alex went on to explain how Pastor Patrick O'Fallon showed from the Bible that soul winners are like high-flying eagles. Pastor O'Fallon had titled his sermon "High Is the Eagle."

Jackson shook his head in wonderment and smiled. "I'm so thrilled to hear this! That's a tremendous way to describe soul winning! And, gentlemen, let me say this, I am so glad to know that *you* are *my* brothers in Christ!"

Suddenly, gunfire roared from the walls of the city, and the American cannons quickly responded. Within seconds, the Kane brothers and Lieutenant Jackson were once again blasting away at the enemy troops on the wall.

22

The Mexican troops under General Juan Morales inside Vera Cruz put up a stiff resistance, and fighting went on day after day.

When night fell each day, the guns on both sides went silent. At dawn, the guns would roar once again.

The casualties on the Mexican side were quite obviously a great deal higher than those of the Americans because of the American cannons.

On the afternoon of March 22, General Winfield Scott was certain his cannons were taking a more devastating toll than ever. There were now large fractures in the stone walls that surrounded the city, and more and more American artillery was taking the lives of Mexican soldiers.

At sunrise the next day, General Scott once again sent a rider with a white flag to General Morales with a message demanding that he surrender or more bombardment would come. Morales angrily refused.

Determined to conquer the city, General Scott had his cannons bombard the city heavily day after day. Finally, at sunrise on Saturday, March 27, Morales led what was left of his troops out of Vera Cruz, and they fled speedily toward Mexico City.

The Americans then captured the city.

The next day, General Scott collected all of his troops, including those who had come with Colonel Leyden from Fort Polk. He announced that a total of 243 American soldiers had been killed in the Vera Cruz battles, and that the few wounded men who were still alive were doing well with the help of medics. Scott told the troops that from what he had gathered from some of the citizens of the city, nearly 1,200 Mexican soldiers had been killed.

The general then told the troops that since President Polk had given him full charge in leading the American troops in Mexico, he had decided to attack Mexico City now, which was just over one hundred fifty miles west of Vera Cruz. He reminded the troops that the president's orders were to capture Mexico City and bring the war to an end.

Scott explained that he would be assigning 800 of them to stay and occupy Vera

Cruz under the command of Colonel Leyden. The few wounded men would remain with Colonel Leyden for further care. This would leave Scott some 10,700 men to go with him to capture Mexico City.

With the help of several officers, the names of the 800 men who were to stay with Colonel Vince Leyden were called out, and those men gathered with the colonel in a large spot nearby.

General Scott then spoke to the crowd of soldiers who had gathered in a semicircle before him and told them that when they headed for Mexico City, they would have to move slowly. Along the way, they would take several days to simply stop and rest in order to give both men and horses time to recover some of the energy that was expended in the Vera Cruz battles. He assured them that if they could capture the capital city, the war would be over.

Scott's 10,700 men cheered him, letting him know they agreed with his plan and would fight for victory.

The general then called Colonel Leyden to him and told him to put some of his men in one of the boats the Mexicans kept on the beach at Vera Cruz and have them go to the U.S. Army post at Corpus Christi Bay and send a telegram to President Polk, informing him of the victory at Vera Cruz. They were to take the list of the 243 American soldiers killed in the Vera Cruz battles and put the names in the telegram so the president could have the list published in newspapers across the country. That way their families, who had a right to know, would be informed of their deaths. In the telegram, they were also to inform President Polk that he and his 10,700 men were heading toward Mexico City to capture it and bring the war to an end. Colonel Leyden replied that he would send the men to Corpus Christi Bay right away.

Scott ordered the men who were going with him to Mexico City to immediately prepare for the trip. They would leave within the hour.

When it came time to pull out, General Scott bade farewell to Colonel Leyden and the 800 men who would remain with him at Vera Cruz, and took his 10,700 troops westward toward Mexico City. Among those troops were the Kane brothers, Captain Ulysses Grant, Captain Robert E. Lee, and Lieutenant Thomas J. Jackson.

When General Scott and his forces — which included ammunition, food wagons, and the cannons attached to the wagons — were some three or four miles from Vera

Cruz, the general halted the wagons, infantrymen, and cavalrymen and called for Captain Lee to come to him.

Lee rode his horse up to where the general sat in his saddle. "Yes, General? What can I do for you?"

"I want you to take fifty cavalrymen, ride ahead of us, and scout out this road that leads to Mexico City for several miles. I have a feeling that General Morales may be contacting Mexican military posts on his way to Mexico City to set up a trap for us."

Lee nodded. "Could be, sir. How far ahead do you want us to go?"

"Far enough to allow yourselves to make it back to us by sundown. If you don't see any sign of a trap, I'll send you farther ahead tomorrow. You can pick the fifty men to go with you."

"All right, General." Lee nodded. "See you at sundown."

Moments later, Captain Lee and his fifty chosen cavalrymen rode westward at a gallop. General Scott and the rest of the troops kept moving their relatively slow pace.

The hours passed, and at sundown General Scott and the troops were setting up camp when Captain Lee and his cavalrymen came riding back.

Lee trotted up to Scott, who was in conversation with a few soldiers, and drew rein. Dismounting quickly, Lee stepped up to the general, his face pallid, and said, "Sir, there's a trap set up, all right. Santa Anna himself has entrenched several thousand men in Cerro Gordo Pass. I estimate it to be about thirty-five miles west of Vera Cruz . . . some twenty miles or so from where we stand right now."

General Scott rubbed the back of his neck. "Wow. Santa Anna himself. He must've figured we would be victorious at Vera Cruz and head for Mexico City."

"That's exactly what came to my mind, General," Lee said. "My men and I hid our horses in a draw and crept up close to the pass on foot. We actually saw Santa Anna moving among his men, and we recognized some of the Mexican soldiers from the Vera Cruz battle. No doubt they joined up with whatever troops Santa Anna had already entrenched in Cerro Gordo Pass. We looked the Mexican troops over carefully, and we estimate that altogether Santa Anna has some 12,000 troops occupying the pass."

The heavyset general squared his jaw and looked straight into Lee's eyes. "Captain Lee, I very much appreciate this information. Let me tell you, though, that with my 10,700 men, we can whip Santa Anna and his 12,000."

Lee smiled. "I have no doubt of that, General. We sure will."

Scott grinned. "We'll continue our march in the morning. Then we'll find a good hiding spot and take several days to get everybody rested up before moving on and engaging in battle with Santa Anna and his troops in Cerro Gordo Pass."

"Sounds like a good plan to me, sir."

On Tuesday afternoon, April 6, Pastor Patrick and Angela O'Fallon rode their buggy onto the Diamond K Ranch, waving at some of the ranch people as they headed for the big ranch house, where they expected to find Julia and her children. The ranch people smiled and waved back.

When Patrick guided the buggy up to the front of the big house, Adam, Abram, and Andy were playing tag near the porch. All three spotted their aunt and uncle instantly. The two younger boys ran toward the buggy while Adam made a dash up the porch steps and through the house to let his mother know that Aunt Angela and Uncle Patrick were there.

Less than three minutes later, Adam preceded his mother, who was being followed by two-year-old Amber, onto the front porch. When Julia saw Patrick and Angela hugging Abram and Andy, she smiled. "Well, if it isn't my favorite pastor and his lovely wife!"

Angela giggled, let go of Andy, and rushed to Julia, who was standing at the edge of the porch. She hugged Julia's neck tightly, then leaned down to open her arms to Amber, who smiled and said, "Auntie Angela," leaning into her grasp.

When Patrick had hugged Adam, Julia, and Amber, he pulled a folded newspaper from under his belt. "Julia, I've got some news here in today's edition of the *Washington Post* about General Scott and his troops. Have you seen it?"

Julia shook her head.

"Is Papa Abram in the house?" Patrick asked.

"Uh-huh." Julia nodded. "He's in his room."

"How about we send Adam to go bring Libby and Vivian so they can hear the news, and I'll go get Abram?"

"Sure." Julia turned to her oldest son. "Adam, will you go get Aunt Libby and Aunt Vivian for me?"

"Sure!" replied the ten-year-old as he took off running in the direction of their houses.

Less than fifteen minutes later, the Kane

family was gathered together on the front porch of the big ranch house, and all were comfortably seated except Patrick. He stood before them with the newspaper in his hand. Little Amber was now on Grandpa Abram's lap.

Patrick then read them the front page article of the *Washington Post,* which told of President Polk having received a telegraph message a few days earlier from Colonel Vince Leyden at Vera Cruz. Colonel Leyden had informed the president that the American troops under General Winfield Scott had won a decisive victory over the Mexican troops at Vera Cruz.

Patrick went on to say, "In the article, it tells that some 1,200 Mexicans were killed in the battles fought there and only 243 American soldiers were killed. Some were also wounded."

Angela's husband noted the fear that claimed the faces of the adults and the three boys. He smiled. "Don't be afraid. I said this was good news. There is a list of the 243 American soldiers who were killed, and Alamo, Alex, and Abel aren't on the list!"

There were sighs of relief, and the three boys clapped their hands.

"I'm sorry that Americans were killed," Patrick said, "but I have to praise the Lord that our loved ones are still alive. Wounded maybe, but still alive."

Grandpa Abram said, "The way we've prayed, they're probably not on the wounded list either!"

Everyone spoke their agreement. Then Patrick went on to tell them the newspaper said that on March 28, General Scott left Colonel Leyden with 800 troops to occupy Vera Cruz and headed toward Mexico City with some 10,700 men. General Scott intended to capture and occupy Mexico City, which he believed would bring the war to an end.

There was much rejoicing among the Kane family at the Vera Cruz victory. Adam summoned Cort Whitney, and Pastor Patrick told him the story as well. Cort told the family that he would quickly spread the word to the ranch hands and their families.

As Cort hurried away, Patrick led the Kane family in prayer, thanking the Lord that Alamo, Alex, and Abel had not been killed in the Vera Cruz battles and asking Him that if any of the three had been wounded, He would heal them quickly. He then gave praise to the Lord for this important victory and asked Him to give victory to the American troops when they moved in to capture and occupy Mexico City and bring the war to an end.

When Patrick closed his prayer, Julia's three boys stood to their feet and happily praised the Lord that their papa and uncles were still alive. Julia left her chair, wrapped her arms around her boys, and shed tears of relief. At the same time, the other members of the Kane family were embracing and shedding tears of relief that their loved ones had not been killed in the Vera Cruz battles.

On April 14, Mexican president Antonio López de Santa Anna and his twelve thousand men were ready to do battle with the American troops they had observed coming toward Cerro Gordo Pass. Well positioned, they opened fire as soon as the Americans were within rifle range.

With bullets speeding toward them, the adept General Scott led his troops quickly to cover amid rocks, gullies, ditches, and small forests that would strategically place them to do battle. Within minutes, the Americans were returning rifle fire, causing the Mexicans to run for cover in the pass.

Moments later, things got much worse for the Mexicans: the American cannons were rolled into place and began to bombard them. The Mexicans had no cannons.

A bloody battle ensued, with cannonballs

striking Mexican troops where they were entrenched in the high areas of the pass.

The fighting went on until darkness fell, and then there was silence.

General Scott led his troops to a forested area out of sight from Cerro Gordo Pass, and they set up camp amid thick trees and heavy underbrush. The general assigned a sufficient number of men as lookouts to keep watch all around the camp in case Santa Anna sent troops to sneak up on them.

When the men who served as cooks had prepared the evening meal for the troops, the Kane brothers and Lieutenant Jackson sat on the ground and ate supper together.

During the meal, the Kane brothers asked Jackson to tell them about himself. He told them he was born and raised in Clarksburg, Virginia. He was an only child. The early death of his father, who left little support for the family, and his mother's subsequent death shortly thereafter caused him to grow up in the homes of relatives in Virginia. He had little opportunity for formal education in his early years, but he received an appointment in 1842 to the U.S. Military Academy at West Point. Immediately after graduation in the spring of 1846, he was assigned to serve under General Scott.

Jackson then asked about the Kane brothers, and they told him of their grandparents' and parents' Irish backgrounds and of growing up in Boston and how the three brothers ended up in Texas on the Diamond K Ranch. Jackson was interested to learn from Alex and Abel that their youngest brother's name was actually Alan and how he obtained the nickname Alamo because of his courage and exceptional military service related to the battle at the Alamo in March of 1836.

When supper was over, the Kane brothers and Thomas Jackson had a time of prayer together in which they praised God for their salvation in Jesus Christ and asked Him for victory at Cerro Gordo Pass and Mexico City. They read their Bibles together just before slipping into their bedrolls for the night.

At dawn the next morning, under General Scott's orders, the well-armed American troops positioned themselves, along with their cannons, at strategic locations and began bombarding the Mexicans with bullets and cannonballs. The Mexicans answered with rifle fire.

The battle raged for days. At dawn on Sunday morning, April 18, the roar of American cannons filled the air, chillingly announcing the beginning of another day of warfare at Cerro Gordo Pass. As the morning hours passed, the rifle fire from the Americans was as intense as the cannon fire. Men were being killed and wounded on both sides, but the Mexicans were by far getting the worst of it.

As bullets ripped away at the Mexicans and cannonball shrapnel took its toll, the Americans could see many wounded Mexicans lying on the ground. Their intense body movements showed their physical pain, and some cried out loudly in agony.

As General Scott hunkered low behind some four-foot-high boulders and looked around at his men, suddenly Alamo dashed to the general's side, hunkered down with him, and pointed over the tops of the boulders. "General Scott! Do you see what's happening out there in the pass?"

Scott blinked and glanced at Alamo blankly. "What do you mean?"

Still pointing, Alamo said, "Take a look! Those Mexican soldiers on their feet are shooting their wounded men in the heads, killing them!"

General Scott bit his lower lip as he took note of the killing of the wounded and nodded. "I've heard that this has happened under Santa Anna before. He gives his soldiers orders to shoot their wounded to put them out of their misery."

Alamo looked around at the Americans who were firing from their assigned positions, and he could see their eyes bulging as they watched Mexican bullets killing Mexicans.

As the day wore on, Santa Anna could see that he and his men wouldn't be able to withstand the enemy's cannon fire. He began telling his troops to retreat out of Cerro Gordo Pass at the west end a few hundred at a time. Then he jumped on his horse and led in the retreat.

General Scott and his men saw what was happening. Scott swung into his saddle and ordered his troops to follow him as he headed into the pass after the retreating Mexicans. There were shouts of victory among the American soldiers as they entered the pass, their guns ready.

On the summit of a sharp-peaked hill in Cerro Gordo Pass, some forty Mexican soldiers — rifles in hand — who had not yet retreated were standing under a Mexican flag on a tall pole, watching the Americans coming toward them.

Among approximately the same number of American soldiers who were closing in on the Mexicans were the Kane brothers and Thomas Jackson. Guns blazed on both sides, but the Americans were much more accurate than the Mexicans. As all the Mexicans went down from the American gunfire, Jackson dashed to the flagpole, flattened it to the ground, and ripped the flag off the pole. He waved it over his head, shouting to his comrades, "We've captured the Mexican flag!"

The Americans cheered wildly.

Before the sun had set that day, Santa Anna and his remaining troops had completely vacated Cerro Gordo Pass in fear and confusion, leaving some 5,000 dead Mexican soldiers behind.

Before darkness fell, General Scott had his officers take a count of the dead and wounded American soldiers. There were 46 wounded men being cared for by the medics. The officers reported to General Scott that they had 198 men to bury. For those 10,400 who were still unharmed, the road to Mexico City was now open.

The next morning, after the dead American soldiers had been buried near one of the forested areas, General Scott stood before his men and told them they would stay there and occupy the pass until they could get reinforcements to accompany them to Mexico City. He then assigned several of his cavalrymen to ride back to Texas immediately and round up more soldiers from some of the nearby army posts.

When the cavalrymen had ridden away, the general turned his attention on the Kane brothers, who were standing in the crowd near the front with Captain Grant, Captain Lee, and Lieutenant Jackson. "Captain Kane," he said with a smile, "I need to talk to you and your brothers."

The Kane brothers approached the general, and he led them to a spot where he could talk to them without being heard by any of the other men.

Scott ran his gaze from one brother to the other. "I want you men to take a wagon and go to the army post at Corpus Christi Bay. Captain Kane, I want you to send a telegram to President Polk for me. Tell him about the battles here at Cerro Gordo Pass, how many Mexicans were killed, how many we lost, and tell him that we need more men with which to go to Mexico City, conquer it, and occupy it, which will end the war."

"We'll be glad to do that for you, General," said Alamo.

Alex and Abel both nodded their assent to Alamo's words.

"Thank you, men," Scott said. "Now, I

know that the Diamond K Ranch is not too far from Corpus Christi Bay, so after you send the telegram for me, while you're that close to home, I want you to go there and spend a day and a night with your family. After that, of course, hurry back here."

This put happy smiles on the faces of the Kane brothers. They each shook General Scott's hand, assuring him that they would stay only one day and night with their family.

Alamo took his eyes off the general long enough to look at his brothers and say joyfully, "Oh boy! A soft bed under a sound roof, some good ol' home cooking, with my lovely Julie and my beautiful children around the table. It doesn't get any better than that!"

"Amen!" Abel responded. "And, of course, most of my time will be spent with my beautiful Vivian!"

"Right!" said Alex. "And mine with my beautiful Libby!"

In Washington, D.C., on Friday morning, April 23, President Polk was at his desk in the White House when his secretary entered with the telegram that had been sent from General Winfield Scott by Captain Alamo Kane. The president was pleased with the message of victory for the American troops in the battles that took place at Cerro Gordo Pass and that the cocky Santa Anna had been put on the run. Polk was saddened at the deaths of the American soldiers at Cerro Gordo but elated to learn of the large number of Mexican soldiers who had been killed.

Polk instantly wired forts in southern Texas, ordering that troops rush to Cerro Gordo Pass, where they would join with General Scott and his troops in marching to Mexico City with the intention of capturing the capitol city and bringing the Mexican-American War to an end.

23

On Monday, May 3, Julia Kane and Daisy Haycock were having a busy morning changing all the beds in the big ranch house and washing the sheets and the blankets. Spring had definitely come to southeast Texas, and the sun was shining down brightly from a cloudless sky.

Julia, with Daisy's help, hung the sweet-smelling laundry on the clothesline in the backyard while a warm, gentle breeze flapped the clean sheets and blankets in the bright sunshine.

Daisy looked up toward the sun and gasped.

Julia looked at her, frowning. "What's wrong, Daisy?"

The gray-haired woman replied, "Honey, where has the time gone? By the position of the sun up there, it's almost noon, and we're having guests for lunch. I don't know what I'll fix for lunch this close to noon."

Julia grinned. "That's okay, Daisy. It's only Lance and Andrea, and I'm sure they're not picky about what they have for lunch. In fact, they're so enamored with each other, they probably won't even know what they're eating!"

Daisy giggled. "You're right on that score, honey! I'm sure we have some chicken left over from supper yesterday. I'll head for the kitchen right now and make up some chicken salad. We have bread I made early this morning, and there's some freshly churned butter. There's also some cornmeal sweet cake and apple pie. I think we'll be all right."

"Sounds delicious to me, Daisy," Julia replied, smiling. "You go on now, and I'll finish hanging up the wash. I'll be right in to help you."

"Okay," Daisy said cheerfully, as she hiked up the hem of her dress a bit and hurried to the house.

Within a few minutes, Julia had finished hanging up the wash. Bending over to pick up the basket that had held the wet laundry, she rubbed the slight ache in the small of her back, tucked some stray curls back into the bun at the nape of her neck, and glanced at the sheets and blankets on the clotheslines as they flapped in the breeze.

Smiling, Julia said in a low voice, "Nothing smells as sweet as laundry dried under God's warm sun and soft breezes."

Just as she turned to head toward the house with the laundry basket in hand, Julia heard happy shouting and laughter coming from the front of the house.

Setting the basket down, she ran in that direction. Seconds later, she rounded the corner of the house and nearly fell at the sight before her. Alex and Libby were embracing, as were Abel and Vivian. Alamo was bending over and hugging his three boys with his back toward Julia.

Adam looked past his stepfather and saw his mother. "Papa, there's Mama!"

Alamo let go of the boys, spun around, and spotted Julia. She was running toward him, her cheeks wet with tears. Alamo picked her up off her feet and swung her around, hugging her tightly. "My sweetheart! My sweetheart!"

At that moment, Grandpa Abram, who had been watching little Amber inside the house, came out the front door with her in his arms.

"Papa!" shouted Amber as her grandfather descended the porch steps.

As Abram drew up with Amber, she reached toward her papa. Alamo took her into his arms. "My *other* sweetheart!"

Julia giggled at Alamo's words, wiping happy tears from her cheeks while he hugged and kissed his little daughter. At the same time, Abram was hugging his other two soldier sons. After a couple of minutes, Abram came to Alamo with his arms open wide. Julia took Amber from her husband and stood her by her brothers, then watched Alamo and his father clamp hugs on each other.

Julia dashed to Alex and Abel, hugged them both, kissed their cheeks, and welcomed them home, saying that she had read about their victorious battle at Cerro Gordo Pass in the *Washington Post* and she was glad they had not been wounded. She then hurried back to her husband.

When Alamo and his father let go of each other, Abram stepped back, knowing that Julia wanted to be in Alamo's arms again. Alamo wrapped Julia in an embrace and held her close to his heart.

More happy tears ran down her cheeks, and she said with a shaking voice, "Oh, darling, I'm so glad you're all right. You haven't been wounded. I just told Alex and Abel that on Saturday we had read about your victorious battle at Cerro Gordo Pass in the *Washington Post*."

"Yes! Praise the Lord, we won that one too!" said Alamo.

Then Julia looked at her brothers-in-law as they were hugging Lance Brooks and Andrea Voss, who had just arrived. Alamo spotted Lance and Andrea at the same time.

When Lance and Andrea had been hugged by all three of the Kane brothers, Julia went into her husband's arms again. "How long will you be home, darling?"

Alamo glanced at his brothers and their wives. "Julie, sweetheart, we just have tonight. We have to head back to Cerro Gordo Pass early tomorrow morning. General Scott is waiting for reinforcements to arrive. Then we're going to Mexico City. Total victory is almost in our grasp!"

Suddenly Julia noticed the captain's bars on the shoulders of her husband's uniform. "Oh, Alamo! You're a captain now!"

"And our husbands are first lieutenants!" spoke up Libby, her voice full of pride.

"But they haven't had a chance to tell us about why they got the promotions!" Vivian said.

"*You* tell everybody the story, Alamo!" Alex said.

"Yeah!" agreed Abel.

Alamo then told everyone the story about how he and his brothers, along with their friend Lieutenant Ulysses Grant, were given promotions for saving the life of Colonel Vince Leyden in the Buena Vista battle.

The entire group congratulated them for their efforts.

Then a big smile spread over Lance's face. "Tell you what, folks, as long as we're giving good news here, I have some too!" Every eye was fixed on Lance as he looked at the blushing Andrea, then back at the Kane family, and said, "Andrea and I are engaged! Show them your ring, sweetheart!"

There were gasps, along with laughter and applause, as Andrea lifted up her left hand so everyone could see the engagement ring on the third finger.

When the applause faded out, Alamo looked at the future groom. "So when is the wedding going to take place, Lance?"

Lance grinned. "That depends on when this war with Mexico comes to an end. We haven't set a date yet because, Alamo, I want you to be my best man at the wedding."

"And I do too, Alamo," Andrea said.

"So Andrea and I have agreed," Lance continued, "that we will set the wedding date once the war is over and the Kane soldiers have come home."

Alamo's eyes misted. "I . . . I am so

honored that you want me to be your best man, Lance."

Lance walked over to him, gave him a hug, then looked into Alamos' eyes. "If it weren't for you, my dear friend, I wouldn't be alive to marry Andrea. If you hadn't picked me up on that blazing battlefield and carried me to safety, I would have burned to death." He took a deep breath. "And what's more, I'd be burning in hell right now."

"I was headed for hell too, Lance," Andrea said, "but because Julia led me to Jesus and Alamo led you to Jesus, we'll both be in heaven together forever."

There were cheers from the Kane family.

Andrea then went to Julia and said so all could hear, "Because you led me to Jesus, I want you to be my matron of honor."

Julia wrapped her arms around Andrea's neck and held her close. "I am deeply honored!"

At that moment, Daisy, who had been preparing lunch and was unaware of what was going on in front of the house, stepped out onto the front porch. She put her hands to her cheeks and said with wide eyes, "Alamo! Alex! Abel!"

The Kane brothers made a beeline for Daisy, and after all three had hugged her, Alamo explained that they would have to leave for Cerro Gordo Pass in the morning.

Daisy told them that she had read the article in the *Washington Post* about that battle and how glad she was that all three brothers were all right. She looked around at the group. "I was about to announce that lunch was ready, but I only prepared enough food for Julia, the children, Papa Abram, and Lance and Andrea."

Libby and Vivian told Daisy that they would each like to go to their homes and prepare lunch for their husbands so they could have some private time together.

Daisy chuckled. "Well, good! That's where you *should* be for lunch . . . privately together!"

Everyone laughed at Daisy's wisdom.

Daisy then told them she would prepare a big supper for all of them that evening — including Lance and Andrea.

Both couples told Daisy they would take her up on the wonderful offer and headed for their own houses.

Andrea turned to Daisy and asked her if she could help her prepare supper in Julia's place. Daisy smiled and said, "Of course, honey. That way Julia and Alamo can spend the whole afternoon together with their children. They'll love that."

"Great," Andrea said. "That's what I had

in mind. If you can use any more help, I'll enlist Lance. He knows how to peel potatoes!"

Both women giggled and Daisy said, "I'm sure you and I can get it all done together, sweetie."

Andrea laughed. "Okay. That's fine with me." She paused. "Lance usually has to take a nap in the afternoon anyway. He still has some fatigue problems due to his wound."

Daisy nodded. "That's fine, honey. You and I will handle it, I'm sure."

Moments later, in the dining room of the big ranch house, Alamo's heart was pounding with joy because he was with his wife, children, and father. Grandpa Abram led in prayer, and everyone dug in.

During lunch, Alamo filled everyone in on the details of the battle at Cerro Gordo Pass and the victory of the American forces. He explained the details about the reinforcements that would be coming to the pass and of General Scott's plan to capture Mexico City and bring the war to an end. Everyone was pleased to hear of the plan.

That evening at supper, a joyful group crowded happily around the large dining room table. Because Alamo, Alex, and Abel would have to return to the war, there was

·a slight undercurrent of sadness.

Later that evening, after the guests had all gone and the children and Grandpa Abram were asleep in their own beds, Julia was sitting at her dressing table in the master bedroom, removing pins from her hair.

Alamo was sitting on a chair by the dresser taking off his boots and looking at his wife with adoring eyes.

When the pins were all removed, Julia's long, dark brown hair fell in luxuriant waves over her shoulders and down her back. Picking up her hairbrush, she began her nightly ritual of brushing her hair.

Alamo stepped up quietly in his stocking feet and reached for the brush. "Julie, sweet love, please let me brush your hair for you. It's one of the small, intimate joys that I miss so much when I'm away from home."

Julie looked up at him, gave him a big smile, and placed the brush in his hand. "Thank you, darling," she said softly. "I miss this special time too."

Alamo bent down and placed a delicate kiss on the lips of her beautiful upturned face.

The next morning, the Kane family shed many tears as Alamo, Alex, and Abel rode away to go back to war.

When the Kane brothers reached the American army camp at Cerro Gordo Pass, where General Scott and his men had been waiting for more troops to arrive, they found that over 900 new troops had already arrived from Texas army posts in response to General Scott's request for reinforcements.

When the Kane brothers had assured the general that the telegram was sent to President Polk from the army post at Corpus Christi Bay, he was certain that even more reinforcements would be coming. Within a few weeks, troops indeed began to arrive as a result of President Polk's telegrams to the officers in command at forts in many parts of Texas.

It took time to get a sufficient amount of men there, but by mid-August, General Scott had some 13,400 troops. Because of a request by President Polk, all of the reinforcements brought a supply of gunpowder and cannonballs for Scott's cannons and cartridges for the rifles and revolvers.

Feeling that 13,400 troops would be sufficient to accomplish his planned task, on Monday, August 16, the general led his men westward toward Mexico City.

On the afternoon of Friday, August 20, General Scott and his troops drew near the city known as Churubusco, a southeastern suburb of Mexico City that Santa Anna had personally fortified with a large number of troops in order to stop Scott's troops from reaching the capital city. This became apparent when, with field glasses, Alamo spotted Santa Anna at the edge of the town on his white horse with thousands of Mexican soldiers flanking him.

Alamo quickly dashed to General Scott, who was on his horse, handed him the field glasses, and told him to take a look.

After looking through the field glasses, the general's mouth popped open. "Captain Kane," he said. "It's Santa Anna! And he's got a lot of troops! I'm sure glad our ammunition supply has been replenished!"

Captain Ulysses Grant was close by on his horse. He moved up beside the general. "Sir, that's a big bunch of soldiers! And did I hear right? Santa Anna's leading them?"

Scott handed him the field glasses. "See for yourself."

When Grant spotted Santa Anna on his white horse and the massive number of troops scattering toward the defensive positions they had erected, he said, "General Scott, we don't dare turn around and run for cover, do we?"

Scott jutted his jaw. "No! They'd cut us down! Bring up the cannons, and we'll cut loose on them right now!"

This was done quickly, and as American cannonballs began bombarding the Mexican troops and Scott's men unleashed with their rifles, a fierce battle began.

Although the Mexicans did not have cannons, Santa Anna's sharpshooters were firing from behind solid defenses against the relatively unprotected American assault force. Though the Mexicans were taking a toll on the Americans, soon General Scott's cannons began to take a much greater toll on Santa Anna's men. By the time darkness was falling, a dispirited Santa Anna led what was left of his troops away from Churubusco.

The Americans were now just over three miles from Mexico City.

By morning, General Scott and his troops had learned from citizens of Churubusco that in yesterday's battle, some 4,000 Mexicans had been killed, including some wounded men who were ordered shot by Santa Anna, to put them out of their misery.

The count of the American dead was 1,053, and 139 had been wounded. General Scott was still set on capturing Mexico City to bring the war to an end, but at that time he was forced to halt and rest his weary troops. In spite of their victory at Churubusco, fatigue plagued the American troops. Also the loss of over 1,000 men in the battle on August 20 persuaded Scott against attempting an immediate assault upon Mexico City.

After explaining all of this to his troops, Scott encouraged them by saying that because 4,000 Mexican troops had been killed in the battle, August 20, 1847, would go down in the Mexican calendar as a sad day. Despite their weariness, Scott's more than 12,000 men cheered him with great emotion.

In Texas, in Washington-on-the-Brazos, and at the Diamond K Ranch, news came of the Churubusco battle and how many American and Mexican soldiers had been killed. There was heaviness of heart among the Texans because they hadn't been given the names of the American soldiers who were killed and were left to wonder if their loved ones were among the 1,053 who died at Churubusco.

Everyone figured that General Winfield Scott and his some 12,000 troops would soon be launching their attack on Mexico City to capture it and bring the war to an end. They were also quite sure that the Mexico City battle was going to be exceptionally fierce and bloody.

At the church and at the ranch, much prayer was offered for the Kane brothers and other men of the church who were with General Scott.

General Winfield Scott allowed his men to rest for three weeks in a forest a few miles southwest of Churubusco, where the medics also cared for the wounded. The general's heart was heavy because they hadn't been able to bury the 1,053 men who had been killed on August 20.

On Tuesday morning, September 14, Scott led his troops, including food and ammunition wagons and the large number of cannons, as they headed for Mexico City. They drew near Mexico's capital city just before noon.

The general sent a few scouts closer to the city, and when they returned, they told him that they had learned from two elderly Mexican men taking a walk outside the city who spoke English that the civilian inhabitants of Mexico City were holed up in their houses and business buildings and were full of fear. The old men, who admittedly had been against Mexico's war with the United States, estimated that Santa Anna had fewer than 8,000 fighting men fortified inside the city, but they were ready to defend it against the Americans, whom they had seen coming.

The Kane brothers and Lieutenant Jackson were together as General Scott led the charge into the city. From the streets, American cannons roared, and rifles and revolvers thundered as the fighting raged in alleys and between buildings all over the city, as well as on the streets.

When night fell, the fighting continued. No one got any sleep, including President Santa Anna, who was in a secret hiding place.

The battle continued all day Wednesday, but great numbers of Mexican troops were being killed, especially by American cannons. Gunshots still sounded when darkness fell. There was a three-quarter moon in the clear sky over Mexico City.

About midnight, as bullets were flying on a street in the business section of Mexico City, Alamo became separated from Alex, Abel, and Thomas Jackson, who had chosen to fight alongside the Kanes because they were his Christian brothers.

Amid the gun smoke and the bullets hissing through the air, Alamo found himself in an alley, the sounds of battle coming from every direction.

Suddenly, by the silver moonlight, Alamo saw a wounded Mexican soldier lying on the ground in the alley. Kneeling beside him, Alamo could see that the soldier had been seriously wounded by two slugs in his chest. Though he was conscious, he was most certainly dying.

Touching the wounded Mexican's shoulder, Alamo asked, "Do you understand English?"

The droopy-eyed soldier looked at him blankly.

Alamo's mind flashed back to the day at the battle in San Jacinto when Mark Nichols, a member of the church in Washington-on-the-Brazos who spoke Spanish, translated for him while he led a dying Mexican soldier to the Lord. He wished Mark was with him now.

Alamo did what he could to make the dying man comfortable. Suddenly he looked up, and by the moonlight he saw two Mexican officers coming toward him, their revolvers trained on him. One was a captain. The other, a lieutenant.

The captain stopped before drawing up to Alamo and the dying soldier, said something to the lieutenant, then turned and hurried away.

The lieutenant stepped up, his gun

pointed at Alamo, and spoke in perfect English. "Tell me, American Captain, what are you doing with this wounded Mexican soldier?"

Holding his gaze in the bright moonlight, Alamo replied levelly, "This man is dying. I was trying to ease his pain as much as possible."

The Mexican lieutenant was obviously stunned to hear this, and it brought a frown to his brow.

The wounded soldier gasped suddenly, took a short breath, let it out, and went limp, his eyes closing.

The lieutenant held his gun on Alamo as he bent low and studied the soldier's features. "He is dead."

Alamo laid a hand on the side of the lifeless man's neck, feeling for a pulse. There was none. "Yes. He is dead."

The Mexican lieutenant frowned again. "Tell me your name."

"Alamo Kane," came the quick reply.

"So you are *Captain* Alamo Kane?"

Alamo nodded. "Yes."

"Well, Captain Alamo Kane, I appreciate you being so kind to a dying enemy soldier, but I still must follow orders."

Alamo's brow puckered. "What do you mean?"

The Mexican lieutenant raised the cocked revolver in his hand, pointed it between Alamo's eyes, and pulled his lips into a thin line. He gave Alamo a sharp, weighing, penetrating look. "You saw the captain with me."

Alamo nodded.

"Well, Captain Alamo Kane, before leaving the scene here, my captain told me to shoot and kill the American captain."

Alamo's heart was suddenly filled with a strong peace from the Lord, and he desired to win the man to Jesus. "If you kill me, Lieutenant, I know I will go to heaven because the Lord Jesus Christ is my Saviour."

The lieutenant blinked and frowned.

"Let me ask you, Lieutenant," Alamo said, "have you repented of your sin and received the Lord Jesus Christ as your Saviour?"

The Mexican looked at him blankly and shook his head. "I have not. I don't know what that means."

"God's Bible says that when you die, you will go to hell and burn there forever because you have not repented of your sin and received the Lord Jesus Christ as your Saviour."

There was a tightening of the Mexican's

face muscles, and he went pale as he lowered his gun.

24

Since the Mexican lieutenant's revolver was now pointing at the ground, Alamo felt a little more peace. Even more peace came as the Mexican put his thumb on the hammer and eased it into place, out of the cocked position.

As guns still roared all over the city, Alamo breathed a silent prayer of thanks to the Lord and then looked the man in the eye. "You know *my* name, but I don't know yours."

The Mexican's face was still pale. "My name is Reynaldo Sanchez, Captain Kane."

Figuring him to be in his midtwenties, Alamo said, "Well, Lieutenant Reynaldo Sanchez, how did you learn English? You speak it so well."

"I was born on a cattle ranch just outside of Mexico City, but when I was in my early teens, my parents and I moved to California. My father and I worked on a cattle ranch.

We were there for six years, and during that time, both my parents and I learned to understand and speak English. We returned to Mexico when I was nineteen. My father bought another cattle ranch near Mexico City, and we took up our Mexican citizenship. Both of my parents died just over three years ago of cholera."

"I am sorry about your parents." Alamo's heart was heavy for the soul of Reynaldo Sanchez. "Reynaldo, do you know who Jesus Christ is?"

"Yes, I learned about Him when I was a boy. I learned more when we were in California. He is God's virgin-born Son."

Alamo took it from there, and while the gunfire continued all over Mexico City, he told Reynaldo again what the Bible said about hell and that without Jesus as his Saviour when he died, he would go there and burn forever.

Reynaldo holstered his revolver and listened intently as Alamo quoted passages from the Bible on the gospel, salvation, and repentance. After nearly an hour, he had the joy of leading Lieutenant Reynaldo Sanchez to the Lord. He then quoted Scripture passages to give him assurance of his salvation, followed by passages concerning baptism, which would be his first step of obedience to God after salvation.

Reynaldo wiped tears, thanked the American soldier for explaining about the cross of Calvary; the death, burial, and resurrection of God's Son; and salvation in Jesus. "Captain Alamo Kane," he said, "I must tell you that I have never liked the leadership of Santa Anna in this country. The man is so brutal and bloodthirsty. Now that I am a Christian, I am going to desert from the Mexican army. I wish I could go back to the United States."

Alamo smiled and told Reynaldo that he owned a large cattle ranch in southeast Texas called the Diamond K Ranch. He added that he was quite sure the Americans were going to be victorious in capturing Mexico City and bringing the war to an end.

Reynaldo nodded. "I think you are right, Captain Kane."

Alamo smiled again. "You are my new brother in Christ. If you want to go to Texas with me, since you're experienced at cattle ranching, I'll give you a job as a ranch hand if you want it."

A broad smile spread over Reynaldo's dark face. "I would *love* it! I enjoy cattle ranching!"

"Then you're hired!" Alamo reached out and patted his shoulder.

At that moment, Alamo saw movement at the end of the alley from the corner of his eye. He turned his head quickly, and by the bright moonlight he saw that it was his brothers and Thomas Jackson. As they headed toward him, Alamo could tell that they were relieved to see he was all right. But by the time they drew up, he could see their puzzlement at finding him in a relaxed position and talking in a friendly manner to an enemy soldier.

With gunfire still echoing all around the city, Alamo said, "It's all right, fellas. This young man is my brother in Christ."

"Oh?" said Alex. "Tell us about him!"

The Alex, Abel, and Thomas moved closer and listened as Alamo told them the whole story, including that Reynaldo's captain had told him to shoot and kill the American captain, which Reynaldo had not done. Alamo had just led the young Mexican lieutenant to Jesus. Smiling, Reynaldo confirmed that it was true; then Alamo introduced his brothers and Thomas to him.

Alex, Abel, and Thomas gave praise to the Lord that the Mexican lieutenant didn't kill Alamo as he'd been ordered to do and that Alamo had led Reynaldo to the Lord.

Alamo told them of Reynaldo's background in cattle ranching, both in Mexico and California, and that when the war was over and they returned to Texas, Reynaldo was going with them. He had just hired him as a ranch hand a few minutes ago.

Then the gunfire in the city began to fade out, and within a few minutes, it became completely silent.

Joyful shouts of American soldiers could be heard.

Alamo looked at his brothers and Thomas. "Sounds to me like it's over. Let's go see!"

The three men agreed. Alamo said to his new hired hand, "Wait right here, Reynaldo!"

The new Christian nodded and watched as the four Americans dashed to the street, turned to the right, and disappeared.

When they reached the center of the city, they were pleased to see that the Mexican troops were surrendering to General Scott and that the American troops were taking their guns from them. Captain Robert E. Lee and Captain Ulysses Grant had noticed the Kane brothers and Lieutenant Jackson draw up. "Guess what?" Lee said. "President Antonio López de Santa Anna deserted his troops when he saw how the battle was going and ran away into the night."

Alamo chuckled. "Why doesn't that surprise me?"

Lee laughed.

Alex, Abel, and Thomas smiled.

"I'll go get Reynaldo," Alamo said to them. "If you can get General Scott's attention, tell him I'm bringing a Mexican soldier I want him to meet."

All three nodded.

Alamo dashed back to the alley where Reynaldo was waiting and told him that the Mexican troops had surrendered and that Santa Anna had run away.

Minutes later, when the two of them drew up to the center of Mexico City, the Kane brothers and Thomas were talking to the general. When Alex saw Alamo and Reynaldo coming, he pointed to them. "Here they are now, General Scott."

Scott smiled at Alamo as he led the Mexican up to him. "I understand you want me to meet this man."

"Yes sir." Alamo nodded. He quickly introduced Lieutenant Reynaldo Sanchez to the general and told him how Reynaldo disobeyed orders from his captain to shoot and kill Alamo. Reynaldo was deserting the Mexican army and wanted to go home with Alamo and his brothers and live and work on the Diamond K Ranch.

The general thanked Reynaldo for not killing Captain Kane as ordered by his superior officer and gave him permission to go with the Kane brothers to Texas, putting him under Captain Kane's authority.

By sunrise, Thursday, September 16, General Winfield Scott and his troops had all the over 4,000 Mexican soldiers who were still alive in custody. Just over 3,000 Mexican soldiers had been killed in the Mexico City battle. Of the American troops, 139 had been killed. The battle was over, and the Americans had won decisively.

Some of Scott's men raised an American flag over the city, and the citizens of Mexico City showed the Americans that they were glad the fighting was over. They also expressed that they were glad Santa Anna was gone.

Later that day, the American soldiers who were not assigned to stay and occupy the city prepared to leave. Most of them were going straight home.

Just before the group with whom Thomas Jackson was traveling left, he talked to the Kane brothers as Reynaldo Sanchez stood with them. Smiling, Thomas patted Alamo on the back. "I'm sure that because of winning this Mexican soldier to the Lord, you must be flying high!"

Alamo nodded with a grin. "I sure am!"

Alex and Abel Kane laughed with joy as

Thomas said, "Yes sir, Alamo! 'High Is the Eagle'!"

Thomas took a moment to tell the Kane brothers good-bye, saying if they never met again on earth, he would see them in heaven. Alamo, Alex, and Abel warmly agreed.

When Thomas was gone, Reynaldo looked at Alamo and frowned. "What does this about an eagle being high mean?"

Alamo walked over to him and put an arm around his shoulder. "We'll tell you all about it on the way home."

It was a crisp autumn morning on Monday, September 27, when the Kane Brothers and Reynaldo Sanchez arrived at the Diamond K. Some of the ranch hands and their wives and children spotted them riding toward the big ranch house and waved to them. The Kane brothers waved back, knowing that the ranch people understood that their boss wanted to see his wife and children first and that Alex and Abel would want to see their wives before talking to the ranch people.

As they continued in the direction of the big ranch house, Alex said, "Boy, is it ever good to be home — and to know that this time, we can stay here!"

"It sure is!" said Abel.

"Amen to that!" said Alamo.

As they drew up to the front porch of the big ranch house, the door swung open, and Adam smiled at his stepfather and uncles. He turned slightly and shouted back into the house. "Mama! Mama! Come see! Come see! It's Papa, Uncle Alex, and Uncle Abel!"

Seconds later, Julia came out the door with Abram on her heels carrying little Amber and with young Abram and Andy following close behind. In back of them were Libby and Vivian, followed by Patrick and Angela with Lance and Andrea. Alamo was giving a bear hug to Adam, who was squeezing back.

Alamo's line of sight went to the love of his life as she ran toward him. Adam chuckled and said, "We'd better let go of each other, Papa, before Mama moves me!"

As the boy spoke, Alamo released him, and less than five seconds later, Julia and Alamo were in each other's arms. He picked her up, twirled her around three times, and placed her back on her feet.

"Oh, darling, you're home!" Julia said. "Thank You, dear Lord! Thank You!"

Alamo stepped back to get a good look at his wife. "Yes, sweetheart, I'm home."

"We all read the newspaper report of the

victory at Mexico City!" she said with delight. "You're home for good now, aren't you?"

"Praise the Lord, I sure am, sweet one!"

"Oh, glory be!" Julia exclaimed, tears misting her eyes as Alamo held her close. She placed her head against her husband's broad chest and heard the steady beating of his heart. All was now right in her world. She breathed a prayer of thanksgiving.

Alamo kissed Julia once more before dashing to the rest of the family, including his two younger sons and his little daughter, and passed out hugs speedily. He greeted Lance and Andrea warmly then returned to Julia.

While all of the family members, including the O'Fallons, were still in the process of hugging each other as Lance and Andrea looked on, Julia suddenly saw a new face in the group. She looked up at Alamo and blinked at the tears in her eyes. "Honey, who is your friend?"

"Oh my." Alamo shook his head. "I got so caught up in loving on my family that I completely forgot my manners!"

Alamo walked over to Reynaldo, who had put on civilian clothing before leaving Mexico City, and placed his arm around the young Mexican's shoulder. "Hey, everybody! I want you to meet someone special!"

Giving Alamo their attention, the group looked on as he said, "This is our friend and brother in Christ, Reynaldo Sanchez." Alamo grinned at the group, who was gathering around him and Reynaldo with quizzical looks on their faces. Knowing he had stunned his family and friends with this surprise, Alamo told them that Reynaldo had been a lieutenant in the Mexican army at Mexico City. Then he told them the whole story of how Lieutenant Reynaldo Sanchez was ordered by a higher-ranking Mexican officer to shoot and kill him . . . but instead Alamo was able to witness to Reynaldo and lead him to Jesus.

The group showed their joy. Alamo then explained Reynaldo's cattle ranching background, told them of his deserting the Mexican army and that he had offered him a job as a ranch hand on the Diamond K, and that Reynaldo had gladly accepted the offer.

When the realization of what Alamo was telling them finally penetrated to their minds and hearts, the adults of the Kane family walked over to Reynaldo, introduced themselves one by one, and welcomed him into their midst as a ranch hand and, more importantly, as their brother in Christ.

Pastor Patrick then introduced his assistant pastor, Lance Brooks, and Lance's fiancée, Andrea Voss, to him.

When everyone had greeted Reynaldo, he stepped up to Pastor Patrick, telling him that Alamo quoted Scripture to him after leading him to the Lord about his first step of obedience to the Lord after being saved — to be baptized.

Looking squarely into the pastor's eyes, Reynaldo asked, "May I be baptized next Sunday morning?"

Patrick smiled. "You sure can! My assistant pastor, whom you just met, is scheduled to do the baptizing next Sunday."

Reynaldo smiled at Lance. "That will be fine with me."

Alamo then turned to Lance and Andrea, with Amber in his arms and Julia at his side. "Now that the war is over and I'm home for good, when do you two want to get married?"

As Lance and Andrea held hands, smiling, Lance said, "Well, we just whispered back and forth to each other during all this excitement, and we agreed that since this is Monday, we'll get married next Saturday, October 2." He turned to his boss. "All right, Pastor?"

Patrick grinned. "Of course. I'll spread

the word among the church members about the wedding right away."

An hour later, when the ranch people were allowed to gather in front of the big ranch house and welcome their boss and his brothers home for good, Alamo introduced Reynaldo Sanchez to them and told his story. Cort quickly said he would assign a spot in one of the bunkhouses for Reynaldo and would put him to work right away. Reynaldo told him how happy he was to be a ranch hand on the Diamond K Ranch.

On Thursday, September 30, young Adam had a happy eleventh birthday party at the big ranch house. He was so thrilled that his stepfather and his uncles were there.

Later that evening, after the party was over, Alamo was relaxing in the swing on the front porch of the big ranch house, enjoying a last cup of coffee in the cool fall air. He was reveling in the peace of the war being over, of once again being a civilian, and of being home.

Looking toward the myriad of stars twinkling over the quiet land, Alamo once again thanked the Lord for keeping his brothers and himself safe through the many battles they faced. "And thank You, Lord," he said, "for helping me to be a witness for You and for those souls I had the privilege of leading to You. Thank You also for protecting our loved ones and employees here on the ranch and for protecting the ranch itself."

At that instant, Alamo heard the front door of the house open and turned to see Adam step onto the porch and walk toward him. Smiling, Alamo placed his coffee cup on the small table next to the swing and scooted over to give the boy room to sit beside him. "Adam, my boy! Come join me!"

As the eleven-year-old sat down on the swing beside him, Alamo said, "I thought after the big birthday party you had, you'd probably be fast asleep by now."

"Mama is putting my brothers and sister to bed and praying with them right now, Papa Alamo, but I . . . I just needed a moment with you."

Sensing the serious tone in Adam's voice, Alamo waited for the boy to go on.

"Sir," said the boy, "since you are my stepfather, most of the time I have called you Papa Alamo."

"Yes."

Adam gently cleared his throat. "Uh . . . sometimes, I, well, sometimes I sort of slip and just call you Papa."

Alamo grinned. "Mm-hmm."

The boy cleared his throat again. "Uh . . . I want to ask you . . . from now on, could I just call you Papa? I love you as much as if you were my *real* father instead of my step-father."

Putting his arm around Adam's shoulders and drawing him close to his side, Alamo swallowed the lump in his throat. "Son, nothing would please me more. I was — well, I was hoping that the time would come when it would always be just Papa. Thank you for giving me this honor. I will try to be the best papa possible to you as the Lord gives me guidance."

Adam turned, lifted his arms, and wrapped them around Alamo's neck. "Oh, Papa, you are already the best possible papa to me!"

25

Just after one o'clock in the afternoon on Saturday, October 2, 1847, Alamo and Julia Kane drove into Washington-on-the-Brazos in a Diamond K buggy. They were ahead of the others from the ranch who would be attending the wedding since they both had a part in it.

Sitting close to her husband, Julia looked up at the clear sky. "Darling, this day is so bright and sparkling that it almost hurts my eyes."

"Yes, it is, sweetheart," Alamo responded. "But you know the old saying 'Happy is the bride that the sun shines on.'"

She chuckled. "Well, I know this much — Andrea can't be any happier than this bride is!"

Alamo smiled and looked at her with loving eyes. "Bless you, darlin'. I'm so glad that I've made you happy enough in our marriage that you still consider yourself my bride."

Julia matched his smile. "You sure have."

Alamo leaned over and kissed his bride, then said softly, "Julie, sweetheart, no woman could ever have made me as happy as you have!"

Julia smiled at him again. "Darling, we are so greatly blessed by our heavenly Father."

"Indeed we are, my precious bride. Indeed we are!"

At two o'clock that afternoon, a large crowd was in attendance at the wedding.

Alamo was thrilled to be the best man.

Julia was also thrilled to be the matron of honor since she had led the bride to the Lord and Alamo had led the groom.

The wedding was beautiful yet simple and perfectly suited the young couple as they pledged their love to each other before Pastor Patrick and repeated the age-old solemn, sacred vows.

When the pastor pronounced Lance and Andrea husband and wife, he looked at the groom. "You may kiss your bride."

Lance took lovely Andrea into his arms, pressed his lips to hers, and held them there until people in the audience were gasping for breath.

When the kiss ended, Pastor Patrick widened his eyes, looked at the audience, and said, "Wow!"

Everyone applauded.

Lance looked down into Andrea's bright eyes. "I love you so much!"

Andrea flashed him a smile. "And I love *you* so much!"

The next day, Sunday, October 3, when the pastor finished his sermon and gave the invitation, five people walked the aisle, four to receive Christ as Saviour. The fifth was Reynaldo Sanchez. While the counselors were dealing with the other four at the altar, the pastor had Reynaldo give his salvation testimony. He shared only that he had been a lieutenant in the Mexican army and that it was Captain Alamo Kane who had led him to the Lord. But he did not give the circumstances.

The testimony caused many an eye to swing to Alamo, who was sitting with his family on a pew near the front of the auditorium. The church members were proud of Alamo's record as a soul winner.

Moments later, standing in the baptistry with Reynaldo, Assistant Pastor Lance Brooks briefly told the story of the incident during the Battle of Mexico City when Reynaldo disobeyed his superior officer's command to kill Captain Kane and how Alamo then led him to Jesus.

The place was then filled with "amens."

When the new convert had been dipped in the water and raised to stand on his feet, symbolizing the death, burial, and resurrection of the Lord Jesus Christ, the crowd applauded.

From his seat on the platform, the pastor looked at Lance and told him to keep Reynaldo there in the baptistry for the moment.

Lance nodded.

Pastor Patrick then stepped up to the pulpit. "In a few minutes, those who came and received the Lord Jesus as their Saviour this morning will be baptized. At this moment, I want to remind the members of this church of the sermon I preached on Sunday, June 7, 1846, the day Lance Brooks first came to this church after Alamo had led him to the Lord at the Battle of Palo Alto."

Many heads were nodding.

The pastor then looked at Alamo in the nearby pew with his family and smiled. He turned around, pointed to Reynaldo, then looked back to Alamo. "High is the eagle!"

Tears filled Alamo's eyes, as well as Lance's eyes. People shouted the same words all over the auditorium.

At the same instant, Alamo and Julia both jumped to their feet, hugged each other, and shouted in chorus, "High is the eagle!"

EPILOGUE

On February 2, 1848, an official document of surrender was signed by government authorities in Mexico. It had been designed to reestablish peace and friendship between Mexico and the United States and to ensure concord, harmony, and mutual confidence in the future.

In spite of the differences between President James K. Polk and General Zachary Taylor near the end of the Mexican-American War, General Taylor ran for president of the United States in November 1848 and was elected. He served from January 1849 until July 1850, when he died some eighteen months after taking office.

As our readers know, when the American Civil War took place from 1861 to 1865, Ulysses S. Grant, Robert E. Lee, and Thomas J. Jackson — who had fought side by side in the Mexican-American War — were also deeply involved. General Jackson and General Lee were on the Confederate side in that war, and General Grant on the Union side. Grant later became president of the United States and served in that office from 1869 to 1877. Jackson was dubbed "Stonewall Jackson" by the men who fought under his command because of the courage he showed in the heat of battle.

Antonio López de Santa Anna carefully sneaked out of Mexico shortly after the Mexican-American War and moved to Jamaica. In 1874, Santa Anna was allowed to return to his homeland of Mexico. He died there, poor and blind, at the age of eighty-two, on June 21, 1876.

ABOUT THE AUTHORS

Al Lacy is a preacher and best-selling author of more than one hundred historical and western novels, including the Angel of Mercy, Battles of Destiny, and Journeys of the Stranger series, with more than 3 million books in print.

JoAnna Lacy, Al's wife and longtime collaborator, is the coauthor of the first two books in the Kane Legacy series, as well as the Frontier Doctor, The Orphan Trains, Mail Order Bride, Shadow of Liberty, and the Hannah of Fort Bridger Series. The Lacys live in the Colorado Rockies.

The employees of Thorndike Press hope you have enjoyed this Large Print book. All our Thorndike and Wheeler Large Print titles are designed for easy reading, and all our books are made to last. Other Thorndike Press Large Print books are available at your library, through selected bookstores, or directly from us.

For information about titles, please call:
(800) 223-1244

or visit our Web site at:
http://gale.cengage.com/thorndike

To share your comments, please write:
Publisher
Thorndike Press
295 Kennedy Memorial Drive
Waterville, ME 04901

481